FOR LOVE AND HONOUR

Antonia Van-Loon

A STAR BOOK

published by
the Paperback Division of
W. H. ALLEN & Co. Ltd

A Star Book
Published in 1979
by the Paperback Division of
W. H. Allen & Co. Ltd
A Howard and Wyndham Company
44 Hill Street, London W1X 8LB

First published in the United States of America by St. Martin's Press, Inc.,
1978

Printed in Great Britain by
C. Nicholls & Company Ltd, The Philips Park Press, Manchester

ISBN 0 352 30418 9

FOR LOVE AND HONOUR

'Oh, there won't be a war. I'm so tired of hearing . . .'

'No', she said quickly. 'But only because I'm not a gambler.'

'Hah! It's because you're a realist.' He glanced at his watch.

'Promised my brothers I'd go fishing. I'll be back for that wallet.'

'Shall I order you a ceremonial sword while I'm about it?'

'God, no. I said there'd *be* a war. I didn't say I wanted to lead the troops or even follow in the rear guard.'

'But you seem so anxious . . .'

'I said I'd *have* to fight. They'll shame me into it.'

Also by Antonia Van-Loon in *Star*

FOR US THE LIVING

In memory of my mother,
Bernadine Smith

PROLOGUE: 1873

The dying man leaned forward and said to Emily, "Most people know a time that's right for them. For some it comes in adolescence. Others don't find it until they're old. For many, like Beth and Kent. the best time is now, the middle years. I think it's a mistake for people to force themselves out of their own golden age. The change must evolve naturally. If this doesn't happen, then a person should relax and suspend himself in his personal era. To hell with conforming more than you have to." He paused, then asked, "Is your time still to come, Emily? Or has it passed? And if it's passed, will you ever try to find it again?"

FOR LOVE
AND
HONOR

PART 1

CHAPTER 1

On a hot July day in 1860, Emily Stevens looked through the window of her father's store and caught her breath. Passing on the opposite side of the street was a man who looked just like Roger Martin. He was tall, black-haired, lean, and he walked with a certain careless stride that was distinctive of Roger. She shook her head. Ridiculous. Roger had been in the West for three years. Even if he had come back—and he had sworn he never would—she would have been the first to hear about it. Every bit of news worth mentioning circulated through Stevens' Store before it traveled up toward the common, out through the town, and on to the farms beyond. The passing figure must have been a mirage. The day was so hot that she was sure mirages could exist here in Massachusetts no less than in the Western deserts. But more likely it was simply a man who looked like Roger. A stranger passing through on his way to Springfield or Worcester, though why he would detour through out-of-the-way Lanston, Emily could not guess.

She walked away from the window, slapping at insects, reminding herself to replace the flypaper. Going over to the spice shelf, she began to check inventory. The town was quiet today, as it always was during haying season. Business would be slow, so there would be a chance to take stock, order supplies, clean and rearrange merchandise.

Emily Stevens was twenty years old, attractive in an athletic-looking way—tall and lean with small breasts and graceful movements that suggested long walks in all seasons. Her face was by no means perfect. The cheekbones were too low, the chin a shade too pronounced, and the severe chignon she usually wore accentuated the problems. But occasionally, as on hot days like this, Emily pinned her dark blonde hair in a way that made her flaws go unnoticed. With her hair piled up so that it stood wide about the temples, her cheekbones were lifted and her chin shrank into proportion. Her neck, another good feature now fully revealed, became a creamy pedestal to a face that sometimes seemed beautiful: large blue eyes, a straight, chiseled nose, and lips that were well-shaped if not full.

She was not, however, thinking about her looks. She was thinking about Roger Martin. Growing up on adjacent farms, the two of them had been close friends in a brother-sister way. They had attended district school together, later plodding through all sorts of weather to attend the new free academy here in the center of town. Where Emily was serious about higher education, Roger took the whole matter lightly, teasing her about her discipline and drive, declaring that she was the proverbial Easterner while he was a freer Western man.

"Western!" she had laughed. "You'll never get farther west than the Connecticut River."

"I'll scale the Rockies and the Sierras."

"You'll scale the stone fences at the end of your father's pasture."

"Ar you'll *sit* on fences," he retorted, "memorizing your Shakespeare. You know what the East is like, Em? Like those poems we memorize in school. As predictable as iambic pentameter."

"Then why do you stay in school?"

"Maybe some day an original idea will come streaking down from the master's platform," he said.

Oh, pshaw! You're making excuses. You're here to learn, your dull disciplines, and your future is as predictable as the East."

So they had insulted each other, walking the three miles back and forth to town, while their friends Abby Blake and Jack Lawrence strolled behind them, holding hands and talking of their future together. Roger was a tall, gawky boy of seventeen. His face was undistinguished (though Abby swore there was potential there). Emily looked upon him as the surrogate brother he was, reassured by the thought that Roger, for all his talk of leaving, would always be around.

They had never been more than friends. Roger pined away for Abby's older sister, while Emily loved other boys. But they were close to each other—and not just for teasing. When Emily had been twelve and her mother died, Roger came by to help with the chores. He didn't say much, but he was there. As he was during haying and harvesting and sugaring—as he was almost every day of her life.

Two weeks after graduating from the academy, Roger said, "I'm ready to leave."

"To *leave?*"

"I'm keeping my promise to the ghosts of Lewis and Clark."

She laughed, but the laugh was brittle. And then it died altogether. He meant it. He really *meant* it!

There had been an occasional letter, though in the past year not even his family had heard from him. But letters could not change the fact that a familiar rhythm had stopped. A pleasant song, scarcely noticed until it had ended.

She was still at the spice shelf, staring blankly at a bottle of ginger, when the front door swung open and she heard heavy footsteps. A man's footsteps. And almost before she had turned around, she knew that they were Roger's.

For a moment they stared at each other. Then she said, so softly that she would not have known whether she was uttering the words or thinking them, "You came back."

"Yes."

"But you said . . ." She trailed off, studying him. He had changed so! Though his height was the same as when he had left (five eleven or six feet) he had filled out considerably and was handsome now—deeply tanned, mustachioed, his black hair thick and tousled, his teeth very white against the dark skin.

"I said I would never come home," Roger completed her sentence. "But here I am." He took a step closer. "It's good to be here."

Emily, whose aplomb was rarely shaken, found herself trembling. Finally she asked, "Are you home for good?"

"I don't know yet."

"When—when did you get here?"

"Late last night."

"Oh."

It was Roger, but it wasn't Roger. She did not know how to talk to him. In the old days it would have been easy. She would have said, "Well it's high time you came to your senses" and he would have laughed, "Senses indeed! I only came home because I ran out of money." Now she stood here staring at a man who was more a stranger than the man she had known. And she could think of nothing—playful or serious—to say.

She was suddenly aware of the apron she was wearing. There was a blotch of molasses on it and she had meant to change it earlier. And oh, her hair! She could feel where the perspiration had glued tendrils to her forehead.

Roger said, "You've done wonders with Mike's old place." He looked around the store at the neat shelves, the polished coffee grinder, the cuspidor that was meant to discourage patrons from spitting at the stove, the two tables at the windows where farmers rested and drank coffee or iced tea, depending on the season, before making the long trek home. He said, "I'll never forget how surprised I was when you wrote that you and your Pa had sold the farm and moved to town."

Emily was still gaping at him, only half listening. But she managed to say, "Were you surprised?" Then she recovered a little. "But tell me about yourself. Why are you back? Did you like the West?"

He grinned. "Which question should I answer first?"

"Sit here, pour yourself some tea, and think about it. I have to go into the back room and get"—she thought fast—"some ginger."

In the back room, among the barrels, she flung off her apron and pushed hairpins into place. Her father, walking in the back door, saw the frenzied toilette and asked, "Going somewhere?"

"No, Pa. Just freshening up." She looked at the tall, spare man and added. "It's hot."

"Noticed that," he said.

She ignored the remark and quickly fluffed the damp blonde tendrils with her fingers. Then she said, "There. All set." She strode into the front room, her father following with a box of children's slates that had just been delivered.

When Matt saw Roger sitting at the front table, he said quietly, "Hello there, son," as though Roger had just returned from a five-minute walk. How typical, Emily thought. If President Buchanan himself were at that table Pa would greet him in the same laconic way. He rarely displayed emotion. But he could laugh heartily at times. He had once laughed himself senseless because Merton the dog had chased Jesse the cat into the woodshed. Emily had watched him roar, waiting for the punch line. But the chase, apparently, had *been* the punch line.

"How'd you like the West?" Matt asked Roger.

"Very much," Roger smiled. "Very much, sir."

Emily stood next to the table, trying to look as casual as Pa, trying not to fiddle with her hands or otherwise betray her nervousness.

Matt said, "Mary'd be mad if you didn't drop by the house."

Mary was Emily's stepmother. Matt was extending Roger an invitation to supper, for it was after five o'clock.

Matt continued. "Em, why don't you show him where the house is?" He paused. "Tell Mary I'll be working late tonight. Doing the ledgers."

He was telling her that he did not expect Emily, who normally did the accounts, to come back to the store this evening. He expected her to take Roger home for supper and spend the evening reminiscing. For all his apparent indifference, Pa never missed a trick. Emily could have hugged him. But she and her father never hugged each other.

It seemed that half the town was assembled when Emily Stevens emerged from the store with a swarthy young man.

People she hadn't seen in weeks had suddenly materialized; they must have seen Roger enter the store and spread the news that a handsome stranger had come into their midst. Now they were clustered on Center Street trying to think of something to buy at the Stevens' place. It was Danny Winstead who first recognized the "stranger." "Why, it's Jep Martin's lad come back from the West! Sakes, I'd hardly recognize you."

There were greetings all around, the men shaking hands and clapping Roger on the back, the older women offering formal pleasantries, the younger women blushing and smoothing their skirts. In this manner, they progressed down Center to the corner of Dawson, Roger telling people that yes, he had seen Indians and yes, he had seen San Francisco and no, he hadn't found gold but yes, he had done some mining and no, he hadn't decided whether he would stay in the East.

As they rounded the corner of Dawson, leaving the townspeople behind, he said to Emily, "Out West you can ride for a hundred miles and never see another human being."

"And you wish you were there now?"

"Let's just say that it will take time to adjust."

"Then you *will* be staying in the East?"

"I still don't know."

"The farmhouse must be crowded," she said.

He nodded. "With my brothers married and the two little nieces, I'm sleeping on the floor in the parlor."

"Really?"

He grinned. "I came prepared. I have my blanket roll. But there's an old cabin in the woods near Whitney Road that I plan to fix up for myself. Since there's no room for me in the inn, I'll just take my swaddling clothes and lay me . . ."

She laughed. "I remember that cabin. Your sister used to use it as a playhouse. She and I once brought our dolls over and left them overnight. Then it rained and the roof leaked . . ."

"Yes," Roger said. "Lee spent a week trying to revive the poor doll."

They talked for a while of the old days, but the Stevens' small frame house was close by, and it wasn't long before

Mary was swooping down on Roger with questions, exclamations, and orders to stay to supper and no excuses. She had known Roger since he was a baby and was happy to see that he'd had the common sense to come home.

Mary was a mousy-looking woman, dark and lean with close-set eyes and a much abbreviated chin. But her kindness and sensitivity went a long way toward concealing her shortcomings. In romantic matters Mary was as astute as her husband Matt. Over dessert she surreptitiously glanced from one to the other, and once she nodded her head as though making up her mind that the match was meant to be.

"You like the blueberry pie?" Mary asked Roger.

"It's delicious. I've missed the New England touch."

"That why you're back?" Mary asked. "For good cooking?"

"It's one of the reasons," Roger said. "I also missed my family—and my friends." He did not look at Emily, and Mary did not turn either. She knew her stepdaughter too well. In the past, Emily had determinedly resisted Mary's matchmaking efforts, announcing that she would prefer to make her own selection. The best way for Mary to encourage a courtship was to say little or nothing about the man, leaving Emily to praise his merits on her own. Thus it had been with two former suitors, each of whom Mary had liked, each of whom Emily had liked but had finally decided not to marry because "I didn't really love him."

Mary and Emily were close in many respects, but there was nothing filial in Emily's attitude toward her stepmother; they simply had a warm friendship. Mary tried to respect Emily's stance even though she often wished the girl weren't quite so independent.

She understood Emily's reasons. Emily had been making decisions for most of her life. An only child, she had lost her mother at the age of twelve and had spent the next five years nursing a rheumatic grandmother while simultaneously doing farm chores and trying to get an academy education. After her grandmother died, Emily had urged her father to sell the rocky farm which depressed him so much that he had to drink cider all day long to keep himself going. She suggested they buy a general store, that they run it together while Matt also worked at the one craft he loved: cabinetmaking. Matt had improved so much after the move that he had summoned the courage to ask Mary, a childless widow, to be his wife. Emily had been warm and enthusiastic. But after marriage, when Mary began making motherly overtures to this seventeen-year-old girl who was already running a store, Emily had looked at her incredulously, as though proclaiming that she was too adult to need all this maternal protection.

Mary, however, had deemed it her duty at least to caution the girl about the ways of men. She was sure old Martha Stevens, the grandmother, had never covered this subject. Rumor had it that before her marriage Martha's reputation had been notorious. While not exactly a prostitute, she had dispensed her favors widely. And though with age Martha had grown dour and downright religious, Mary felt that she would never have been so hypocritical as to give stern lectures to Emily on modesty and virtue.

Mary therefore took it upon herself to guide her attractive stepdaughter along a safe path to matrimony. After a while she had realized that Emily was already discerning about men—almost too discerning. She never dressed in a manner calculated to attract the opposite sex. She dressed to please herself. And as for dreaming up schemes to win husbands, the girl was just too busy to bother. Rarely did she flirt, and when she did, Mary wasn't sure it was flirting. The smiles she turned on pleasant young men seemed no different from the smiles of any person enjoying herself. In time, Mary began to worry. Didn't Emily care about getting a husband?

As soon as dessert was polished off, Mary shooed Roger and Emily into the backyard as though they were a couple of chickens getting in her way. It was early evening, and the air was cool. Seated in the wicker chairs, looking up at the darkening sky, they were finally able to talk with ease.

"Was it what you expected it to be?" she asked. "The West?"

He nodded.

"I'm glad, Roger."

"Are you? But you used to tease me so."

"I know I did, but I should hate to have had you come back disappointed. Tell me what it was like."

"Well, I've talked myself dry on the subject, but I'll try. How can I explain that the West is more than mining and trapping? It's more than mountains, deserts, canyons. Actually, it's something greater than the sum of its parts—if you can picture concepts like that after all the geometry you've had hammered into your brain."

She flared. "Are you going to start in on my 'disciplines' again? Of *course* I can understand what you mean."

He shook his head. "Same old Emily. No, I'm not 'starting in on your disciplines.' After all, I studied geometry too."

"Darn right you did, and I'll bet you can remember every axiom." The more she talked to him, the more he began to seem like the old Roger. She was looking at a man twenty-one years old, one of the most attractive people she had ever seen, but she was talking to the seventeen-year-old boy.

He said, "Actually, I admired you and your disciplines, but I was damned if I'd let you know it." He paused. "Excuse the language."

"I've heard worse in the store. Why wouldn't you let me know it?"

"We were always happiest when we were insulting each other," he said.

"That's true."

"But you had an ambition any man would envy. Hell, you had the farm and all the aggravation but you still got the highest marks in school. We boys had to sit there and hear a girl deliver the commencement oration. A *girl*, for God's sake! Outrageous."

Emily smiled. "None of you fools ever bothered to study. You and Rafe would go fishing while I struggled with *Caesar's Gallic Wars*. I kept winning by default."

"Whatever the reason, you won."

After a while she said, "As long as we're in an admiring mood, I have something to say too."

"Yes?"

She cleared her throat. "You're the only one I've ever known who had a dream and actually pursued it."

He was silent for a long time, studying her face. Emily was uncomfortable. They had, with their uncharacteristic compliments, ventured into uncharted territory. And Roger, who kept looking at her intently, was carrying them further afield. She felt the need to say something, to fill the void until she could adjust to the new situation. What she said was, "What have you been doing since you got home?"

That broke the spell, all right. He leaned back in his chair and said, "I only got home last night, remember? But tomorrow we start haying at our place. Next it'll be the Lawrences, then the McDowells, then the Blakes."

"I must get out to the farms to help the women," Emily heard herself say. Never once, in the three years since moving to town, had she visited a farm during haying time. Emily loathed all farm chores, but she most hated cooking for swarms of men in hundred-degree kitchens with the sweat pouring down and the flies attacking in legions. Now, however, with Roger joining the crew, the prospect of serving up beans and chicken and of carting water out to the steaming fields didn't seem so bad. She would tell Pa that the farm wives needed her. Pa would be happy, for Emily's absence would give him a legitimate excuse for staying in the quiet store rather than toting a pitchfork to the farms of old friends.

Night descended and the stars came out. A train rumbled by and discharged a passenger. Though the Stevens house was on the right side of the tracks, it was still near the tracks and peaceful nights were periodically shattered. Across the narrow Fort River they could hear the faint sound of singing. The Irish worked twelve- to fourteen-hour days in the sweltering woolen mill and in smaller factories, yet they still managed to sing of the old country—or perhaps it was the new. Emily could not, from this distance, discern either tune or lyrics.

Roger talked of mining camps and blustery towns that sprang up quick as tornadoes, of Indian villages, trading posts, the towering Rockies and the gentle Platte. But he lingered longest on accounts of the empty undulating prairies, where wheat grew freely and cornstalks stretched high, straight and defiant.

Emily talked of the store, the lyceum movement she was helping to organize, the Lanston Mozart Quartet in which she played the piano, the success of the Independence Day pageant, the quarrel at town meeting about allocations for the academy. She thought, as she talked, that all this must sound hopelessly dull to him, but he kept saying, "Go on," and she did. She told him about some of their classmates. Joan and Kurt had married. Each other. Christine was unofficially promised to Rafe. Rafe was still at Harvard and Artie at Yale, but both were home for the summer. Some of the boys wanted to enlist. With Lincoln running for president, people were worried about war. But all things considered, nothing much had changed since he had gone off.

They might have gone on talking all night, but Roger had to get up early, and he still had a three-mile walk ahead of him. As they stood at the gate saying goodbye, she thought for a moment that he was going to kiss her. But he took her hand instead and covered it with both of his. Then in a soft voice he said he was glad to be home. He walked off with the distinctive gait she had recognized from the store window. She watched until he had turned the corner of Dawson Street.

Though it was now one in the morning, Emily was not sleepy. Thinking of Roger—of the way his hands had felt when they held hers—she began to pace restlessly. The pacing led to a walk upstreet where the town lay sleeping under the moonlight. She stood at the corner of Dawson for a while, reluctant to walk farther lest she rouse an alarmed constable who would assume a thief was prowling.

Lanston was a town typical of New England, though it had a disproportionate number of wealthy because it was growing rapidly. At its heart was the green or common, its grasses kept trim by grazing sheep. At the south end of the common was the imposing Congregational Church, still the ranking meeting house in town, though four other churches existed. Next to this was the parsonage, occupied by a histrionic minister named Reverend Mitchell. At the other end of the common were the immense houses of two rich landed gentlemen and their families. Along the right side was Maple Street. Here stood the houses of other old families (there was a clear distinction between old wealth and new, and Maple Street meant "aristocracy"). Directly across from Maple was the town's main thoroughfare and business district, Center Street. (Most towns called their main streets Main Street but the founders of Lanston, Emily reasoned, must have fancied themselves more imaginative.) It was on South Center Street that Stevens' Store was located.

Emily stood for a moment before going home, looking around and remembering things Roger had said when he was a student. He had looked at the winding roads east of Maple Street, where new money was moving in, and proclaimed them "Maple's Tributaries." He had called the poor area across the river "The Nether Regions," alluding to the manner in which the new rich referred to hidden parts of the body. "Yes," he had growled, "they'd rather believe that those hungry people over there just don't exist."

So Roger had fled from it all, denying the East as the rich denied The Nether Regions. In doing that, hadn't he been as intransigent as they? Perhaps that was why he was back. Perhaps he was ready to admit it. But she'd see. He would be home for a while at least, and they would talk about this and other things. On the walk home, she began to smile, wondering what other things Roger was ready to admit.

CHAPTER 2

Abby Blake Lawrence nearly dropped her soup spoon when her best friend Emily showed up at the farm on the first day of haying and announced that she had come to help with the cooking.

"I don't believe it," Abby said, standing in the kitchen door.

"Don't believe I'd do a good deed for a friend?" Emily walked inside.

"I don't mean that," said Emily's former neighbor and classmate, now a young mother of two. "I think you'd lay down your *life* for a friend—rather than help one at haying time."

"I come here out of the goodness of my heart, and you, you ungrateful wretch . . ."

"I'm sorry," Abby said, stooping down to hand her toddler the spoon. "Do forgive me. You've come with the best of intentions, of course, and I shall accept your generosity in the proper spirit. So here on the counter is the chicken. And there in the pantry is the celery. And on a higher shelf, you dedicated little cook you, is flour for the dumplings. Oh yes, and out in the fields is our neighbor Roger Martin looking more delicious than the food."

Emily's mouth fell open.

Abby grinned. "I have two pails of water that I was going to cart out to the men. Would you mind awfully if I prevailed upon you . . ."

"Is it *that* obvious?" Emily blurted.

"Only to me," Abby said. "I took one look at him and knew you'd invent some excuse to come out to see us rural folk. But I was sure you'd wait until after haying."

"Did he say anything about—the other night?"

"He said you'd become very pretty."

"He did?" Emily brushed at her dark blonde hair. "Anything else?"

"He said I was looking good too, the liar." Abby had lustrous black hair, but she was short and plump and her face was too round to be considered beautiful. Yet her husband Jack, one of the most handsome men in the town, had chased her for most of his life. When Abby deprecated her looks, as she often did, Jack would get angry. He could not understand why Abby did not know she was beautiful.

Emily asked, "And that's all Roger said? That I was pretty?"

"No, there was more. Though Roger's not the sort to kiss and tell." Abby paused. "Well, did he?"

"Did he what?"

"Kiss you."

"I'm not the sort to kiss and tell."

"That means he didn't, or you'd be blushing all over yourself."

"At least I have the grace to blush," Emily retorted. This was an allusion to their early adolescent years, when Abby, the most earthy and frank young woman she had ever known, had talked freely and enthusiastically about sex, leaving Emily crimson but fascinated. Not only had Abby explained the facts of life to her naïve friend, but she had gone on to experience those facts firsthand as soon as she and Jack came of age. When she had told Emily about this, Emily had gasped. "But suppose you get with child? The wedding's year off."

"I probably won't. If I do, we'll get married."

"But what do you mean by 'probably won't'? You yourself told me that anyone who lies with a man . . ."

"But a clever man can prevent it," said Abby.

"Really?" This was interesting news. "How?"

"He . . ." Abby had hesitated. How to describe this? She had finally resorted to the Biblical explanation. "He spills his seed upon the ground."

"Onan," Emily had mused. "I remember that passage but I never understood what it meant. So there's an actual seed. Is it as small as an apple seed or is it . . ."

Abby had hooted, her round body shaking. "It's not an 'it.' " And she had gone on to explain what was meant in this case by "seed."

"But if men are so clever, why do so many women have so many children?"

"Well," the expert had explained, "I didn't say all men were like Jack. Maybe most of them think it's sinful and the rest can't control where they spill the seed."

"Oh." Emily had been disappointed. For a moment she had wondered if she too might indulge without benefit of clergy. Though outwardly proper, Emily was open-minded on the subject of sex. Her grandmother, in her studied avoidance of the subject of her past, had also, as Mary had guessed, spared Emily tiresome lectures on morality. But Emily was also practical. Lying with a man would be too risky. She could end up either an unwed mother or wed to a man she did not love.

Abby had told Emily other things too. There was, in sex, a sensation so allegedly unspeakable that no lady would dream of mentioning it but which, in Abby's opinion, all brides should know about so that they would go to their husbands' beds with more enthusiasm. It was called "spending." Though even the frank Abby had been too embarrassed to describe the sensation in detail, she had assured Emily that there was no experience in all the wide world to compare with it. To this day, Emily remained curious.

Now Abby said to Emily, "Are you going to take those pails out to the field or would you rather I took them so that you can do what you love—make soup."

"You really think you're funny, don't you?" Emily moved toward the pails.

"I think the situation's funny. To think that you'd end up with a farmer when you swore on your life that you'd live some incredibly exciting life."

"End up? I've barely had a chance to say hello." Emily picked up the pails.

"Well, don't be surprised if he acts fast. I think he has this idea that you two understand each other just because you grew up together."

"Why do you say that?" Emily set down the pails abruptly. "Did he say something to that effect?"

"Not exactly. But he was here last night reminiscing away, and your name came up in every other sentence."

Emily's heart began to thump, but she said airily, "Well, don't go making wedding cakes until we progress from 'hello' to 'how are you.' "

"But," Abby continued, "just because you were neighbors doesn't necessarily mean you belong together forever. For one thing, you're not suited to farm life."

"Did he say he was going to buy a farm?"

"No, but he probably will. And he'll need a wife with a love of livestock and a green thumb."

"I like animals," Emily said.

"But that thumb of yours is better suited for turning the pages of account books or arranging displays in the window. Whatever color your thumb is, Emmy, it isn't green."

"Maybe we'll go out West," Emily said, unaware that she already saw herself married to Roger.

"There's a thought," Abby said. "I can see how you might be happy as a clam running a general store in some mining town and trying to undersell the man down the street."

Emily grinned. "Yes. And Roger down at the creek panning for gold."

"Not exactly the exotic trips abroad you used to talk about," Abby said, "but close enough."

"Don't hold me to my childish fancies. I've outgrown them." This was not true. Emily was still a dreamer, though she liked to keep the fact hidden. She read romantic literature in private, like a secret drinker, sighing for the worlds novelists depicted or yearning for love as true and enduring as Shakespeare described in his sonnets. Her dreams usually ended with the love, however. She rarely took her imagination beyond the altar.

"So here's to you and Roger," Abby said, pointing at the pails. "A gold strike in California and a store with branches from San Francisco to St. Jo."

"Will you quit this, Abby? I've got to go out there and see the man. If you keep talking this way, I may slip and ask him what names he's considering for our first child."

All of a sudden Abby's face was serious. "*Would* you marry him if he asked you?"

"I don't know. Give me a chance to get to know him again."

"Take it slow," Abby cautioned.

"Oh, I will," Emily assured her.

When the men saw Emily arrive, they hooted and hollered and descended on her like Bastille stormers. The temperature was 95 degrees, and the sweat was pouring off them. They greeted her with grunts, took up the dippers, plunged them into the pails, and guzzled like men who had been stranded for months in the Utah deserts. Roger was one of the last to appear. His hair was slicked down by perspiration, and his opennecked white shirt was drenched. But unlike the others he greeted her warmly before seeking his bracer.

As the men moved off to sit down for a spell, Roger, grinning, rolled his eyes heavenward and recited a much-quoted New England prayer:

Oh Lord, thou knowest we do not want Thee to send us a rain which shall pour down in fury and swell our streams and carry away our haycocks, fences and bridges; but Lord, we want it to come down drizzle-drozzle, drizzle-drozzle for about a week. Amen.

Emily laughed and said, "You're in a cheery mood considering that you've been working since dawn."

"I don't mind haying that much," he said. "There's something almost exhilarating about it. You feel your body in motion, yet your mind soars free."

She knit her brow. His mind soaring free? Out here in the frying fields with straw in his hair, down his back? Exhilarating? Perhaps the sun had gotten to him. More likely he was joking. But he didn't seem to be joking when he went on to tell her of haying on the prairie or of scything wheat or of the satisfaction he derived from that open-to-the-sky feeling. As she listened, Emily tried mightily to imagine herself on the prairie in order to understand what he might have experienced. All she could come up with by way of analogy was the feeling she had had years ago, sitting at the edge of a meadow, propped against an oak tree, reading *Jane Eyre*. This was Emily's idea of open-to-the-sky.

They talked briefly of Abby, Jack and their children, and then, as the men went back to work, he asked when he could see her again.

"I'll be up at Abby's for now," she said. "And then I'll follow from farm to farm, just as I" she was about to say "always do" but changed it, in the interest of honesty, to "used to do," hoping that he wouldn't notice the tense. He didn't. He smiled broadly—God, but he was attractive!—and said, "I'm happier when you're around."

"Why?" Her voice was almost a whisper.

"I guess it's because we've always been—oh—a part of each other."

The words made her shudder with excitement. Abby had read him correctly, all right. Yes, it did seem as though he intended to court her.

Emily remembered his words as she helped Abby and two other women prepare and dole out dinner. She murmured them to herself later as the men, finished for the day at last, trudged in to supper. She thought of them through the serving and the mounds of dishes. And she finally began to assimilate them when Roger, after smoking a cigar, suggested that he and she take a walk.

She had planned to spend the night at Abby's and was tired enough to flop into bed right now, but Roger's invitation gave her such vitality that she felt as she did at eleven o'clock on a brisk spring morning. They walked through fields that had just been scythed and over to the dark line of the woodland. Here they sat among pine needles and mosquitoes, looking out into the warm night.

When he put his arm around her, she said nothing. Normally she would have feigned indignation. Such intimacies had to be worked up to, over a period of a week at least. But she and Roger, old friends that they were, had no need of such formalities. He had said it himself; they were part of each other. He caressed her shoulder with his hand but did not attempt to kiss her.

"Tell me what you've been doing," he said.

"You mean the store . . ."

"No, not the store. I mean what are your plans?"

"Plans?"

He came straight to the point. "There must be men interested in you."

"Oh, that. Yes, a few."

There was a long silence. Then he said, "Any from the old crowd?" He was referring to boys who had liked her when she was seventeen—boys Roger had usually found some fault with. She said, "There's Eddie Michaelson."

"Eddie wants to marry you?" His body tensed slightly.

"No, no. I mean, I don't know if he does or not. You asked if there are men interested in me. Yes, there are. But I'm not planning to marry right now."

"So you've discouraged them?"

"You could say that."

"You always did have common sense, Em." He paused. "Does Eddie still brag all day long about his magnificent horse?"

Emily grinned. "He's really very nice, Roger."

"Yes, well maybe I was jealous," he admitted.

"Why didn't you ever tell me?"

"And make a fool of myself?" He tried to smile.

"It wouldn't have been foolish at all."

He looked down. "There was another reason I never told you how I felt about you. I didn't want you thinking I was going to stay in the East. You see, I wanted so badly to go West . . ."

Here the conversation came to an abrupt halt. Emily was thinking that the West had meant more to him than she had. Roger was hearing her thoughts as clearly as if she were speaking them.

"I was young then," he said, as though answering a question she had put to him. "My priorities have changed."

Without thinking, she asked, "Suppose you had come home and found me married?"

"I would have been miserable."

There was, she decided, nothing more he could have said. At least he had been honest. Besides, it was not the man sitting here who had left her behind while he struck off for parts unknown. It was a seventeen-year-old boy who had done that. A boy too young to have known his own mind.

He smiled. "When I decided to come home, I thought it was because I missed New England. It wasn't until I got here that I realized it wasn't Lanston I wanted to see but only certain people who lived here. In less than a week, I've come to see that the town hasn't changed one iota. In fact it's drearier than ever. But a special young woman who lives here is as lovely as I remembered her." He paused. "You're the only part of the trip home that hasn't in one way or another disenchanted me. In fact, you've done quite the reverse."

He locked his arm more firmly around her. For a while neither spoke. Then, without prelude, he bent down and kissed her. It was a brief, discreet kiss, his mouth firmly closed against temptation. She responded just as primly, and they returned to their customary positions, not looking at each other but staring out into the hayfield. It was only when they rose to walk back to Abby's that he kissed her as she wanted to be kissed: his lips on her face, on her neck, in her hair, his lips finally parting to coax open her own; his hands moving from her back to her waist, along her arm, and then quickly grazing her breasts. She responded eagerly, panting, wanting more of him. But they knew they were on dangerous ground, and he finally moved away, murmuring her name in a hoarse whisper. Then he took her hand and said, "Better go in."

"Yes." Her voice shook and her knees were weak, but she felt peaceful and secure. When he took her hand, on the walk back to Abby's house, Emily knew that Roger shared her emotion. Their experience in living apart—the separate adventures that each had undertaken since graduation—had come to an end. They were together now, as each had always known they would be. They were together and the world was safe and the future would be good.

For the first time since moving to town, Emily found the

store a dreary place. After the haying idyll, which had lasted a week, each day punctuated by passionate kissing and caressing in the woodlands of various farms, going back to work at the store was like coming home from a tour of the world. For Roger was the world and life was wherever Roger was—but Roger, at the moment, was milking cows three miles away and Pa needed her in town. They were far behind in account entries, behind in the ordering, and the place was dirty, too. Matt had never been fussy about dust or flies, and Emily had to spend one night after closing scrubbing and dusting and using chloride of lime to rid the place of the smell of cats.

Adding to her irritation was the fact that she didn't know where she and Roger were to go from here. He had hinted about marriage but had not formally proposed, and seemed undecided about how long he would have to work at various farms before undertaking a mortgage to buy a farm of his own. He needed time to plan, she told herself, and she would give him all the time in the world. For he had her in the palm of his hand, and he knew it. This might have disturbed her pride had she not known beyond a doubt that she was just as indispensable to him. Abby had noticed this and remarked upon it. The rolling stone, she said with amazement, had come to a halt when he rediscovered Emily. At the moment, however, nothing was happening. Emily was back at the store, Roger was fixing up the old cabin for himself, and meetings would be limited to Sundays and perhaps one evening a week.

News of the Emily-Roger courtship reached Center Street almost as soon as it commenced. One of the town women had gone out to the Blake farm one day during haying to make her famous blueberry tarts. She had witnessed the affectionate glances between Roger and Emily, had deduced everything, and had rushed back to town to spread the word that Emily Stevens was in love.

Most of the townspeople were too genteel or too disinterested to come tearing into the store demanding confirmation from Emily, but Rosie Barrington knew no such scruples. The daughter of the harness maker/constable, she was a big redheaded woman a year older than Emily, and an incurable romantic. People liked her, in spite of her insatiable curiosity, because Rosie was never afraid to admit to an emotion or to say what was on her mind. She was not a pretty woman, being large-boned and somewhat masculine in build, but she was forever telling men she loved them and, to everyone's amazement, exacting similar avowals in return. Until recently she had weaseled out of engagements, because the world was too full of other men. But Rosie had finally found her true love—a shy thirty-year-old widower, new to the town, whose trade was mending watches and other gadgets. He was as different from Rosie as soft is from loud, but they adored one another and planned to marry in winter.

Rosie walked into the store one morning in late July clad in a lacy, flowered pink dress that clashed with her red hair and was much too dainty for her large frame. But for some reason the outfit was as right for Rosie as it would have been wrong for anyone resembling Rosie. She didn't waste time with amenities but came straight to the point. "I hear Roger Martin is madly in love with you."

Emily fought a smile. She too had always liked Rosie, mostly because Rosie generally told her what she wanted to hear. But Emily said, "Oh, pshaw! We're just good friends."

"He's absolutely gorgeous, Emily. That black hair, those dark brooding eyes. Oh, a woman could drown in them!"

Rosie, Emily thought, was able to express the sentiments that Emily felt profoundly but which, under pain of death, she would never utter aloud. Rosie, at the moment, was Emily's heart and brain talking. But Emily said, "Honestly! You do get carried away. Can't we just say he's a nice looking man and leave it at that?"

But Emily hoped Rosie would not leave it at that, and her friend did not disappoint her.

"He's exotic, mysterious, yet somehow so pure. He's a Greek god, Emily." She paused. "Has he asked you to marry him?"

"Aren't you getting a little personal?" Now Rosie had gone too far.

"Don't worry. He'll ask. I'm so happy for you, Emmy. I've known since school days that you and Roger were meant for each other. He's so vital and passionate, and you—underneath that cool veneer you're a seething cauldron . . ."

"God save us! What dime novels have you been reading lately? Why don't you save these speeches for Ed?"

"Ed." It was the one-syllable nickname of her fiancé, but Rosie caressed it with her voice as though it were as long as a sonnet. Then she looked up and said earnestly, "I know I must sound silly at times. I'm too romantic, I exaggerate all over the place. But Ed says he loves me because I give the world more zest. He says I try to find more in life than what's actually there. There's nothing wrong in that, Ed says."

"No, I suppose not. But you can't blame the rest of us for not feeling things so—so intensely." Sometimes Emily wondered if Rosie was real or just someone she imagined.

Rosie sighed. "Mrs. Harrington says my brain is up to date but my emotions are those of a child."

"She may not mean that unkindly," said Emily diplomatically. "After all, the poets say we should try to feel things as children do. Christ Himself thought that."

"Yes, He did, didn't He?" Rosie smiled at the thought of Christ Himself taking her part against the widow Harrington. "Well, now for a bit of gossip. Rafe and Christine are finished." Rosie grinned more broadly. Her dislike of Christine was as intense as her love for Ed Jamieson.

Christine was from the set Emily called "the embroiderers," wealthy town snobs who spent their days trimming trousseaus and gossiping about Emily and other women who committed the crime of doing men's work.

"Rafe and Chris finished?" Emily repeated in astonishment. "But they were going to be married."

"She's never loved anyone but that blackguard Don Benton. As for Rafe, I think Harvard has changed him, and I'm glad. He's too good for her."

Raphael Taylor was the son of a Maple Street aristocrat (old money with ancestors trailing back to the Bay Colony). Christine, a black-haired town beauty, was the daughter of a quarry owner (new wealth and no pedigree, though the latter could be bought in a generation or so). Her family lived on one of Maple's Tributaries, not yet worthy of the boulevard itself. Years before, Emily had suffered through a crush on Rafe, who had eyes for no one but Christine. This had infuriated Emily at the time—unfairly, since she had never let him know of her feeling.

So Chris had left him after all. Or had he left her? It

wasn't Emily's habit to make inquiries of this sort to Rosie or anyone else. She listened to gossip all day long, but to participate in it by asking too many questions or by letting people guess her opinions was bound to lead her into some warring faction, automatically pitting her against its opponents. Worse, she might become known as a gossip and lose the business of valued customers. As matters stood now, Emily's function was much like that of a tavern keeper in the days before temperance. Just as he had been obliged to hear the confessions of besotted male patrons, so Emily listened to the female community. To tell Rosie what Chris thought of her or to tell Chris what Rosie thought of *her* would be most unwise. Though Emily disliked Christine every bit as much as Rosie did, all she would say now was, "Perhaps the two just weren't suited to each other." She hoped Rosie would now go on to tell her who had initiated the breakup. But Rosie either didn't know or didn't consider it important.

After delivering another rhapsody on the wonders of Roger Martin, Rosie was off, down the street where she, like Emily, helped her father run his shop. Flowery pink dress notwithstanding, Rosie would spend the day making or repairing harnesses.

Emily spent the morning waiting on customers, grinding coffee, and thinking of Roger. He was coming to supper tonight and she must remember to take some cinnamon home so that Mary could make one of her spice cakes. She wondered idly if Roger knew that Rafe's long romance had come to a bitter end. Rafe and Roger had once been close friends even though Rafe was rich and Roger so poor that he would never have entered the academy had it not been tuition-free. For that matter, Emily too would have ended her education at common school. It occurred to her that she was now living in splendor compared to the old days on the farm. Yet she sometimes looked longingly at Maple Street and its annexes, wishing she had enough money to live as Rafe, Christine and the rest of them did.

That afternoon Rafe himself came into the store asking if the wallet he had ordered was in. It hadn't come yet, but she was sure it would be delivered the following week. Rafe was a tall, lanky, sandy-haired man. His eyes were dark blue and his features classic enough to be described as patrician.

But his crooked smile, together with his slouchy gait, cancelled the aristocratic effect. The rest of his family looked as though they belonged on Maple Street. She had never been able to figure out just where Rafe belonged.

It was his smile she had fallen in love with years before when they were fourteen and in the first term at the academy. They had sat in the back of the room in proper alphabetical order: Stevens, Emily and Taylor, Raphael. He was always making her laugh by writing in his copybook his comments on dull lectures or poems he considered silly. She recalled in particular a poem called "The Bells." The master, who thought it patriotic to give attention occasionally to American writers rather than spending all his time on Latin and English classics, had been trying to illustrate the unique cadences in Poe's poetry. He strutted back and forth, chanting the stanzas in a loud resonant voice. Each of the verses ended with the word "bells," repeated over and over again—for *effect*, he said:

> Keeping time, time, time
> In a sort of Runic rhyme
> To the tintinnabulation that so musically wells
> From the bells, bells, bells, bells
> Bells, bells, bells—

And Rafe, who could stand it no longer, had scrawled in his copybook, "I think he has bells in his belfry."

Emily had laughed so hard that the master reprimanded her. This didn't stop further observations written or whispered, from Rafe. Nor did it quell Emily's laughter. That had been a time in her life when Emily needed to laugh. Her sickly grandmother rarely cracked a smile, and her father's mirth was seldom prompted by anything but the antics of the animals. Abby, Jack and Roger were sometimes jolly during the long walk to school. But in winter they became as grouchy as Emily herself, overwhelmed by chores and homework and the unrelenting cold.

So Rafe, for a brief time, became the focus of Emily's life. His ready grin and his kindness endeared him to her. She would come into class, shivering, late for the algebra lesson after the three-mile walk in sub-freezing weather. And

Rafe would whisper. "We're doing motion problems this morning, Em. 'A', as usual, is driving the fastest train. 'C' is creeping along at five miles an hour. Do you suppose 'C' will *ever* do anything right? . . . Here, take my jacket, Em. You look frozen."

No one, not even Roger, had guessed how much these gestures meant to Emily. Rafe himself hadn't a clue, and he had spent many classroom hours gawking at raven-haired Christine. Emily's love had persisted for a good three months before pride quelled passion and she decided that he could take his Christine, the simple-minded bonbon, and choke on her.

All this had happened five years ago. He had pursued the beauty for more than two years, had won her at last from Don Benton, and now it was over. She searched his face for any signs of regret. There appeared to be none, and this piqued her. It was only fitting that he suffer a bit as she had once suffered for love of him.

They made pleasant conversation, however. Rafe had not changed much since the old days and could still make her laugh as heartily as she had laughed then. No, he wasn't suffering at all, and this led her to believe that it was he who had left Christine. But as they chatted on, she found that it didn't matter. Since Roger had come home she was feeling as forgiving as Father McNulty, who abolished sin every Saturday night in the small Catholic church across the tracks. (Though Emily was a Congregationalist, she sometimes envied the Catholics. How good it must feel to be free of the threat of hell for a few hours every week.)

Rafe said that he had seen Roger once, when he passed on the Whitney Road. "I mean to get out to the farm before I go back to Harvard. If I wait till the next holiday, he may be gone."

"Gone where?" she asked.

"Out West, of course."

"What makes you think he's going back there?" she asked.

"Did Daniel Boone return to the frontier?"

"Roger's different."

"Roger will never be dif—" Rafe stopped and then

smiled slowly. "Ah yes. The love of a good woman. You may be right at that."

"So you've heard."

"Who hasn't heard? I'm surprised they didn't post broadsides. There must have been a problem about the headline. Couldn't decide who should get top priority: You and Roger or Chris and me."

Again Emily waited for details. Again she was disappointed. All Rafe said was, "Oh well, there are plenty of girls in Boston. And after I graduate, there'll be a war to keep me busy."

"Oh, there won't be a war. I'm so tired of hearing . . ."

"Care to take any bets?"

"No," she said quickly. "But only because I'm not a gambler."

"Hah! It's because you're a realist." He glanced at his watch. "Promised my brothers I'd go fishing. I'll be back for that wallet."

"Shall I order you a ceremonial sword while I'm about it?"

"God, no. I said there'd *be* a war. I didn't say I wanted to lead the troops or even to follow in the rear guard."

"But you seem so anxious . . ."

"I said I'd *have* to fight. They'll shame me into it."

If Rafe was anything, it was honest. Not for Rafe any grand exhibitions of patriotism. He was firmly abolitionist but he was no breast-beating hero. Therefore his comment about being "shamed into it" was curious. Rafe was irreverent and defiant, constantly questioning conventions and getting away with remarks about religion that anyone outside Maple Street would have been tarred and feathered for. Yet Rafe was going to shoulder a rifle because the town would expect it. She was surprised.

Rafe said goodbye and left the store, while Emily stood at the counter wondering if there *would* be a war. Rafe seemed so certain. Well, Roger wouldn't go, at any rate. He had told her that he was a pacifist, opposed to killing no matter what the circumstances. If only everyone felt that way, there would never be another war. But there was no sense worrying about it now.

Rosie and Rafe were the only two customers that day to mention Roger by name. Other patrons were more oblique. One elderly farm wife asked, "Think your father'll be getting a clerk in here?"

"He already has Danny Winstead part time."

"I mean full time. Case you get married or something. You're the one pretty much runs the place."

"Well *in case* I marry, I guess Pa will get a clerk."

"Hope the new man don't let the place go to seed."

They were already saying goodbye to her, Emily realized, and the thought made her sad. As Roger's wife she would still be part of the town, but never again would she have so much importance. Stevens' Store was as central to Lanston as its common. For three years she had struggled to make it that way. In the beginning she had advised Pa to paint the clapboard exterior a snowy white. She herself would design and paint the sign. After agonizing over the merits of "Stevens' Market" and "Stevens' Grocery" and "Stevens' Emporium" and "Stevens' General Store," she had decided finally that the simplicity of "Stevens' Store," coupled with the whiteness of the edifice itself, would project a feeling of honesty, cleanliness, and general rectitude. Matt had listened to her, incredulous. He told her that white showed the dirt, that a general store was what the place was. But in the end he had done as she suggested, warning her not to blame *him* if folks didn't find "rectitude" in colors and signs.

But these changes, reinforced by Emily's insistence on absolute spotlessness, enabled Emily to end the monopoly of Zeke Masterson's General Store. As the postmaster, Zeke was always patronized and people bought from him while they collected their mail. Zeke also claimed the cracker-barrel set, especially since he had never posted a rule against spitting at the stove. Any man with an ounce of spirit was bound to prefer Zeke's rough-and-tumble store. But not their wives. The new place hadn't been open a week before wives were ordering their husbands, "Don't go to Zeke's sty, you hear? Go to Stevens'. Least they don't have mice living off the stock." And the men found it simpler to go to Stevens' and mind their manners at the window tables than to amuse themselves at Zeke's and come home with mouse droppings or weevils in the flour bag.

After that, Zeke had gone on a cleaning spree and won back some customers. But no one forgot who had started the sanitary trend, and most of the women at least stuck with Emily. For a while the two stores shared the town about equally. Then Emily would suddenly lower the price of tobacco or Zeke would undersell her on sugar. They still engaged in this practice from time to time, just to keep things lively, but Zeke had let cleaning standards slip. He seemed content with his gabbling men and the few dollars he garnered from patrons who made quick purchases while picking up the mail. For some time Stevens' Store had been number one in town. It lost a few customers among the Irish because the mill owners built a store near the company houses that was more convenient. But many of the immigrants still traipsed over to Emily's store, where goods were more reasonably priced and orders more speedily filled. Their comments on the superiority of her place over the mill store delighted her.

Emily was grinning as she thought about the history of Stevens' Store. Her father walked in and asked, "Something funny?"

"No. Just thinking."

"Thinking, huh. Well, I just saw him down by Acton's. Oughta be here any minute."

"Excuse me, Pa?"

"The Martin boy. Ain't that what you're thinking about?"

"No," she said.

"Hmmph," muttered Matt, disbelieving.

But Emily was surprised at herself that five minutes could go by without a thought of Roger.

"Better scoot on home," Matt said. "He's coming to supper, ain't he?"

"Yes."

"Good man," Matt said.

Emily nodded. She knew that Matt was seeing her married to Roger.

"Good man," Emily agreed.

CHAPTER 3

Emily first saw Roger's cabin in mid-August. She and Roger were trailed through the woods by his sisters, who served as chaperones. Roger had repaired the roof and cleaned the fireplace, but the cabin remained dismal. A table, one straight-backed chair, and a wing chair with the stuffing coming out of the cushions and arms constituted the furnishings. Strewn among these were a blanket roll, a rifle, a pitcher and basin for washing, canteens, an oil lamp, a few newspapers, and two leather bags stuffed with God knew what. The rafters of the single room were festooned with cobwebs and the remains of an old bird's nest. The windows were opaque with grime.

His sisters gasped at the sight, Lee going so far as to feign a swoon. Emily bit her lip and said nothing. The group remained for only a moment before Lee decided that they ought to go back to the main house for tea.

In September, on her second visit to the cabin, Emily and Roger sneaked in without stopping at the farmhouse first. This was a special occasion, he told her, and he didn't want his sisters intruding. He preceded her in and stood proudly in the center of his cave. Assuming he had summoned her here to witness the improvements he had made, she looked around vainly trying to find one. After a desperate two-minute search she thought she saw it. The moldy wing chair had been covered with a brown furry throw. Roger, beaming, identified this as a buffalo robe. Emily tried to feign enthusiasm, though the robe added little zest to his abode. But the robe, it seemed, was not the reason he had asked her here. Walking into a cluttered corner, he produced a bottle of burgundy wine, explaining that he had bought it in intemperate New York before returning to teetotaling New England. A ceremony was about to take place. Was he finally going to propose formally?

Setting the wine on his broken table, Roger asked her to sit in the wing chair which was too low for the table but was somehow more fitting, draped as it was in buffalo, than the rickety pine chair he himself took.

"Well?" he said. "Here we are."

"Here we are," she echoed, puzzled but delighted as always to be with him.

He remembered at that moment that he had forgotten the glasses and reached up to get them from the windowsill while she, dismayed by her pettiness, noted that the bird's nest still dangled overhead. But the glasses were honest-to-God wine glasses, sparkling clean, bearing no relationship to the murky chipped vessel he kept near his water basin. She was so touched by his thoughtfulness in having thought to buy or borrow them that she tried to ignore the fact that the cobwebs in the place were growing as thick as drapes. With an indulgent smile Emily watched him fill her glass and then his own. He said, "To us," and they sipped their wine. By the time she had finished a glass, Emily was feeling mellow and affectionate. Sensing that it was the perfect moment, Roger presented her with a small box wrapped in blue paper. She carefully undid the wrapping, folding it solemnly, and opened the box. Inside was a gold ring with a stone Roger said was green agate. As she exclaimed over the jewel, examining it carefully, he told her he had found the stone himself in Minnesota. A goldsmith in Dawn Hills, a town ten miles north of Lanston, had made the ring.

"It's exquisite," Emily said, her throat constricting with emotion.

"Shall we put it on your finger?" he asked quietly.

"Which finger?" In an effort to keep from crying she was resorting to teasing. But the fact remained that even now he had not said the words "Will you marry me?"

"You know which finger," Roger said. "Don't make me say formal things in formal ways. We don't need that."

By "formal things" he also meant the words "I love you," which neither of them had yet uttered even in the throes of frenzied caressing. It was not that they didn't love each other, she thought. It was simply the reluctance to use those particular words. What was it about them, anyway? Were they inadequate to express the emotion? Or were they too full, too naked, too—too soul-baring?

She placed the ring on the third finger of her left hand. Both of them studied the ring and the hand. They drank more wine and smiled shyly across the small table. Then Roger said, "We ought to settle on a date."

And on other things, she thought. Like where they would live. He was the second son in a clan adhering to the tradition of primogeniture and so would not inherit any portion of the family farm. They could stay here, of course, until they found a farm to their liking. But in spite of the wine and in spite of the ring, the thought of making a home in this dismal one-room shack was repellent. Even with ceiling, curtains, carpets and flowers, it would still be one room. Where would she go when she wanted to be alone? And then she remembered that married people weren't ever supposed to want to be alone.

He said, "I sort of thought we'd get married in February or March."

Emily nodded. Plenty of time. But were they going to live *here*?

Roger brushed at his hair and looked up at the ceiling. "I have a question to ask, Em. It's—it's been on my mind for weeks but—it's . . ."

"What is it?"

"Do you want to stay here in the East? Or would you consider going West?"

She had been half-prepared for this question ever since she and Abby had joked about mining towns. Rafe's assertion that Roger would always be a Daniel Boone had also caused her to wonder if he meant to return to the West. Having prepared herself, therefore, and having despaired of the pathetic cabin, she answered with a rush of relief, "I think I'd love to see the West." In her mind "the West" was San Francisco. No longer the swashbuckling town of '49, it was nevertheless a center for the new Western culture. She could picture the Pacific before them, the blue mountains looming behind. She saw a neat little house on a steep, twisting street—a street full of forty-niners and fishermen and trappers, each with stories to tell of the gold rush or struggles at sea or harrowing adventures in the mountains. She saw housewives much like herself—young, adventurous, casually attired in the free Western style. They would walk with their children down to the ocean, see the sea gulls wheel, watch the ships come in. As a woman with children she could not run a store, but in a town as lively as San Francisco, excitement would lap like the Pacific itself against the walls of their snug little house.

"You do seem enthusiastic," he said, noticing the shine in her blue eyes. "I was afraid you wouldn't be." He paused, then said quickly, "Of course we can always come back." He was thinking, "on visits." What Emily thought he meant was "when you're ready." This was reassuring. On the off-chance that she didn't like San Francisco, it was good to know that Roger would lead her home again.

Her lips parted in anticipation. How exciting it would be, sailing west in a great white wagon, camping at night, and, oblivious to the threat of Indians, making love under the prairie stars. And afterward, sitting by the open fire, she would read aloud to him from Dickens. No, he wouldn't like Dickens. He'd want—what *would* Roger want? Knowing him, he would probably want to contemplate the moon. There should be no poetry or music interpreting that gleaming ball. Roger was romantic but his was a romance she had never quite understood. With Roger it must be the moon for its own sake. *Luna gratia lunae.*

By night they would gaze at the moon, then. And by day they would roll across the plains, up past the timberline of the Rockies, down again into the hot Utah valleys, up into the majestic Sierras, down once more in the last lazy descent to the port of San Francisco. Then they would buy a small house and Roger would get work in the—she was about to ask him what sort of work he meant to do. Fishing? Mining? Running a livery stable? But he was looking at her intently, misinterpreting the dazed look on her face as an invitation for a kiss. She could see that this was not the time for detailed plans for the future. And anyway, she wanted very much to be kissed.

When at last he lifted her to her feet and embraced her, Emily, who had just consumed her third glass of wine, responded with an emotion she had never before experienced. Always—even in her most delirious moments—there had been the voice of caution—a voice resembling Abby's— warning her that passion led to babies and that only experts knew how to control "the seed." Roger might be her love and the quintessence of all things perfect but there had been, until now, doubts about his expertise in this dangerous area. Now, however, with the ring binding her to him, and the wine dulling the voice of Abby Lawrence, Emily had ceased to worry.

Before she knew how it happened, the buffalo robe was on the floor, and she and Roger, still fully clothed, were lying on it. She drew his fingers into her mouth, closed her eyes, and tasted them. She heard him moan and then felt his lips on her cheek and his free hand caressing her basque. Then she heard her own voice—a low moan that seemed to come from all over her body, turning her arms and legs to liquid, causing her breath to come in gasps. Her hands stroked his arms and his chest. His flesh was firm and muscular and she pressed her body against his, craving more of his hardness, knowing somehow that this action would make her more yielding, more liquid. She realized dimly that her dress was being unbuttoned. Eager to be free of restraints, she found herself helping Roger to remove her clothing. She did not think about what she was doing, for her practical mind was asleep and all thoughts were focused on his body. At last, lying naked on the buffalo robe, she felt the hardness she had been seeking. He drew her hand to it and both of them moaned and then she saw him shudder in desperate convulsions and then she felt warm liquid on her hand, like the juices that were flowing in her own body. Feeling the slickness of him and of herself, she began to move in abandon, in a longing so intense that her body began to hurt. Roger stroked her then, in the place where desire was concentrated, and her body arched, and she moaned and gasped. Then he was kissing her breasts and entering her. Though the pain made her wince for a moment, her body strained toward his. He moved against her, the rhythm like music she had never heard, its tempo increasing, transporting her upward to a place that was all sensation, concentrated and acute. And just as it seemed that she could bear no more, the pleasure diffused in waves over the length of her body like a series of sighs.

She was depleted, and barely aware of Roger's continued movement. By the time she did come out of herself sufficiently to notice, he was holding her tight, panting and moving rapidly. She heard groans and a hoarse cry, and then he seemed to melt into her, crushing but not hurting her. His hair was damp against her cheek.

They lay still for a while, both of them too tired to speak or even to think. Then Roger moved from her body and lay beside her, his hand running along her breasts. He said, "So beautiful."

Emily saw a different kind of beauty. Blissfully in love, satiated, she knew now how men had first conceived the idea of paradise.

He said, "Are you—do you feel all right?"

"Yes."

"You're shivering. Let me get you a blanket." He grinned. "Of course I don't really want to cover you . . ."

"I *am* cold." She was also a bit embarrassed.

He fetched a blanket, covered her, and then crept under it himself. Closing his eyes, he ran a finger along her throat, down to her breasts, along the line of her hip and thigh. "My God," he murmured.

But for Emily sobriety was coming back quickly. Even as they clasped one another in a mutual savoring, she began to wonder if Roger had controlled or not controlled the seed. At what point was the seed released? Had that been the liquid she had felt on her hand? And when he entered her, had any of it still been there? How much of the liquid did it take to make a baby? Or the half of a baby that would be Roger's? She did not want to ask these questions directly so she said with studied casualness, "Will there be a baby, do you think?"

"I hope not."

He *hoped* not? Then he hadn't been careful after all.

"We can't have a baby just now, Roger."

"I know that."

"Yet you—uh—seemed to forget that."

"*I* seemed to forget? Let me remind you that you didn't exactly fight me off."

"It was the wine," she said, coloring.

"The wine," he repeated, grinning.

"We have to be careful," she said. "Have to—have to be *prepared* for the child." As though to emphasize this, she wrapped the blanket more tightly around her.

"Yes. I understand. Practical to a fault, aren't you?"

"Someone has to be," she said pointedly.

"But I—but you—Yes, you're right. We'll be practical." He sighed.

After they were dressed, they ate some crackers—the only food he had about—and then he walked her home.

"Happy?" he asked as they strolled leisurely down the Whitney Road.

"Oh, yes."

"Aside from the—the risk, you did like it?"

She colored. "Very much."

"The first thing I'll do when we get to Nebraska is make the biggest, sturdiest bed in the—"

"Nebraska?" she repeated.

"Well, yes. That's where we're going to settle."

"In *Nebraska* territory?" Her voice was at soprano pitch.

"Well, yes. Where did you think we were going?"

"To—to San Francisco."

"What gave you that idea?"

"Why—why I don't know," she said in amazement. "I just imagined . . ."

"I'm a farmer, Em. I want to raise wheat."

"*Wheat?*"

"You look so shocked."

"I just imagined other things, that's all. I mean one doesn't think of wheat when one thinks of the West. Gold, yes. Tumbleweed, sandstone . . ."

"You can't raise children on tumbleweed and sandstone."

"Children?" she croaked. "In Nebraska territory?"

"They've been known to survive there," he said dryly.

"Oh, I should have realized that you meant to farm." Now that she thought about it, his accounts of towns had been brusque newspaper recitals, his accounts of the prairies sheer poetry. And how could she have forgotten Roger in that haying field talking about his mind soaring free? How could she not have seen that Roger was, and always had been, a Nebraskan Thoreau? Well the answer to that was plain enough. She hadn't wanted to see.

He said, "Don't you like farming? You always seemed so good at it. I know your Pa never had a yen for the land, but you seemed to like it."

"I—I—" she broke off in amazement. And she had thought he knew her so well. And she had thought she knew him.

"The prairies are so beautiful, Emily."

"Yes, you've told me." She thought, miles without a human being in sight. Huts made of sod. One-room hovels that would make his cabin look like a palace.

"We could live near a town," he said hopefully.

What he meant, she realized, was a trading post. She said, "Why Nebraska? Aren't there other states that are just as fertile?" She was hoping for New Jersey.

"I'm an abolitionist, Emily. Too many slaves in Kansas."

She admired his ethics but was surprised that the choice must be Kansas or Nebraska. What about Illinois or Iowa? Not fertile enough? Too Eastern? Imagine thinking Iowa Eastern. . . .

For a long time she was silent, stunned. He asked her what was wrong and finally she told him. Bluntly. "I don't want to live in Nebraska."

Silence. Silence. Was he going to change his mind? Was he considering San Francisco? Was he going to stay right here? Finally he spoke. "I know you'll miss the folks," he said. "But I know you love adventure too."

"Oh?"

"Nebraska will provide you with plenty of that."

Yes, she thought. But what kind of adventure? Endless tussles with the elements? Matches of wits against tornadoes and prairie fires? The thought of the isolated prairie was enough to make her crave Indian raiders for company. "We have different definitions of adventure, Roger. For me, *people* are an integral part of all . . ."

"You haven't even *seen* Nebraska, Emily! Why are you closing your mind to the whole territory?"

He had touched a nerve. There were two things Emily could not bear to be called. One was "afraid," and the other was "close-minded." She said, "I'm *not* closing my mind."

"Aren't you?"

"No!" She thought a moment and then mumbled, "You said we could always come back . . ."

"Yes."

"All right. Then I'll go." Already she could picture them coming back.

He clasped her hand, and as they walked into Lanston, she tried to concentrate on the positive things and to remember in every detail the moment on the buffalo robe. When it came right down to it, that was the sort of adventure she basically craved. The rest of her problems, she was sure, could be dealt with somehow.

Emily smiled and turned to him. "Nebraska, ho!" she said wanly.

Wedding plans were quickly drafted. Though the event was months away, Mary began immediately to clean the house from attic to cellar to the remotest recesses of the pantry. Old receipt files were recovered and menus were planned. There were trips to Winters' Dry Goods to examine white silk and lace. Matt began putting extra money aside for the event. Abby, who was none too happy about her friend's plans to move, nevertheless pondered guest lists and tried to look enthusiastic. Rosie advised Emily on trousseaus, ignoring Roger's warning that they could take little with them. The railroad did not yet run near the area in which he was planning to settle, and it would be difficult to ship items out.

Emily told her father that it was a bit too soon to start interviewing clerks to take over at the store. Matt was puzzled. He had expected her to discard her apron and spend the next few months mooning about—knitting, embroidering, or whatever it was prospective brides did.

Under prodding by his family, Roger appeared the following Sunday morning to accompany Emily to meeting. A godless soul he might be, but the least he could do, his family told him, was to get to know the minister who would marry him to Emily. Reverend Mitchell was one of the last of a dying breed. He had come down to Lanston in 1858, trailing clouds of Calvin, openly scorning the liberal attitudes of the newer ministers in Massachusetts and elsewhere and stressing the stern Puritan philosophy that enlightened Congregationalists had long since abandoned. He was a fifty-year-old widower with consuming dark eyes, and if the townspeople did not take his sermons to heart, they were nevertheless mesmerized for the moment. All agreed that he preached a lively sermon. Reverend Mitchell's God was an angry tyrant such as Jonathan Edwards might have depicted. But sometimes during his sermons, and always at funerals, the preacher would speak of the Almighty's infinite mercy. Thus God became a human being, not unlike hot-tempered men the townspeople knew, and one who bore astonishing resemblance to Zeus and other Greek deities. God raved and roared and generally damned mankind, but at times He could have a charitable heart. Though a good number of citizens, Emily among them, were appalled by Reverend Mitchell and the God he presented, the majority were fascinated by this mercurial Deity. They went off to meeting with interest, wondering what sort of mood God was in today.

On this particular day, God was spitting fire. As Roger, holding Emily's arm, walked down the church steps, he stammered, "Where—where did that insane preacher *come* from?"

"Excuse me?" Emily was smiling as she waved at a friend.

"That raving lunatic in there. Don't tell me you didn't notice him."

"Oh him. Reverend Mitchell," she said absently.

"Yes, *him*."

She turned her attention to Roger. "That's right. You were gone by the time he came to town."

"Thank God I was. Who the hell is he? Beelzebub in disguise?"

"Lower your voice!" she hissed, smiling at other parishioners.

"Crazy as a hoot owl," Roger said in a lower voice. "Can't we get a Baptist to marry us? Or that pleasant Methodist minister—I forget his name."

"We're not Baptists or Methodists," she said.

"A justice of the peace then. What difference does it make? We can't have that raving Puritan performing the ceremony."

When he talked this way he reminded her of Rafe. Two years earlier Rafe Taylor had quit the Congregational Church for good. He hadn't gone Baptist or Methodist or Episcopalian. He'd done something which, according to the citizenry, was worse than becoming a Roman Catholic. To the horror of Maple Street and most of the town, Rafe had proclaimed himself a deist—one who believed that perhaps some Creature *had* created the world, but if so, he had taken no further interest in it. Deists did not believe in supernatural happenings or in the Blessed Trinity or in God's interference with the laws of the universe. Most deists were considered downright heathens.

Only Charles Taylor's son could have gotten away with an announcement like that. And only Charles, a lawyer and statesman who had served several terms as first selectman, could have explained it. Once after meeting she had heard Charles say to a fellow worshipper, "My son? (chuckle). Why, he's still a Harvard man. Young, experimenting with new ideas, you know. Paine's beliefs, Franklin's beliefs. Yes, he will outgrow it. (chuckle.)" And so Charles had managed to link Rafe's outrageous philosophy with the finest school in the state and with the architects of American independence.

But Emily would have no clever apologist to explain her breaks with convention. To Roger she said, "Be reasonable. Your parents and mine will expect Preacher Mitchell to marry us. I know he's a maniac. I know he's made the church as grim as Hades. The only reason I go at all is that I can't afford not to. Snubbing the church would be very bad for business."

"So it's not our wedding then. It's our parents', the community's."

"I'm talking about *business*, Roger. Pa's store. If customers thought an atheist was running Stevens' Store . . ."

"An atheist?"

"Why else would I get married by a judge or stay away from meeting?"

"To worship God in private," he said.

"In Lanston there's no such word as 'private.' "

"My point exactly." His tone was smug.

"All right. All right. But we'll be leaving soon enough."

"God speed the day!"

As they walked across Center and over to Dawson, she studied his profile. Never before had she realized just how thoroughly he despised the region of his birth. And with each passing day his discontent grew. How on earth was he going to survive the winter here?

That Sunday and every Sunday they ate dinner with his family or hers, then went on long walks or on visits to friends. Never, after the day of their engagement, did they stop at his cabin. They decided that it would be safer to walk through the brilliant-hued woods, stealing kisses under the drifting leaves, holding hands near the brook that ran along the edge of the Martin property. They were careful not to arouse one another, so careful that their conduct was more discreet than it had been since his first kiss in Abby's woods. But each kiss, each touch, was a tantalizing reminder to Emily that soon they would need no restraints. It was that vision that occupied her thoughts in the following weeks. Leaving home, becoming a farm wife on the prairie, adjusting to a life she was doubtful she would like—all these problems seemed unimportant when she considered the happy ending. Roger's arms around her, his lips on her face, on her breasts; his hands on her thighs; Roger entering her, Roger moaning, moaning, murmuring, "So beautiful." Oh yes, she would think, walking through the red and gold woods. Oh yes!

Roger was frustrated by the long wait, but he would not let it show. Lonely months on the trail had taught him how to deal with his drives. He did not want to get her with child—not while they were still in New England with doting women around who would urge her not to go West in her condition, who would make them wait for the baby and then fall in love with the baby and keep the three of them prisoned here for the rest of their lives. And so, every Sunday before seeing her, Roger satisfied himself twice. After that it was easy to be chaste.

He was saving money by hiring out as a hand on some of the wealthier farms in the fertile land to the north. By spring he would have enough for the trip itself and for the 200 acres in Nebraska. And then . . . like Emily, he savored the promise. The two of them lying together at night, touching and stroking and sharing, happily tired from the long day, from the satisfaction of jobs well done. As Roger walked with Emily under the fiery trees of a New England autumn, he would see her naked on a summer night in Nebraska. As he listened to her chatter about the trouble the lyceum committee was having getting a speaker for November, he would imagine her lying in the weeds, her breasts outlined in the moonlight, her lips parting as she turned toward him with moans of pleasure. . . .

In this way the courtship progressed, each of them dreaming of consummation, neither thinking too hard about the long hours leading up to it.

Election day in Lanston was a busy one at the store. Farmers came in from every outpost, often bringing their families and making a holiday of it. Voting this year was on North Center Street at the new Williams Hall, named for the retired Maple Street judge who had funded the building. Between the hall to the north and Stevens' Store to the south was a solid block of humanity, some on the gravel street itself, others on the common, others spilling into Acton's Apothecary, Winter's Dry Goods, Zeke's General Store, the blacksmith's shop, the bootmaker's—every place in town overflowed.

This year the crowds were denser than ever because the election was national and particularly important. Lincoln, of the new Republican Party, was running against two Democrats, Douglas and Breckinridge. Breckinridge was expected to sweep the South and get few Northern votes. The contest in the North between Lincoln and Douglas was the crucial one.

Lincoln was a newcomer of undistinguished background. He was sincere about abolition, but many in Lanston doubted his ability to run the country. Douglas, on the other hand, was taking too soft a line with the South. He was opposed to forcing the Northern view upon them and was worried about the many threats of secession.

In Stevens' Store pandemonium reigned as shoppers mingled with political zealots and old rural folk hailed town cronies they had not seen in months. Matt, Emily, Mary and the part-time clerk Danny Winstead worked steadily, taking time occasionally to listen in on a heated argument but making sure they did not betray their own political feelings. All of them favored Lincoln, though neither Mary nor Emily was able to vote for him.

A tanner named Jason Gibson and Abby's father, a farmer, were among the many friends greeting each other today. But they soon fell into a raging argument about the South.

"Don't matter *who* they put in," Gibson asserted. "Lincoln or Douglas, he won't do no more'n Buchanan's doing. If it was me, I'd order the army to blast them rednecks to kingdom come."

"What good'd that do?" asked Abe Blake.

"What *good* would it do? It'd get rid of troublemakers."

"But you'd be killing half the country," Blake said.

"Just the half that's rotten," Gibson declared. A small group was gathering around him, nodding.

Abe Blake stood alone at the end of the counter. "Easy for you to stand here saying we're better folks than they are 'cause we don't have slaves. Well I'll tell you something, Jason. 'Taint true. It was New England sent the biggest slavers to Africa, New England made a pile of money off selling black men. Only reason *we* gave up slaves is 'cause we couldn't afford to keep 'em. It was cheaper to hire a hand for the summer and dump him into the cold when we was done needing him."

"Do you stand with the South?" Gibson bellowed.

"'*Course* I don't stand with the South! I'm just saying that truth is truth. You wanna bring the South round to our way of thinking, you don't go shooting people to do it. Won't be no one left to hear the preaching."

"Then what *would* you do?" Gibson challenged.

"Ain't figured that out yet. Just know war ain't the answer." Abby's father still stood alone.

"Know what I think?" Gibson shouted. "I think you *believe* in slavery." There were a few indignant nods, and Emily, watching Mr. Blake's shocked expression, had to bite her lip to keep from telling the group that the Blake farm had for years been a station on the underground railroad. At considerable risk, the family helped smuggle slaves to Canada. Emily had found out about it when she was ten years old. She had barged into the Blake kitchen one day and found Abby's mother hastily shooing three black children up the stairs. But Mrs. Blake hadn't been fast enough; Emily had seen everything and had to be sworn to secrecy. In the following years, Emily sometimes assisted the Blakes, bringing food to the Negroes or helping Abby sew garments. Eventually Matt learned of the matter, and after the store opened, he and Emily became contacts for wagon drivers carrying Negroes. Every so often a man posing as a teamster would stop at Stevens' Store, asking directions to the Blake farm. Matt or Emily would give the directions and also give the man some food for his "cargo" to eat.

Because she could not divulge this secret, Emily now attempted to stop the battle by asking Gibson how he wanted his tobacco mixed. The recipe took some time to recite, and in the interval Blake stalked out. Emily looked after him sadly. What would the townspeople think when they eventually learned the truth? On the day the slaves were freed and the Blake heroism became known, Gibson and other self-righteous folk would turn crimson with shame. She hoped she would be around to witness the spectacle.

Next to politics and the slaving issue the most popular subject for debate was temperance. Tipplers and abstainers alike pointed to the Good Book as the final authority. Espousers of the Demon Rum referred to the wine-drinking episodes in the Bible as proof that even the Lord had indulged. Temperate folk insisted that "fruit of the vine" referred to grape juice. Drinkers hooted that they could not imagine grape juice being the magic potable at Cana. So the arguments continued as they had for forty years. Prior to that time, alcohol had been a staple of most New England diets, with children as well as adults drinking moderate amounts. But eventually religious leaders and others had begun to associate alcohol with loss of inhibition (the wonder, Emily thought, was that they had not stressed this connection back in 1620) and drinking was now officially condemned as contributing to loose morals. In the privacy of the home, of course, people like Matt still took their liquid solace. But in stores and taverns not a drop was in evidence.

Roger did his civic duty, ferrying infirm gentlemen to and from the polls in a carriage provided by Rafe's father. Periodically through the morning he stopped in to see how Emily was doing, amazed that she could be so calm in the midst of this mob. He would suffocate, he told her, after half an hour of it. His comment made her remember that this might be her last election day at the store. It was becoming more and more obvious that once they got out West Roger would not want to come back. The thought made her so sad that she snapped. "Well, if you don't like the store, then by all means leave."

"I didn't say the store itself was . . ."

"You never stop, do you? Can't you for once, just once, say something nice about this town? About Massachusetts? About *anything*?"

"What's wrong with you?"

"Nothing!"

"It isn't as though you don't know how I feel."

"I'll say! You never pass up an opportunity to let me know *exactly* how you feel." These last words were hissed into his ear, for a customer, sensing a battle brewing, had edged up close to hear. The customer was Christine Osbourne, Rafe Taylor's ex-fiancée, a condescending young woman who felt that all the world should feel deprived because they weren't Christines. As Emily turned to glare at her, she realized that there were plenty of people in town whom she herself disliked. Why was she getting so sentimental over the election day holiday? Why was she risking her future with Roger for a town that had a goodly number of Christines in it? Looking beyond to the door, she saw two more irritating characters—Sam Jackson, who hated all Irishmen, and Jimmy McGarrity, who loathed all Yankees. They were staring each other down, and for a minute she thought there was going to be a fight. But Sam marched in toward the stove and Jimmy stomped out to the street.

Roger had not moved from his position in front of the counter. He was either riveted to the spot by the shock of her unexpected outburst or was waiting for an apology. She motioned him into the back room and said, "I didn't mean it, Roger."

"I think you did. And you have a point."

She stared at him, questioning.

"You'll miss the place, won't you?"

"Oh—a little," she admitted.

"Then there's only one thing to do," he said.

For an instant she brightened, thinking he would suggest that they stay in the East. What he said was, "I have to try to understand."

"Excuse me?"

"I'll try to make it easier, Emily. And I'll start by keeping my big mouth shut. As proof of my good intentions, I'll not say another word about Preacher Mitchell performing the ceremony."

She smiled wanly. He meant well, but giving in on the Mitchell issue was hardly her idea of "trying to understand." What he ought to understand, she thought, was that she was giving up a way of life that challenged her: the store, the concerts, the lyceum, the clatter and commotion, excitement and gossip that swept her from day to day, piqued her curiosity, engaged her brain. But how could she, who had never been an attention seeker like Christine or Rosie, who in fact often fled the noisy store to get home to her quiet books, explain to Roger that she needed people?

A customer called into the back room and she hastened back to work while Roger went off to ferry another voter. It was just as well, she thought. If she once told him how she really felt about the store, it would not end until the engagement ring was on the floor and the words "close-minded" were ringing in her ears. She had promised him. And she was neither a vow-breaker nor a coward.

As if to reinforce her sense of self-sacrifice, every friend she had dropped into the store that day, hailing her with anecdotes about the old days or questioning her about a concert where she was to play, a committee meeting she was supposed to attend. News was traded, jokes were told, and everyone seemed to be laughing. Why, she thought angrily, couldn't they have walked in with scowls on their faces, oaths on their lips? Why couldn't they have made her good and mad, anxious to escape to Nebraska?

One of the last to arrive was Abby, carrying her baby and trying to maneuver her toddler daughter around three men, two of whom were laughing themselves senseless because the third had called Lincoln "Old Ape."

Abby said, "They'll be laughing out of the other side of their mouths by tomorrow. Oh, it's exciting, isn't it?"

"Yes and no." Emily did not want to be excited. She wanted to hate everything she was leaving. So she said, "Rafe was in here just before he went back to Harvard. He was almost certain there'd be a war."

Abby nodded. "Jack thinks so too."

"Well, maybe they're right."

Abby shrugged. "What does Roger think?"

"He doesn't talk about war. He's a pacifist."

"A pacifist? Seriously?"

Emily nodded.

"Never even killed an Indian?"

"I doubt it."

"Anyway, you won't have to worry about the war on your doorstep. You'll be hundreds of miles away."

"More than a thousand," Emily said, her normally low voice sinking to new depths.

Abby studied her face. "Are you sure you'll be happy out there?"

"Yes! Yes I'm sure!" Emily was almost bellowing now. Then in a calmer voice she said, "If not, we'll just come home."

Abby bit her lip and changed the subject.

On the morning after the election, the townspeople moved from Center Street to the railroad station where the telegraph office was located. The outcome would not be one hundred percent certain. It would take weeks to collect every last vote from every last county in the Union. But by early morning most newspapers were saying that Massachusetts had gone solidly for Lincoln. So, apparently, had most of the North. Emily, who had decided not to think of Nebraska until the territory was there confronting her, was in the crowd at eight A.M. when the telegrapher shouted the news: "It's Lincoln and Hamlin. Definite. One hundred eighty-three electoral votes."

She ran upstreet to bring the news to fellow shopkeepers. Behind her she could hear cheers. A few firecrackers went off, set no doubt by the boys who had been waiting since dawn for confirmation. A buggy rolled past her, the horses dancing, the rider shouting "hurrah!" She reached Center Street, breathless, and called the news in to Pa. Then she stopped at the harness shop to tell Rosie and her father. As she entered Acton's Apothecary, she could hear people behind her shouting, "Lincoln! Lincoln!"

Andy Acton greeted her at the door. She said to him, "I gather you've already heard."

He nodded, smiling.

"Missed my chance to be Paul Revere," she said.

"You're doing well enough. Here, sit down. You're breathless."

Andy nodded toward a chair that seemed lost under the cluttered shelves of potions and nostrums and candies. Acton's was a tiny place but it served the community well. The three doctors in town were impressed by Andy's knowledge of chemistry and by the speed with which he filled prescriptions. The children loved Andy because he also had a widely varied stock of sweets. Soon they would be coming up from the station and Andy, because this was a special occasion, would be dispensing free confections by the wagonload, even though it was early morning.

"Any comment from the South?" he asked.

"About seceding? I didn't stay long enough to find out. The city papers will be full of news."

Andy drew up a chair and sat down. He was a large, heavy man, twenty-eight years old and prematurely bald with close-set eyes that were lost in his round doughy face. Rosie had once said of Andy, "Oh, if only he were handsomer. If only he weren't so—so *lumpy* looking; the girls would pine away for him. He's so *good*, Emmy. If only some girl would look beyond his body and appreciate his sterling soul!"

But many did appreciate Andy's soul. He was one of the best loved men in town, and one of the few devoutly religious people who actually lived his creed. It was unfortunate that he was not a Quaker. As a Quaker he could, in conscience, say that he would not fight. As a Methodist he could not. It was this that was troubling Andy now, and Emily said, "Even if the South does go, that doesn't mean there'll be a war."

"There will be."

"Well—but you don't have to go. I know how you feel about the slaves, Andy, but you've got a mother and sisters to support. And the doctors rely on you . . ."

"Ma and the girls are getting lessons in pharmacy."

"You can't mean that!"

He grinned. "Are you afraid they'll poison you?"

"No, of course not. I just don't want you to go."

"But I must. It is my duty, Emily."

Coming from anyone else, these words might have sounded sanctimonious. Coming from Andy they were the simple dictates of heart and mind. Rosie was right. Andy was so good. Emily had sometimes wondered why she had never seen him as a possible husband. Was it simply that he hadn't been attractive? Or had she wanted a man with a few unsavory traits, if only to balance her own? Whatever the reason, she had often wondered about it.

Having failed to fall in love with Andy, she joined Rosie and others in wishing someone else would. She had seen him shyly pursue girl after girl, had seen his heart broken, had marveled when he came through the ordeals with gentleness intact and charity undiminished. In his position she would have been silently cursing the empty-headed young fluffs who used him to get to dances and later discarded him for other men. But Andy, she guessed, never cursed anyone, not even silently.

He had never, however, pursued Emily. The reason, Rosie thought, was that he feared a rebuff, however kindly phrased. For Emily's part, she had never led him on either. never flirted with him to get herself a partner for a skating party or picnic. Now, of course, because she was engaged to another man, it was easier to be friendly with Andy. No longer need she fear his asking her to a party. No longer did she have to arm herself with excuses as to why she couldn't go. Since her engagement to Roger, Emily and Andy had become good friends.

"Think it over," she cautioned. "Don't join up until war's a certainty. Promise me."

"I can't promise that. But thank you for caring."

In the old days these words would have caused her to change the subject before he got the wrong idea. Now she could say with sincerity, "I care very much what happens to you."

He lowered his large head and swallowed. "Thank you," he whispered.

At that moment the door swung open and a group of children rushed in. One was shouting, "Did you hear, Mr. Acton? It's Lincoln! It's Lincoln!"

Andy stood up and shouted, "Free candy for everyone!"

As other children surged in, Emily left the apothecary shop. There was something about him—a strength? a resolve?—that made her wonder if she loved him after all, not in the romantic sense but with the love one feels for God or country. Andy was intelligence and safety and security. Andy was always there at seven every morning and he never left his post during working hours, not even to go to the telegraph office on historic occasions. He rose at any hour of the night to mix medicines for the sick and dying, never grumbling, never turning anyone away. And he was there to comfort the children when they were afraid to go home with their failing grades, when they came in weeping because the schoolmaster had used the switch. If Andy went to war, one of the bracings of the town would collapse. Lanston would not be the same place.

It was a good time to be leaving, she thought. Andy was going; other men would follow. The character of the town would change and the profile of the nation as well. Perhaps the West would be a better place after all. At least there would be no war in Nebraska. Only one question remained to disturb her. What on earth, besides chores, was there to *do* in Nebraska?

CHAPTER 4

The Mozart Quartet, in which Emily played piano, had prepared an all-Bach program for their semi-annual performance. It was something of a joke in Lanston that the Mozart Quartet was forever playing Chopin, Mendelssohn or Bach. The cellist had suggested that the name be changed, but it was always old Wolfgang who spurred the group on.

It was a cold night in December but Roger loyally attended, all decked out in his meeting clothes, using his family's wagon to squire Emily to Williams Hall. For Emily it was an exciting night. She had practiced the music for months, yet somehow never grew tired of it and was looking forward to sharing Bach's genius with the town. Though she was sure that Roger would not like the concert, she was touched by his insistence on attending tonight. Just before she went on stage, he told her she looked elegant in the deep blue silk Mary had made for the occasion. He told her too that he would find some way to get her own piano out to Nebraska if he had to hire a separate wagon. When he said this, her hand reached out for his and she grinned with delight. With a piano out there in the soddy, she would not feel severed from the world. And who knew? Perhaps there would be a town close by after all. She could organize a group of musicians. At the very least, she would have time to compose. That was one thing she could say for the prairie: no one would interrupt the creative process. At home, whenever she started notating her own pieces, there was someone knocking on the door or Mrs. Dawson calling over the back fence.

For a moment, as she walked onto the stage, she saw herself returning from Nebraska in triumph. Emily Stevens, first major woman composer in America.

In the audience, several people were studying her. Her parents and fiancé thought she looked lovely and confident. Andy, anxious to hear the recital itself, was thinking of her talent. Rosie was agonizing for her, feeling the stage fright, hoping that Emily would not make any mistakes.

But elsewhere in the hall were some whose thoughts were less benevolent. Christine Osbourne was thinking that Emily looked too conceited, gliding to the piano as though she were a soloist in a Boston concert hall. Mrs. Joan Armstrong, one of the town's richest gossips, was also frowning. She would not be here tonight had her nephew not been the violinist in this tedious group, for she thoroughly loathed Emily Stevens. In her view, the girl was too smug, too self-satisfied, and had a tongue like a razor. Once, when Mrs. Armstrong had made a perfectly innocuous comment about the dirt in shantytown, that snip Emily had arched an eyebrow and said, "Mrs. O'Rourke is here in the store, Mrs. Armstrong."

"I am aware of that. But I don't see what it has to do with me."

"In plain English, Mrs. Armstrong, you're being rude."

"This is a free country."

"But the store is not free. The Stevens family owns it. And we won't tolerate customers being insulted."

The O'Rourke woman had actually gloated, holding her head high as though no one knew that her daughter dispensed her favors to every taker in town. And then Emily, outdoing herself in arrogance, had said, "You will apologize, Mrs. Armstrong."

"To *that* woman? I most certainly will not."

"Then you will take your business elsewhere."

In due time everyone heard about the incident. There were, of course, two diametrically opposed versions: Mrs. Armstrong's and Mrs. O'Rourke's. People tended to mesh the two. Many had been annoyed with Emily, though none who shopped at her store could be induced to go to Zeke's. Only Mrs. Armstrong had suffered the weevilly flour and cat odors of Zeke Masterson's establishment. The memory of the incident still made Mrs. Armstrong boil.

Just who did the girl think she was? Well if *she* didn't know, the town certainly did. For one thing she was the granddaughter of a tart from Dawn Hills. Old Judd Stevens had tried to make her respectable, but the history could not be erased. And Matt Stevens was that woman's son. And his wife Betsy had come from a London family of the poorest stamp. Emily herself, for all her bluestocking airs, was still a nobody. And she had only made matters worse when she opened that store with her father and began competing for business like a man. There was nothing more repellent than ambition in a woman. Everyone had remarked upon it.

There were, however, kinder townsfolk in the audience. Old Judge Williams, old widow Harrington, Rafe's parents, Dr. Nelson and his wife—all of Maple Street—saw Emily in a different light. To them she was simply a young woman of principle who liked to work. If not descended from American Puritans, she nevertheless embodied the Puritan spirit. For Lanston's aristocracy, Emily's resourcefulness mattered more than her family history. As for the O'Rourke incident, they had at the time supported Emily's stand. The people of Maple Street prided themselves on their tolerance. Puritan background was important, but this was the age of the enlightened Yankee—the militant abolitionist and fighter for equal rights. The Browns, the Beechers, the Sumners, the Stowes were making New England the headquarters for Christian charity. The children of the Pilgrims had been chosen to lead the way to the New Jerusalem. And that meant being kind to the poor misdirected Irish as well as the chattel slave.

Particularly impressed by Emily was the widow Harrington, a wealthy old eccentric who stumped into town meetings demanding, among other things, that women be given the right to vote. She liked Emily to the same degree that she disliked Rosie and that silly piece Christine. Emily was strong. She never cried or carried on or used feminine wiles to get her way. And now the girl was getting married. She hoped Emily would have sense enough not to have five babies in succession, thus chaining herself to the farm forever. If the girl had to go West, Mrs. Harrington thought, she ought to employ her talents in giving the new land a distinctive character. No self-respecting Yankee man would think of doing less. It was time for women to match them.

The concert was, by Lanston standards, satisfactory. The town was not one for standing ovations and demands for encores. Only Jenny Lind, the Swedish nightingale, would have gotten more than polite applause here. But Andy Acton and Rosie made up for everyone else's reserve, Andy weeping at the end of an adagio, Rosie sniffling loudly and ostentatiously passing the embarrassed Andy a handkerchief. In this way, Rosie meant to show Emily how profoundly the music had moved the audience. Mary, on the other side of the hall, was seated between Roger and Matt. She had spent the better part of the evening nudging the men to stay awake, hoping Emily hadn't noticed. But Emily had noticed and was neither surprised nor annoyed. She hadn't expected either one to attend to the music.

After the concert, Mary, trying to make up for the dismal behavior of husband and future son-in-law, invited the spirited Rosie and the sensitive Andy to the house for a late evening snack. Rosie brought her fiancé Ed along. He and Andy had good voices, and the party soon became lively. Emily banged out Stephen Foster songs on her secondhand pianoforte. In this way, she, Andy and Ed managed to drown the voice of the off-key Rosie. Matt and Mary joined in when they knew the words, and Roger, trying hard to make up for falling asleep earlier, taught them a Western ballad. But he was trying too hard, Emily noticed after a while. There was a perpetual smile on his face that seemed stiff and strained. He was not enjoying himself, though she could not guess why not. He had always respected Andy, he liked Ed and Matt, and he had always liked Rosie too in small doses. Was that it? Was he getting too strong a dose of Rosie?

When the others went into the kitchen for sandwiches, she asked him, "What's wrong?"

"Not a thing." His smile was like a crescent glued to his face.

"Are you sure? You looked pained."

"A little tired. That's all."

"Is it Rosie?"

"Not really. I'm just not used to crowds."

Seven people constituted a crowd? She did not believe it. "You mean the singing's too loud, don't you? Then we'll stop."

"Oh no!" he said heartily. "No, please have your party. We should celebrate your performance tonight."

She said, "It's late, and you have a trip ahead of you."

"I can stay another hour."

"Please don't," she heard herself say. "I mean, don't feel you have to. We can celebrate at Abby's on Sunday. She and Jack feel bad because they couldn't come tonight. They've invited us to dinner." Four people, she thought. Would that be a crowd for Roger too?

"Well if you insist that I leave . . ." he began, looking vastly relieved.

"Yes, I do insist. Here, I'll get your coat."

"I feel terrible about the whole evening," he muttered.

She smiled. "You shouldn't, Roger. I know you can't abide Bach."

"I never said . . ."

"You didn't have to. Heavens, if you can't stand Eastern ways and mores, how on earth could you like Bach?"

"He was a German," Roger said, puzzled.

"Yes. But his music depicts all the rhythms you despise. He's a classicist. You're a romantic. Or are you even that?"

"Excuse me?"

"I sometimes think you're just Roger. No epithets apply."

He grinned. "Is that a compliment?"

"It is." And she meant it. In many ways she envied him. He could live comfortably within himself, rarely requiring outside stimulation to give definition or purpose to his life. Alone on a desert island, Roger would never be bored. Yet Roger had finally recognized that he did need someone. And from all possible choices, he had selected her.

At the door, she placed a hand on his cheek. "I think you've complimented me as well," she said.

"Oh? How?"

"It would take too long to explain. Some day, when we're settled, I'll tell you."

He kissed her good night and she kissed him back eagerly. She was beginning to sense what being married to him would mean. He would look only to her for sustenance and approval. Not to his friends or to the world beyond. Only to her. She felt important—indispensable. And kissing him again, she vowed that she would never let him down.

On the Sunday of Abby's dinner, the sky was overcast and snow was predicted. Roger and Emily rode in a farmer's wagon as far as Spruce Road, then set out for Abby's on foot while the farmer took a left turn and drove home. They had walked a short way when Roger remembered some cigars he had meant to bring Jack. They weren't far from Roger's cabin and they had half an hour before they were due at Abby's—at two. They walked off the road and into the woods. The snow began to come down. It was only the second snow of the season, and they greeted it with delight. They held hands and watched the skies sprinkle sugar on the evergreens. The wind was picking up, and the temperature was dropping as they walked. But in the woods they did not notice this too much, and they continued to stroll at a leisurely pace until they reached the cabin.

Was it the snow outside or was it the fact that the bird's nest was gone from the rafters? Emily did not know, but she was feeling exhilarated this afternoon and so in love that she didn't even frown at the sight of the cluttered hovel. Roger searched through his heaps for the box of cigars while Emily sat down on the buffalo-robed wing chair remembering her last visit here. Rising with the cigars, looking at her face, Roger remembered too. Remembered so vividly that the cigar box was placed on the table and his lips were grazing her hair.

"Emily," he murmured, taking her arm and easing her out of the chair, into his embrace. It was difficult kissing with coats, scarves and hats on, so Roger, glancing at his pocket watch, said he'd build a little fire so that they could warm up. If they were late, they could always explain to Abby that the snow had delayed them.

Emily, afraid of what might happen, told him they must not be too late because Abby had gone to great pains with the dinner. Roger nodded as he arranged the logs and set fire to the twigs. "Just half an hour. Take off your coat."

She deliberately piled her outer garments on the buffalo robe so the robe would remain on the chair. But Roger, seeing this, casually removed them to the pine chair by the table. He himself sat in the wing chair and drew her into his lap.

"Cozy," he said.

"Yes. Very."

He traced his finger along her forehead, her nose, down to her chin, down to the nape of the neck, where, giving her a penetrating look, he stopped.

Her look was equally penetrating, and he took this to mean, "Go ahead." Then, closing his eyes, he grazed each breast, feeling little under the heavy poplin, stays, and chemise, but apparently liking what he felt. Emily said in an unconvincing voice, "We really must go. We'll be too late."

"Late," he repeated dully, sinking into a trance as his grasp of the poplin became firmer. His hand crept toward the buttons of her dress and he murmured, "Please. I'll be careful. I'll make sure nothing happens."

She was too aroused to argue with him, especially since he *had* said he'd be careful. He whipped her clothes off with a deftness that made her wonder how many Western stays he had practiced on in order to develop such skill. But soon she was beyond considerations of jealousy, lying by the fire, trembling with anticipation. How many times had she dreamed of the moment. Every day for more than two months. And every night. Every night. . . .

He kissed her breasts quickly and touched her thighs. But before she could feel the sensations she had experienced the first time, he was inside her, moaning, moving up and down very rapidly. Then, abruptly, he was outside her, crying hoarsely, spewing liquid onto her abdomen. With a sigh, he collapsed beside her and closed his eyes.

The sounds of his pleasure had excited her, but she was feeling unaccountably disappointed—as though something more should have happened but had not. Turning to kiss him, she saw him smile, a lazy, satisfied smile. His hand reached out, stroked her breasts, and then dropped as though from exhaustion. She wanted to tell him to keep caressing her but knew that such a request would sound shockingly forward. Instead, she picked up his hand, hoping he would take the hint.

He grinned, stretched, and sat up. "I'm coming. I'm coming. I don't think we'll be too late."

She almost laughed at the irony. Now it was Roger worrying about the dinner appointment and she wanting the lovemaking. As he stood up and began hastily dressing, he asked, "Was it good? Did you feel—uh—good?"

"Oh, very good." This was true as far as it went. Her only wish was that it had gone farther.

"I was very careful," he said. "I'm almost certain there won't be any babies. But I wish we hadn't been in such a hurry. I don't think you actually—uh—"

"Was able to spend?"

"Where did you learn that word?" He frowned.

"A girlfriend of mine told me what it meant years ago." By this time Emily too had risen and was getting dressed. She arched an eyebrow. "You didn't think I discussed our—that time with anyone, did you?"

"I didn't know," he said.

"You should know me better than that!"

"I'm sorry."

But Emily was angry. The lovemaking had left her frustrated and his implication that she gossiped about their personal life had outraged her. "You *should* be sorry."

They finished dressing in silence, Emily bitterly disappointed that the moment she was always dreaming about—the moment that was supposed to make up for everything else—could be over so quickly and with such unsatisfactory results. Here they were carping at each other not ten minutes after Roger's final cry of pleasure. She tried to tell herself that it wouldn't have been that way had they not been in a hurry, but her rationalizations did no good. As they set out into the storm, she was still fuming.

The snow had become heavier. Roger suggested that they take a shortcut through a wood road rather than go around by the main roads where the force of the wind would be stronger. This made sense to Emily. She had seen enough New England storms to know how to cope with them. The best way, of course, was to stay indoors—especially at night. She had heard about men who had gone outside in blizzards to check the cows and had not been seen again until the first thaw revealed their bodies. But she doubted that the storm was as bad as all that. It was still daylight, after all, and though the snow lessened visibility, the wood road, marked on both sides by trees, would keep them from straying off course. She wasn't thinking of the hayfield ahead of them, a quarter of a mile square with not a tree in sight. She simply plodded behind Roger, shivering uncontrollably, hoping that her foul mood would miraculously vanish before they got to Abby's.

It wasn't a long walk to the hayfield, but the trek seemed endless because she was anxious to get somewhere warm. They felt rather than saw the hayfield, for the wind here was fierce and the granular flakes of snow drove into their faces like needles. Here they halted and Roger shouted above the wind, "Hold on to me!"

She grabbed a fold of the back of this coat.

"I said *hold on*."

"I am! I'm holding your coat!"

"Don't let go!"

"I won't!"

"We have to feel for wagon ruts. That's all we have to go by here in the field."

"I know that."

"Stay behind me, then. That way both of us can feel for the ruts."

Emily said nothing. She well knew how to conduct herself in a blizzard and was insulted that he would think she did not.

"Are you afraid?" he shouted after a while. "We can still turn back."

She had thought of making that suggestion herself, but the word "afraid" had its usual effect on her. "Of course I'm not afraid. What do you think I am? A child?"

They dragged ahead in silence, chilled to the bone, trying to feel for wagon tracks. At one point she was sure they had strayed. "We're off course, Roger!"

"No, we're not."

"Yes we are. I can't feel any ruts."

"Well, *I* can. Step heavier. Kick. You'll feel them."

The snow was sticking to her eyelids and the wind was numbing her face. She kicked at the ground, felt an indentation, and nodded to herself.

"Well?" he called over his shoulder.

"All right." She had lost the grip of his coat while concentrating on the kicking. By the time she realized it, he had gone a few paces ahead. "Roger!"

"Yes!"

"Get back here."

A dark form loomed into view. "I lost my grip," she said.

"You certainly have," he muttered, emphasizing the double entendre. "Just thank me for not having lost the trail."

"Oh, hush up and let's just get out of here!"

Progress was slow. She was sure they had traveled a mile and had gone off course. The tracks must have run into a ditch and they were following the ditch to the edge of the world. She asked Roger to halt while she wrapped the scarf around her face so that it half-covered her nose. He tightened it and pulled her woolen hat lower over her forehead. "Are you all right?" His tone was soft, concerned.

"Fine," she said, pleased by his sudden solicitousness. But she wasn't fine at all. She was cold and numb and afraid they were going to die out here.

After an interminable time, they could feel no more ruts. They were either on the main road or they had lost the trail. They walked fifty paces to the left looking for a tree, a sign that they had reached the road. No tree. They walked a hundred paces to the right. Still no tree. No bush. No haymounds. Nothing. Where were they? Where the hell *were* they? Blinded, lost in a world of white, they could only stumble around reaching out with their hands or kicking with numb feet, hoping to feel something. Anything. She was now holding Roger's arm rather than his coattail because they no longer had a need to walk one behind the other. But the effort was still exhausting. Her impulse was to drop her arm and suggest that they build a snow wall to shield them from the unrelenting wind. But she knew she must keep holding on and that they must keep moving. They must not stop moving.

Finally she felt something with her feet. A shallow ditch or a wagon rut? She shouted for Roger to stop. They bent down and dug at the snow with their mittened hands until two parallel ditches presented themselves to their limited view and a patch of dried grass emerged between them. The wagon tracks. But in which direction should they go?

"Let's not worry about it," Roger said. "One way will lead us to the Blake Road, the other back to the woods. What matters is that we get out of the hayfield."

She wondered what he intended to do after leaving the hayfield. Even if they managed to get to Blake Road, how would they find Abby's house? And if they stumbled back into the woods, how would they locate the cabin? Well, if they could at least find trees and bushes they might make some sort of shelter and a fire.

She was now so tired from holding on that she demanded they change positions, Emily in front and Roger holding onto *her* coat. The maneuver was made, and they shuffled along. As leader, Emily took the full brunt of the wind, weaving so badly that she was nearly blown off course and had to be steadied by Roger's grabbing her waist. By now she was visualizing the search parties tomorrow coming upon their frozen bodies. She saw Reverend Mitchell muttering over the coffins. At funerals God was always kind. . . .

Eventually she stopped thinking altogether and moved along like a dumb beast, kicking, kicking, stumbling, kicking. It was a moment before she realized that with that last kick she had felt nothing. And then she heard Roger, as though from a great distance. He was saying, "Trees!"

They were on the road, finally, walking at right angles to the wind. The snow didn't pierce their faces so much but they were too numb to realize it. Where was Abby's house? Somewhere to the left, of course, set back from the road, but how many paces from here? It was now too dim to see even the snow. As they walked along, they listened for the sound of animals. All they could hear was the wind shrieking. And then Roger thought he heard a cow.

"Are you sure?" she asked. "I didn't hear anything."

They stopped and listened. "Are you sure?" she asked again.

Then she heard it. A faint, far-off "moo" coming from

behind them. They walked in the direction of the sound, up off the road, counting the paces as they went, in case they wanted to descend again. But there were no more cow sounds, and so they stopped. Together they began to shout. "Abby! Jack! Help! Abby! Abby! Jack!" They shouted in unison until they were hoarse. Finally they heard an answering sound: the "moo" of a cow, and close by. The Lawrence farm was constructed in the shape of an "L." Its barn was connected by sheds to the main house. If they could only find the barn . . .

Instead of calling for Abby and Jack, they began now to call for the cows. Emily mooed and Roger mooed and after a while a cow obligingly answered. They moved closer, mooed louder, were answered, moved closer. And then they were walking into the wall of the barn.

As they felt their way around to the barn door, Roger said, "We make wonderful cows." And Emily, who had thought she would never smile again, began laughing in sheer relief. They opened the barn door and stumbled past the stalls of the beasts who had saved them. Roger lit a lucifer match, and the two went from cow to cow, gently patting each on the head. Then they were feeling their way through the dark sheds and into the warmth.

Abby and Jack, having finished dinner long before, were sitting in the kitchen drinking hot cider when the two burst in from the ell-room. The children, playing with the dog on the floor in front of the stove, screamed at the snowy apparitions. Jack and Abby, rushing toward the pair, were shouting, "Good Lord, what happened?" Emily was shaking so hard that she could not speak. But Roger, grinning, said in a soft drawl, "Sorry we were late."

At this, Emily found her voice. "Are you trying to be *funny*, Roger? Is this your idea of *wit*? Because if it is . . ."

Abby cut in quickly. "Come on. Let's thaw you two out."

They were rubbed with snow and given dry clothing and warmed with brandy and covered with blankets and finally, when they were fully thawed out, they were fed. Through the reheated pot roast dinner, Roger told and retold the story. Emily, still reeling from the terrifying experience, silently picked at the food. Later, sitting by the fire in the parlor, Roger and Jack began talking about other blizzards, while Emily half-dozed in a chair. Upstairs in the children's room Abby was fixing up a spare bed for Emily. It was heaped with a dozen quilts. Roger would sleep on the couch in the parlor.

Emily was fighting hard to stay awake until the bed was made. She opened her eyes and shifted herself into consciousness, trying to concentrate on the men's conversation. But all of a sudden she was wide awake and concentrating fully, for Roger had said to Jack, "This? This blizzard is *tame* compared to the ones you see in Nebraska territory."

From the other side of the fireplace came Emily's voice, as icy as the wind outside. "What did you just say?"

Roger looked at her. "Nothing. Why don't you go back to sleep?"

"Tame? Did you call that storm *tame*?"

"I—I just said that I've seen worse."

"Have you! Do tell me about it."

"Emily, you're tired. Why don't you just . . ."

"And when you're finished with the blizzards in Nebraska, why don't you brag about the tornadoes and fires? And when you're done with that, be sure to ask me if I'm afraid to go out there and live in a hut. Or better yet, I'll save you the trouble and tell you right now. Yes, I'm afraid. I don't want to die young. I'm *close-minded*, Roger."

"It's late and you've had a scare. You don't know what you're saying."

"Yes I do. Oh yes I do!"

Abby had walked into the room and was frantically motioning for Jack to get up. Jack finally took the hint and the two exited into the kitchen, closing the door.

"I can see it all now," Emily continued. "The ten children and me alone on your two hundred acres waiting for you to come back from the trading post in a blizzard more horrible than New England's finest."

"It won't be that bad."

"Hah!"

"You really should go to bed and get some rest, some warmth . . ."

"It won't change my mind, Roger. I'm not going."

"Not going?" he repeated dully. "Then what—what will we do?"

"That's up to you, Roger."

"You mean you want me to stay here?"

"Or to compromise. San Francisco, some decent sized town."

"I can't," he said in a ragged voice.

"And I can't either. Call me a stick-in-the-mud. Call me a coward. I don't care anymore *what* you call me. If you want to be a pioneer—a noble savage or whatever—that's your choice. I have to be a mother, which means I'm not about to risk my life or that of the children to prove I'm a heroine."

"Plenty of women are living on the plains."

"Fine. I admire them. I stand in awe of them. But I don't have to *be* one of them."

"It's your store and your activities," he said, his voice hard. "Your—your civilization."

"That too. My dull old civilization. The masses of men living lives of quiet desperation. Civilization, the scourge of mankind with its wicked doctors caring for the sick and those loathsome housewives helping during the lying-in and those terrible schools educating the . . ."

"Very clever," he said. "But how do you suppose all this civilization got here in the first place? If everyone were like you, the Pilgrims never would have left England."

"And if everyone were like *you*, they wouldn't have stayed in town after the population leaped to seven. Each stage of development requires a different kind of hero. The fearless explorer generally isn't the one who drafts the plans for the meetinghouse. Could you imagine Columbus busying himself with plans for the first Catholic church in the colony?"

He was growing weary of the analogies. "Are you giving me an ultimatum?" he demanded.

"Yes." She leaned forward in her chair.

"Then I—I'm sorry."

She leaned back and sighed. "So am I."

The house was deathly still except for the crackle of the fire. They looked at each other for a long time, as though each was subject and camera both, taking and posing for mental photographs. Then she said, "I'm going to bed. We'll talk in the morning."

He sighed with relief. By morning she would be herself.

"Good night," he said.

"Good night."

The next day Roger borrowed Jack's cutter to take Emily home. As the runners glided smoothly over the frozen white land, he said, "This doesn't have to be final. You can always change your mind."

"Oh?" She looked up at the cold sky and all along the chill horizon. She was so anxious to get home to the warmth that she could barely concentrate on what he was saying.

"Do you think you might?" he asked.

"Change my mind?"

He nodded, tugging the reins to get the horses back on course.

"I don't know," she said.

"But there's a chance?"

"I have to think . . ."

"That makes it easier," he said. "The thought that people change. Situations change."

"Yes," she agreed. He was right. It was possible that a year from now they might compromise on Illinois. It was possible, therefore, to say "au revoir" and not goodbye.

"Well," he said, "we'll just write to each other and see how we're feeling."

"Yes," she said. "A good idea."

They rode along, not talking, until they could see the town ahead, looking today like a collection of snowballs scattered among the trees. He said, "I guess I'll leave in a couple of weeks then."

She had expected this announcement. "Can you get work in winter?"

"There's a farmer I know who lives near Omaha. He'll hire me. I don't need so much money to make the trip now that you've decided . . ." his voice broke and he cleared his throat. He busied his hands with the reins until he had collected himself. She watched him, swallowing, feeling sorry for him, sorry for herself. They rode the rest of the way in silence.

They saw each other several times before he left in late December. They renewed their vows to write, renewed their pledges to keep the door open in case either one changed his mind. And then one day they walked down to the train. Roger was carrying the two bags she had seen in his cabin. And it occurred to her as he set them down and kissed her, that he had never actually unpacked them.

He said, "I have a feeling that this won't be the end."

"I have the same feeling," She smiled brightly, wishing she believed what she was saying.

"Anyway, you're still wearing my ring."

"That's right. And I'll keep wearing it."

The train began to move and he leapt aboard. "I'll write," he shouted.

And then he was gone.

CHAPTER 5

Emily told her parents and Abby the truth: that there had been a difference of opinion on where to settle and that she wasn't sure there would be a wedding. Others who asked why she hadn't gone with Roger were told simply, "I decided to wait until spring or summer." A few asked her if she intended to go at all, but most customers did not press her even though some guessed accurately that Emily just wasn't suited for the plains.

Had the times been different, Emily's and Roger's parting might have filled gossip vacuums in Lanston homes just as the dissolution of Rafe's and Christine's engagement had intrigued people four months earlier. Snippets of drama like these were what kept people interested in getting up the next day. When all else failed, folk had been known to gossip about couples who were too *happy*, speculating that such situations were unnatural and wondering what troubles or scandals lay behind the serene facades.

But this December there was genuine drama for people to sink their teeth into. Excitement was running high as national issues dwarfed all local doings. Lincoln would not take office until March, but already the state of South Carolina had seceded from the Union and other states were about to follow. Militia units were forming, abolitionists were declaiming, the quietest Yankee farmers were beginning to rumble like cannon. There were few arguments at the front tables in the store these days. Rather, there was a feeling of camaraderie, of "we'll show 'em," and "the Union now and forever!" The younger men, eager for war, joined the older ones at the tables, buying slates or pencils from Emily and making crude maps illustrating maneuvers that would bring the South to its knees.

Emily did not like the war talk, but she had to admit that it served a purpose so long as no actual war followed. Even in dreary January, customers were pouring into town like a volunteer army. Everyone seemed anxious to get out of their stuffy houses and share their feelings with fellow patriots. The discussions were distracting, they filled the coffers with money, and they helped Emily to endure the first weeks without Roger.

Only Rosie, who had been married the previous month and was deliriously happy, would not let the issue of Roger drop. Being Rosie, she felt that her discoveries about love's magic must be shared with the world. She would stand at the counter, her loud animated voice competing with the war prophecies emanating from the tables beyond, talking of the profound and glorious changes that marriage brought, wishing that all might know the beauty she herself was experiencing.

One day she said to Emily, "There's nothing more important than love. Nothing in the world. You and Roger *love* each other. And you should be—you *must* be—together."

"Rosie, will you please drop the subject?" Emily scrubbed the counter with angry vigor.

"But it's my Christian duty to help you see what you're doing to yourself. I care about you, Emily, and it breaks my heart to see you standing here trying to keep up a brave front when inside you're sobbing because you miss him so."

"Rosie . . ."

"You're too independent, Emily. No, don't interrupt me. Just hear me out a minute. Do you know what love means? It means submerging your spirit in that of another, of making his ways your ways. It's all there in the Book of Ruth. 'Whither thou goest, I will go. Whither thou lodgest . . .' "

"Then why didn't Roger lodge here?" Emily snapped.

"Because like it or not, the man is the king. He is the decision maker. He . . ."

"You said 'like it or not.' Well, I don't like it."

"But the Bible says . . ."

"I don't give a *hoot* what the Bible says."

"That's blasphemy, you know."

Emily shrugged.

Rosie, never too religious herself, tried a different approach. "If you're not willing to follow your man, you'll never know what love really means, Emily."

Emily stopped scrubbing the counter and glared at her friend. For the first time in their acquaintance, Rosie was telling Emily things she did not want to hear.

Rosie continued. "The others agree with me, you know."

"*Which* others agree with *what*?" Emily clenched her teeth.

"Women I've talked to. You know. They all say the same thing. You should have gone with . . ."

Emily took the rag she was holding and hurled it into the back room. It flew in an arc and landed with a thud ten feet away. Matt, sitting with the men at the front tables, stopped talking for a moment, hoping to find out why Emily, normally so neat and industrious, would suddenly be so lazy as to throw, rather than carry, a rag into the back room. Oh, well. He guessed everyone had a right to be lazy once in a while.

Emily hissed to Rosie, "I will *not* have my private life analyzed by the whole town. I won't have the chorus of women out there trying to tell me, through your big mouth, what I'm doing wrong. And as for you and your Christian advice, do me a favor and peddle it elsewhere." Emily shook her head. "I can't get over you, Rosie. Ever since you married, you've been self-righteous to the point of obnoxiousness, to the point of—oh, no, Rosie! Don't!"

Rosie had started to cry noisily, the tears splashing onto the counter, the large shoulders heaving. Fortunately, the men were too occupied moving imaginary armies through North Carolina to notice the outburst.

"Rosie, stop! I didn't mean obnoxious. I meant—well— that Christian charity ought not to be carried to extremes. I meant you're too happy to understand that some of us have different ways of looking at—oh, Rosie, take this handkerchief, please."

Rosie blew her nose. "I'm sorry," Emily said.

Rosie nodded but continued to weep copiously.

"Oh, do please stop crying!"

Rosie hiccupped. "It was only because I cared about you."

Trying desperately to make amends, Emily promised, "I'll think about what you said, Rosie."

"Are you serious?" Rosie sniffled.

"Yes," Emily said gravely.

Now Rosie was moved to retreat a bit. "Maybe I *was* too outspoken. Maybe it's just that you didn't love him enough." She dried her eyes. "I'll bet when the right man comes along it'll be different."

"I've no doubt it will." Emily was anxious for the crying to end and would have said almost anything to speed up the process.

"I hope so," said Rosie. "You look beautiful when you're in love."

"Thank you." Emily, fingering the agate ring, couldn't help wondering if this was true.

"Some day you'll know what I'm talking about, Emily."

"I'm sure I will."

Emily had thought she would forget Rosie's comments as soon as the big redheaded romantic vanished through the door. But she did not forget. In February and March letters came from Roger. They were mostly descriptions but always included references to Emily ("If you ever come out here, you'll see for yourself how the sky seems to glow with an almost supernatural light. . . ."). And she would remember what Rosie had said and wonder if Rosie was right and wonder if Roger still loved her.

In March the boys who had joined the militia held a drill on the common. One Saturday afternoon the whole town turned out to see them. In the lead of one platoon was Andy Acton, looking very soldierly for all that he was thirty pounds overweight and had only been accepted on the condition that he slim down. A hat covered his balding head and the line of the uniform minimized his girth. Rosie declared that he looked positively dashing. Emily would not go that far, partly because the word "dashing" could never describe Andy and partly because the spectacle before her gave her a sense of foreboding. Of course there was no war yet. Horace Greeley and others were urging that the South be permitted to "go in peace." The new president too was hopeful that the catastrophe could be prevented. But how this miracle could be brought about, no one knew.

In Charleston Harbor was a federal post called Fort Sumter. Here a Major Robert Anderson commanded a small garrison. But South Carolina was no longer a part of the country that Anderson was supposed to be defending. The South wanted Anderson out. The North wanted to send down provisions and reinforcements. In January, an attempt to deliver reinforcements had been opposed by battery fire. The steamer had withdrawn, and the lame-duck president, Buchanan, always a fence sitter on the slavery issue and doubtless reluctant to have a war commencing in the last months of his administration, had chosen to ignore the incident. Now, two months later, Anderson was still in Charleston Harbor and badly in need of food. The nation was waiting to see what the newly inaugurated Lincoln would do. Would he withdraw the men from the fort and effectively acknowledge the Confederacy? Or would he send another steamer to Charleston?

Emily watched the troops march up and down, bugles blaring, drums thumping. Children squealed with delight, women brushed at their eyes, and men gruffly cleared their throats. Emily watched and thought of Andy leaving, of thousands dying, of herself growing old in Lanston with other old ladies and no more men. The thought was so devastating that she hurried from the common, breathing hard, trying to concentrate on something cheerful. Soon the snows would melt and the trees would bud, and out in Nebraska Roger would begin the planting. Spring in Nebraska. Somehow it didn't seem so appalling as it had last December. Spring in Nebraska with the new-plowed fields and Roger's tanned face and nine whole months in which to build a house. She had only to send a letter and pack a trunk and her loneliness would be over. Then perhaps if she could learn to give more of herself, to submerge her spirit in his—then happiness might be possible. Heady with the thought, she went back to her father's desk and extracted a piece of paper from the clutter. She carried it out to the counter and began to write standing up. "Dear Roger," she began. And the pen stopped moving. She had better think this over carefully.

That night, as on every Saturday, the store was crowded. Mill workers, holding their week's pittance, carefully combed the store for supplies. Emily and her father always extended credit to those in need—a gesture that rankled some of the townspeople and farmers who claimed that the Stevenses weren't so understanding about *their* credit. But the truth of the matter was that there was a great deal of anti-Irish prejudice in the town, a prejudice which the Irish returned in full measure.

By all logic, Emily thought, the Irish and the descendants of the Puritans should have understood each other, both having a common enemy—the English crown—and a history of fleeing the British Isles for religious freedom. But to Irishmen, Yankees were just transplanted Englishmen. And to Yankess, Irishmen represented the abuses of the Church of England (which was actually the Roman Catholic Church, Henry the Eighth having done little more than rename it). The Irish blamed Yankees for everything from Cromwell to the famine. The Yankees somehow blamed the Irish for the sufferings of the Puritans. But fundamentally they hated each other for two reasons: the difference in cultural background and the fact that the Yankees had gotten here first.

Today, perhaps because of the martial atmosphere outside, Irish-Yankee animosity had been running high. There had been a fistfight between two bands of youths on the lawn in front of Williams Hall, in the vicinity of John Adams' statue. One of the Yankee boys had hit his head on the statue's base and had been carted over to Dr. Nelson's with a head injury that had turned out to be minor but could easily have been a concussion. In the store this evening were the two archenemies, Sam Jackson and Jimmy McGarrity. They hadn't been here together since election day, but to Emily's dismay they were staying tonight long after the rest of the crowd had gone. Each occupied a window table. Each was flanked by two henchmen.

Emily whispered to her father, "I wish they'd leave. They're making me nervous."

Matt nodded wearily. "I'll close the store."

He took the night's haul of money into the safe in the back room, then went outside to carry in boxes of supplies that had been delivered today but not brought into the store because they had been too busy. Emily began tidying up. She was replacing a box of smoked herring on its designated shelf when out of the corner of her eye she saw Jackson rise and glare at McGarrity. Jackson was a town blacksmith, McGarrity a foundry worker. Both were stocky, powerfully muscled men. Now McGarrity also rose and the four other men present fell silent. Jackson and McGarrity strode toward one another until they were standing face to face.

"One of our boys got hurt today," Jackson said.

"And ain't that a crying shame."

"Seems to me these things should be settled by bigger men."

"I'm after thinking the same thing," McGarrity growled.

Emily did not see whose fist shot out first. One minute they were glaring at each other and the next minute they were bouncing from wall to wall. Emily ran over and stood between them, shouting for them to stop. They sidestepped her and continued to swing at each other, reeling dangerously close to one of the windows. She tried to grab Jackson's arm and was shaken off with oaths. In the meantime the four others had sprung to their feet, shoving Emily back to the counter. "This ain't no place for a woman," one of them said, with ludicrous chivalry.

"It's no place for *you*," Emily shouted helplessly. "It's *our* store."

Her logic was lost on the fighters. Fists flew, curses rang, and by the time Matt came in from outside, bellowing for order, Jackson was knocking McGarrity through the plate glass window and into the street.

Emily tore out, crouched down beside the unconscious

McGarrity, and applied pressure to a spurting artery. Andy, who had heard the commotion from two doors down, came running over with bandages. Both of them shouted for someone to get Dr. Nelson as they hastily applied a tourniquet. McGarrity's two friends knelt by their hero, getting in everyone's way. Jackson and his friends stood off to the side, immobilized. They didn't care about McGarrity but they didn't want homicide on their conscience.

Rosie's father, a constable, arrived soon afterward followed by Dr. Nelson, who was breathless, followed by half the town, who were also breathless—with curiosity.

As four men carried McGarrity back into the store, he began to come around. Aside from scratches, cuts, and a bleeding artery, he seemed to be all right. Dr. Nelson doused a handkerchief with chloroform, gave McGarrity a whiff, and began hastily stitching the artery. Constable Barrington questioned the witnesses. The three Yankee participants said that McGarrity had started it. The two still-functioning Irishmen said that Jackson had started it. Matt had arrived too late to see *who* had started it. That left Emily as the only witness. It was Jackson, she said, who had risen first, Jackson who had spoken first, and Jackson who had thrown McGarrity through the window. She did not see who had thrown the first punch. But both men, she said, had been spoiling for a fight since they had walked in.

Mrs. Armstrong, who had arrived with other curiosity seekers, was assuming the role of nurse to two of the Yankees who had sustained minor cuts. She saw her chance to right the unforgettable wrong of the O'Rourke Apology Incident. In a voice loud enough for the constable to hear, she remarked to another woman, "Emily Stevens sees what she *wants* to see."

The constable turned to Mrs. Armstrong. "That so? Were you here to see different, Mrs. Armstrong?"

"No."

"Then let me find out who was." He turned to Emily. "You say Jackson threw McGarrity through that window?"

"That's right."

Barrington looked around. "Anybody here say different?"

No one could possibly contradict the story since McGarrity was the only one with glass all over him. Mrs. Armstrong's face fell.

"So Jackson is the perpetrator," Barrington said, "but McGarrity's guilty too." He glared at all offenders. "If I ever see something like this again, you'll be in the wagon and on the way to the county jail before you feel the other one's punches. Understand?" Of course McGarrity, out with chloroform, did not understand a thing. But Barrington raged on as though McGarrity were all ears. "I seen this fight coming a long time ago, and I'm telling you right now this is the last time any of you will pull a stunt like this." He stared each of the men down, including the unconscious McGarrity. "All right. Get out of here."

"Not just yet," Emily said. "We've got one broken window, a broken table, and damages Pa and I haven't had a chance to look at yet. Someone had better pay for this or Pa will take the matter to the justice of the peace." She turned to her father, who nodded.

"Then Jackson pays for the window," Barrington said. "He broke that. Now what about the table? Anyone know who . . ."

Jackson roared, "That Mick started it and that Mick'll pay for everything."

One of McGarrity's cohorts said, "We'll not be paying a dime. We'll go to the justice."

"All right," said Matt laconically. "That's what we'll do then."

Jackson's men and the Irishmen exchanged angry glances. On the floor, Dr. Nelson tended to McGarrity. In the crowd outside people were chattering about what had happened. For the first time in months a local incident was lively enough to silence the war talk. Emily, Matt, and Andy stood off to the side. Andy was watching Dr. Nelson at his craft. Matt and Emily were glaring at the "perpetrators." Mrs. Armstrong was glaring at Emily.

Suddenly a group at the door parted to admit the eminent Charles Taylor. Rafe's father was no longer first selectman but might as well have been, considering the influence he had in the town. Charles was a prominent attorney, renowned throughout the state. He was a tall, slim and dark-haired man with greying temples, a socially minded

Brahmin who was forever suggesting peaceful settlements among warring factions. As first selectman he had earned himself the affectionate title "Great Conciliator." Rafe, who was still at Harvard, did not appear with his father, but another son, also a lawyer, entered on Charles' heels as though to observe the technique.

Charles addressed Matt. "I understand that none of these gentlemen wishes to pay damages."

"That is correct," Matt said. Anyone encountering Charles Taylor—with the possible exception of his son Rafe—adopted formal speech instantly. "That's right" became "that is correct," "darn shame" became "unfortunate situation," "wrecked the place" became "destroyed valuable property." Charles, without realizing it, corrected grammar and encouraged the use of vocabularies that were normally dismissed by Matt and others as "fancy speech."

Even though Charles no longer occupied any town office, having declined the honor this year because of his busy law practice, he stood and took testimony like a judge presiding in court. After all accounts of the event had been repeated, he handed down his opinion:

"In view of the fact that both parties will doubtless be judged equally guilty in intent if not in deed, would it not be advisable, considering that both plaintiff and defendants are here assembled, to settle the matter with dispatch, thereby eliminating the need for disturbing Justice Dale at this late hour?"

Not everyone could follow the rises and dips of Charles' sentence, but the two sets of perpetrators, along with the crowd jammed in the doorway, nodded assent. Whatever he meant, it had to be the right thing. Charles Taylor always did the right thing. By the time Dr. Nelson finished his task and McGarrity drifted back to consciousness, the matter had been settled. Each of the ringleaders would pay half the damages. To the extent that they were able, other offenders would contribute. In this the drowsy McGarrity concurred. And that, it seemed, was the end of that.

But that, Emily soon found out, was only the beginning. Shortly after Charles went home, an incensed Mrs. Armstrong began gathering neighbors into her house on

Patterson Street, which ranked second only to Maple in importance. (The Armstrongs were a wealthy landed family but had come to the town a mere fifteen years earlier, making them "new people.") Mrs. Armstrong and her equally outraged husband were declaring that something had to be done about the Irish before it was too late. Who were these people anyway? Illiterate ungrateful newcomers who had plunked themselves down on land that the forebears of some of those present had shed *blood* for. They were criminals with dirty houses, immoral women, men who broke the temperance laws without batting an eye. How dare they swagger all over Center Street and the common as though they had the right to be here, as though they'd done something to deserve the privilege! And now—the absolute limit—they were knocking Yankee children senseless and picking fights in the general store. And what were the constables doing? Nothing at all. And what was Charles Taylor doing? Conciliating! And what were the Stevenses doing? Going out of their way to defend them!

If the citizens of Lanston did not do something, Mrs. Armstrong declared, those Hibernian barbarians would overrun the town. Why, the situation was serious enough already. That savage, McGarrity, was getting away with assault and battery while their respected blacksmith was being accused of the crime.

A man named Mr. Allen, sitting in the back of the elegant parlor, said, "But Miss Stevens *said* that Jackson started it."

"Miss Stevens," said Mrs. Armstrong, "is biased."

"She's always been fair," insisted Mr. Allen.

"Fair to the Irish and no one else."

Mrs. Armstrong went on to remind the group of how Emily Stevens had ordered her out of her store. "I made the simple suggestion that the Irish clean up the streets over there and Emily *ordered* me to apologize to that O'Rourke woman. Apologize for *what*, I asked. And without a word, she turned me out of the store. Without a word, I tell you! If you want my opinion, I think that girl takes the part of the Irish because she comes from a family of no distinction whatsoever. She's envious of our people and will stop at nothing to make us grovel."

"Really, Joan!" Mr. Allen sighed, as others exchanged amused glances. Mrs. Armstrong could not make much claim to distinction herself, they thought. But a few listeners, including one of the owners of the mill, were beginning to wonder if Emily had in fact distorted the truth about the incident this evening. It was possible. And the situation with the Irish was indeed serious. Why, a body wasn't safe in the streets anymore! If Emily changed her story or if she suddenly remembered a significant detail, and McGarrity was locked up for a while, well, at least those people would learn a lesson.

The next morning one of the mill owners—Mr. Price by name—called at Stevens' Store. Matt was out making deliveries and Emily was alone at the counter wearing a shawl and shivering. The window had not yet been replaced and a blustery March wind was gusting through the place.

"I'm here, Miss Stevens, because something must be done," said the portly man.

"About the window? But Mr. Taylor was kind enough to . . ."

"About the Irish, Miss Stevens."

"I don't understand."

"Are you sure of what you saw last night?" He leaned across the counter.

"Of course I'm sure."

"You couldn't possibly be mistaken?"

"No." She was puzzled.

"We have evidence that McGarrity provoked that fight."

"You do? What sort of evidence?"

"I will detail that later," said Mr. Price. "The point is that McGarrity belongs behind bars and we need your testimony to put him there."

"Absolutely not. Jackson started that fight. Any testimony of mine would put Jackson, not McGarrity, behind bars. Besides, Constable Barrington let them both go free on the condition that they never . . ."

"Can you afford to distort the facts, Miss Stevens?"

"Distort—but I'm not distorting any . . ."

"Because, Miss Stevens, if you insist on telling untruths, the people will not patronize your store."

Now she understood. Her eyes narrowed and she said in a barely controlled voice, "And who might 'the people' be?"

"A substantial portion of this town." Actually, there had only been five willing to go along with Price's plan.

Her face turned red and her voice rose. "Well, you and 'the people' can do whatever you wish. Stevens' Store will remain open. To everyone but you and 'the people'! Get out of here!"

When her father came back, Emily was standing near the broken window, oblivious to the wind, her hands on her hips and her mouth set with rage. She told Matt what had happened, then proclaimed, "That does it! I'm going to Nebraska. This town is as rotten as the barrel of apples old man Burke tried to palm off on me." (Many people traded produce, cheese and eggs for store items and a few of these cheated unmercifully.) "Roger's right," she continued. "Why am I staying here anyway when I could be with him?" She paused. "What are we going to do, Pa?"

He shrugged. "Tell the truth, I was thinking of selling the place anyway. Want to hook the lathe up to a water wheel and see what I can do."

"A furniture factory?"

"Small one."

"Do you think you could compete with the big places?"

"Don't know. Just said I'm thinking about it."

"I think you should try, but don't give up the store, Pa."

"Huh?"

"Take out a loan for the factory and try it out first. Don't burn your bridges behind you, Pa. I can run the store."

"What store? You just told me there ain't gonna be no customers. 'Sides, you're going to Nebraska."

"Well, not right away. We have to *fight* this, Pa."

Matt scratched his head. Never would he understand his daughter. Did she love that rover or didn't she? Was she going to Nebraska or wasn't she? Did the girl know her own mind?

He said, "One minute you're running to Roger and the next minute you're fighting the town." He sighed. "Why?"

"Oh, I don't know, Pa. Right now we have a crisis on our hands."

The boycott of Stevens' Store was arranged by Mrs. Armstrong, Mr. Price, and three others who possessed more finesse than either. The five let it be known that the Stevenses condoned the criminal behavior of the Irish. The reasons why this might be so were matters for speculation. Had Emily ever been involved with an Irish man? The departure of the Martin boy *had* been rather precipitous. Could he have been jealous? But whatever the reason, the girl had been distorting the truth. A brief boycott of the store would show Emily and the Irish alike that such abuses were not to be tolerated.

Most of the townspeople—and this included the "embroiderers" and their parents—just did not believe that Emily would lie. They were, nevertheless, intimidated by the five prosperous citizens who did. Instead of boycotting Stevens' Store by going to Zeke's, they simply refused to shop at all, saying that they were all stocked up. This went on for three days, though many people made a point of defying the edict, among them Charles Taylor's wife, the cane-stumping widow Harrington, an outraged Rosie, and a group of farm wives organized by Abby. But everyone on Center Street lost business while the rest of the community hid in their homes. Emily, who had been determined to smoke the people out by waiting until they were hungry enough to take a stand, felt compelled to act now before Acton's, Winter's Dry Goods, and others paid the price for her battle.

On the third day of the boycott she stormed up to Charles Taylor's office on North Center. He took her arm and guided her to a leather chair. He said, "I am so sorry about this unfortunate situation, Miss Stevens. Of course you realize that neither Mrs. Taylor nor I will tolerate it."

"Yes. Your wife came in yesterday morning." Emily had been impressed. Marie normally sent her cook to do the shopping.

Charles said, "Other citizens share our indignation."

"I know that, sir." She paused. "I came to discuss a matter bearing on the situation."

"Oh?" Charles lit a pipe.

"Do you know *why* we're being boycotted?"

"As I understand it, there are several in this town who believe you were—er—mistaken in your testimony."

"Did you also know that Mr. Price came into the store and demanded that I commit perjury?"

Charles frowned. "That is a very serious allegation, Miss Stevens."

"But it is the truth. He said, and I quote, 'McGarrity belongs behind bars and we need your testimony to put him there.' What name would you give to such a request, Mr. Taylor?"

Charles nodded but said nothing.

"What shall I do about it, sir?"

"Mr. Price is a very influential man in this town," said Charles.

"Then you're saying it's his word against mine."

"Yes. Though there are doubtless many who would believe you." Charles' expression indicated that he might be one of them.

"Do you think it's useless to make the charge?"

"I would not say that. You must give me time to ponder the particulars, to define the scope of the problem, as it were."

"But Mr. Taylor, time is of the essence here. Other people are losing business too."

"I understand that. But I must determine the most effective way to proceed. Please give me a day to think about it."

"Very well, sir."

That evening a gentleman named Mr. Allen came to see Emily at home. "I'm going to put an end to this," said the man who had been in the room during Mrs. Armstrong's tirade and had pleaded the case for Emily. He was the owner of the iron foundry.

"How do you propose to do that, sir?"

"By telling the truth." He then described the meeting that had taken place that night. After Emily, open-mouthed, had listened to all this, Mr. Allen said, "I should have come forward earlier but I've had my own troubles with the Irish. McGarrity, after all, is one of my workmen. However, I do believe in justice."

Emily told him about Mr. Price's attempt at coercion. Mr. Allen did not seem surprised. "I expected that he might try something of the sort."

"What shall we do about it, sir?"

"I shall tell other people what I've just told you. And if you wish to bring charges against Price, I shall appear as a character witness."

"Thank you, sir. But all of this could take weeks. Oh, I wish we could just put a platform on the common and have you stand there describing that meeting. You're an excellent mime, sir."

"Thank you. Yes, anyone knowing that group will know how well I can mimic them. Perhaps I've missed my calling. Do you happen to know if Edwin Booth needs an understudy?"

Emily laughed.

"But unfortunately these matters can't be resolved on a platform," Mr. Allen sighed.

Charles Taylor, however, found a way to do just that. After talking again to Emily and to Mr. Allen, he began collecting petitions for a town meeting. The annual town meeting had been held, as was the custom, just two weeks earlier on the second Tuesday in March. But Charles said that they had failed to resolve an important question: the need for a public library. Shouldn't this be discussed at once? The people, knowing that the town would never vote funds for a library building, sensed that something more than books was at stake here. They crammed into the hall that night anxious to find out what it was.

Mr. Allen was the first to speak. He had a loud, clear voice, and his enunciation was perfect. As Emily had suggested, he might have been an actor.

"I propose," he intoned, "that a committee be appointed at once to ascertain the need and the cost of building a library in Lanston. Now why, you may ask, does Lanston need a library?" Long pause. "Those of us able to afford books cannot know the deprivation of the impoverished. They toil long, weary hours in many industries, including my own, with never a bit of poetry or fancy to lighten their hearts at the end of the day. All their wages must go for food, for bits of clothing, for sticks of furniture. How splendid it would be if these unfortunates were given access to books. Then they might fly for brief hours from the tired world, losing themselves in lovely Herrick poems, traveling with Gulliver, sharing observations on man's condition with Alexander Pope or Francis Bacon . . ."

A few Irishmen in the hall exchanged incredulous looks. How many mill workers were going to spend their evenings curled up with Bacon and Pope? Most of them did not have time for a weekly newspaper.

But Mr. Allen was now coming to the real issue. "Yes, we need a library," he said, "and we need a great deal more for these citizens. But first we must stem the poisonous tide that is rising in this town. A tide of fear and hatred the like of which has not been seen since the days of the Salem witch hunts!"

"The issue is libraries," interrupted the first selectman.

"Yes, of course." Mr. Allen paused. "As I said, the need for a public library is urgent. This fact was eloquently demonstrated at a meeting I attended in the house of Mr. and Mrs. Armstrong several nights ago." Mr. Allen took a deep breath and stepped forward as though he were about to deliver a Hamlet soliloquy. "At that meeting Mrs. Armstrong said"—here his voice rose to contralto level and he waved his arms in an attempt to mimic her—"she said, 'If the citizens do not do something, those Hibernian barbarians will overrun the town. They . . .'"

"What has this to do with a library?" the selectman roared. "Will you confine your remarks to the business at hand?"

Mr. Allen ignored him. "And so Mr. Price *did* 'do something.' He threatened Emily Stevens with boycotting if she did not change her testimony about the McGarrity-Jackson incident. He said"—and now Mr. Allen bared his teeth and lowered his voice to suggest the criminal in many a melodrama—"our noble Mr. Price said to Miss Stevens, 'McGarrity belongs behind bars and we need your testimony to put him there.'"

There was a commotion in the audience. The first selectman pounded for order. Mr. Allen shouted above the gavel, "That man tried to coerce a fine and just young woman into committing perjury! Perjury!"

There were gasps and whispers, and the first selectman continued to bang with his gavel until Mr. Allen was forced into silence.

"Next speaker!" the selectman roared.

"Sir, I'm not finished."

"Next speaker!"

Allen shrugged and walked off. Old Judge Williams limped to the lectern and began to speak. He too thought a library was needed. He agreed with Mr. Allen that free books might benefit the Irish who had little to cheer them in their toiling lives and were now being defamed unjustly and to a shocking degree as all had heard Mr. Allen describe. As the first selectman pointed out that the judge's remarks were irrelevant, the latter simply went on talking as though he were too deaf to hear. He was retired now, no longer presiding in court, and considered some matters just too important to be impeded by parliamentary procedure. The judge said that it was time for the town to practice Christian tolerance. It was time to end the hatred that crippled Lanston and penalized upstanding citizens like the Stevenses. It was time for the town, no less than the divided nation, to reform.

Finally Charles Taylor spoke. After making the obligatory reference to libraries, he assured the assembled group that there were only a few people who were guilty of the heinous offenses against the Irish and the Stevenses. The rest were good, fair, upstanding citizens who loved their neighbors as themselves. The people in the hall solemnly nodded, each perceiving himself as one of the loving neighbors. The weary first selectman told Charles he was getting away from the subject at hand. But Charles did not have to shout or feign deafness. The people themselves were cheering for Charles to continue. As the first selectman sat back with his head in his hands, Charles launched into a full-length speech.

In heart-rending language Charles described the problems that Puritans and Irish shared in common. He pictured sick Puritans dying during New England's first winter, then compared their plight to that of the victims of the Potato Famine. He alluded to the children. The innocent children suffering on land, dying at sea, some of them coming at last to the shores of America. Pilgrim and Irish children alike, believing in their new world and then seeing their dreams brutally shattered. Children starving and dying because of hatred. Because of intolerance. Because people had turned away from Christ. Lanston would not turn away, he declared. Lanston's good people would not be misled by the wicked. And Lanston's immigrant children would know what it meant to be free.

There was more in this vein, and by the time Charles finished there were few dry eyes in the hall. But the meeting was supposed to concern itself with a public library. And so, amid the tears, a quick vote was taken to appoint a committee to examine the library situation.

As people left the hall, those Yankees who had always been friendly with the Irish were making a great show of reaffirming their feelings. Rosie hugged a friend named Ellen Murphy. Those less demonstrative than Rosie found excuses to chat with their neighbors who lived across the tracks. Emily heard one Yankee loudly shout to an Irishman named Mahoney, "Say, Ed, why don't you come round the house for dinner Sunday? We keep asking you, but you haven't been over in weeks." The tables had turned. Tonight the town's leading citizens were those who had always mingled socially with their Irish brothers.

The next day the store was jammed with people who were anxious to jump on the brotherhood bandwagon. Emily knew that many of them were hypocrites and many more were cowards who had not had the courage to defy the mill owner and his cohorts. She knew too that the newfound love for the Irish would not last the day. But she had been advised by the religious Andy to forgive the people one and all for they knew not what they did. And she was rather enjoying her role as heroine, watching everyone squirm as they foraged for explanations. ("I didn't need any flour this week." . . . "I couldn't come by 'cause the baby was sick." . . . "I thought Price would do something to me if I came in. I read about them picket lines, you know.")

Emily and Matt sent warm notes of thanks to those who had defended them at the town meeting. They stressed the words "courage," "statesmanship," and "fair-minded." The pleased men thanked them when they came into the store—which they did as often as possible in the week after the meeting. They were not above basking in praise.

The conduct of the ringleaders became a town-wide scandal. Mrs. Armstrong was ostracized by all but a few like-minded bigots. She and her husband began thinking of moving away. The two other partners at the mill offered to buy out Price, who had lost respect and standing in the community. For a week the town talked of nothing but the incident. And then one day the Irish issue died in an instant. For on April twelfth three words clattered over the telegraph wires: "Fort Sumter bombarded." The next day another announcement jolted the crowd at the telegraph office: "Anderson surrenders." And on April fifteenth came the message they had all been expecting: "Lincoln calls for 75,000 volunteers."

CHAPTER 6

All over Massachusetts militiamen were answering the call. On the sixteenth of April, amid bands, flags and tears, the local company massed at Lanston station on their way to join the regiment. It was a sad moment for Emily, made worse by the thought that Andy had no girl to kiss him goodbye. All the other men were being kissed by wives or sweethearts. Andy, to be sure, had his mother and sisters, but dispersed through the group were the faces of women who had used the gentle man to further their own ends and then had dropped him. Couldn't one of them, in the interest of patriotism at least, give Andy a kiss and wish him well? He might never come back. Didn't anyone realize that?

She was seized by the impulse to kiss him herself but found herself taking his hands instead and shouting above the strains of *Hail Columbia*, "Be careful."

"Don't worry," he shouted back.

Now was the time to kiss him, but before she could bring herself to do so, Andy was swept along with the others to the screeching train. Then he was mounting the steps and waving goodbye. So like Roger, she thought. And in that moment she realized that she hadn't thought of Roger since the day Mr. Price had threatened her. Did that mean she hadn't missed him?

As the train chugged into the distance, she thought again of Andy. She had meant to give him that kiss. But he had left too fast. She must think of some way to make it up to him when he came home.

In May of 1861, President Lincoln began calling for three-year volunteers. The militia had been inducted only for three months, and though Andy and others wrote home to say they would certainly reenlist if matters got worse, Lincoln was not about to take any chances. There had been a riot in Baltimore in which pro-Southern elements had attacked the Sixth Massachusetts on their way to defend Washington. Four soldiers had been killed. Heavier fighting was expected, even though, for the time being, the troops remained massed in the capital doing little more than disrupting the Washington routine.

Andy wrote to his mother that his regiment was quartered in the Capitol building itself. Troopers were sitting at the desks in the House of Representatives, conducting mock sessions of Congress with much whooping and laughter, scrawling letters on stationery belonging to their august leaders. Some of the Washingtonians were shocked and dismayed by such conduct, but Andy felt that these shenanigans said something about democracy. Where else but in America could privates and corporals park in the aisles of the House and Senate? He had never laughed so much in his life. When Mrs. Acton read this section aloud to her, Emily was pleased. She was glad that Andy was laughing and hoped the war would be over before his mirth ended.

In June Rafe Taylor and other college men came home for the summer. There would, of course, be no real summer for any of them. The regiment quartered in Dawn Hills was forming quickly and in a matter of days Rafe, Artie, and other friends would be enlisting for a three-year-term.

On the morning after Rafe came home, Emily saw him and other men in their early twenties playing cricket on the common with the little boys. They were running and stamping and clowning and yelling "Not fair!" It was their last fling at childhood. Emily, along with other people, stopped and watched for a while, understanding their need to cram as much fun as possible into the few days left to them. When the first game was over, Rafe looked in her direction, shielding his eyes from the sun, and then waved for her to wait. He came striding across the common and over to her. His thin face was sunburned and his fair hair disheveled. He stood in his slouchy stance and said, "I haven't seen you in months. How have you been?"

She told him she'd been fine. He inquired about Roger and she gave him the usual evasions, ending with the standard phrase, "I'll be joining him one of these days." Then she quickly changed the subject. "By the way, congratulations." Rafe had graduated from Harvard three days earlier.

"Congratulations yourself. I understand you single-handedly brought the Armstrong-Price cabal to justice."

"Not single-handedly. Your father and other men meted out the justice."

Rafe nodded. "Father told me about it. You managed to run the lot of them out of town." Mr. Price and his family had moved, and Mrs. Armstrong was in the process of packing.

Rafe continued. "After I quit the church a few years ago, that Armstrong harpy used to trail me like a hound. She found me here on the common one Sunday morning leaning against a maple and smoking a cigar. This was too much for the self-righteous hypocrite and before I could take another puff, the cigar was on the ground and she was howling like a banshee. How dare I defile the Sabbath by smoking right in front of the meetinghouse! Had I no respect for the Lord? I told her that the Lord lived inside the church with Preacher Mitchell and that I wasn't exactly puffing in His face. She said I was the most arrogant blaspheming young churl she had ever encountered and wondered how poor Charles Taylor could bear such a cross. After that, whenever I met her, I would throw my jacket on the ground with a Walter Raleigh flourish and say, 'Charles Taylor's cross—I mean *crossing*, Madame.' "

Emily was laughing. "I wish you'd been here during the boycott. I could have used some cheering."

"I wish I'd been here too. Wish I could stay here now."

"It's a volunteer army, Rafe."

"I know that."

"You've never before hesitated to do what you wanted to do."

"But this is different."

"Why?"

"I can't sit here and watch the rest of them march off to die."

The smile was gone from his face, and his eyes were glazed. But he quickly recovered himself and said, "My brothers are hollering for me. Got to go."

She watched him as he ran back to join his team. Rafe would never, in a hundred years, use the word "honor." Yet he was joining the army not, as he'd said, because "the town was shaming him into it" but because of honor and nothing else.

Life for Emily went on as usual. The Irish incident had ceased to be a topic of conversation and she was once again just "the Stevens girl." Emily and Roger were still exchanging letters, and Emily still wore the ring. But she hadn't made any final decisions and was stalling for time. Roger, meanwhile, had bought his two hundred acres, and his hopes for success were high. He wrote poetic descriptions of the land itself and said that one day a great house would stand here. In the first three weeks of June there were no letters from him. Emily thought nothing of the lapse, attributing the delay to transportation problems. Letters had to go by stage to the end of the railroad, and either conveyance might be raided, lost or stalled. But in the last week of June a long missive arrived that startled her.

Sandwiched between descriptions of the landscape were allusions to the family Roger had worked for during the winter. In paragraph three he mentioned the oldest daughter who was "very kind." More descriptions of prairie followed and then, in paragraph five, he identified the daughter. Her name, it seemed, was Anne. She was not only kind but "very capable" and "born to the land." There were two pages about a harrowing trip to Omaha before Anne reappeared on page six along with a description of her cooking talents. There was no mention of Anne's beauty or charm but that, Emily decided, was because Roger did not want to hurt her feelings. Nor was there a word about Roger's romantic interest in Anne. Instead, he went into a long digression about beautiful Minnesota, where he had found the agate stone for Emily's ring. It could never be right for anyone else, he declared. The letter concluded with a comment on the tragic situation in the East and the hope that Washington would not be attacked. It was signed, "As ever, Roger."

Emily did not know what to make of it. Did he want to marry Anne or was he forcing Emily to make a decision? If he wanted Anne, why didn't he just come out and say so? Why all the circumlocutions about the ring being right for Emily and "no one else?" Why any double talk at all? Was he testing her? Was he waiting to see what she had to say about Anne? Was he waiting to hear that she was on her way out to Nebraska? Emily read and reread the letter, trying to force herself to make a decision. She studied the words "capable" and "born to the land." She paid special attention to the cooking accolades. Then she thought of Rosie's advice about submerging spirits. And throwing the letter across the bedroom, she muttered aloud, "I can't. I just can't."

After calming down, she wrote a brief letter to Roger telling him of local events and saying that yes, she would always treasure the ring "no matter what happened." She posted the letter and waited.

Federal armies would call the battle Bull Run and Confederates would refer to it as Manassas. By either name it would spell disaster for both sides. For months the Northern papers had been hounding the army in Washington to get a move on and end the rebellion. "On to Richmond!" had been the rallying cry that finally provoked the unprepared General McDowell to lead his green volunteer armies into Virginia. Here, on July twenty-first, at a site so near Washington that picnickers came across the Potomac to watch, the first major battle of the war was joined. Though the Confederates would claim victory because they had defended their state and caused the federal army to go streaming back to Washington, even the South was forced to admit that they could have done better. Casualties had been appalling.

The telegraph office had been a busy place for the past

year, but battle rumors, interspersed among messages that the 6:05 out of Dawn Hills would be ten minutes late, were not enough for the townspeople. They wanted to know the details and who the casualties were. For that they must wait for the big city papers or telegrams from officers on the field.

In the case of Andy Acton the telegram arrived first. It was a simple message, as direct as the bullet that had hit him: "Regret to inform you that your son, Andrew P. Acton, died of his wounds following valorous charge near Centerville Va. Letter follows." It was signed by his captain.

When Mrs. Harrington came into the store to tell her the news, Emily did not cry. But she could not work either. Urged by her concerned father to go home, she stumbled down Center Street, seeing nothing, unable to think of where she was going, forgetting momentarily to pay her respects to the family. Others in town were also stunned. On the common the young boys quit their ball game and sat on the ground, their heads in their hands, some of them weeping. On Maple Street people were talking almost in whispers. At Charles Taylor's office the shades were drawn. Matt closed down the store, and other businesses followed. The bells of the Methodist Church began to toll.

Andy was the only one killed, but two other boys sustained minor wounds. The war of flags and slogans, of maps drawn on children's slates, of drums and fifes and smart platoons drilling had become a war of bleeding men. The impulse now was to *do* something.

Though all spring long the sewing circles had busied themselves making uniforms, rolling bandages, scraping lint and the like, there came a move now to set up an official committee to gather these items, along with food, delicacies and inspirational literature, and distribute them where most needed. Emily was appointed to the committee, which was called the Lanston Victory Association. One of her tasks was to set up a depot in the store for collecting donated items.

In the commotion following Bull Run, Emily busied herself so that she would not have time to think about Andy. The Mozart Quartet was preparing a benefit performance for the relief of the war wounded. Emily concentrated on the music itself, which was to be a grim program of funereal pieces, and not on the reason for it. Running from committees to rehearsals to the store, she had little time to think and managed to work herself into such a state of exhaustion that sleep came easily. In the midst of all this, a letter came from Roger:

"Dear Emily,

Almost nine months have passed since we last saw one another, and much has happened. While my feelings for you will never change, my need for a wife and a family remains strong. Though at first I was convinced that you would change your mind and join me here in Nebraska, I have come to the conclusion over the months that such is not your intention. The fault lies neither in you nor in me . . ."

She dropped the letter and muttered, "But in our stars." After a while she picked up the letter and wearily read on to the end.

In elaborately formal language, Roger cited the basic difference in their natures. Then, in a two-page prelude to the inevitable announcement, he outlined the reasons why farmers needed wives. Then came the news that he had met a young woman who could be such a wife. It was the selfsame Anne he had mentioned in an earlier letter. Did Emily remember his mentioning Anne? And so the letter went on, leading to the statement "We would like to get married" and ending with the words "I'll never forget you, Emily."

So now it was done. Emily had expected this, but seeing the facts in black ink did jolt her. One year ago he had walked into the store—the tanned, handsome adventurer who had decided that they must be meant for each other because they had grown up together. How naïve he had been, yet how appealing. She remembered the time they had kissed in Abby's woods, thought of the wine glasses gleaming on the broken table, of the feel of the paper as she unwrapped the ring, of the buffalo robe on the floor.

It was over. No changing of minds was possible now. She wanted to talk to someone—to Abby, who had warned her all along to take it slow; who had, after Roger left, consoled her with, "You did the right thing, Emmy." But Abby had her own troubles these days. Jack had joined the army, and Abby was trying to run the farm alone with the occasional aid of a younger brother. Emily shrugged. Perhaps she could talk to

Rosie. But what would Rosie say? More homilies and Biblical quotations and "Don't worry, Emmy, one day you'll find true love"? Emily rarely shared sad feelings with her stepmother, Mary. This was partly because Mary had always looked up to Emily as a strong young woman and Emily had not wanted to shatter the illusion. If she went to Mary now with her tale, Mary would surely be a comfort. But she would also be alarmed, and her cure was apt to be radical. She would probably search all over town for young men to fill the void. No, she wouldn't tell Mary or anyone else just yet. She would handle this crisis as she had handled most of the others in her life: alone. Time would pass and things would get better. . . .

One of the projects of the Lanston Victory Association had been to locate the body of Andy Acton and have it shipped home. In late August a train bearing a pine coffin creaked into Lanston station. It was late at night, but much of Lanston came out to witness the tragic homecoming. The funeral was held the next day at the Methodist Church on Dover Street. All the pallbearers were in uniform, Rafe Taylor and Jack Lawrence among them. They had come home on leave from the training camp in Dawn Hills to carry the coffin of a fellow soldier. Burial was in a small cemetery on a knoll overlooking the town. Everyone was there, from the most reticent farmer to the liveliest little boy. Mothers held babies in their arms and old people leaned on canes. The sun burned down on the bowed heads as the minister mumbled his ritual phrases. Beneath them lay the deserted town and Emily, looking toward it, remembered words from *Ode on a Grecian Urn*:

> What little town by river or sea shore,
> Or mountain-built with peaceful citadel,
> Is emptied of this folk, this pious morn?

Not wanting to think of what was taking place in the six-foot trench in front of her, she escaped into more Keats, into the part of the poem where the poet celebrates the fact that the trees and the figures captured on an urn can never die:

> Ah, happy, happy boughs! that cannot shed
> Your leaves, nor ever bid the Spring adieu;
> And happy melodist, unwearièd,
> For ever piping songs for ever new;
> More happy love! more happy, happy love!
> For ever warm and still to be enjoy'd
> For ever panting, and for ever young;

There was comfort in that, at least; in knowing that Andy would always be young; that he had died loving life and that his goodness was forever preserved like a figure in clay.

But such comforts were not enough. As she watched the people around her weeping, as she gritted her teeth so that she would not cry herself, she thought, But he deserved more of life and never lived to find it.

The services ended and the crowd dispersed. A breeze blew in, stirring the trees and ruffling the womens' black skirts. She walked back to town with Pa and Mary in a group so quiet that all she could hear were the shuffling feet. She guessed that all of them must be tormented by the same question: why did Andy, of all people, get cheated of life?

The store was quiet that afternoon. While Matt dozed in a chair by the counter, Emily busied herself in the back room with the accounts. She heard a customer enter, and hoping that Pa would rouse and take care of him, turned back to her work. Today she was in no mood to talk to anyone. The footsteps continued to the threshold of the back room. Sighing, she turned around. It was Rafe Taylor, looking as he had that morning, when he had shouldered the coffin of Andy with five others: very rigid and grave and unlike the Rafe she knew. In his blue uniform with scabbard and sidearms, he looked every inch an officer. The sight of Rafe so clad disturbed her. She did not want to be reminded of soldiers.

"I'm saying goodbye to everyone," he said. "This is probably my last furlough. The regiment's about ready to march."

Her mouth fell open. She hadn't realized they would be leaving so soon. Then Jack would be going too. And Artie and so many others. Boys she had grown up with, boys she had gone to school with, boys she had loved—like Rafe himself. She remembered the whispered jokes in the back of the classroom, the master's reprimands. She remembered coming in on cold mornings searching for Rafe's face in the corner near the coat racks.

She looked up at the sandy-haired man, half expecting to see the familiar crooked grin. Instead she saw strain and sadness. "Sit down, Rafe." She motioned him toward a chair. "I can't believe you're going."

"Neither can I . . ."

"This morning when you were all at the church . . ." Suddenly she knew she was going to cry. She had managed to get through the funeral and burial dry-eyed, but the tears had been close to the surface. In an effort to keep Rafe from seeing her cry, she rose and strode toward the window, gulping and blinking rapidly. Ten deep breaths and think of something pleasant, she commanded herself. The last thing a departing soldier needed was a weeping woman on his hands, especially one who hadn't cried in five or six years. That added up to a heavy reserve of tears, and if they once began to flow they might not stop until Thanksgiving.

She felt a hand on her shoulder. "Don't be embarrassed. Cry if you need to."

He had once made her laugh. Now he was encouraging her to cry. She tried to concentrate on the irony of this, hoping that the mental effort would stop the tears. It didn't work. She found herself in Rafe's arms, sobbing against his shoulder.

After a while he asked, "Do you want to tell me?"

"It's Andy," she choked, though it was probably also her mother's death and Roger's departure and the boycott of the store and just about everything else she had refused to cry over at the time the event had taken place.

"I know you were close to Andy," he said.

"They used to call him lumpy Andy," she sobbed. "Did you know that? And all the girls used him, broke his heart. And—and I didn't even kiss him when he went away," she finished incoherently.

Rafe held her firmly, stroking her hair. "Did he ask you to kiss him?"

"No."

"Then why do you feel so guilty?"

"Because—oh, I don't know," she stammered. "Tell me his death meant something. Tell me that, Rafe."

"He died very nobly," said Rafe, who had never before uttered the word "nobly" with a straight face. But for Andy, he had to admit, the word applied.

"I know he died nobly, but to what purpose?"

"I don't know," Rafe said helplessly, wishing he could think of a reason to give her. "His—uh—country."

Though the occasion was grave, he was distracted by the feel of her breasts against him and was seized by an impulse to kiss her. Gently he removed his arms from hers and led his distraught friend to a chair. Handing her a handkerchief, he sat down himself.

"Now about Andy and his broken heart . . ." Rafe began.

"Yes?" She pushed stray strands of dark blonde hair into place.

"What makes you think his heart was shattered?"

"Do you know Nancy Adams and Becky Garvey?"

"Of course."

"Well, they used him and—and then dumped him," said Emily, who rarely gossiped.

"No, they didn't. They pleased and delighted him. If anyone did any dumping it was Andy. In his own genteel way, of course."

She looked up, blinking.

"I grew up with Andy. I knew him at least as well as you did. If he'd wanted to marry at all, he wouldn't have chosen Nancy or Becky. He would have found the right woman with no problem."

"If he wanted to marry at *all*?"

"Has it ever occurred to you that he might have preferred being single?"

"I—no, it never did."

"And as for your failing to kiss him, are you saying you think *you* broke his heart too?"

"Why, I . . ."

Rafe was finally grinning. "You're awfully modest, aren't you?"

She wanted to give an indignant retort but could not

think of one fast enough. Actually his teasing had relieved her of an enormous amount of guilt.

"Of course he liked you," Rafe said. "He liked everyone. But he wasn't the type to moon over unrequited love."

"You may be right," she said slowly, thinking about it.

Rafe leaned forward. "May I ask you a personal question?"

"It depends on what it is."

"Whatever happened to Roger? I mean, why all the guilt about Andy when you and Roger were planning—" He broke off. She was struggling against tears again. Rafe could not understand why she fought so doggedly. How different she was from other women who pumped up tears as though they were cranking windlasses. He said, "If you don't want to answer . . ."

"No," she swallowed. "No, I'll answer. Roger's going to marry someone else." As Rafe set his teeth in anger, she added, "Don't blame him. It was my doing. I refused to go West with him when he wanted me to and I dragged my heels all winter and spring. I wasn't sure I wanted to marry him, and he knew that. It was inevitable that he'd find someone else."

Rafe nodded. "I never took you for the pioneer type. But I didn't know it was over. No one has mentioned . . ."

"No one knows. You're the first one I've told."

"Really? Did you just find out?"

"No, I've known for weeks."

"Weeks? And you haven't said a word to anyone? No wonder you're in such a state." Rafe shook his head. "I know your type, Em. You wear your pride like an iron shawl until you buckle under the weight of it. In your place I'd be crying on any shoulder available."

"Oh, you would not. You never cried about Chris."

"Only because when the end came we were both too bored to care very much."

"I didn't know that," she said. "Yes, I do miss him, but let's drop the subject, Rafe. You came to say goodbye, not to console a damsel in distress."

He touched his jacket. "But have you forgotten? I'm Sir Walter Raleigh. Alias, Charles Taylor's Cross."

"I forgot to ask you that day—did Mrs. Armstrong ever step on the jacket you offered?"

"No. But the third time I tried it she stepped on my hand. All one hundred sixty pounds of her."

Emily laughed. "Don't say you didn't ask for it."

He nodded.

"You haven't changed from school days," she said.

"I guess not. Except that then I was never afraid."

"And now you are?"

"Scared to death."

She wanted to tell him not to worry, wanted to assure him that he'd come home in one piece. She said nothing.

They talked for a while longer and then he stood up to leave. She rose too and looked at him, thinking of Andy's departure a few months earlier. She had meant to kiss Andy. She had wanted to kiss Andy. But the train had come in. . . .

Rafe, however, was not Andy. Without asking permission, he suddenly stepped forward and crushed her in his arms, kissing her on the lips. Closing her eyes, Emily kissed him back. Their hands caressed each others' backs and their lips moved over the planes of each others' faces. And then, with effort, she pulled away and stood looking at him. Both were trembling.

Rafe studied her face for a moment and then said, "Goodbye."

"Goodbye, Rafe." She walked him to the door, watched as he crossed the street, and then, sighing, returned to her ledgers.

PART 2

CHAPTER 7

Second Lieutenant Raphael Taylor was the first from his family to enlist in the War of the Rebellion. His older brothers were encumbered by their families and careers. His younger brothers had not yet completed their education. So Rafe became the warrior, carrying on a tradition of selfless devotion to country that had distinguished progenitors on both sides of his family. The mantle, he thought, could not have fallen on less capable shoulders.

Though he had predicted this war, he had always hoped that events would prove him wrong. He had damned Buchanan and damned the slaveholders and he did not believe in easy compromises either. Yet always, in the back of his mind, he had relied on the hope of miracles. Even as he spoke of armies, he had not been able to picture himself in one. Even as he shouted that the slaves must be freed at all hazards, he had never imagined himself in the midst of those hazards. And now here he was.

He did not enjoy marching around the training grounds, issuing orders to young men who had once been close friends and now muttered under their breaths every time he gave a command. He was overwhelmed by the number and variety of maneuvers, weapons, and strategies listed in his tactics manuals. He detested the sight of blood, cringed at the thought of his bones being mashed by a shell, vowed that he would swallow cyanide before suffering untended on some distant battlefield. Night after night he lay awake on his cot wondering if he would be the first to run from battle. With all his loathing of warfare, he was equally repelled by cowardice and had nightmares about coming home in disgrace. Even death was preferable to shame of that magnitude.

As he walked the short distance from the store to his house, Rafe tried not to think of Emily, though he could still feel her lips on his, her hands on his shoulders. And he was still trembling with his unexpected need for her. She had been there all his life, a pretty girl he was fond of, accustomed to. But until now he had not fully realized that she was no longer a girl. She was a woman, and a very desirable one. Thank heaven he hadn't gone further than that one kiss. To have done so would have meant disaster. This was no time to be thinking of love.

In an effort to put Emily from his mind, he began to think hard about the cause for which he was leaving Emily and everything else he wanted. Thus far Lincoln was trying to keep border slave-owning states from seceding by claiming that this was *not* a war to free the slaves. It was an effort to save the Union and that was all. There were some willing to accept this explanation, but Rafe was not among them. "Saving the Union" was too feeble an ideal for him. The North and South were so different in nature that both sides might be better served if they indeed split apart into independent nations. As far as Rafe was concerned, the war should be fought for one objective: emancipation. And if Lincoln, a known abolitionist, was not admitting this truth, it was only because he could not afford to lose the border states. Rafe respected Lincoln and felt certain that, if the North did win the war, emancipation would quickly follow.

In order to maintain his courage, Rafe decided, there was only one thing to do. Before every battle he would make himself remember why he was there. He would call to mind every story of slavery he could remember from the accounts of the slave ships to the more recent descriptions of bondage in the South. With these ghastly images burning in his mind he would somehow summon the resolve to charge the enemy lines.

Rafe reminded himself that in order to be an effective soldier he must try not to think of anything but the objective. He must close off the thought that the rebels he would be slaughtering might be innocent crackers who owned no slaves or men who had been conscripted against their wills. He must forget every college discussion in which peaceable means of resolving the crisis had been suggested. It was too late for college solutions. He must forget that murder was a despicable act and try to believe that the slaying of men was sometimes justified for the greater good. War was all emotion and action. Reason ought to have no part in it. This troubled him, for he could not imagine enduring for months on end without using his brain.

Rafe walked into his house frowning. Downstairs in the summer kitchen the cook was preparing supper and the smell of food improved his spirits. He walked in and took a large hunk of bread. His two younger brothers, seated at the long wooden table, had already demolished three-quarters of a loaf. Annie, the round, red-faced cook, shook her fist in mock anger, warning them as always that they'd spoil their appetites for supper. The three boys laughed at her and continued to gorge, reaching occasionally for the pitcher of lemonade. The kitchen had always been their favorite haunt and Annie, for all her muttering, never failed to indulge them.

Neighbors had always thought the Taylor family to be an ideal one, and they were right—up to a point. The father, Charles, was of course a model human being of great probity. The mother, Marie, was attractive and sensitive. What few people realized was that Charles' frequent absences on behalf of his many causes were resented by his children, who felt that he ought to pay more attention to them. And Marie's sensitivity, which might send her into raptures over a blossoming tree or the beauty in a child's face, was just as likely to plummet her into a two-day depression over the fact that winter is cold. At times, when Charles was off campaigning for a worthy representative of the people and Marie was pacing about snapping at everyone because one child had left his boots on the stairs, the children would retreat en masse to the kitchen. Here the indulgent Annie consoled them with cookies and jolly chatter about life in old Kerry before the famine.

The older boys were off on their own now, but there were still five children at home: three boys, now twenty-one, seventeen and sixteen, and two girls, fourteen and thirteen. They formed two groups, neither of which had much in common with the other though the affection between them was strong.

Marie peeked into the kitchen, reminded Rafe to pack the socks she had knitted for him, and then went up to her room to brood upon her son's fate. She was a thin, pale woman with wispy blonde hair and delicate features indicating that she had once been beautiful. But her fine skin, which had been admired by many suitors, was now starting to wrinkle. The forty-six winters were beginning to show, even though her fair hair blended nicely with the gray outcroppings.

But Marie had never been one to fuss about her looks. Her husband Charles was quite satisfied with them. Too satisfied, if seven children and four miscarriages were any indication. Seven children. Even now she wondered how she had survived it. Other women apparently had no problems in raising such a brood, but for Marie, the only child of a quiet professor and his equally bookish wife, the experience had been overwhelming.

In the beginning motherhood had been a challenge. Her first two boys had been eagerly awaited, and she gave of herself joyfully. "Our sons!" she would exclaim to her husband as they stood with linked arms at the door to the nursery, their hearts overflowing with the wonder of it all.

For five years all had been bliss. Then, after giving birth to Rafe, the shine of motherhood began to tarnish. It started with the realization that babies did not remain chubby bundles of joy. They grew up, acquired character, acquired little habits of which she did not approve. The nurses were able to handle some of the problems but the responsibility for molding Christian character fell upon the parents. Since one parent was rarely around, it was she who had to assume the awesome task.

But character was only one problem. What drove her to distraction were the incessant questions. The older boys, though annoying, had been satisfied with simple answers. (What makes the sun shine? God makes the sun shine.) But with Rafe there had never been any peace. She remembered a typical conversation when Rafe was about eight.

"Does God hear our prayers, Mother?"

"Indeed He does."

"Everybody's?"

"Yes. Everybody's."

"How can He listen to all those people praying at the same time? Doesn't He get mixed up?"

"He has no human limitations, Raphael. He is divine, and His abilities are not understood by men."

"Does He *look* like a person?"

"I don't know, Raphael."

"Is there anyone who knows?"

"No."

"You mean no one's ever *seen* God?"

"No. That is, yes. In the form of Christ."

"Christ only had two ears, didn't he?"

Sighing. "Of course."

"Then how could He hear all our prayers?"

"It's a mystery, Raphael." This through clenched teeth.

"If it's a mystery, how do we know it's true?"

"Well, I—perhaps you ought to discuss this with your father."

"I did. He said you could explain it better."

Oh the coward! "I see. You must simply have faith, Raphael. Now why don't you run outside and pick some berries? We'll bake a . . ."

"Does faith mean believing things that aren't true?"

"It means believing things that haven't been proven."

"Why should I do that?"

"The berries, Raphael!"

Rafe was the first to tax her patience thoroughly. By the time two more sons were added to the household, making a total of five, she was ready to commit herself to a lunatic asylum. Life was reduced to shouts and banging doors, sodden mittens whitening mahogany tables, muddy boots resting on oriental carpets, frogs scampering over sofas and chairs, skinned knees, bleeding fingers, bruised foreheads, servants fleeing the commotion to take posts with sedate elderly couples. . . .

Into this bedlam Charles would sail, happy to be home again after arguing cases in the county court. He was puzzled when his lovely wife snarled at him, or, pleading a headache, escaped to her room. And his wife was ashamed and guilty. Why was she taking it out on poor Charles? None of this was his fault. And the boys, after all, were basically good children. "Boys will be boys," the saying went. What was wrong with her?

In time came the two little girls: familiar letters ending a line of runes. They were lively and mischievous, true, but at least they represented a sex with which she could identify. In raising them she felt a resurgence of the old maternal buoyancy. Here were characters she knew how to mold! To them she communicated all the lessons she had learned in life's hard school, the most important of which was, "Don't be in a hurry to marry, girls. Cultivate your minds and abilities while you still have the chance."

While you still have the chance. It sounded like the advice one might give to those given six months to live. But that was how she always seemed to phrase it even though the girls were nowhere near marriageable age.

Marie sighed and walked over to the closet to change for dinner. It was to be a farewell dinner for Rafe, and she was dreading it. Why, at the very moment when that squirming mass of males was metamorphosing into a dignified group of young gentlemen, was the Lord deciding to take them from her? She jerked a brown muslin from the closet and blinked back angry tears.

Rafe's older brothers, who lived in towns near Boston, had not known that he had managed to get a pass and so were not present at what Rafe was calling "the last supper." The rest of the family was there, though, seated in uncharacteristic silence as they waited for Charles to deliver the blessing. All were staring grimly at Rafe as though, he thought, they were already imagining how he would look in a casket. Rafe couldn't bear it. He lowered his head and kept it down until the blessing was concluded. Then he cast about in his mind for some tale to relate. No training camp jokes. He mustn't remind them of the army. No allusions to Andy's funeral. In desperation, he said, "Beautiful weather we're having."

"Splendid," Charles agreed.

"Yes, " Marie added, trying to sound bright. "Quite breezy for August."

Rafe could think of nothing to add to this, so he picked up his spoon and began sipping his soup. To his relief, his younger brothers began talking about yesterday's game on the common. Someone was breaking the silence, thank heaven, but his sisters and parents said nothing.

Rafe looked up and met the eyes of his father. He could not read Charles' expression. Was he sad? Proud? Uncertain? Rafe could not tell. He turned away and began talking with his brothers.

Charles Taylor, as the incident with the Irish had demonstrated, was known as the people's lawyer. There was no man too humble and no case too trifling for Charles. He was friend to the farmer, spokesman for the laborer, and yet highly respected among the elite. The workers up at the mill applauded him as he argued for shorter hours. Yet the mill owners somehow had the impression that Charles sympathized with their problems. In the end, hours were cut back, the mill owners feeling benevolent, the workers triumphant, and Charles retaining his title as the great conciliator. In church matters too he was deft. During the summer, a group of distressed Congregationalists had approached Charles and said that the town had tired of its reincarnated Cotton Mather but was reluctant to hurt his feelings by asking for a resignation. Charles canvassed the state, found a pastorless parish willing to take neo-Calvinists, and told the grim preacher that since other towns had too long been deprived of his wisdom, Lanston, though grieved, would not want to deny these souls the privilege of boasting a minister of his caliber. Soon Reverend Mitchell was on his way and an amiable young minister was presiding at meeting. Charles had not had much time to devote to the school board but this was to be his next project and he was now scouting about for decent teachers to staff the academy—a problem at a time when most of the college men were enlisting.

Charles was a remarkable man. His only failing, aside from being away from home so often, was that he expected his sons to be just like him. From infancy each boy had been advised of his destiny. He must serve God or man in one of four professions: the ministry, the law, medicine, or education. Theirs was a family of privilege, and since God had so favored them, it behooved everyone to go forth and aid his less fortunate brothers. Charles' older sons had answered the call—one becoming a minister, the other a lawyer like his father. But Rafe had shown interest in none of these vocations, and this concerned Charles.

The name Raphael had been chosen for his third son during a period when he and Marie were much taken by Renaissance art. As the boy grew older, however, they had agreed that if this Protestant child was destined to have a Papist name Galileo would have been preferable. At an early age the boy had besieged them with an unending list of questions about the movement of planets, the composition of matter, the structure of the body, the effects of gravity, and on and on. They had answered him as best they could, but when Rafe began questioning them about God, they had balked.

When Rafe became a deist and then an agnostic, Charles was upset but not surprised. For years Rafe had been a stranger to him. If father and son had not borne such a close physical resemblance, Charles would have sworn that Rafe was the product of an encounter between Marie and some natural philosopher. But Charles was a tolerant man. He had accepted his son's defection in a democratic spirit. What he was finding it difficult to accept was the fact that Rafe was leading his younger sons down the same road.

Among the three boys, nothing was sacred. They saw humor in all achievements and institutions. Fine art, literature, politics, music, religion, the press, the law, the government—all were subjects for their gibes, as were people, from temperance leaders to schoolmasters, who took themselves too seriously. In all fairness, Charles had to admit they did have their serious moments. And none of them was in any way malicious. But their godless stance had led them into a world where there was no point of reference, no ultimate authority. Every truth was open to question, and while they might find this sport enjoyable for the moment, what would they do when they needed some Absolute to turn to? How would Rafe feel when death threatened and there was no God to help him, no thoughts of heaven to comfort him?

These were the thoughts that had plagued Charles all through dinner. As the family rose from the table, he said to his son that he wished to speak to him in the library.

"Yes, Father?" Rafe said when he was seated in the leather chair in front of the massive bookcases.

Charles also sat down. "I wanted to have a short talk before you left." He cleared his throat. "When do you think you will be getting your marching orders?"

"The colonel thinks within the week."

"Are you nervous, son?"

"A little."

"If only there had been a way to prevent this war!"

"I'm sure there were ways, Father. But hotheads on both sides refused to explore them." Already he was thinking in an unsoldierly manner. Must stop this, Rafe told himself. Must think only of the objective.

Charles decided to come straight to the point. "I wish you believed in God, Raphael."

"I wish so too, Father."

Charles hadn't expected this reply. "You do?"

"Of course."

"Then why . . ."

"Because wishing can't force a being into existence."

"I see. And you are quite sure that the being does not exist?"

"Not sure, Father. I'd say it's a ninety-eight percent probability. The shadow of doubt makes me an agnostic, not an atheist. I've explained before why I . . ."

"Yes. Yes, you *have* explained. But that two percent chance, son. Would it not be wise to consider it now? Now that you are facing—great danger?"

"Father, I understand your concern. I know you're saying these things because you care for me. But I can't make myself believe what you want me to believe. I'm sorry, Father."

Charles sighed. Had he really expected his son to change? "Very well," he said.

Rafe said, "You're a remarkably tolerant man, Father. Years ago I used to cower at the thought of confronting you with these beliefs of mine. But I finally found the courage to tell you—and you were quite reasonable. I respect you for that, sir."

Charles looked carefully at his son. There was no hint of mockery in those clear blue eyes. Raphael meant what he was saying, and Charles was deeply moved. Not trusting himself to speak, Charles simply nodded. For a while both were silent, then Charles nodded and rose. He did not wish to monopolize his son's time when there were other family members waiting to say goodbye. Rafe would be leaving at six the next morning and it was already getting late. Before leaving the library, Charles gave his son a pat on the back. "Do I dare say 'God go with you'?"

Rafe smiled. "I know what you mean, sir."

Charles blinked back tears and strode from the room. "I will see you in the morning," he said from the hallway.

"Yes. Good night, Father."

"Good night."

Rafe remained in the library a while longer, looking at the law books, the leather chairs, the heavy oak desk, the gilt framed paintings of his paternal grandparents. He wanted to remember it all. Rebellious though he could be, Rafe loved his home and his family so much that he was less inclined than most of his friends to seek companionship elsewhere. His social and intellectual life were bound up in these rooms, in the rich cultural environment his parents had created. His younger brothers were his closest friends and confidants, and his sisters were dear to him. It had been a happy household, for the most part, though he sensed that his mother had problems coping with the pandemonium. In recent years, without realizing it, she had handed the responsibility for raising the younger boys over to Rafe, while she occupied herself with the girls and Charles assumed the burdens of society at large. Rafe did not particularly resent his fatherly role, but he did get irritated when his parents blamed him for his brothers' transgressions and unorthodox ideas. What else could they have expected? Having entrusted the boys to an unorthodox brother, they would have to put up with the results.

What really bothered Rafe, however, was that he loved the boys almost too much. He was loath to have them join the army, and though they had promised their parents that they would wait, both were champing at the bit. Rafe was certain that within a few months they would be enlisting with or without parental sanction. This was all he needed—to fret about his brothers while simultaneously leading men into battle. Again and again he had urged them not to enlist, but neither had listened.

"You're enlisting, aren't you?" seventeen-year-old Bill had said defiantly.

"Yes, but that's different."

"Why is it different?" asked Johnny, who was a year younger than Bill.

"Because one of us has to go. But all of us . . ."

"So you've decided to be the martyr," said Bill.

"Of course not. Not a martyr. Just . . ."

"If you can risk your life, so can we," Johnny said.

"No! God! Supposing you were killed?" Rafe shouted.

Bill said, "But we want to help."

"If you really want to help, you'll stay right here, goddamn it."

Every time they talked about it the argument ran the same course. Rafe had never been a worrier, but now his days were filled with agitation. Fear of his brothers' dying, fear of dying himself—well, at least he no longer had a woman to stew about. Many of his friends were agonizing over the thought of losing their girls to stay-at-home cowards. He, on the other hand, had already terminated his relationship. Or, more accurately, the romance had died of natural causes. Why had it taken him so long to realize that Christine Osbourne was nothing but a pretty face? For years he had deluded himself that she was all he could want in a woman. He had woven illusions about her that were shattered every time she opened her mouth. And yet he had ignored the facts. Ignored them because her full lips were sweet and her breasts—that one time she had actually let him touch her basque—had been so soft.

His craving for Christine had begun to abate during his third year at Harvard when he first found sexual release in the parlor houses of Boston. Though his encounters with women of pleasure were few, they were enough to make him realize that sex and love were not to be confused. Better to spend a lifetime paying for the services of these lonely women than to commit himself to someone as vapid as Christine. The ideal solution, of course, would be to find someone both physically and mentally stimulating. Someone like Emily Stevens . . . but he was not going to think about Emily Stevens.

Rafe left the library and went to say goodbye to the rest of the family.

The troops marched at the beginning of September, passing via a roundabout route through a string of small towns that had contributed companies to the regiment. The men were bound for the Connecticut River, where steamers would carry them south. All along the route, crowds flanked the roads, shouting, waving handkerchiefs, crying, tossing flowers, singing. As they passed through Lanston, Rafe tried to pick out his family. There they were at the end of Prospect Street in a small phalanx. His father looked tall and stoical, as though standing in review; he gave a dignified wave as his son passed. His mother and sisters each tossed a flower. Annie and another servant alternately waved handkerchiefs and wiped away tears. And his brothers were shouting someting inaudible as they tapped their feet in accompaniment to the infantry band which was rendering "John Brown's Body" for the tenth time in two hours. Rafe nodded at them all, his throat hurting, his steps faltering. He was anxious to get away now—away from the temptation to fall out and walk home with the family.

As they marched on through the outskirts of town, he could hear the bells of the meetinghouse pealing as though already celebrating a victory. A bit premature, he thought irritably, remembering that poem of Poe's that had driven him crazy in school: "The bells, bells, bells, bells, bells, bells." He had written Emily a note about it: "I think he has bells in his belfry." How she had laughed at that! He smiled, remembering, and wondered if by any chance Emily recalled the incident. He turned to see if she might be here in the thinning crowds at the south end of town. He hadn't seen her when he passed the store.

But she had been there, in the shadow of the awning, watching Rafe pass on the opposite side of the street. She would have been moved to know that Rafe's last thoughts upon leaving his boyhood town were of her.

CHAPTER 8

The camps on the shores of the Potomac in Alexandria, Virginia, formed a city of tents. Various regiments were represented by uniforms so widely ranging in style and color that Rafe sometimes wondered how the rebels would be able to distinguish the Yanks from their own men. Across the river in Washington, higher officers strutted about with Napoleonic pomp while Lincoln, their considerably less pretentious commander in chief, wondered when and how this loose coalition of volunteer forces raised by the separate states could be formed into a cohesive national fighting unit. Rafe's days were spent giving lectures on tactics, maneuvers, chains of command, cleanliness, orderliness and cooperation. In addition, he regularly drilled his platoon in a series of complicated steps designed to move men from marching columns into battle lines. Over and over again they rehearsed this ballet of war, muskets loaded in the prescribed manner, commands issued by hand signal and bugle, simulated charges, advances, and marches. They practiced so often that everyone was anxious to see how the choreography would work in an actual battle. Even Rafe began to long for a genuine confrontation. Endless rehearsals were tiresome, and he wondered how career military men could endure year after year of peace, when their *raison d'être* was war. It must be frustrating. And it explained why so many problems were resolved by war. With a standing military body bored with play-acting and eager to practice its craft, any dispute was apt to bring men running with rifles cocked.

Rafe's platoon sergeant was his old schoolmate, Jack Lawrence. The two became good friends during the first few weeks in this alien country. There were other Lanston men in the company, many of whom had once been closer to Rafe than Jack, who had lived on a remote farm. But the transplanting of men to Washington had altered relationships, partly because Rafe was now an officer in command of old chums and partly because the Lanston boys were finding new friends and diversions in this unique war fraternity.

Neither Jack Lawrence nor Dr. Bob Nelson, a middle-aged man who had been a neighbor of Rafe's, was inclined to seek adventures in the back streets of Washington. Faithful married men, they were both rather straitlaced. Recreation consisted of playing chess in Nelson's tent, singing (Jack could play a mean banjo), and temperate drinking (Rafe had to sneak alcohol to Jack, who, because he wasn't a commissioned officer, was not supposed to imbibe). There was also a lot of talk of home—especially from Jack, who desperately missed his wife Abby.

The first few weeks passed in this way—organizing the camp, engaging in innocent recreation. On a pass, Rafe saw the sights of Washington but did not participate in its fabled nightlife—mostly because there was no one to participate with him. He needed some crony, someone who did not hail from Lanston or a neighboring town and so would not write home describing Taylor's unseemly behavior should he ultimately be lured into a brothel or dingy bar.

He found two such companions in a roundabout way. They were brigaded with Pennsylvania and New York regiments. Thus far there had been little communication among the units except when high-ranking officers were obliged to confer with one another. But late in September, an outbreak of camp diseases felled a good number of the Massachusetts boys, including Rafe, who came down with measles. Dr. Nelson and his assistant surgeons were staggering with dysentery. There were also cases of scarlet fever and typhoid. Meanwhile, in one of the New York regiments camped near them, everyone was disgustingly healthy. Dr. Nelson wondered why this was so. Had the hand of God concentrated the dread miasma on only one camp? Was the Almighty displeased with the state of Massachusetts, the most voluble champion of abolition? Perhaps God was on the side of the slaveholding states, just as its leaders claimed.

Dr. Nelson decided to make his way over to the quarters of one Kent Wilson, senior surgeon of the healthy New Yorkers, and ask for help. Wilson was a man in his early thirties, not known for his charm or bedside manner. But his record as a surgical resident at Bellevue Hospital in Manhattan indicated that he would probably be more than capable on a battlefield.

Dr. Nelson dragged his thin frame toward Wilson's tent, slapping at flies that kept landing on his gray hair and wondering if this infernal dysentery was going to kill him. Wilson was seated in front of his tent, bent over a table scribbling something. He was a thin wiry man with a shock of blonde hair that was always in disarray. Tales of his temper and profanity had reached the puritan Dr. Nelson and he was hesitant to ask for assistance. But there was no alternative.

"Major?" Bob Nelson barely had the strength to address his cocky young colleague.

Major Wilson looked up. "Good God, man! What the hell's wrong with you? Go into my tent and lie down on the cot. What do you have?"

"Dysentery. A bad case. That's why I'm here. We need help. Half the men . . ."

The younger doctor was yanking him by the arm into the tent. "Jesus Christ, why didn't you come sooner?" He assisted Nelson onto the cot.

"I thought we could handle it." Wearily he reeled off a list of statistics, ending with his observation that the Almighty seemed to have a grudge against the Bay State.

Wilson began to laugh. No, Nelson. The problem is that most of you have never been exposed to these diseases. You're from inland communities, pure as mountain streams. Half of our men grew up in the Five Points or its neighborhood. Even the wealthiest have been drowned in New York effluvia and those who survived to tell the tale are probably the healthiest men in the army. At least *now* they are. If the army diet gets any worse, I'll expect them to keel over too." He paused. "You have an emergency over there?"

"To put it mildly."

"I'll contact all available doctors in the brigade. In the meantime I want you flat on your back." He bellowed to an orderly, "Get a stretcher for Nelson here and carry him back to his quarters. And tell Captain Shepherd to get the hell over here on the double."

"Yes, sir!" the orderly shouted from outside the tent.

Kent Wilson asked Nelson a few questions about what supplies they needed and then introduced him to the breathless, gangling young man who had answered Kent's summons. "Major Nelson, Captain Shepherd, my assistant surgeon. Tell him where to begin."

The team of Wilson and Shepherd took command of several tents at the regimental hospital. In the beginning Rafe was scarcely aware of their existence. The fever, hacking cough, and itching rash of the measles made him oblivious to everything but his misery. But as the disease ran its course he began to notice these two doctors. They swept through the hospital tent like a rush of wind, dispensing medications, taking pulses, roaring commands to scampering orderlies, and generally acting more like officers leading a charge than like the folksy doctors Rafe was accustomed to. The senior surgeon, Rafe noticed, had a Boston accent. One morning Rafe asked idly, "What's a Massachusetts man doing in a New York regiment?"

Kent Wilson shrugged. "I moved to New York a few years ago."

"Why?"

"Is this a matter of personal concern?" asked the doctor.

"No," Rafe snapped, instantly angry. "I was just trying to make conversation. Actually, doctor, I don't give a damn where you came from—or where you're going either."

Wilson ignored the comment. He took Rafe's pulse and felt his forehead. "You're better," he said. "Another day in bed, then slowly resume normal activity. *Slowly*, Lieutenant. Occasionally there are complications with measles."

Rafe looked up at him, his face sullen.

"Did you hear me, Lieutenant?"

"How could I help it," Rafe growled.

"Look here, Lieutenant, I'm a busy man. If I did not respond in kind to your attempts at chatter, I hope you will bear in mind that I don't have time to converse with every patient. More to the point, however, is the fact that Massachusetts has unhappy associations for me. If you must know, I left Boston after my wife and infant daughter died."

"I'm sorry," Rafe murmured.

The doctor nodded shortly. "You understand my instructions then?"

"Perfectly, Major."

The doctor moved on to the next tent. His assistant surgeon turned from a nearby patient and walked over to Rafe. "I couldn't help overhearing that exchange," he said. In this small tent, accommodating eight patients, private conversation was impossible. "Don't be angry at Wilson. He's always gruff."

"Don't concern yourself, Captain . . ."

"Shepherd. Pat Shepherd."

"Rafe Taylor. I suppose everyone's nerves are on edge. It's all right." He paused. "Can you tell me how our own doctor is faring?"

"Nelson's still quite ill with dysentery. But he'll recover, I think. There's talk of consolidating the hospitals so that any doctor in a division will be authorized to treat any patient. There'll be no more depending on the regimental surgeon." He paused. "These camp diseases are miserable, aren't they?"

Rafe nodded. "And I thought all we had to worry about was dodging bullets."

"Disease is the major killer of armies, Lieutenant—Taylor is it? I suggest that you take good care of yourself."

"Let's be realistic, doctor. Shouldn't I drink and be merry while there's still time?"

Pat Shepherd smiled. "You have a point. As a matter of fact, that's my philosophy."

"Good. Then perhaps you might tell me—where's the best place in Washington to be merry?"

"There are a number. Consult with me again, Taylor, when you're able to stand up."

"I'll do that, doctor." Rafe smiled at the tall young man. He guessed that they were near the same age, the doctor possibly a year or two older. He was thin and awkward and his brown hair was tousled. Like his senior surgeon, he was clean-shaven—a rarity in the heavily bearded and mustachioed army (Rafe himself had grown a mustache upon arriving here). In Pat Shepherd, Rafe sensed a kindred spirit, and he resolved to find out more about the merry places in Washington.

It was a full two weeks before the epidemic in Rafe's camp showed signs of abating. During that time, Rafe became well acquainted with the young New York doctor. In the process, he was also thrust into the company of Pat's surly senior officer, Wilson. The doctors returned to their own regiment but Rafe continued to see them. One night he and Pat journeyed across the river to Washington. There Rafe had an encounter with a woman almost too refined to be considered a prostitute. Afterward, he and Pat reeled from bar to bar in a night so utterly debauched as to be sublime. Toward dawn, they lurched down a street toward a run-down hotel singing "Annie Laurie" at the top of their lungs. The next day they staggered back to camp with heavy heads and churning stomachs, vowing never again to take a drink. Two days later they were sharing a bottle of bourbon.

Rafe's first real contact with the realities of war came a few days after the Washington excursion. Farther north on the Potomac, a detachment including many of Rafe's Harvard classmates had been sent across the river to attack a rebel position. The engagement, known later as the folly of Ball's Bluff, had decimated the Yankees. Men fleeing in retreat were forced to swim across the river because there was not enough transport. Wounded died on the few skiffs available, others drowned, and some were shot as they swam. When the casualty lists were posted, Rafe was stunned. Two college classmates were dead, others were missing, and many more were seriously injured, among them Wendell Holmes. In camp, Rafe sat on his cot, too numb to move. When Pat came by, Rafe was staring dully into space.

"You must have had college friends in the twentieth," Pat said.

"Yes." Rafe's tone was flat.

"I'm sorry."

Rafe shook his head. "It's just the beginning, isn't it? There'll be more and more. Soon all my friends and yours will be lying in some river or ditch with bullets in their heads. My brothers will join too, and they . . ." He stopped short, remembering that Pat had a brother in the infantry. He offered whisky to Pat, who drank healthily and then handed the bottle back to Rafe.

Rafe drank the equivalent of two more shots and said, "Never send to know for whom the bell tolls. The bells bells bells bells bells bells bells . . ."

"You're mixing poets."

"I know, but Emily thought it was so funny." Rafe continued to drink.

"Emily?"

"Girl back home."

"She pretty?" Pat was trying to change the subject from death to romance.

"Yes. Very pretty." Rafe's voice was quite thick.

Pat snatched the bottle from Rafe's hand. "She wasn't your girl, was she?"

"No. Girl's name was Christen—Christine. Emily's—girl I went to school with."

Pat said, "I think you ought to be getting some sleep, Rafe."

"Um. Yes. Awful drunk."

"I daresay." Pat yanked Rafe's boots off, then eased him into a supine position on the cot. Rafe was already asleep when Pat left the tent, thinking, "Already a casualty of war and he has almost three years ahead of him."

They remained in the Washington area throughout the winter. A bright, aristocratic young man named George McClellan was named commander in chief of the Army of the Potomac. His task was to organize the army and prepare for an advance into Virginia. There were endless drills and parades. The camp resonated with patriotic music and military bluster. More bars, brothels, and gambling establishments were erected, and soon even the most religious men in Rafe's regiment were being lured into sin. Rafe's friendship with Pat Shepherd and Kent Wilson grew stronger, and the three spent many evenings in Wilson's tent discussing medicine, women, science, women, sports, women, philosophy, mathematics, and women. Neither doctor had any scruples about taking his pleasure where he found it, and Kent advised Rafe to buy a device called a condom, asserting that certain deadly diseases could be prevented by its regular use. It also had the side effect of preventing pregnancy, Kent said. Pat had a younger brother named Joe who disapproved of Pat's loose morals. He warned Pat that excessive indulgence would affect his relationship with some future wife. But at Christmastime, Joe, on a drinking binge in Washington with Pat and Rafe, found himself unable to resist a certain red-haired lady who was lounging in a parlor house. After that they suffered no more lectures from Lieutenant Joseph Shepherd.

By March, Rafe had become accustomed to the routine of army life. He no longer thought in terms of battles or death. His concerns ran to seeing that the mess hall was clean, making sure latrines were dug to specifications, overseeing drills and rifle practice, settling arguments among privates, and cheering up Jack Lawrence when he yearned for his wife Abby. Alternating with the dreary mind-dulling work were occasional pleasures: bars, parlor houses, chats and chess games with the New York doctors, and mail from home. He was relieved to hear that his brothers had not yet enlisted, and he hastened to write them that army life was a thumping bore. He said also that he expected McClellan to detain the army in Washington until hell froze over. Perhaps Lincoln and Davis would come to terms before another shot was fired.

The last of his letters in this vein had just been sent off when word reached Rafe that the army was planning the advance on Richmond down to the last detail. No vague rumors this time. This was the real thing. They would not go overland, as Rafe would have expected, but would approach the Confederate capital by way of Chesapeake Bay, being transported to the tip of a swampy peninsula in the Norfolk area. Disembarking there, they would march past Yorktown (where Cornwallis had surrendered to Washington), past the colonial city of Williamsburg, and into Richmond. With any luck, the war would be over in two months.

The two months were used up just getting close to Richmond. Muddy roads and McClellan's caution made progress slow. The rebels obliged them by abandoning Yorktown. There was a fight at Williamsburg, but Rafe's units were not involved. The Yankees continued to advance to the gates of the capital, where the rebels would certainly put up a stiff fight.

With a genuine battle imminent, Rafe's excitement grew apace. At last he would see the results of all the drilling. To awaken his courage and resolve, Rafe again called to mind the cruel accounts of slavery he had read, trying to remember the black men who had come to America shackled in the bowels of ships. He would be fighting for them, he told himself. For the dignity of men. Whenever Pat or Kent pointed out that the war would have little effect on the Negro or anyone else he tried to close his ears. But one night on bivouac they became embroiled in a heated argument. It was a sweltering evening in late May and mosquitoes were attacking them like enemy legions. Ambulances were jolting out of camp, carrying men to a base far behind the lines. The soldiers were down with malaria and typhoid as well as the ever-present dysentery. Rafe wasn't feeling well either. The doctors were so overworked that they had little patience with Rafe's apologies for war. Pat and Kent were sitting on the ground near the hospital tents having a quick smoke before returning to duty. Rafe was standing, gesturing with his arms, saying, "Of course I'm scared. I'm not ashamed to admit it. But the cause is just, and that's what I . . ."

"Just?" Kent interrupted. "You're incredibly naïve, Rafe. Don't you realize that this war will change nothing?"

"You're the one who's naïve, Kent. You never consider reality at all. You expect men to settle differences with words followed by handshakes and when they don't you stomp around like a child."

Pat finished a cigar and threw it down, grinding it out with his heel. He said, "Very well, Rafe. We know what a hardheaded realist you are. We've all heard how you buried your pacificism in the sand and faced the fact that, people being people, war was inevitable. But do you realize *this*? To the extent that you sanction murder, no matter what the sacred cause, you insure the inevitability of future wars."

"Well, if I sanction murder, then so do you, you sanctimonious ass. Why else are you in the army?"

"We're here to save lives," Pat intoned.

"How touching! How noble! But you're still wearing the uniform of the United States Army. If you really want to impress me, then go the hell back home and stop trying to keep us warmongers alive."

Kent muttered. "Don't be so damned histrionic. You're giving me a headache."

"You! Giving *you* a headache," Rafe shouted. "If anyone ought to be suffering around here it's me. As a matter of fact, I am feeling sick. Do you realize that within a few days I may be dead? Or minus an arm? Christ almighty, how can I summon the courage to fight with you two naysayers constantly undermining the cause." Rafe was shaking with rage.

At last Pat admitted quietly, "You're right, I guess. Our views on this debacle aren't going to change anything. You're committed. All our arguments about how things ought to be can't alter the fact that you're going to have to fight."

"Exactly," Rafe nodded. He was still shuddering, so he sat down on the ground.

Pat said to Kent, "I think that the best service we can render the infantry is to keep our mouths shut, don't you think?" Kent did not comment. "Well?" Pat persisted. There was still no reply, and now Pat noticed that Kent was staring fixedly at Rafe. Pat said, "What is it, Kent?" Then he turned to look at his friend and murmured, "Oh, Jesus."

Rafe was not trembling in terror. He was suffering chills. The doctors had seen the symptoms often enough to guess that he was coming down with typhoid or malaria.

"Guess what?" Kent said, waving his pipe. "You're not going to have to fight in *any* battles this month."

"Oh? Do you have intelligence to that effect?" Rafe said wearily. He was now slumped against a tree.

"The best of intelligence," Kent said. "Tomorrow you will be lying on a pile of straw." He rose, picked up a lantern from the ground, and examined Rafe closely. "I'm afraid you're ill."

"Malaria?" asked Rafe, his voice bleak.

"Typhoid, I think."

"You mean I'm not going to die in a blaze of glory? I'm going to die like a dog in this swamp?" Rafe was rubbing his head, which was beginning to hurt. Kent and Pat each took an arm and led him fifty paces back to the hospital tent. As Kent prepared to dispense a dose of Dover's Powders, Rafe held up his hand and said, "Take that stuff away. I want someone to record my last words."

Kent said, "Don't be in such a hurry to go to your reward. You might find a warmer reception than expected." But Kent was not smiling.

Rafe, tossing on the straw, insisted, "Will someone write down my last words?"

"Very well," Kent said. "Pat, get a pad and record this idiot's pearls of wisdom."

Pat yanked a pad from his breast pocket and Kent handed him a lead pencil. "Proceed," Pat said.

Rafe began: "I only regret . . ."

"Only regret," Pat repeated, scribbling down the words.

"That I did not have a longer life to lose . . ."

"Hold it. All right. 'longer life' . . ."

"To lose for my country." Rafe said.

Pat, dabbing imaginary tears from his eyes, read back the dictation. "I only regret that I did not have a longer life to lose for my country."

Kent bowed his head. Then the two stepped forward and, while Kent held Rafe down, Pat shoved the Dover's Powders into his mouth. Soon Nathan Hale was fast asleep.

A few days later Rafe's regiment distinguished itself in the Battle of Seven Pines. Rafe, tossing with fever, was too ill to care that after ten months of rehearsal he had missed his opening day performance by less than a week.

He was sent away from the front in a rickety ambulance that took him back to a base on the Pamunkey River. There was no question of shipping him out of the miasmatic peninsula and back to New England. The army wanted its sick to stay put until they recovered (*if* they recovered, typhoid having a mortality rate of 25%). Rafe's fever rose daily and soon he was passing in and out of delirium, calling for his brothers and for a childhood nurse, occasionally carrying on conversations with his father. There was no one here who knew him. Pat, Kent, and his regimental doctors were all up at the front performing amputations on Rafe's comrades. Weeks passed before Rafe had any clear idea of where he was, and during that time he was transferred to another base, Harrison's Landing.

The army, meanwhile, was beaten back from Richmond, made a gallant stand at Malvern Hill, and finally retreated to join the sick in dismal Harrison's Landing. By this time a month had passed. Rafe had barely been restored to health when his friends came marching back, accompanied by ambulances filled with moaning men and wagons bearing the plank coffins of officers (ordinary soldiers had been buried on the battlefield). The peninsula campaign was over, though no one realized it at the time. It was August, 1862, almost a year after Rafe had marched off to war.

His platoon sergeant, Jack Lawrence, who had taken command of Rafe's unit, related in detail all the events of the past month: charges and countercharges, the remarkable gallantry of certain privates and corporals they had expected to crack under fire, the remarkable cowardice of boys who had always seemed fearless. He rattled on in a nonstop monologue, and Rafe, annoyed that it had not been he leading the men, gritted his teeth and mumbled, "Good work, Jack. Proud of you and the men."

Pat had another side to the story. After telling Rafe how glad he was to see him healthy and well, he launched into a tale of front-line surgery that made Rafe nearly as ill as he had been two weeks earlier. Rafe was deeply depressed, not only because he had missed the opportunity for which he had been training these many months but also because two Lanston friends lay in graves near Richmond and others were being sent home armless, legless, or not right in the head. The only comforting thought was that his brothers had missed the carnage and, according to their last letters, were enrolling at Harvard for another year. Rafe was relieved. By next year the war would be over. If he was lucky enough to survive it, he would at least be able to return to a whole family, to the small town and the life he loved.

CHAPTER 9

At long last the weary army was hauled out of the peninsula like a dinosaur being wrested from quicksand. In early September they had word that the new Confederate commander, Robert E. Lee, was leading his army up toward Maryland. The Army of the Potomac dutifully took off in pursuit of this audacious Virginia gentleman, but their own commander, McClellan, did not seem in any great hurry. He was a cautious man who was convinced that Lee's army outnumbered his own and was not about to undertake any rash action before weighing all contingencies. The soldiers adored Little Mac, for he considered his men's welfare more important than mere victories. Yet because of McClellan's prudence the army missed its one real chance of winning the war in '62. As the cautious Yankees made their way toward Sharpsburg, Maryland, Lee had ample time to assemble his army, which had been dangerously spread out, to meet the Northern foe in force. The engagement, which would later be called the Battle of Antietam Creek, took place on September seventeenth. And Rafe, at last, was healthy enough to participate.

They had passed through a friendly little Maryland town called Frederick, a village of Union sympathizers who flew United States flags and cheered the soldiers while pretty girls dispensed food and drink. It was a refreshing change from the peninsula, which had been hostile enemy territory. Moreover, Maryland was bursting with end-of-summer bounty: corn, peaches, apples, plump pigs ready for the slaughter. The march proved to be almost pleasant until they reached a pass in South Mountain called Turner's Gap and Rafe first saw the areas where advance Union units had recently fought the rebels. Here lay the unburied bodies of Confederates blackening under the indifferent trees. And here Rafe had his first actual view of a battlefield. He felt that he was going to be sick. This would be the ultimate degradation. How would it look for the men to see their leader sinking to his knees and vomiting? But, God, he couldn't stand that smell of decay. And not from the carcasses of animals either. From men. From human beings.

"Lieutenant?" It was the voice of Jack Lawrence, still Rafe's platoon sergeant, though he had been recommended for promotion following his valor on the peninsula. "Lieutenant, you look green, sir."

"Um."

"It's all right. Lots of men were sick down on the peninsula. Guess you're entitled."

"Wouldn't look good, Jack." Rafe was panting. He was now breathing through his mouth for fear that using his nose would bring on an attack of nausea too overwhelming to fend off. "I'm green in more ways than one, as you well know."

"But Rafe—but Lieutenant," Jack corrected himself, "it can't be helped. Everyone has to learn war the hard way, even officers. There's no sense pretending . . ."

"I've got to set a good example for the men," Rafe said.

They tramped along in silence, Rafe looking fixedly at the units ahead of him instead of glancing around. He never knew when his eye might light on another rebel corpse. At last he asked, "How are things at home, Jack?"

"Abby?"

"Yes, Abby." Talk about anything, he thought. Anything but this.

So Jack spoke quietly, almost caressingly, about his wife—a girl whom Rafe had always found rather plain and undistinguished. Now, however, he forced himself to concentrate on Jack's accounts of Abby's capabilities on the farm, her succulent meals, her way with animals, her gentle humor, her smile. Rafe wished he had a wife to think about, but in lieu of this he relived moments with Christine. By the time they reached Antietam Creek, he had successfully lifted himself out of the corpse-strewn battlefield and into a world of lovers strolling along summer paths.

It rained steadily on the night of September sixteenth, and the high command had ordered no campfires lest the rebels, who were facing them across the creek, ascertain the position of the army. Everyone fully expected battle the next day, and Rafe, wondering if this night would be his last on earth, cursed the rain for making his final hours so dismal and the generals for denying them the campfires on which he might brew a cup of coffee. The regiments were in position now so that he didn't even have his medical comrades with him to share macabre humor about the coming doom. There was only Jack—sad and preoccupied—and the nervous unit Rafe commanded. Most of these men had seen battle before, but their fears did not seem to diminish at the prospect of another one. And he was supposed to be keeping their spirits up. Hah!

The night wore on—fear of the morrow disturbing everyone's sleep—and Rafe was still half awake at first light when, off to the north, batteries began blasting into the misty dawn. He sprang to his feet, instantly awake yet somehow very tired as though he had been fighting all night long. Black smoke hung suspended upstream over the trees, and this was all he could see of the battle.

"We can pretend we're watching a thunder cloud," he muttered sardonically to Jack as the two stood with mouths agape looking toward the smoke. The cannon fire became so steady that individual reports could not be distinguished. This in a sense was good, for the unrelenting crash masked other sounds that supported it like a harmony: thousands of muskets, rebel yells, the screams and moans of wounded men.

The rain had ceased, and because it was daytime,

campfires again flickered along the line. Rafe gulped his coffee but for once was too nervous to taste it. Afterward he reviewed his men. All was in readiness. They couldn't have been more ready, he thought, wishing to hell they could just plunge in and get it over with. But they had to wait. And wait. Six o'clock, seven o'clock, seven-thirty, eight . . . The sun was sucking the bracing moisture out of the air and the day promised to be warm.

At last the command came down the line and the corps was marching. Grateful for something to do, preferring to chase death rather than to sit idly by while it skulked up to him, Rafe got the men into line and followed the column, wading through the creek in water up to his hips, halting at the other side so shoes could be emptied and socks wrung out, plodding on behind the Irish Brigade toward he knew not what. Would the terrain be full of trees and afford them some protection? Would they be out in the open?

They passed ambulances with men howling inside them, they saw walking wounded limping toward the rear, and everywhere they heard beaten troopers talk of the carnage, some going so far as to admit the possibility of defeat.

They came at last to a hill and suddenly the Irishmen ahead of them were plunging down the side, running across an open field, waving their flags and cheering, sweeping head on into a sunken road, which served the rebels as a rifle pit. The charge was suicidal, and even as Rafe and his men came to realize this, they were being sent in to relieve the battered Irish Brigade.

When Rafe finally charged into battle, the thought of avenging slaves was the farthest thing from his mind. He ran partly because there was nowhere else to go, partly because the long wait had produced impatience, partly because he had the sense that his destiny was inevitable, and mostly because he was enraged at the rebels who wanted to kill him. But forward he ran, into the deadliest fire imaginable, his enemy hidden and blasting from the sunken road, his comrades toppling like tenpins. It was all so insane that he rose to the occasion, yielding to the madness, wailing in terror and relief. He was ahead of his men (no coward he!) shouting "come on!" as they charged toward the rifle pits, shouting "let's go!" as the pits were overrun and the rebels went fleeing to the rear. He picked up the rifle of a fallen corporal, loaded it, and shot at the backs of the scampering rebels. Then, as he came up close, he used his revolver.

They crashed through a second line and down into a hollow. Rafe was exhilarated. He did not want to stop. But the enemy was receiving reinforcements. Rafe's platoon was called to a halt, and now the shooting continued without that rush of motion sweeping under them.

The division commander was not at all daunted. Soon orders came down for the officers to dress their lines, and Rafe, still experiencing an insane euphoria, began bellowing orders like a general, telling the troops that with one more charge the rebels would surely be routed. He had a brief glimpse of Jack's smoke-blackened face and felt a flush of triumph. He'd done it; he'd led his men into battle and earned their respect. But there was no time now to exult. He must see to the next charge, crush the enemy.

The next charge, however, was never ordered. Richardson, the division commander, was shot and carried off the field. His superior had seen too much carnage today to risk any more of it. And McClellan, as was his custom, advised caution. Gradually the fight on Rafe's portion of the field sputtered out, though a monumental one was raging to the south. As the shots became fewer and fewer, Rafe's mind began to clear until he gradually became aware of where he was and what he had done. Then he and his men started to dig in.

All through the afternoon there was sporadic fighting. Rafe's main task, however, was to see that emergency aid was given to the wounded on the field and that men were detailed to carry hurt comrades to the medical stations or ambulances. There was no time to do anything about the dead except ignore them, leaving them where they lay, some with tense expressions still on their faces and others evidently at peace. There was one young private staring with unseeing eyes up at the sun, as though contemplating the meaning of truth. A bullet had entered his temple, and brain matter had spilled onto the dry ground. Rafe knew him. He was the son of a neighbor and a good friend of his younger brother. Rafe looked at him, fought off nausea, and turned away. This was Dave and he ought to be feeling something for the dead boy who just this morning had been laughing as he emptied his waterlogged shoes, saying, "Can't fight, sir. Got cold feet." That was Dave and he ought to be feeling something. But this morning was long ago, and Dave had existed in a world Rafe could no longer imagine. Still, he ought to be feeling *something*.

What he felt then and all through that day was the need for a cup of coffee. Some voice was telling him that he was behaving like an animal and he knew it was true. But he still wanted a cup of coffee.

He thought of coffee constantly as he inspected arms and urged men to be calm. Warm, comforting coffee. He had to have it. Had to. As the afternoon waned, Rafe, without orders from above, detailed a private to gather all available twigs and build a fire.

"Coffee for the men," he proclaimed. "They must remain alert!"

Dark came over the field. The firing died in the blackness, and nervous men began to talk to one another. Jack complimented Rafe on his courage. Rafe clung to the accolade as a man being swept by a current clings to a stray log. Courage. It was one redeeming attribute. He had slaughtered men, shot them in the back, ordered others to kill—howling with exultation all the while. Courage he had, but he was not particularly proud of himself.

If Rafe had slept little the night before, he slept even less at the end of this bloody day. There were wounded to tend to and comrades to calm and the gnawing apprehension over the battle they must face the next morning. Rafe unrolled his blanket at three in the morning and stared up at the dark sky thinking until his thoughts became too oppressive to bear and were bludgeoned to death by sleep.

There was no battle the following day. Toward nightfall, Lee withdrew and when dawn came again on the nineteenth the Army of the Potomac lay alone in the fields with thousands of bloating corpses to remind them that there had been a battle. Burial parties were detailed, and some men strode around examining the carnage. But Rafe had no stomach for it. Lee had gone; this was all he cared about. Was the war over? He hoped so, though he doubted it. But at least he had lived to see another day.

He wanted very much to talk to Pat. Pat had become the confessor not only for Rafe but for other distraught soldiers. When Rafe arrived at the field hospitals, however, he saw horrors far worse than any he had seen in battle. The dead bodies had looked gruesome, had smelled terribly, but at least they had been silent. Here there was moaning, screaming, cries of terror as men were lifted onto the doors, supported by sawhorses, that served as operating tables. Pat and Kent looked like butchers with their bloody smocks, their scalpels and saws. He didn't know them, didn't want to know them, and was prepared to flee the barn when Pat shouted, "You made it, Rafe!" and the latter realized that a human being existed under that splotched apron.

"Yes, I made it," Rafe muttered.

"What? Can't hear you." Pat and two orderlies were lifting another man onto the table. Kent was shouting for more chloroform.

"Nothing!" Rafe shouted back, striding furiously out of the barn, stepping over the writhing mangled bodies outside the barn, and plunging at last into the woods and the relative serenity of camp.

The company commander had managed to get a bottle. He motioned Rafe into his tent and offered him a belt. The two men drank in silence until Rafe's senses were sufficiently dulled. Then the captain ordered him back to the barn to start compiling casualty lists.

Rafe reentered the inferno of screams and began his job in a kind of stupor, entering names on a pad the captain had given him. He wrote: "Robert Carson, thigh; Michael O'Donnell, arm; David McMahon, chest; Allen Barker, groin." His hand shook as he wrote the word "groin." He looked steadily at the moaning Barker, thought of the girl who was waiting for him in Lanston, and silently wished for the boy's swift death.

It was not until much later that Rafe learned what the Battle of Antietam had meant. Lee had been trapped between Sharpsburg and the Potomac. One good thrust along the entire front might have finished the Confederacy, driving the army into the river. Instead, McClellan had hesitated. First there had been the cannonading on the right which

Rafe had seen in the damp morning air. When this attack ended in stalemate, the center (including Rafe's regiment) had initiated a charge. This second assault was stopped by the nervous McClellan. Finally, the left had surged toward the enemy, only to be repulsed by the thin rebel line. The result was that the battle had not been decisive. Both sides maintained essentially the same positions with only the shape of the lines altered. Lee had retreated not because he'd been beaten but because his troops were exhausted. McClellan, far from being commended as a hero for driving the foe from Northern soil, was berated by Lincoln as having been too cautious. On November seventh the little general was removed from command.

The army was back in Virginia when Burnside took over, and though most were sad to see McClellan go, Rafe had no emotions about it. There were arguments pro and con, each valid enough. It came to sacrificing soldiers for victory or sacrificing victory for soldiers. A swifter punch might have ended the war more quickly, but a great many men now alive might be dead. On the other hand—but he refused to dwell on this question or any other military speculation which did not involve him personally. There were other ways in which to occupy one's time. Rafe read books he had sent away for or asked his parents to forward to him. He read several novels and a few texts on civil engineering. He became interested in railroads and read about their function. Kent Wilson was well versed on these subjects, and the two spent evenings discussing pistons, tractive forces, the problems of braking. In turn, Rafe listened to Kent's theories about the nature of contagion. The craggy doctor had seized on the idea, first propounded by an obscure Hungarian-born doctor named Semmelweis and also considered by Harvard physician Oliver Wendell Holmes, that contagion could be passed on surgeons' hands and instruments. Accordingly, Kent was using chloride of lime between operations, a procedure that took a good deal of time and earned him the ridicule of his colleagues. According to Kent's statistics, however, the method seemed to be working.

Kent was a fine intellectual companion, a scientist to the core, and Rafe respected him. But when it came to sharing confidences, Kent would freeze. With a brush at his blonde hair or a wave of his pipe, he would suddenly claim that he had to see a patient. Leaving Rafe and Pat behind, he would vanish into a hospital tent or into the trees.

"I don't understand him," Rafe said to Pat one chilly November evening as they warmed their hands over a feeble fire. "The minute I mention missing home or family he disappears. All right, I know he's a widower. I know he must be sad at times. But it isn't only family. It's everything involving feelings. Almost as though he's afraid to admit to having any."

"Some men are like that," Pat said. "Either by nature or circumstance. With Kent there's a natural reticence abetted by personal loss and the war itself."

"Guess you're right," Rafe said. He thought a moment. "Actually, the war has changed me too."

"How so?" Pat passed a cigar to Rafe and then lit one for himself.

"I used to be—what's the word—carefree, I suppose. Nothing much bothered me. It wasn't just the fact that my village is peaceful. People there are terribly earnest about life. If they hadn't had real problems, they would have invented them or the minister would have reminded them of what scoundrels they were." He paused. "But I was happy. Summers with my brothers, the years in college . . ."

"Your girl," Pat added.

"Yes. Chris was fun in the beginning. A challenge, though I always knew it wasn't a serious challenge." Rafe paused for a moment, thinking of Christine. "I was carefree, but I wasn't without feelings. I had normal reactions to events like—people dying."

"And now?" Pat prompted.

Rafe confessed to his crimes in a rush of words. "I shot men in the back, Pat. In the *back*! And I howled with glee while I did it. And later—the coffee. I watched my brother's friend—brains on the ground—and I thought of coffee. And then—God!—I came across another friend shot in the groin and I just stood there scrawling the boy's name and hoping he'd die soon. And then . . ." he broke off, then said, "So I don't have a right to criticize Kent, do I?"

"Did he die?" Pat asked.

"Who?"

"The boy shot in the groin?"

"Yes," Rafe whispered.

"Didn't mean to interrupt," Pat said. "Just curious." He puffed his cigar, watching the smoke swirling up to blend with that of the campfire. "You and Kent are quite different," Pat said. "You make an effort to feel emotions; you struggle for it. Kent does just the reverse. But it's true that the war will deaden you. It's done that to me, Rafe. After all, I hack off the arms and legs of friends thinking all the while of the cigar I'm going to smoke later. The cigar serves two functions. It's the promise of pleasure and it's also something to concentrate on while I'm mutilating men." As Rafe shuddered at Pat's choice of words, Pat continued. "But there's no help for it. There'll be more battles for you and me. If we're to survive we have to control feelings. Actually we don't do this consciously. The body does the job for us. Unlike your brain, your body has your best interests at heart. In other words, it tells you, 'Don't think about that dead man. Thinking will only make you sick. Drink coffee instead.' It says, 'If you wait too long to shoot that rebel you'll give him a chance to shoot you. Therefore, shoot now.'" Pat turned to look at Rafe. "Later your higher nature is appalled by what your lower form has done. But in the next situation of stress your body will invariably take charge."

The next situation of stress was called the Battle of Fredericksburg. This was followed in spring by a situation named the Battle of Chancellorsville. In each case Rafe repeated his insane performance at Antietam.

But everyone seemed to be repeating performances. Each Northern general duplicated the caution of the previous leader. Each defeat resulted in Lincoln's replacing the man in charge. Even Robert E. Lee was repeating a performance. He had decided once again to invade the north.

CHAPTER 10

The name of the town was Gettysburg, but Rafe had difficulty remembering it. During the forced march north he had been poring over war maps studded with "burgs" of every variety. Woodensburg, Middleburg, Emmitsburg, Chambersburg, Harrisburg. And now a messenger had come puffing past the tent shouting that they were breaking camp. They'd have to hurry to this—Somethingburg—where advance corps had met legions of rebels.

Rafe was talking with Kent when the summons came. As troopers ran to and fro and bugles blared into the dark, Rafe muttered. "I haven't been wounded yet. Do you suppose this is my last chance?"

"Perhaps you don't remember when your mother dipped you in the Styx," Kent said.

"I do remember. She held me by the head."

"Was she trying to strangle you?"

"It'll be the head, Kent. I know it."

"Bullshit. You'll get rheumatism and be discharged with an aching knee."

"I'm serious. I had a dream that a bullet was coming to-

. *143* .

ward my head. For some reason I could see it. I tried to dodge . . ."

"Well, for God's sake don't dwell on the damned dream," Kent snapped. "Or are you trying to fulfill the prophecy?" He strode away toward the ambulances, roaring a command to an orderly, as Rafe stood looking after him. The gruff parting remark, he knew, had been Kent's way of saying, "I don't want you to talk of dying because you're my friend." Why then couldn't he have said exactly that? On the eve of what he felt in his bones would be his last battle, Rafe thought that the son of a bitch could at least have shaken his hand.

Rafe was now a captain and Jack Lawrence a lieutenant in another company. Old friendships were being severed— men dying, men sent home wounded, men transferred to new units, strangers taking everyone's places. Pat and Kent were the two he could depend on, and at times like this Rafe needed them. Yet at times like this Rafe always seemed to be alone.

It was just like the old days, Rafe thought, as he stood in place behind what was left of the Irish Brigade and listened to instructions from his breathless commander. They were to follow the sons of Erin down a hill and into a valley. The colonel pointed. Could Captain Taylor see the position? Captain Taylor could not. Captain Taylor saw only a valley of smoke. But he said, "Yes, sir." Captain Taylor did not know or care about the exact position. He'd just follow the green flags into any old hell they found. To the colonel he nodded again, "Very good, sir," and he waited for the order to advance, angrily muttering one of the commander's favorite poems:

> Theirs not to make reply
> Theirs not to reason why
> Theirs but to do and die:
> Into the valley of Death
>   Rode the six hundred.

Cannon to the right of them,
Cannon to the left of them
Cannon in front of them
    Volley'd and thundered;
Storm'd at with shot and shell
Boldly they rode and—

The command came down, and Rafe was leading his troops down the hill and into the fray.

All Rafe ever saw of the Battle of Gettysburg was a dense cloud of smoke with a mad jumble of legs rushing under it and tangling in the golden wheat. In five minutes his command was scattered; in three more he was down. It was a merciful bullet that glanced off the frontal bone, leaving him with only a scalp wound. But the impact caused him to fall, breaking his leg. And both pains together delivered him into blessed unconsciousness.

Periodically over the next half hour, Rafe drifted into consciousness, felt the blinding pain, and then passed out again. He was choking in the acrid smoke, and during one period of lucidity he attempted to drag himself a few feet as though this motion would carry him to pure air. Groaning, vomiting, clawing furiously at the matted wheat, he made scant progress before abandoning the idea as hopeless. He murmured "wounded" and looked around, knowing full well that no one could hear him. The pain in his leg was unbearable. His head throbbed acutely. Blood was running all over his face and he was whimpering like an animal, oblivious to everything but his pain, plunged into a primitive state. The war roared around him but he did not see or care—except when someone stumbled over his prone body. He begged the wheat for morphine and urged it to take his leg off. The blow to his head had cut off memory, and he did not realize that his leg was only broken. He was sure he had been hit by a minie ball. To the wheat he murmured over and over again, "Take it off. Take my leg off." And he was still chanting these words when the stretcher bearers reached him.

The pain of being moved caused him to lose consciousness again. He did not come fully awake until he was back at the field hospital. Pat Shepherd's face was swimming into focus and Rafe looked up, muttering, "Hurry up and amputate."

Pat began cutting away Rafe's trouser leg and feeling the bone.

"Ow! Stop!" Rafe roared. "Just take it off, for God's sake. Don't fiddle with the—Jesus Christ!"

Pat removed his hand, smiling, and Rafe moaned, "What the hell's so funny?"

"Nothing. Relief. You've got a simple fracture of the tibia and a flesh wound on the temple. Possible concussion, but you'll live, I'm afraid. With both legs too. When I first saw you I thought you'd been shot in the head. But as soon as I heard you begin to complain . . ."

Rafe heard no more. The knowledge that he would retain the leg had buoyed his spirits as much as spirits can be buoyed while the body is in acute pain. But after two minutes of contemplating a normal future, Rafe, who was not one to suffer in silence, was demanding sedation.

Sedation came in the form of a handkerchief doused with chloroform. He was on an operating table and Kent was preparing to stitch the scalp and set the bone. An orderly was holding the suffocating cloth against Rafe's nose.

"Take that stuff away. Can't breathe!" Rafe cried, the handkerchief muffling his words.

Kent said sharply, "Shut up, Rafe."

"Shut up yourself, you cold-hearted bast . . ." the rest of the word was lost as the anesthesia began to take effect.

"Corporal, hold this lunatic down, will you?" Kent was smiling. He too was relieved to see how relatively minor Rafe's wounds were.

Rafe came to consciousness in a two-man pup tent. He was lying on straw and his leg was in a splint. Next to him a sergeant was staring up at the canvas. Outside it was dusk, but it seemed like dawn in a barnyard. The sounds of the wounded were closer to mooing, crowing and braying than to any human cries. Rafe shuddered, pressing a hand to his aching bandaged head. He was still in agony but those around him sounded as though they were in even worse straits. The sergeant retained only half his left leg and was wincing in pain.

"Can I help, sergeant?"

The man turned his head slightly and attempted a smile. He spoke in a brogue. "With your leg in a splint? I appreciate it, sir, but there's nothing you can be doing."

"I can talk, sergeant."

"Ay," the man said wearily.

"Are you in the Irish Brigade?"

"Ay."

"Seems we're always following you lads down a hill."

"To your glory, sir?"

Rafe smiled. "To our doom. Why do you have to be so damned courageous? You shame us into imitating you when at heart we're cowards."

"Something to be said for cowardice, sir. Keeps your arms and legs with you."

Rafe had hoped to avoid talking of the sergeant's missing limb. His plan had been to concentrate on the young man's bravery, thereby making his torture seem worth it. This hadn't worked, so now he changed the subject abruptly. "Do you suppose we can get any water in here?"

"If anyone ever comes by."

Rafe frowned. From the sound of things outside, no one would be likely to enter the tent for hours. Days, perhaps. They'd been shoved under canvas and abandoned. "I suppose we could shout," Rafe said.

"Shout? And do you think they'd be caring with all the screaming out there?"

"No. You're right. But we've got to think of something before we die of thirst."

"All respect, sir, I'd as soon be dying."

"Sergeant . . ." Rafe began, knowing there was no way to avoid discussing the wound. "You can get fitted with an artificial limb. Why, they're quite realistic looking and they . . ."

"I know that. But 'tisn't just the leg, sir. Got it in the belly too."

Rafe's eyes widened. He had not guessed that the man had another wound. A dingy grey blanket, too small to cover the man's entire body, did hide the abdominal dressings.

God! The poor man must be in excruciating pain. "I'll get you some sedation somehow," Rafe said, his voice urgent.

"Ay. Thank you sir."

Rafe tried shouting but nobody came. He looked around for something to throw. Digging into his shirt pocket he pulled out a penny and heaved it forward as best he could from his horizontal position. No luck. It was getting dark anyway. He shouted again, calling in turn for Pat, Kent, General Hancock, and General Meade. No one outside paid the slightest attention.

The sergeant said, "You might try singing, sir."

"Singing?"

"No one would expect to hear singing. Might notice that. Start singing and then shout 'help!'" The sergeant's voice was growing weaker and Rafe turned toward him in alarm. The light was too dim to see the man's pallor but he guessed that the sergeant was pale, if not blue.

"All right. I'll try it," he said quickly. "A song. Let's see. Something to contrast with the word 'help'. Something cloying." He settled on a piece called "Weeping Sad and Lonely," and soon his bass voice was rolling across the field. He was amazed, considering his condition, that he could summon such vocal power. With his head throbbing accompaniment to every lyric, he bellowed,

> Dearest love do you remember (Help!)
> When we last did meet (Help!)
> How you told me that you loved me
> Kneeling at my feet.
> (Pat! Goddamn you!)
> Weeping sad and lonely
> Hopes and fears so vain
> (Sons of bitches!)
> When this cruel war is over
> Praying that we meet again.
> (Jesus Christ, doesn't anybody hear me?)

He began a second chorus using stronger curse words for contrast, and at last a young orderly poked his head into the tent. It was Kent's assistant, Tim Kelly. He said, "Sir! Your language, sir! The chaplain . . ."

"The chaplain be damned. Where's Kent?"

"Operating. Quarter of a mile from here."

"I need opium for this man."

Tim reached in and felt the man's pulse. "Gone, sir."

Rafe gulped. "Dead?" He shook his head. "I was just talking to him. I—I never even learned his name."

"Sorry, sir. Will that be all? Need any water?"

"Yes," Rafe said. "The sergeant here and I were trying to figure out how to get some. We—Uh, yes. Please bring me some water."

"You in pain, sir?"

"Quite a bit."

"Laudanum's run out, sir."

"Any whiskey?"

"I can try," said Tim.

"Please."

Two men came in a few minutes later to take the sergeant away, and long afterward Tim returned with water and whiskey.

"Major Wilson's own bottle, sir. Not much left, but let me prop you up. Drink it fast 'cause I gotta be getting back. Major wants the bottle for water. By the way, he says you're not to move. Not one inch, he said, until he can get plaster for a cast."

Rafe took several frenzied swallows, trying simultaneously to get news of the battle from Tim.

"What happened to my men?"

"Don't know, sir. Ask Dr. Nelson. He knows the men in your regiment."

"Where's Dr. Nelson?"

"Don't know, sir."

"Can't you tell me anything?"

"Afraid I might start to cry. Major said try not to. Captain Shepherd and me, we were crying like babies and the major said we'd never get any work done unless we . . ."

"About what? What were you crying *about*?"

"Everyone, sir." Tim snatched the empty bottle from Rafe's hand and ran out into the night shouting, "Awfully busy, sir. Sorry."

Sometime during the night a new patient was placed next to Rafe in the tiny tent. This one had bandages around his head and was either heavily sedated or so asleep that his being moved had failed to rouse him. He was still unconscious when Rafe woke the next morning, acutely uncomfortable and very thirsty. Rafe turned and saw to his amazement that the man was a rebel. What was a prisoner doing in here? Had the medical staff gone crazy? Well, he would have to think about it later. At the moment, he wanted water.

Rafe tried shouting, had no response, and began singing "Weeping Sad and Lonely" without the curse words. This brought a curious orderly who wondered why this wounded officer was singing so lustily. Rafe explained, to his later sorrow, that singing was the only way he could attract attention. He was parched and needed water for his canteen.

"Bring me water and I won't bother any of you again," Rafe said. "I don't expect luxuries like food and medicine, sergeant. Just water. And a bedpan if you have one."

"A bedpan!" the sergeant roared. "You're joking, sir."

"All right then. If someone would just change the straw once in awhile. Or better yet, get me crutches and I'll find a latrine."

"Crutches, sir? We won't get crutches for a week. 'Sides, you shouldn't move until that leg's in plaster."

"Well, then. Bring me anything you can spare, sergeant, beginning with water."

"Yes, sir."

The water arrived an hour later, and Rafe drank greedily, saying "Ah!" to his tentmate, whom he now realized was comatose. He pried open the man's mouth and dribbled some water into it. Somehow the rebel was able to swallow. Rafe refused to speculate about him. He was still thinking of the nameless Irishman, reminding himself that he mustn't weaken himself further by developing an attachment to a man who was nameless, inert, and an enemy too. He contented himself instead by carrying on a one-way conversation. "Say, soldier, what day is it? Thursday? Friday? Friday, you say? Oh, and we're in the village of Middleburg. No, Emmitsburg, right? Wait, now I remember. It's Burgburg. Right, the model for all burgs. . . . Am I going crazy, Johnny Reb?"

In the afternoon there was a nightmarish cannonade which continued for two hours. This sound, blending with that of the howling wounded outside, drove Rafe into babbling idiocy. Laughing hysterically, he said to his comatose companion, "I have a hunch that there are people out there who're mad at each other. . . . You think so too? . . . Someone ought to call it a draw. . . . Exciting, though, isn't it? Never know when one of those cannon balls will land right here. . . . There, there now, don't be scared, Johnny Reb. Old Rafe'll be here, yes indeed."

The cannonade died at last and the afternoon wore on. Dr. Nelson came to look in on him, told him to keep up his spirits, and left before Rafe could ask him about the outcome of the day's fighting or about the casualties in his command. Rafe chatted at the Confederate until, exhausted from his own monologue, he fell asleep.

The following day it rained steadily. Rafe had one caller, an orderly, who threw some salt pork in his general direction, shouted that Pat would be by soon, and disappeared into the torrent. On the following day the face of a grey-haired woman appeared in the tent opening. After introducing herself as a Sanitary Commission Volunteer, she passed a bowl of pea soup in to Rafe, waited until he had finished it, and then left him with crackers and jelly sandwiches, dried apricots, and a pamphlet. It was the first time in the war that Rafe was able to weep, but he had to control himself lest his tears drip on the crackers and make them soggy. He ate greedily, saying to his tentmate, "Mighty good victuals. I'll save a few crackers for you in case you wake up. Got something to read, too. Things are getting better, lieutenant. . . . The battle? No chance to ask about it."

The pamphlet, titled "The Soldier's Friend," described the organization of the Sanitary Commission, a civilian organization that gathered donations from all over the country and sent them where most needed. The text was deadly dull, but Rafe read it through three times, asking the lieutenant, "Did you know, sir, that there are five divisions in the commission? . . . That's right. Medical Inspection, Special Relief, Hospital Directory, Statistical, and Publication . . . Isn't that fascinating? . . . Don't look so excited, Johnny. I'm not giving away military secrets after all. . . ."

The pamphlet concluded with hymns, psalms, and patriotic songs, all meant to give comfort to the soldier. Rafe spent an hour chanting psalms to the lieutenant before sinking into glorious sleep.

The next day he discovered that he and the lieutenant needed more water. This time he chose a hymn from the pamphlet in order to get the attention of a pair of legs racing past the tent opening. His voice boomed,

> Father, when the child is dying.
> On the bed of anguish lying,
> Then my every want supplying,
> To me love display.

The legs did not stop, so he resorted to a more familiar hymn:

> Rock of ages cleft for me
> Let me hide myself in thee,
> Let the water and the blood
> From thy wounded side which flowed
> Be of sin the double cure,
> Save from wrath and make me pure.

No luck. They were onto his tricks. And to make matters worse, a voice was floating back to him. Someone was warbling another hymn, only this was in Russian. Rafe sighed. He'd started a goddamned international chorus! There was nothing for it but to add a few curse words to "Rock of Ages" and bring down the wrath of a chaplain.

> Rock of ages cleft for me (God damn!)
> Let me hide myself in thee (Oh hell!)

A long skirt appeared in the tent opening. Rafe heard a gasp, the crack of bones, and then a face was looking in. It was the dear old lady who had given him the pamphlet and the food. Rafe was profoundly ashamed.

"I'm sorry, Madam," he muttered, blushing.

"And well you should be, young man!"

"It's just that nobody ever comes in here unless I sing. I

need water. Also fresh straw. There are no bedpans, Madam, and surely you understand . . ."

"Yes. Yes. I'll do what I can. But oh how *can* you desecrate our sacred hymns? Howl or shout or—or even curse if you must. But don't ridicule God, young man!" She paused, swallowing.

"I'm awfully sorry. It was a thoughtless thing to do. You see, I'm desperate. The lieutenant here and I . . ."

"You and everyone else are desperate. I'll get you water and what food I can find. But try to understand, young man, there are thousands worse off than you are. You can't imagine! Many have no shelter at all. Those poor boys are . . ." She broke off.

"I am sorry," he said lamely. Then he tried to change the subject. "Do you happen to know who won the battle?"

"Why, we did! It was a great victory."

"The war's over, then?"

She frowned. "I hope so. Our army is driving their army back to Virginia."

"When did they start the pursuit?"

"A day or so after the battle. They say General Meade was cautious. He wanted our men to rest."

"Goodbye, General Meade," Rafe sighed.

"Captain, I have no time to waste chatting about the generals. I'll personally see that you're fed twice a day. But I want you to do something for me, too. Be patient. *Patient*, young man! Why, there are men in agony, *dying* men who are showing more forbearance than you!"

When at last she left, Rafe felt thoroughly guilty. Like a spoiled, complaining child. "Trouble is," he said to his silent companion, "I'm not a very good sufferer. Can't stand pain, Johnny Reb. Not a heroic type at all. You know, Pat talks about bodies speaking for us. Afraid that's the case with me. When I'm suffering, I yell. Can't help it. . . . I know I'm not supposed to do these things, not supposed to value my own skin. Supposed to think of the cause, right?

"What do you think of the cause, Johnny? Somehow you don't look like the slaveholding type. . . . Wishful thinking, I guess. . . . Can you hear me, Johnny? There are times when I think you can. . . . Wish there were something I could tell you. . . . Don't know much about the South but I'll sing 'Dixie' if that'll help. What the hell, Johnny, are they gonna courtmartial a wounded Yank for singing 'Dixie'? If they do, I'll tell them I'm not right in the head. Maybe they'll discharge me. Scalp wounds have advantages. . . ."

Rafe sang "Dixie," "Maryland my Maryland," and "Swanee River." Then he began to talk again:

"All right, enough of the South. Let me tell you about where I come from." Rafe rambled on about William's hill in winter, the spruces under the snow, the leaves of October, Barrett's Pond, the snug little houses, the mores and morality of Lanston. "Guess you'd tell me people behave pretty much the same down South. I've never met a Southern girl but I hear they're pretty. Magnolia skin, right? You call them Georgia peaches, don't you? . . . Our girls are pretty too. Did I ever tell you about Christine? The blackest hair I've ever seen and the whitest skin and the rosiest cheeks. We used to go walking in the wintertime. She looked so beautiful against the snow. Like part of the landscape. . . . But I couldn't marry her. Beauty isn't enough for me. If there's anything I learned in Cambridge and Boston it was that. . . . What else did I learn in college? The classics. Always the classics. . . . The world is changing, Johnny, but you'd never know it up there. The professors go on reading Cicero and Plato as though civilization had never passed beyond the borders of Greece. . . . Strange . . . The world and its values don't make sense to me, Johnny. Never did. . . . This war, for example. It should never have been fought. The problem could have been solved through science. That's right, science. History tells us that the master/slave situation began to change when exploiters found animals or machines to do the work of men. You don't see men hauling stones the way they did in Egypt, do you? You see trains doing the job, right? And now people say that it's inhuman to make men—even slaves—do the work that horses or machines can do. Moral rectitude follows the curve of comfort, right? Men with machines don't need to exploit other men just as starving people with cattle don't need to eat other people. . . . But does your government understand the underlying principle? Does ours, for that matter? We have the machines now, Johnny! With more development both the slaves in the South and the serfs in the North can be liberated. But people get in the way. They always will. Kent's right about that. The cotton gin should have freed the slaves; instead it created a need for more material. People are selfish, Johnny . . . . Damn, can't figure it all out. . . . Contradict myself. . . . Science won't solve anything. . . . But still, those Egyptians don't haul stones anymore. . . . Or do they? What do you know about Egypt, Johnny?

"God, but it's hot! Here I go, complaining again. But this climate drives me crazy. Back home we're always saying that there are eleven months of winter and one month of summer, and that month is cold. Well, that's not quite true but I do miss the snow right now. . . . Seems I'm always talking about snow. . . . Sometimes it gets too cold, though. When I was in school—the academy—this girl used to come in late all the time. She had to travel a long way and she was always so cold. . . . Funny, I can still see that classroom. I can smell it, too. Damp wool and chalk and the wood fire . . . Seems so far away now. . . . She and I used to exchange notes. I think she thought I was witty. . . . But *you* don't think so, Johnny. . . .

"Did I ever tell you about my brothers? I like the older ones but I don't understand them any more than I understand my father. The younger ones are more like me. They . . ."

On and on Rafe would talk, always hoping that the man would open his eyes or at least move his mouth to give a sign that he heard him. Rafe would tell jokes and anecdotes, sing, read from the pamphlet, even philosophize. It was always the philosophy that lulled him to sleep.

Kent and Pat finally appeared one day, bringing a lovely young woman with them.

"My sister Beth," Pat said, as orderlies dismantled the pup tent and lifted it from the ground, bringing Rafe and the rebel into the daylight.

The young woman looked as though she was in her early twenties. She had dark hair and eyes and a beautifully shaped basque. She smiled down at Rafe and said hello. Then her eye fell on the Confederate lieutenant and she frowned. Kent, who was kneeling beside the unconscious man, opened the lids and closed them, then felt the man's pulse.

Pat looked over and exclaimed in amazement, "That man's Secesh!"

"You noticed." Rafe nodded. "Wondered when someone was going to comment."

"How did he get here?" Pat asked.

"He was drunk and he stumbled in." Rafe smiled and winked at Johnny Reb, as though the man were sharing the joke.

Kent rose from the rebel's side. "He's moribund. Let's get someone to move him."

"You can't!" Rafe cried.

"But the man is practically dead. There's a special place near the burial area . . ."

"He's my friend!" Rafe shouted. "You can't take him away!"

While Pat's sister looked at Rafe, frowning, Kent repeated, "Your friend? You mean he comes out of his coma? I would never have guessed . . ."

"No," Rafe said. "He's been unconscious for the five, six days—however long I've been here."

"Then how is he your friend? Do you have friends in Georgia?"

The young woman understood. "He means, major, that he feels close to the man. They've shared quarters for many days. The fact that they've never spoken is not the point."

"Yes," Rafe nodded. How understanding she was. He asked, "Are you with the Sanitary Commission?"

"No, captain. I've just come down to help my brother."

Kent looked at her, then Rafe. He said briskly, "We've got to be getting on with rounds. I'll leave this man here if you wish, Rafe, but I . . ." He shrugged, then addressed Pat's sister, "Let's go, Miss Shepherd."

"Wait!" Rafe shouted. "Can't you stay and talk a minute?" He was addressing Kent but smiling at Beth.

"Afraid not," Kent said. "Come, Miss Shepherd."

The lovely vision waved goodbye and trailed behind the surly surgeon, orderlies following in their wake. They ascended a small hill and entered a hospital tent.

As Pat examined Rafe's flesh wound and changed the dressing, Rafe said, "Why didn't you tell me about your sister?"

"I did tell you I had a sister."

"But you never described her. Oh, what a scoundrel Kent is, hauling her away like that when he knows I'm desperate for the sight of a beautiful woman. Not only beautiful but sensitive as well. How could he do that?"

"He's in a hurry, Rafe."

"Hurry? Hell. He's in love with her."

"She's only been here two days. How could he be in love with her?"

"All right. He's infatuated, attracted. Old granite face was awfully anxious to get her away from me."

"She's not Kent's type. Nor yours either. She fancies poets and idealists."

"I don't care who she fancies. I'm talking about who Kent fancies. And I'll bet you my Sanitary Commission pamphlet that he . . ."

"Your sanitary what?"

"Never mind. Damn it, if I had the strength I'd pursue her myself. But I'll do Kent a favor. It's high time a woman melted that chunk of ice."

"You *are* going mad, my friend. I was going to move you to a livelier tent. Are you sure you want to stay with the rebel here?"

"Yes, but could you get me something to read?"

Pat nodded. Then he said, "Rafe, wait a minute. I forgot to tell you earlier. Your father's on the way."

"My father? Here?"

"Nelson managed to get a wire to your home town. He'll be here any day to take you home."

"They're letting me go home?"

"You've been in almost two years. You're not supposed to get a pass until fall. But Nelson felt benevolent. I understand he and your father are neighbors."

"How many weeks, Pat?"

"Two."

"Tell him to make it three and I'll give him my Sanitary Commission Pamphlet absolutely free."

"Your *what*? What's this pamphlet you've been . . ."

"I'll explain when I get back. Fascinating story." Rafe paused. "Home," he said softly.

Pat smiled, then said to an orderly, "Change the straw

here before you put the tent together."

After Pat went away, Rafe turned to the lieutenant. "I'm going home, Johnny Reb. Wish you were too. Well, maybe you will be. Who knows? I don't want to leave you until—until . . ." But he could not finish the sentence. He would not tell the unconscious man that he expected him to die.

At about eight o'clock that night the lieutenant's breath began coming in choking gasps, and then Rafe heard the sound men called the death rattle. He had seen dead men many times but he had never before watched a man die. Just as the man expired, Rafe reached out and clasped the still-warm hand. Then he murmured softly, "Goodbye, Johnny Reb."

A few minutes later he shouted hoarsely into the dark, "The lieutenant is dead." Orderlies appeared like a squad of firemen. They never seemed in any great hurry to save the living, but disposing of the dead was another matter entirely. Rafe considered asking the orderlies to try to find out who the man was and where he came from. Perhaps it would comfort his folks to know that he had not died alone. In the end, however, he decided not to inquire. The rebel had been a special friend, part real and part imaginary. Rafe did not want him altered in any way. Especially did not want to make him an enemy.

As the orderlies carried the man out, Rafe turned away. For a long time he stared into the blackness until, numbed by the enormity of what he had seen, he fell into a troubled sleep.

Hours later there was the flash of a lantern and Kent's voice behind it. "Rafe?"

Rafe, jolted awake from his nightmares, nearly cried out. In the eerie light Kent looked ghostlike.

"Did I frighten you?" Kent asked. "Didn't mean to."

"It's all right. What time is it?"

"Four A.M.," Kent said.

"Four? Haven't you had any sleep?"

"What's sleep," Kent growled. He said in a softer voice, "The rebel died?"

"Yes."

"I'm—uh—sorry." Kent was still puzzled about the strong affection Rafe had had for a comatose enemy.

"It's all right," Rafe said.

Kent cleared his throat. "I'm here to plaster that leg." He began to lift the limb.

"Careful! Christ, that hurts."

"Sorry."

They did not speak for a while. Finally Rafe said, "How's the dark-eyed belle?"

"Pat's sister?"

"No. Mary Todd Lincoln."

Kent smiled. "Miss Shepherd is a very capable young woman. She's helping us with laundry, nursing, even assisting with amputations. There's nothing she can't do."

"I daresay."

"What's that?"

"You're smitten, aren't you?"

Kent did not bother to deny it. As he applied the plaster he said, "She doesn't like me. We had words the other day."

"Oh?"

"My fault. I lost my temper." He looked up and said gravely, "Charm was never one of my strong suits."

Rafe struggled to keep a straight face. Understatement of the year, he thought. Aloud he said, "Don't worry about it, Kent."

"She upsets me, Rafe. Her behavior—it's so much like my late wife's."

"Why should that upset you? You loved your wife, didn't you?"

"Too much. That's the problem. I guess I resent Beth for—I'm not sure. Maybe for having the nerve to be so much like Nancy."

Rafe nodded. Never before had Kent been so candid about his feelings. Overwork and late hours must have done it. But Rafe knew that Kent would resent him for having been witness to this outpouring. Rather than risk that, Rafe decided to drop the subject now. "You'll handle it," he said, noncommittally, hoping that Kent would not ask him if he meant handle it by spurning her or handle it by marrying her. Then Rafe rushed on to another subject. "Tell me, how's the war going?"

"How should I know?"

"Did we win or lose?"

"I'm not sure."

"Doesn't anybody know?"

"New York papers ought to."

"Jesus Christ, what a farce! I've been here for a week, Kent, and I might have been in China for all the news I've had. What's happened to my command? Who was wounded?"

"I don't know all the men in your command."

"You know some of them. And what about E company? Jack Lawrence?"

"I haven't seen Jack. I assume he's moved with the army. Rafe, do you really think that knowing the casualty list will speed your recovery?"

"I'll have to know sometime."

"Wait until you get home then. They'll have the lists there. But don't mourn them here." Kent looked away.

Rafe studied his friend's face. "Must have been hard for you and Pat."

"Yes."

When Kent had finished with the cast, Rafe asked, "When can I have a bath?"

Kent just arched an eyebrow.

"This is an emergency, Kent. I'm going home any day now." He stroked his week's growth of beard and fingered his filthy, battle-worn shirt. "They'll never let me on the train."

"What do you think I am? A goddamn manservant?" But as he was leaving, Kent said, "The best I can do is to send a volunteer in to sponge you. As far as clothes are concerned, plan on wrapping yourself in a blanket, toga style."

The bath was administered by Rafe's old friend from the Sanitary Commission. She had managed to find underwear, a shirt, and a used uniform jacket to which she hastily sewed Rafe's shoulder straps. The trousers she produced were of brown shoddy. Cheap, she explained, because she would have to cut one leg off at the knee. She hadn't been able to find crutches but she was certain that Rafe's father could pick them up in Philadelphia. When she bade Rafe goodbye, she was smiling. And she said, with a wink, "You've got a good voice, young man. But please, don't sing hymns on the train." She paused, then said, "Nor rebel songs either."

"You heard that?"

"As who did not?"

"No hymns, no rebel songs? What will I do?"

"Just keep your mouth shut for a change."

He was moved by ambulance to the village and propped, sitting, against a pole in one of the large tents at Sanitary headquarters. The atmosphere here was much jollier than that in the lonely pup tent. Men chatted and played cards, volunteers dispensed coffee, stew, cookies, cakes, and even whiskey. At last he heard a voice cry, "Rafe! Raphael!" and his father was bounding toward him.

"Hello, Father." He smiled.

Charles touched Rafe's shoulder. "How are you, son?" He was blinking back tears.

Rafe swallowed. "I'm fine. Must look worse than I feel. It's just a broken leg and a scalp wound."

Charles told him that the family had thought him dead. The casualty list had said simply, "Raphael Taylor, head and leg," and the word "head" had made them believe the worst. He had wired frantically and received assurances from Dr. Nelson. But no one at home would be convinced until Rafe actually appeared. Charles went on to tell of transportation arrangements. He and Dick Allen had left Lanston with bags of drugs and the intention of bringing home the five boys from town who had been listed as wounded. On reaching Philadelphia they had heard horror stories about the trains leaving the battlefield area. Trying to hire a coach in Philadelphia, they were told that none would be available for days. Dick urged Charles to take a hack so that he might get to his son quickly. Dick himself had no sons and would remain behind to wait for a larger conveyance. Finding a hack driver willing to travel down here had taken time, Charles explained, but the man was waiting outside.

"Who are the other wounded, Father?"

Charles named four young men, three of them in Rafe's company. Remembering Kent's advice, Rafe did not ask what the wounds had been. "Can Mr. Allen handle them by himself?"

"There are volunteers all along the route. But Dick is very capable." Charles paused. "Very well, then. You and I shall go by hack to Philadelphia, by train to Jersey City, by boat to New Haven, and by train to Lanston. Can you manage that, son?"

"I'd travel by tortoise to get out of—by the way, Father, what's the name of this town?"

"You have a strange sense of humor, son." Charles signalled two orderlies. "Here comes your stretcher."

"Really. I've forgotten. What *is* this place?"

"Why, it's Gettysburg. Surely you could not have been here a week and not learned the name of the town."

Rafe considered telling him how he had spent the week, but he didn't want to relive it so soon. "Gettysburg, is it? I'll try to remember it, Father." He paused. "On second thought, I'll try to forget it."

In Philadelphia Charles installed his son in a good hotel and went off in pursuit of a pair of crutches—an errand that took four hours. Rafe, alone in the expensive room, had a choice between reading the Bible and sleeping. No contest. He crawled from his chair to the bed and raised himself to the blissful mattress with the fresh sheets. It was like ascending into heaven. He awoke thoroughly refreshed and anxious to try his assistant legs. Maneuvering proved to be simple enough, and descending the stairs to the hotel dining room less harrowing than he had anticipated, though Charles' presence at his side was reassuring. Over brandy, he asked his father about the casualty lists. He knew who the wounded were; now what were their wounds? And who were the dead? Charles told him that four boys from the area were dead and three were missing. Of the names mentioned, one of the dead and two of the missing had been under Rafe's command. Of the wounded, two in his company had lost legs and one had sustained a chest wound.

Rafe turned pale, shoved his brandy aside, and buried his head in his hands. He had been through this in four previous battles, but every new roster was a new shock. Each name was a boy he had either grown up with or had come to know well in camp. Each was a face and a unique spirit and arms that waved and legs that ran.

> Where are the legs with which you run
> When you went to carry a gun?
> Indeed your dancing days are done—
> Oh Johnny I hardly knew ye.

Everyone was Johnny and he had a brother named Johnny and—No! His brother's real name was Jonathan and ought to be spelled J-O-N-N-Y. Rafe must remember to spell it that way.

Charles was saying, "Don't blame yourself, son. I read about the wheatfield. You could not have saved them."

"I know that," Rafe muttered.

"Try to think of the good things, son. We routed the Secesh and you will be coming home for a while—a hero."

Rafe looked up wearily. "A hero?"

"Why—yes."

"How am I a hero?"

"You were cited for valor at Antietam, wounded at Gettys . . ."

"But I didn't ask to lead a charge or to be wounded. It happened because there was nowhere to go but into the cannon's mouth."

"Raphael . . ."

"I was ordered to fight. I had no options."

"I wish you would not . . ."

"I am *not* a hero, Father."

"Very well, son. As you wish. I was not trying to offend you, merely to cheer you."

"Yes. Well, let's talk of something else. You said the boys are doing well at Harvard? Make sure they stay there, Father. I want to go to their graduation."

As Rafe climbed the steps to his room with Charles behind him in case one of the crutches slipped, he began to groan, "Months more of this. I'll develop awfully strong muscles. Maybe I'll be able to choke a reb with my bare hands. Even more gory than rifles and bayonets, don't you think? Or possibly I'll lose my footing someday and fall. Then I'll also have a broken back to give for my country."

Charles frowned at these sardonic comments; he had always been an intensely serious man. In the room, Rafe studied his father, wondering what Charles would have thought of the profanities sprinkled through "Rock of Ages." He'd better remember to mind his manners and watch his language if his stay at home were to be rewarding. And no confessions about shooting rebels in the back or slurping coffee while staring at dead bodies. It would break Charles' heart, appall Marie, upset his brothers, shock and dismay the town. He could not accept the title of hero, but he still did not want to be thought of as a blackguard. Sighing and brushing his uniform with his hands, he said to himself, "Raphael Taylor: officer and gentleman."

Rafe was the first of the Gettysburg wounded to arrive home. The entire family, including his older brothers, was there at the Lanston station, flanked by friends and town officials. Their greeting was restrained. Since much of the town was grieving for the dead and missing, it would not do to cheer too loudly over Rafe's escape from death. His mother and sisters hugged him, and his brothers shook his hand. Others in the group said solemnly, "Glad to see you home." Rafe greeted each with a hearty "Glad to be here!" To the judge and other dignitaries he was careful to say the correct thing, knowing that this would please Charles.

"Yes, our men behaved in exemplary fashion. . . . Hancock is indeed a noble general and I shall pray for his swift recovery. . . . Well, perhaps Meade *was* a bit timid but the foe was whipped nevertheless. . . . The wound? It troubles me occasionally but I've no cause to complain. There are those who sustained more permanent injuries. . . . Plucky lads . . . Never complain . . . Capital army, yes sir."

After twenty minutes of this, Rafe whispered to Charles, "I'm tired, Father. Let's go home."

Charles, waving his hands and smiling, nodded toward the Taylor carriage and shouted, "Thank you for coming, everyone. Now we must take our soldier home for a good, well-earned rest."

As Rafe maneuvered his crutches toward the waiting carriage, he saw three young women hurrying toward him, down Mill Street: Abby Lawrence, Rosie Jamieson, and Emily Stevens. Emily looked lovely in a simple green dress with no trim. Her hair was up, but she wore no earrings. He waited, smiling, for the women to greet him. Rosie charged over first, gasping, and said, "The train came in early. Oh, we wanted so to be here on time. It's so good to see you, Rafe! Oh, Rafe!"

Rafe smiled at Rosie and at Abby. Then he turned to Emily.

PART 3

CHAPTER 11

Emily had expected never to see him again. The paper said that Rafe had sustained a head wound. Like the rest of the town, she assumed he, had been shot through the brain. He would lie untended until he died. She had imagined him in a long row with other hopeless cases. And she had remembered the Rafe she knew—warm, bright, witty, gentle. She had sat in the parlor, her head in her hands, thinking, no, there is no God.

And then Dr. Nelson had wired that Rafe's wounds were minor. Mrs. Nelson had come to the store to make the announcement. Emily remembered how the people had milled around on the common that day. She recalled her own physical relief—the goosebumps, the tightening in her throat, the tears quickly blinked away. And all these feelings came back now as she looked at him. He was alive. He was whole. Rafe could think and talk and smile. It was as if he had been resurrected, and she could scarcely assimilate it. Now if only Andy too would suddenly appear here. If only things could be as they had been two years ago.

After Rosie had finished her effusive greeting and Abby

her more restrained one, Emily stepped forward, touched Rafe's arm, and said, "I'm so glad you're home."

"How have you been?" he asked.

"Oh, fine."

"I've missed you," he said, gazing at Emily and then, a shade too belatedly, also nodding at Abby and Rosie.

"Yes," Emily said. "We missed you too."

Now Rosie took over with her dime novel profusions and soon Rafe, looking embarrassed, inched his way toward the carriage. He called, "I'll see you soon," and the three young women chorused "Yes!"

They began to walk toward Dawson Street. Abby and Rosie said that Rafe looked tired but healthy enough, considering what he had been through. Emily was silent. She had thought of him often in the past two years, and she was glad he was home.

It had been a busy two years. Pa had started the factory, turning the store over to Emily's management. He had three apprentices and she supervised two clerks. When they talked together after supper, Mary declared that they sounded like a couple of Vanderbilts. In addition to the store, Emily was still active in the Lanston Victory Association, the lyceum committee, the Mozart Quartet.

Emily's time was structured carefully. So much on this project, so much on that one. She had lists of tasks to do and deadlines by which time a job had to be done. Hours and minutes were important to her, and she rarely wasted them. Every so often Rosie would tell her that she was *insane* to approach life this way. So *what* if the new store displays didn't get done by July first? So *what* if she didn't practice her Chopin piece twenty times by Thursday? But Emily did not think her methods were at all rigid. She worked hard but she enjoyed what she was doing and found that the discipline gave her more time to appreciate what leisure she had.

There were two men interested in Emily. One was a classics master at the Lanston Free Academy and the other her music tutor in Dawn Hills. Both were more than ten years her senior. She was fond of them but at present had no intention of marrying either. Barry, the master, was too shy and self-effacing and sometimes made her feel, by comparison, rather masculine and aggressive. Jonas, the tutor, was a moody perfectionist and a bit too stuffy for her taste, though she learned a great deal about music from him. But she had welcomed the attentions of these two men, had enjoyed dressing up for dinner parties and concerts. She was, she felt, living a satisfying life.

Of course Rosie was forever reminding her that true fulfillment could come only from marriage. And a year ago Rosie had added motherhood to the list of essentials. Rosie as a mother was a phenomenon to behold, and Emily sometimes wondered if the baby girl would be talked or smothered to death.

As they walked up the hill, Rosie mused, "If only Rafe had a girl waiting for him."

Abby muttered, "Leave the poor man alone for a couple of days. He looks as though he needs some rest. Besides, the town is full of eager women. They'll go to him." The war had carried away many bachelors, and some envied Emily because she had two men where they had none. Christine, however, was engaged to Rafe's old rival Don Benton and did not envy Emily in the least—which rankled.

The women arrived at Dawson Street where Mary had been tending Abby's children and Rosie's baby.

"How did the boy look?" Mary asked them as they walked into the kitchen.

"He looks good," Abby said. "Thin, though. And there are still dressings on his forehead. There were so many people at the station that I didn't get a chance to ask him about Jack." She sat down at the kitchen table, looking doleful.

"You'll see Rafe again," Mary said. "I expect he'll be here for some time."

Abby nodded and reached for the teacup Mary was setting down. "Will this war *ever* be over?"

Rosie quoted a newspaper headline. "Gettysburg turned the tide."

"It didn't turn a thing," Abby snapped.

Rosie, whose husband had been rejected with a heart murmur, could afford to be cheerful. "Everyone knows it's just a matter of weeks."

"No," Abby said. "Only *you* know that, Rosie."

Abby was in a foul mood and Emily, sensing that Rosie

was not far from tears, quickly said to the latter, "Why don't you get the baby? It's been ages since I've seen her." It had been an hour.

Rosie went into the parlor where little Chastity romped on the floor. Abby pushed away her teacup, lowered her head to the table, and began to sob.

Mary touched Abby's shoulder. "Seeing Rafe must've hit you bad."

"I should have stayed at the farm," Abby choked. "Why did I ever come here today?"

"No," Mary said. "No, coming here was good. Have to get it out, Abby. Being *too* brave ain't natural."

When Rosie came back with the baby, she took one look at Abby and bit her lip. That was one thing Emily could say for Rosie. She did sometimes know when to remain silent.

Eventually Abby collected herself, and the group drank tea and talked about the children. Then Abby and Rosie gathered offspring and belongings and left for home.

Emily said to her stepmother, "I don't know how to help her, Mary."

"Being around's all a body can do."

"But what if Jack's killed? What will she do if . . ."

"He ain't dead yet," Mary said. "So don't let's think on it."

And that, Emily thought, described the attitude of many young women in town. They lived from day to day propelled by the thought "He ain't dead yet." It was ludicrous.

Mary said to Emily, "Forgot to tell you. Widow Harrington's cook was by just before you got here. Lady wants to see you."

"Must be another project for the Victory Association." This group was now a part of the network donating items to the Sanitary and Christian Commissions. Emily made a mental note to drop in at Mrs. Harrington's huge Maple Street edifice later this afternoon. The two had become fast friends in recent years, working on committees together, and Emily was as comfortable with the gruff old widow as she would have been with an aunt. Mrs. Harrington was forever telling Emily that she was a sensible girl with a few tragic flaws, among them a weakness for handsome men and a love of money. Emily generally retorted that Mrs. Harrington had these flaws herself. Her late husband's portrait revealed an extraordinarily attractive man, and the lady was still perched on Maple Street with all her money. Anyone hearing these exchanges marveled at the teasing familiarity. Mrs. Harrington liked few people in town, yet her favorite was a young woman who put her in her place every time.

To get to the widow Harrington's, Emily had to pass the Taylor house. Inside she could hear laughter and chatter. Out in the backyard Rafe's nieces and nephews played. She wished she could stop and join the welcoming party. But friendly as she was with Rafe's mother, Marie (she too worked with Emily on several committees), Emily would not think of intruding today.

The Harrington residence was a huge federal-style building with seven bedrooms. In some of the bedrooms, the lady stockpiled donations for the soldiers and various charities. Some of the bedrooms had, in the past, been used by her neighbor Doctor Nelson as emergency quarters for patients too ill to travel home. But the occupants of the house were at present limited to two, Mrs. Harrington and her cook. The place was badly run-down. Nothing that a little carpentry and paint couldn't cure, but it was dusty and dingy, and its mistress did not seem to care.

Emily's knock was answered by Delia, the elderly cook, who was clad not in black servant's attire but in a bright red and green cotton festooned with clumps of cheap blue flowers and imitation jewelry. She was as eccentric as her mistress, though in a different way. Mrs. Harrington eschewed all decoration in dress and seldom bothered with corsets.

The portly gray-haired widow greeted Emily in the parlor, wordlessly waved her to a sofa, and told the cook to bring in some lemonade.

"It's too warm for tea," the widow declared in her booming voice.

Emily nodded.

"Did you see Raphael this morning?"

"Briefly. He looks well. Awfully thin, though."

"Poor child," Mrs. Harrington shook her head. "Have you read about that battle?"

"God, yes."

"I must have Rafe to tea tomorrow. Yes, we'll fatten him up. I shall tell Delia to make her biggest, richest, creamiest cake." The widow plunked herself into a chair like a sack of feed. "Well, to the business at hand."

"War relief," Emily said.

"No." She paused. "Well yes, in a sense. I would like to get involved in war relief."

"But you already *are* involved. You're head of the committee."

"I mean in Washington, my dear. I am going to Washington City to live with my sister. Lovely house in Georgetown."

"You mean until the war's over?"

"No, my child. I mean permanently."

"You're joking! Why?" Emily would very much miss the old woman.

Mrs. Harrington leaned back and sighed. "I'm sixty-five years old and I haven't that much time left. I'd like to put the years to good use. Washington City is the place for all my—well, for want of a better word, I'll say projects. War relief, abolition, temperance, suffrage. Yes, after the war I shall certainly stump for women's suffrage. And if I'm going to be stumping, it might as well be on Pennsylvania Avenue, don't you think? On Center Street there's not a Congressman in sight."

Emily smiled as she visualized old Mrs. Harrington tapping her cane, marching by the Capitol in the lead of an army of women. No, Emily would not put it past her. "I only wish I could be there to join the parade."

"And I'd certainly like to see you there, but we both know you're tied to this foolish town with a hundred strings."

The cook set the lemonade down and Emily took a glass. Mrs. Harrington waited until the bangled servant had left and then said, "If I put this house up for sale, you know that at least ten families will bid for it."

Emily nodded. The place was a prize plum all right. It was the biggest house on Maple Street, and the new rich on Patterson would fight like tigers for this spot on aristocracy row.

"I see that envious look in your eye!" Mrs. Harrington shook her finger. "Among your weaknesses, my dear, is your poorly concealed lust for this end of town. I wish there were a way to cure you of the malady."

"You can," Emily said. "You can give me this end of town."

"Hmmmph!" the lady snorted. "Now, getting back to the issue, I have to do something about the house. As you know, I *could* sell it for an enormous amount."

Now the reason for this meeting was coming clear. "I know," Emily interrupted, "but you don't need the money, right? And you don't want Patterson Street people moving in here. So you're leaving the place to the town. For what, though? No, let me guess. A library? That's it. And you want me to be in charge of it." Emily sighed. "I swear, Mrs. Harrington, you spend your every waking moment dreaming up things for me to do. Two months ago it was finding inspirational literature for the troops. Last month it was the Christmas-for-the-poor committee. Christmas comes in December, but you had me packing boxes in June. And now a library!"

Mrs. Harrington laughed, choking on her lemonade. It sprayed in all directions, but she continued to roar helplessly until, remembering her manners, she wiped her mouth with a handkerchief. "A library! Oh Lord! No, my child, that is not what I had in mind. You are right on two counts, though. I don't need the money and I won't have those shoddy vulgarians moving in here. But bequests I am not about to make. I do intend to sell the house."

Emily grinned. "What? No Harrington Library to perpetuate your name?"

"The gossip about my ways will keep my name alive for a century. As for libraries, that will be your decision to make."

"Excuse me?"

"I would like to sell this house to you and your family for whatever amount you can afford."

"*What?*"

"You heard me."

"But you know we can't afford a third of what the place is worth, especially in this location."

"Yes, I'm aware of that."

"Then why are you . . ."

"It's quite simple. I like you."

"Mrs. Harrington, I was only joking when I said I wanted a spot at this end of . . ."

"Perhaps so. But now you shall have your wish."

"What can I say? I . . ."

"No speeches. If I wanted speeches I'd be offering the place to that blathering Rosie. Just talk it over with your father. Whatever you can afford, my dear."

"Please explain why you're doing this?"

The widow mopped at her perspiring brow with a hand-kerchief. "I never had any children," she said. "Hence I have never had the opportunity to partake of the ultimate joy of parenthood—illustrating my superior wisdom to callow offspring. Making them see, in other words, that mother was right. Oh, the pleasures I've missed!" She sighed elaborately. "So while you're still single I want you to move here and indulge your foolish fancies. And when you've learned your lesson you may write to me and tell me that Maple Street is as vacuous as the rest of the town. In that will lie my fulfillment."

Emily swallowed, trying to control her emotion. Mrs. Harrington was telling her in her inimitable way that she wished Emily had been her daughter.

"I can't tell you how moved and grateful I . . ."

"I *said* no speeches. All I want from you is the money and an occasional letter praising my keen mind and unerring judgment."

"But let me at least thank . . ."

"Enough! Now let us have another glass of lemonade and discuss your project for the month."

After Emily told her parents of the offer, Matt's first words were, "I don't know."

Emily had rarely heard her stepmother raise her voice. Now she heard a near-screech. "Don't know!" Mary set down a pot on the stove with a clunk.

"We don't belong there, Mary."

"And why not? Just tell me why not?"

" 'Cause we ain't fancy people, that's why not."

"So to prove we ain't fancy we gotta live on Dawson, on top of the tracks, for the rest of our lives?"

"I just think we oughta stay where we belong. If you

don't like Dawson, there's always Jefferson Street. I saw a place there for sale . . ."

Mary flared. "You're crazy, Matt! I mean it. Not only crazy but insulting a great lady. Telling her to take her offer and you know what."

Emily too was angry. "Don't you think we're as entitled to good things as anyone else in this town? Honestly, Pa, if you were a Negro you'd be thumbing your nose at Lincoln and begging old massa to keep you a slave."

"That's enough back talk, Em!"

"But you're as deserving as anyone else, Pa. And it's not as though she's *giving* the place away. She's *selling* it. At a discount. To the owner of a furniture factory and a store."

Matt snorted. "Me on Maple Street with the Taylors, the Wescotts, the Nelsons, the judge? They'll be making me change my outfits three times a day. Mary'll be wanting visiting dresses and all that *Godey's* stuff. We got different ways, Em. I ain't educated. I don't know nothing about painting and literature. Or which fork to use or how to treat a servant. I won't *have* a servant, do you hear?"

"Well, you don't have to have a . . ."

"Maybe you with your fancy schooling can fit in over there, but Mary and me gotta live there too and don't forget that."

Through clenched teeth Mary said, "You mean you think we're peasants? *That* what you mean?"

"I'm saying *I* am," Matt admitted. "Well, maybe one step up."

Emily exploded. "A peasant! Oh, Pa!"

There was a long silence. Then Mary said brightly, "Why don't us two ladies and the peasant here move to Maple Street? Us ladies can pretend the peasant is their servant."

Matt got red in the face. "It ain't funny!"

"Darn right it ain't funny," Mary muttered. "It's sad."

"I'm warning you, I ain't gonna change my ways," Matt said.

Emily said, "You don't have to, Pa."

"Long as that's understood," Matt growled. And this meant "All right, I'll think about it."

Mary and Emily looked at each other, smiling. They knew that Matt would do just fine on Maple Street. No one there changed outfits three times a day. And few people cared that Matt and Mary were poorly educated. Only one or two families would look down their noses at Maple's new occupants. The rest felt as Mrs. Harrington did. Better to have the lowly Stevenses on the street than the pretentious new wealth they so disdained. Judge Williams and Charles Taylor might actually be pleased. Both were quite fond of Matt. When she thought of Charles, she remembered Rafe. In all the excitement today she had almost forgotten him. What would Rafe say when he discovered they were to be neighbors?

Later she thought of the ramifications of the move. Some people would think that the Stevenses were richer than they pretended to be and had hidden money in their mattresses all these years. Others would accurately guess that Mrs. Harrington was having her last laugh at Patterson Street's expense. The howls of indignation from Christine's parents would reverberate through town for a year. But Emily did not care. As she had told Matt, the Stevenses were as entitled as anyone else to the good things in life.

CHAPTER 12

The beginning of Rafe's homecoming dinner, from soup to entree, was a lecture from Rafe to his younger brothers urging them not to enlist. Through the second half of dinner he asked questions of everyone. How were his mother's committees? His father's practice? His brother the lawyer's practice? His brother the minister's flock? How were the younger boys doing at college? And the girls—did Meg or Jessica have any beaux yet? He asked his sisters-in-law about his nieces and nephews (the children were seated at a separate table) and complimented Annie, their cook, on the meal. Rafe soon grew weary of having to watch his language. In commenting on a nasty client of his older brother he said, "Well, why don't you tell that son of—old Boston to go to—another—another lawyer."

When his older brothers had departed for the inn with their families (there was no room at home to accommodate such a brood) Rafe asked his parents if they'd mind if he went to bed early. As a child he had shared quarters with Bill and Johnny but when his older brothers had fled the nest, they had left their room to him. He was aching for the weeks of sleep ahead. The silence! No bugles tomorrow. No marches. No schedules. The thought was enough to make a man weep.

His eyes had just closed when he heard tiptoeing on the oak floor and saw Johnny's face outlined in the moonlight. "Rafe, what was it really like?"

Rafe sighed. "How's the fishing out at Barrett's Pond, Johnny?"

"Please tell me."

So Rafe told him about Antietam and other battles. He did not discuss the deeds he was ashamed of, but he did concentrate on the gore, giving grisly descriptions of the field hospitals. "And if you enlist, Johnny, you may end up minus a couple of limbs, perhaps even your manhood. Would you like that, Johnny? Not being able to perform with a woman? Well, *would* you?"

Johnny said nothing.

"I asked you a question, goddamn it!"

Johnny said, "Most men don't get it *there*."

"Are you giving me statistics? Bullets don't know anything about statistics."

"I know that."

"You know everything, don't you? Are you listening to me, though? Did you hear my descriptions of the hospitals?"

"I heard you."

"So did I." Bill entered the room and sat down on the floor.

"Splendid," Rafe said. "Then you'll both stay in college."

"No," said Johnny.

"Why the hell not?"

"We're not cowards," said Johnny.

Rafe quoted the Irish sergeant. " 'Something to be said for cowardice, sir. Keeps your arms and legs with you.' "

"Now wait a minute," Bill began.

"The discussion's over. I'm sleepy."

Johnny said, "Father said you led a charge at Antiet—"

"Out!"

But the boys would not move. Instead, they proceeded to tell Rafe of their predicament. They had been sitting in college month in and month out while classmates enlisted with whoops and clamor, deriding the Taylor boys for giving in to their Mama's fears. To make matters worse, the town girls preferred the absent heroes to the stay-at-homes. They might flirt with the Taylor boys but their hearts were with the men who were risking their lives on the front.

Rafe finally realized that he could not win. He tried to get them to consider fields other than the infantry. The medical corps needed men. Musicians were important too. The war department in Washington needed clerks. The regiments needed cooks. They could always tell their girls that they had tried for the infantry but that the decision had been taken out of their hands.

"Cooks!" Bill thundered. "Cooks!"

"All right then. Ambulance drivers."

"We are joining the infantry," Bill announced. "We promised Mother we would wait until the end of the year. But that's *it*, Rafe. We're not *asking* you, big brother. We're *telling* you."

"You are, are you? Well you can both go to hell for all I care! Get out!" The boys left. Rafe felt outraged and defeated. He hoped that they would see only one battle and this a conflict in which their units were kept in reserve. Then they could say in all honesty that they had been at the Battle of Glem's Gulch, guns at the ready, thinking of their lady loves and shouting "*Morituri te salutamus*." It wouldn't matter that they hadn't gotten into the battle. The willingness to die was the thing.

The widow Harrington's old cook, clad in green calico with purple and orange trim, came by the next afternoon and told Rafe that her mistress wanted to see him. Rafe had slept until noon and had just managed to get himself into his clothes. He had eaten a large breakfast/lunch and was planning a hobble to the Common today. Though he was fond of the widow, he hoped that the visit would be a short one.

He clumped into the lady's parlor on his crutches. She greeted him with a bear hug that nearly threw him off balance. Grinning stiffly, he half-fell onto the sofa. "Yes. How are you, Mrs. Harrington?"

"Much better than you, I assure you. I have taken upon

myself the task of feeding you. You are a skeleton, do you know that?" She turned to her cook and thundered, "The cake, Delia!"

"Cake?" Rafe croaked. He had just polished off a pound of bacon, six eggs, a plate of fried potatoes, half a loaf of bread, and four cups of coffee. "I've just eaten, Mrs. Harrington. I appreciate your offer, but I'm really . . ."

"I had the cake made especially for you, Raphael."

"Oh, did you? I didn't realize—thank you for the thought. Well, perhaps a small piece." And he thought, oh, God.

The widow grinned. "We can wait a while. You do look rather green."

Rafe nodded and said again, "I've just eaten."

"Well now, let us not waste valuable time chatting about pastry. How are you, Raphael? As I said, you look frightful."

"Why, thank you, madam. A warmer, more thoughtful welcome I could not have hoped for."

"I mean *tired*, my boy. Dreadfully tired."

Rafe nodded.

"Will you have a scar on your forehead?" She frowned, studying the dressings on Rafe's temple.

"A small one, I imagine. I don't think I'll frighten *too* many people."

"To the contrary, you'll look rather dashing. You've always had a touch of the cavalier. If only I were forty years younger . . . ah, well!" She paused. "Now then, can you tell me of some of your experiences?"

"I'd rather not," Rafe said.

"But it's important that I, as head of the Lanston Victory Association, ascertain the needs of the soldier."

"Oh. Well, that's easy. Fewer hymn books and more novels. Fewer patriotic poems and more whiskey."

"But we never send *any* whiskey," said the temperance advocate.

"That's what I mean," Rafe sighed. "We have to *buy* the liquor when we could be getting it free in loving packages from home."

"Enough of that. What else do you need?"

"Artistic portraits," said Rafe.

"Excuse me?"

"How can I phrase this delicately, Mrs. Harrington? Evocative portrayals of spirited young ladies."

"Pictures of naked women?"

Rafe gasped and clutched at his heart. "Oh please, madam! Your unseemly phrasing. My salts! Where are my salts?"

The widow started to roar. "A lot of help *you* are!"

Rafe grinned and sat up straight. "All right. The food we need most is dried fruit. Ten months out of the year my men live on salt pork and beans. The surgeons think the diet may wipe out the army. Kent—one of the doctors—was telling me . . ."

At that moment the door knocker sounded and Mrs. Harrington shouted for Delia. A minute later Emily Stevens was entering the parlor. She was not as neat as she usually was. Her hair had been carelessly pinned up, and she was dressed in limp calico. But she was flushed and buoyant, and Rafe had never seen her look so appealing. She did not see Rafe at first. She dashed over to Mrs. Harrington shouting "Pa's agreed. He said we'd be able to pay about. . ." and then she noticed Rafe on the sofa. "Oh, excuse me. I didn't realize . . ."

Mrs. Harrington said, "That's all right. Sit down, my dear. We shall discuss the matter later."

Rafe wondered briefly what matter they planned to discuss but he was more interested in studying Emily. He was recalling a line of poetry, "A sweet disorder in the dress / Kindles in clothes a wantonness . . ."

Mrs. Harrington said, "I made a cake especially for our hero, and the scoundrel had the effrontery to refuse it." She rang for her cook. "Delia!" She waited, then muttered, "Where has that woman gone?"

"I saw her out in the yard," Emily said.

"Ah me! Then I shall fetch the cake myself, for surely *you* will have a piece, my dear." And she moved from the room like a wagon loaded with granite.

Emily turned to Rafe. "You refused her *cake*? Oh Rafe, she had it made special."

Rafe smiled. "She was joking. I told her I'd just eaten and would rather wait."

"Oh," Emily said. "For a moment I thought you'd committed the sin of sins."

He said, "Thank you for coming to the train yesterday."

She nodded. "We all wanted to be there. Rafe, do you think you'll have time to go out to the farm and see Abby? She's so concerned about Jack."

Rafe nodded. "Of course I'll go see her. If I don't, Jack will give me no peace. That was one of my duties, you know. Consoling Jack."

"How does it feel to be home?" she asked.

Rafe frowned and rubbed his chin. "To be honest, I don't know. It's something I've wanted so much—dreamed about—and yet, knowing it will only be for two weeks makes me feel—what's the word?—indecisive, I guess. I can't make plans, can't really settle in. I'm a visitor."

She nodded.

"In the service, of course, a man gets used to uncertainties. There may be a tomorrow or there may not be. He accepts that idea and takes what pleasures he can find. But at home the attitude permeating everything is permanence, stability. People here think in terms of futures, of lives going on and on. A soldier doesn't fit in."

"After the war . . ." she began.

"Yes. When it's all resolved, I'll feel more comfortable."

The conversation was interrupted by the entrance of Mrs. Harrington and her cake. It was a cake in keeping with the Harrington tradition. No inscription, no frills of any kind. Just big, heavy, and filling. Mrs. Harrington ate two pieces. The others each managed half a serving. Mrs. Harrington resumed her questioning of Rafe, taking notes occasionally. Emily noticed that Rafe was becoming more and more distracted. He would answer, "Yes, we always like to get crackers and preserves," and then would look off into space, not hearing the next question. At last Mrs. Harrington asked, "Are you feeling well, Raphael?"

"Yes, of course."

"I don't think you are. I want you to go home and sleep for a week. Forget the war if you can. And forgive me for having forced you to remember it." She gestured toward the door, dismissing him. "I have business to discuss with Emily."

"All right, then." He picked up the crutches, shoved

them under his arms, and with a brief nod at the women, left the parlor.

Mrs. Harrington said, "I can't rid myself of the thought that if a bullet doesn't get him, his experiences will."

"What do you mean?"

"Some soldiers are driven plumb out of their minds." Mrs. Harrington shook her head and changed the subject abruptly. "Now then, tell me. What is your father prepared to pay?"

In the week following the Harrington cake presentation Emily saw little of Rafe, though she thought of him a good deal. He was squired by his family hither and yon, visiting relatives and friends, attending dinners. And because Rafe was one of the few eligible bachelors in town, there was a parade of visitors from Patterson Street and other tributaries. Mothers with nubile daughters in tow would suddenly find excuses to call on Marie. Rafe was fussed over by practically everyone, and Emily thought he deserved the pampering.

During the second week of his leave, Emily met Rafe on the common. He was sitting on a bench, coaching a new game called baseball, shouting to his brothers and their friends, waving his crutch for emphasis. He seemed more himself this morning—cheerful and grinning, animated. During a break in the game, he told her that he and his brothers were going to Vermont for a three-day fishing trip before he returned to camp.

"Will I see you before you leave?" she asked.

"I'll come back to town first."

She remembered the day in August of '61 when she had kissed him goodbye, and she wondered if he remembered too. Then she turned to walk toward Mrs. Harrington's, wishing him a good trip.

The sale of the Harrington house was no longer a secret. The widow had told Mrs. Nelson about it yesterday and now the whole town was talking. Some people coming into the store today went so far as to ask Emily outright where Matt had gotten the money. Emily was prepared for this. Smiling, she told them, "The Earl of Wessex expired and left us his fortune."

The outrage on Patterson Street was as voluble as expected. Maple Street remained silent, reserving judgment. Out on the farms, people were pleased to hear that one of their own had gained mighty Maple at last, but at the same time they envied the Stevenses' good fortune. Only Rosie fully and enthusiastically shared Emily's delight. "Think of the balls you can have here after the war!" she exulted.

In all the excitement following the announcement, the Stevenses nearly forgot Jenny Lawrence's wedding. Jenny had wanted to wait until her brother Jack came home on leave but since her fiancé had decided to join up, the country wedding was rather hastily gotten together. In the next two days Emily finished a dress which she had been working on in spare moments for months. The project had started last fall when Mr. Winter of Winter's Dry Goods had given her a bolt of muslin while cleaning his shelves to make room for poplins and wools. The style of the dress was chosen by Mary six months later from a sketch in a Boston newspaper. Since then both she and Emily, with advice from Rosie, had worked on the frock from time to time. It was very fashionable, unlike any of the simple styles Emily normally wore. She had been wondering where on earth she would wear this creation. And now, in midsummer, came Jenny's wedding.

The dress was of lemon yellow muslin. It was high-waisted with a square neckline which Mary had assured her would "show off her pretty neck." The sleeves fell gracefully and there were separate undersleeves of white sheer. The wide skirt, which would be supported by petticoats rather than hoops, was ringed at the center and at the hem with petal trim. Every so often Mary or Emily would sit down to make or attach new petals. Emily had hastily completed the task last night. She had a white straw bonnet, and today she had bought some yellow satin with which to line it. She already owned white kid slippers and white silk stockings, but she had to make another trip to Winter's for the lace mitts. lace mitts.

Now, twirling in front of the glass, she admired herself thoroughly. All she needed to complete the picture was Jonas Whiting at her side. But Jonas, her elegant music tutor, was up in Boston and Barry, the academy master, was on holiday.

She would travel to the wedding in the company of her parents only.

At Lawrence weddings (the family had already married three girls) the ceremonies themselves were always private family affairs. Friends arrived later for the afternoon-into-evening parties following the rites. Most brought covered dishes out to the sprawling farm, and some came with "apple juice" (cider) or "grape juice" (wine). Matt's contribution was always cider. The Lawrences had come to depend on him.

The weather was perfect, though rain would not have daunted the merrymakers; they would simply have moved inside. The Stevenses arrived at five that afternoon. Tables were spread out under the trees, amateur fiddlers were tuning up, children were playing in scattered groups, and a few men, already feeling their apple juice, were heatedly discussing politics. Abby met Emily as the latter was rounding the corner of the house to make her grand entrance into the backyard.

"Look at you!" Abby cried. "And you haven't even *moved* to Maple yet. Turn around and let me see the dress."

Emily self-consciously pirouetted. Abby nodded and said, "All the women are dressed up and the men are in shirts and trousers."

"Characteristic," Emily said, admiring Abby's apple green print and wishing Jack were here to see her. Abby had lost a great deal of weight since she'd been running the farm alone. She looked stunning this evening, and Emily told her so.

Abby returned the compliment and said, "Jeremiah won't let you alone when he sees you in *that* outfit." Abby's seventeen-year-old brother had had a crush on Emily since he had been a little boy. "Will you dance with him?"

"Of course," Emily said. "I'll be the worldly older woman."

"Just don't get *too* worldly," Abby said.

Emily grinned and walked on, greeting the newlyweds and other old friends, swapping news, laughing out loud when people told her that she and her family had "crashed" Lanston society. As evening came on and the lanterns were strung up, she doffed her bonnet and joined in the first reel with young Jeremiah. Later she danced with others—boys of Jeremiah's age or younger, occasionally with the father of a friend. Most men of her own age were at war. She ate heartily and drank enough cider to make her tipsy. But she didn't need cider to assist her tonight. The atmosphere of the old days—of other weddings, husking bees, and rural parties—was strong and exhilarating. Only when she happened to think of Roger did her expression become melancholy. If only he were here, the old days would be real again.

She was walking back to the tables, breathless after an exhausting dance, when she saw Rafe. When had *he* arrived? And what was he doing at this country wedding? Then she remembered that Rafe was now one of Jack's close friends and of course would have been invited to the wedding of Jack's sister. He must have come back from his fishing trip today. That meant he would probably be leaving tomorrow or the next day. He was sitting on the ground, his crutches beside him, surrounded by gesticulating men and interested young ladies, and he seemed to be enjoying himself. He waved at her as she passed and she waved back.

It was not until half an hour later that she had a chance to speak with Rafe. He was still in the same spot, a plate of food in front of him and a pitcher of cider at his elbow. The others had moved off to drink or dance. Abby was standing apart talking with Mary. Nell McDonald, a romantic girl of fifteen, was a few feet away, peering at Rafe from behind a rose bush. He did cut a handsome figure, Emily thought, even though he was sitting on the ground. And the scar over his eye, now unbandaged, did not detract from his basic good looks.

Rafe smiled and gestured toward her. "I'm all alone," he said. "Abandoned."

No, you're not, she thought, thinking of lovesick Nell behind the rose bush. But she sat down beside him, handing him her glass of cider while she arranged her petalled skirts, wondering if the petal near the left seam at the hem was going to come off. She had sewn that one on very hastily last night. She asked, "How was your fishing trip?"

"Very pleasant."

"Any extraordinary catches?"

He nodded. "Trout."

"Really? How many?"

"Let's just say we didn't starve to death."

"One?" she asked, smiling.

"One. And Bill caught it. Otherwise we lived on bull-heads. But we had a good time." He paused. "Moving from my undistinguished fishing record to more pleasant subjects, I must say you look lovely tonight."

"Thank you," she said. And feeling flirtatious after all the cider, she added, "You look very dashing yourself."

"Dashing? Really?" He patted the sleeve of his open-necked shirt, looked at his cast, shrugged, and sat up straighter. Then, fingering his mustache, he said, "It must be this."

"It's everything," she said. "I can personally attest that several young ladies here tonight are positively smitten."

"Where are they?" He swiveled his head but not so far as to take in the rose bush. "I hope you count yourself among them."

"But of course I do." She winked and sipped from her glass.

"You're drinking cider, Emily?"

"Just a bit. Why?"

"Cider becomes you," he said, pouring himself another drink. Raising the glass to his lips, he studied her: the flushed cheeks, the tendrils escaping from the upswept hair, the teasing smile. She had never before flirted with him. He moved closer to her, dragging his leg. "May I have this dance?"

She smiled. "Can you dance on crutches?"

"Oh, we needn't get up. We'll dance right here." He drained his glass and said, his voice slightly thickened, "In the army we quickly learn what is called 'field expedient.' For example, if a tent leaks, one might use a greatcoat to cover the spot. If a rifle or revolver is lost in combat, one would probably pick up the nearest stick or stone. Field expedient," he repeated.

"Yes?"

"Here the objective is to waltz with a beautiful woman. But alas, the leg is not working. What can we do?" He stroked his mustache. "We can hold each other and move back and forth."

She smiled. "It's a lovely idea, Rafe, but I'm sure the onlookers would not understand."

"Of course they would. We can hum as we rock. You sing the melody and I'll do the three-quarter beat."

Emily began to laugh. To Rafe's cider-warmed ears, the low-pitched musical sound of her voice was positively sensual. He longed to pull her to the ground and kiss her. She said, "Will they hear our waltz over the strains of the fiddle, do you think?"

"I doubt it, but who cares." Pouring himself more cider, he moved closer still and looked into her eyes. To the other guests, including Nell at the rose bush, the two looked as though they were just having a friendly conversation. They were in a dark spot, away from the lanterns, and no one could see that Rafe's eyes had moved from Emily's face to her square neckline (he was wishing it were a V-neckline). Nor did they notice that Emily, her inhibitions evaporating in cider, was staring back at him just as boldly, her eyes on his lips, her own lips unconsciously parted. And if they noticed that his hand reached out to touch her arm, they might have taken this too to be a friendly gesture, for they could not see his finger grazing the flesh of her wrist, his eyes closing, the beads of sweat appearing on his forehead.

She too wished the wedding guests would disappear and that he would kiss her. But instead of disappearing, the party now advanced upon them like an invading army. Jack Lawrence's father and two younger men plunked themselves on the ground and began asking Rafe about Pickett's Charge. Rafe started to explain for the twentieth time that evening that he had never *seen* Pickett's Charge, only *heard* the blasting from a tent far behind the lines. While he was talking, young Jeremiah Blake came over, grabbed Emily's hand, and snapping his fingers, dragged her off to the dance area for a reel. Emily stood up and gave Rafe a helpless look. Rafe nodded wearily in resignation.

As the reel commenced, Rafe finished another glass of cider. He watched Emily dance and merely grunted at the men who were questioning him. He was feeling the alcohol now, and his body was flushed. The lanterns spun, and under the lights Emily spun, and soon his head was spinning too—with desire and frustration. He couldn't even *dance* with her, much less do anything else. The men continued to talk of war until Rafe could almost hear the cannon rumbling under the fiddles. The music and the laughter and the dancing would soon vanish and only the cannon would be left. He needed a woman to hold—someone to forestall the moment. He wanted total immersion in something soft and liquid. Something that would carry him out of time. But time was relentlessly beating on, foot tap by foot tap, as the reelers reeled and the fiddlers played and Emily's yellow dress flashed back and forth in the dark like a warning lantern. He was so drunk now that he thought he might pass out if he didn't get up, and move, and clear his head. Whiskey he could drink by the gallon, but he hadn't had New England cider for so long that his resistance was low.

With a nod at the men, Rafe reached for his crutches and hobbled off toward the barn. A young girl emerged from behind a bush and opened her mouth as though to speak to him. But she did not speak and Rafe moved past her, rushing toward the barn as fast as his arms could work the crutches. Here in the darkness he could be violently sick as many times as necessary without being observed. After a while he rose, feeling weak but better, and saw that his buggy was parked nearby. He dragged himself up into the conveyance and sat for a while, wondering if he ought to go back to the party. No, he decided. No more frustration. He checked his wallet, saw that he had enough, and started the horses along the Whitney Road to a place seven miles north in Dawn Hills. Here lived a most accomplished professional lady.

When Emily returned to the spot where Rafe had been, she did not find him. For fifteen minutes she walked with apparent casualness around the grounds, wondering where he had gone. Then Jack's father told Matt, within range of Emily's hearing, "The Taylor lad got so drunk he had to leave the party. He'll be sick as a dog tomorrow."

Emily's face fell. Drunk! Oh, damn it! And they'd been having such a good time. If he had been sober, she thought, he surely would have waited for her to come back. Jeremiah asked her for another dance and she shook her head. She went over to a table for more cider, wondering what she and Rafe might have done if they hadn't been interrupted or if the cider hadn't been quite so hard. She was still daydreaming about him four hours later when she fell into bed, quite inebriated herself.

By the next morning, Rafe was clear-headed, sexually sated, dressed, packed, and ready to go. He stopped at Stevens' Store to say goodbye, but Emily wasn't there. (Matt did not tell Rafe that his daughter was home with a hangover.) Rafe asked Matt to say goodbye for him and then left the store slowly, looking up and down the street, hoping that he might see her. But she was nowhere in sight and he didn't have much time. Shrugging, he hobbled home for the family farewells. Within half an hour he was boarding the train.

CHAPTER 13

The Army of the Potomac spent the first cold months of 1864 in a camp north of the Rapidan River in Virginia called Brandy Station. Though General Meade had not been fired after Gettysburg, a new man, Grant, had been named to take charge of both Eastern and Western war theaters. At the moment he was concentrating on the bumbling Easterners, leaving a man named Sherman in charge of the more successful Western corps.

An influx of conscripts and soldiers who were paid cash bounties for enlisting had diminished the quality of the Army of the Potomac. The conscripts, who had been drafted in spite of violent riots protesting conscription in New York, Boston, and elsewhere, were resentful. The bounty men often collected their reward for enlisting in one part of the country, got "lost" on picket assignment, and reappeared under false names at enlistment offices somewhere else to collect another reward. This might go on indefinitely until the criminal was caught. Many, however, were never caught.

These unsavory additions to the army gave rise to unsavory modes of discipline. There were gallows and shooting squads in every corps, and on Fridays the death penalty was regularly enforced. For crimes less heinous than desertion there were less permanent modes of punishment—stockades, balls and chains, gaggings—new tortures were dreamed up all the time.

Rafe's brothers, who had joined the regiment in January but were not under Rafe's command, were appalled when they saw what the army was really like—long cold days on picket duty, unscrupulous comrades-at-arms, terrible food, camp diseases. Where, they wondered, were the battles? They had come in as privates because their mother had decided that officers were likelier targets for enemy guns. But they had few regrets about their noncommisioned status. From the look of things, officers fared little better except if there happened to be a camp ball with ladies from Washington present or some other exclusive festivity. For the most part, line officers and enlisted men shared the same troubles and the same foolish amusements—poker, cock fights, horse races, greased pigs and poles and the like.

Rafe watched over his brothers, sending them to Pat, Kent, and Dr. Nelson at the first sign of a sniffle, asking Jack Lawrence, now a captain and the boys' company commander, to keep an eye on them. He spent hours in their barracks playing cards or talking about home or advising them on proper conduct with women. There were also lectures on battles—how to load a rifle, how to take cover, how to endure long marches, what to carry in a haversack. And one day Bill exploded, "Rafe, for God's sake! We've got sergeants telling us these things day in and day out. We don't need any more advice."

Rafe was no more daunted by these rebuffs than is a parent whose children tell him to let them fend for themselves. The lectures continued throughout the winter, and the boys managed to endure them. They respected their brother, knew he meant well, and he was always there to cheer them when any serious problems came up. Rafe had mastered the fiddle and he played it lustily, rendering "Turkey in the Straw" with skill and verve. He added tempo to such mawkish songs as "Weeping Sad and Lonely" and sang irreverent verses to Stephen Foster melodies. Jeannie dyed her light brown hair a flaming red and Susannah abandoned her banjo-playing lover and took off with a Rocky Mountain miner. Once Rafe invited Pat and his brother Joe, Jack Lawrence. Dr. Nelson, and the Taylor boys to a jamboree in his cabin. Liquor flowed like water, Jack looking the other way as his two troopers guzzled whiskey. The music grew more and more spirited. Soon Pat was doing an Irish jig to "The Girl I Left Behind Me" and Kent was singing his own version of 'When Johnny Comes Marching Home," picturing a group of fat businessmen throwing stones at Johnny because the war was over and their munitions businesses useless. This gave rise to bitter criticisms of civilians, the government, and the army brass. Jack Lawrence denounced many of the generals as pompous, self-indulgent asses. Rafe's brothers were stunned by their commander's remarks. But their own brother was ranting about the hypocrisy of Northern leaders, whose main concern was not for the slaves but for crushing Southern representation in Congress. Even their folksy home-town physician, Bob Nelson, grew angry that night, and soon the happy jamboree had degenerated into a sullen coalition of potential mutineers. Rafe's brothers thought to themselves, this is the same army that's described by the Northern press as gallant and fiercely patriotic.

But the following day all was as usual. Rafe, Joe, and Jack were again the stern commanders. Pat, Kent, and Bob were the noble Apollos of the medical corps. And Bill and Jonathan Taylor were the properly subordinate enlisted men.

The boys were particularly fond of Dr. Pat Shepherd, a professional ladies' man who regaled them with stories of his sexual adventures. Rafe and Kent would scoff, telling Pat that no man could possibly have ten successful encounters in one night. Rafe asked if perhaps a god had sired Pat—in which case anything was possible. Pat sometimes admitted that he was exaggerating—but not too often.

Pat could be quite serious about the subject of sex, however. His warnings about using protective measures were as stern as Kent's. And when he discussed the art of love he was often cool and clinical. There was an anatomy book which he usually kept under lock and key, fearing that frustrated men might tear pages out. Pat removed the work on special occasions, however. Pointing to sketches of the female body, he would show selected gentlemen where a woman's center of pleasure was located and advise them on techniques of awakening the erotic potential of women. The boys were fascinated and so, they noted, was their older brother. After Rafe went to Washington on the one-week pass he finally managed, he came back looking smug. "It worked so well," Rafe said, "that she never charged me a dime."

Battles were a long time coming that year, but when they came it was with a fury. In May, 1864, Grant led them south into a place called the Wilderness. Here men slaughtered one another in woods so dense that officers found it impossible to keep their men in line. The underbrush was dry and soon gunfire had precipitated raging forest fires. Wounded men, too weak to crawl to safety, burned to death. No one could see the enemy. Officers wondered where their men were located or if they had been swallowed into rebel lines. Rafe, leading his ragged company into the brush piles and pines, hesitated before giving the order to fire. He wondered if they would be shooting their own men.

It went on for three days, a blind fight that accomplished little. The smell of burned bodies mingled with that of the gunfire and wood smoke. At night Rafe accompanied his men into the forests and tried to drag the wounded out, but most of their efforts were futile. He clenched his fists in frustration as the screams pierced through the blaze and the nauseating odor of burned flesh rose around him.

It was the most ghastly battle Rafe had ever seen, yet he had survived it and so had his brothers. He had a chance to speak with them briefly as the army was forming for another march. (Lee had slipped away from the Wilderness, and the battle was over.) Bill and Johnny were standing together in the long column, their faces smoke-blackened, their expressions grim. When Bill saw his older brother approaching he said, "Don't say 'I told you so.' Just don't say it, Rafe."

It was hard to resist, but Rafe resisted and said, "I won't."

Johnny was on the verge of tears. "One of my friends burned to death. I saw him. I saw him, Rafe, and I couldn't help him!"

Rafe shook his head. "I'm sorry." He would not ask who the friend had been, because he still remembered Kent's advice at Gettysburg.

The three brothers had little more to say to each other. The experience had been so revolting that no one cared to relive it. But Rafe tried to comfort them as best he could.

"Usually after a battle like this, the generals let us rest awhile," he said.

Bill asked, "You mean we're not going to chase Lee?"

"Not right away. We'll probably rest first, then mount a new campaign."

"Thank God," Johnny said. "Will we be marching back to Brandy Station?" Compared to this hell, dreary Brandy Station had been an Elysian field.

"I hope so," said Rafe.

But he was wrong. Grant was the first general in the three-year history of the Army of the Potomac to press the fight. There was to be no licking of wounds. To Rafe's amazement, this cigar-chomping Midwesterner began leading them south in hot pursuit of Lee's army. They met up with the cocky Virginian at a place called Spotsylvania Courthouse

The first division of the Second Corps contained Raphael Taylor, his brothers, and almost every friend he had in the army. It had had several commanders in its distinguished history, the latest being a New York lawyer named Francis Barlow who was known to be tough and fearless. Since Gallant Grant, unlike his predecessors, valued victory above all things, he was fortunate to have Brave Barlow in the lead of an assault that more cautious generals would never have completed. They were to set out on a rain-drenched night, cross a vast tract of land, and overun a rebel salient—heavy fortifications and trenches that protruded in an angle toward the Union Army.

Most men, including Rafe, had no idea what they were about to face. They knew only that they were marching toward rebels. How many there were and how their defenses were constructed was unknown, even to the guides. Rafe and his company simply followed in the column of fifteen thousand men (soon to be increased to half the army) and muttered about the foul weather. All officers were ordered to walk and silence was to be maintained. Barlow himself would lead the men.

It soon became apparent to many that neither Barlow

nor any of his aides were sure where they were going. Instructions had been vague, and on this soupy night they were forced to rely on compasses. On they slogged, elbow to elbow, through the mud and into the unknown. Barlow was heard to say to a guide, "For heaven's sake, at least face us in the right direction so that we shall not march away from the enemy and have to go round the world and come up in their rear." The remark was overheard by a staff officer who repeated it to a colonel, and eventually Rafe and his grumbling company heard it. They laughed nervously to think that their own commander would admit that the army could bungle so badly. Another Barlow remark—that he hoped they wouldn't fall into an open canyon between here and the rebel works—brought hoots, more crazed laughter, and Rafe's sharp command that the men shut up before the enemy discovered they were there. But Rafe was chuckling with the others as they stumbled onward into the dawn. Far to his right were his brothers and he hoped they too were having a good laugh. He had been feeling guilty since assuring them that the army would rest after the Wilderness. A march in weather like this was hardly a rest.

But he felt no particular fear on this soggy morning. The rain had stopped and the heavy fog that followed seemed to provide a gentle cover. The sky, the ground, and his uniform were all so sodden that he could not picture the heat of battle. They would just move along in this damp cloud and one day the sun would come up.

Suddenly a line of men coalesced in the fog and Rafe could see Yankee pickets disarming rebel pickets. Rafe said dryly to the lieutenant next to him, "I say, Mason, do you suppose they were telling the truth? There does appear to be a Confederate army here."

The lieutenant, who had a sense of humor much like Charles Taylor's, said, "Of course there is."

"I thought it was something we must take on faith." Rafe said, "like the Blessed Trinity."

This the lieutenant did not find amusing. He studied Rafe's face a moment, wondering if the captain had gone mad, then turned his attention to the hapless rebel prisoners now being marched to the rear. Rafe began laughing helplessly. He was still laughing as the lines ahead of him broke into a run and began shouting like a ravaging mob.

They swept over a ridge, disentangled an abatis, and tore into the enemy's entrenchments. There was no order to this wild charge. It was a mob of scrambled troops howling maniacally as they crashed through the rebel defenses, capturing the salient and four thousand of its unprepared defenders. On they plunged, triumphant over having succeeded at frightening the rebels. Rafe was more crazed than usual today—shouting, yelling, waving his sword like a general. Even when he came up against the solid rebel line, he continued to howl frenziedly.

At Antietam the division's charge had begun in the same way. They had overrun a trench, been stopped by the rebels, and then both sides had given up in exhaustion. But in this battle there was no slackening of fire. It went on and on as though it would continue forever. Rafe's voice eventually grew hoarse, his insane howling died, and he continued to fight silently with the mindless brutality that troubled him in his more lucid moments. The front was narrow and the men on both sides so tightly packed that there was no room to move and no way to dodge a bullet. Men toppled into trenches and others fell over them. Troops moving up to take the places of the fallen were shot immediately and fell headlong into the trenches. At the bottom of one heap of dead was Bill Taylor, shot through the head. Rafe, who was a few yards behind and to the left, did not know about it. He had ordered his men to the rear to clean their choked muskets and was shouting at the men further behind to bring more ammunition forward. The pelting rain had begun again, and as Rafe brought his men back into line his foot sank in the mud. Looking down momentarily as he yanked it out, he saw a familiar face. His brother Johnny was lying face up, pinioned under the bullet-ridden body of an officer who was lying face down. As Rafe stooped to move the dead man, he saw that Johnny's eyes were fixed, not blinking. The horrible truth registered in Rafe's brain and he reached down to pull the officer off the body of his brother. In the act of flinging the man aside, Rafe's body was so positioned that the bullet missed all vital organs but passed dangerously near his heart.

Pat and Kent stood at adjacent tables in a large tent. They were operating at a furious rate, shouting to orderlies and to each other.

"Do you think Rafe's going to make it?" Pat yelled over the din of the wounded.

"I don't know," Kent roared back, tying an artery as he thought about it. "Depends what sort of care he gets."

"Care? What a joke! We can't take him with us. Can't leave him here for guerrillas. We have no choice but to send him to Fredericksburg."

Fredericksburg was the nearest depot for the wounded. To survive the ride there in a jolting ambulance would be a miracle in itself. But the hospitals in Fredericksburg were war-wrecked warehouses. Wounded men were lying untended on bare boards and one floor featured a patina of spilled molasses. Most doctors were required to remain with the army, so there were few who could tend to the wounded left behind. And the townspeople were firmly secessionist. The Yankees had ravaged their homes two years earlier, and few had sympathy for the wounded coming in. The place had been dubbed "charnel city" by one horrified ambulance driver. If Rafe survived Fredericksburg, he would eventually be moved to Washington and a decent hospital. But in his current condition Rafe's chances were not good. He lay in a four-man tent not far from the operating area. Kent had probed the wound and an orderly had been instructed to check his condition periodically. As of now, ten P.M., he was just holding on.

Pat, who had completed an operation, was scrubbing his hands for the next. He shouted to Kent, "Who's going to tell him about his brothers?"

"You are."

"I can't do it, Kent."

"Then find another friend. Don't look at me."

"Most of his friends are dead or missing."

"Bob Nelson, then. He's Rafe's own doctor. He'll know what to say." They both turned to look at Nelson, expecting to see him operating. The grey-haired doctor was sitting on the ground cradling the head of a dead soldier in his arms and sobbing. Kent sighed, handed his patient to the waiting orderlies, and went over to wash his hands. "That brings us back to you, Pat."

"No."

"You craven son of a bitch. You're one of his closest friends. Do you want him to learn the truth by accident?"

"You're his friend too," Pat shot back angrily.

"Yes, well I probed the wound. You can do your goddamned share."

"Like hell!"

This might have gone on indefinitely, but Kent's orderly, Tim Kelly, suggested the toss of a coin. Kent lost.

The next morning Kent crawled into Rafe's tent armed with a hypodermic syringe. He planned to administer the sedative as soon as he broke the news. Rafe was awake, staring dully up at him. The other three patients were asleep.

"How do you feel, Rafe?" Kent asked quietly.

"Give me something for the pain." Rafe's voice was barely audible.

"I have a syringe right here," Kent assured him. "But there's something I have to tell you first."

"Kent, just give me the . . ."

"It's about your brothers," Kent interrupted, looking away.

"I know. Johnny's dead. I saw him." Rafe's tone was flat. Kent frowned, studied Rafe's face. No change of expression, no tears.

"You *saw* Johnny?"

"Yes, I did. Now will you give me the sedative and . . ."

"In a minute. I want to talk to you about Bill."

"Is he dead too?" Still no change of expression. Rafe might have been inquiring about the weather.

"Yes, he is, Rafe. I'm sorry."

Rafe did not acknowledge the sympathy. He said, "I knew it. I've always known it. Now do something about this pain, Kent, and as long as you've got that syringe, make sure it's a fatal overdose."

Kent stared at his friend, dumbfounded. Without another word, he injected just enough to lessen the pain. He waited until the sedative had taken effect and then hurried back to the operating tent.

Pat was in the middle of an amputation. Kent waited until the operation was finished before telling Pat, "There's nothing I can do for Rafe. He's been shocked senseless. At the moment all he wants is oblivion, and I can't say I blame him."

"What did he say when you told him?"

"He asked for an overdose of medicine. Wasn't surprised, though. He says he saw Johnny."

"I've got to talk to him." Pat dropped the towel he had been using to wipe spattered blood off his arm and rushed out of the tent.

But litter bearers had just lifted Rafe and his tentmates into ambulances. By the time Pat reached the area where Rafe had been, his friend was being jolted over corduroy Virginia roads to an unknown destiny.

Rafe's three-year term of service was almost over. If he ever made it home, he would not be returning. Since he lived in Massachusetts and Pat in New York, it was unlikely that they would see each other again.

"I didn't have a chance to say goodbye," Pat murmured aloud as he watched a procession of ambulances make its way up the hill. One of the cruelest paradoxes of war was that it made men utterly dependent on one another and then tore apart the special friendships that resulted.

A nervous young lieutenant came racing up to Pat. He shouted over the clamor of ambulances, horses, and wounded men, "Making casualty lists for the company, doctor. Got a blank next to Captain Taylor. An orderly said you'd know."

"Chest wound," Pat managed to say, his throat hurting and his eyes filling.

"Flesh wound?" the officer shouted.

"Right," Pat answered absently, walking away.

Two days later the anxious Taylor family read in the paper:

TAYLOR, RAPHAEL, CAPTAIN: FLESH WOUND
TAYLOR, JONATHAN, PRIVATE: KILLED
TAYLOR, WILLIAM, PRIVATE: KILLED

The grieved family hung on to a thread of hope; at least Rafe had survived. They had no way of knowing that the thread was on the floor of a Fredericksburg warehouse, almost as dead as his brothers.

Partly because of the severity of his wound and partly because of his mental state, but mostly because of his captain's bars, Rafe Taylor was moved to Washington ahead of many others. Here, in a neat, clean ward, he was given a nightshirt, was bathed and shaved, was fed by legions of motherly volunteers and cared for by skilled army doctors and nurses. Since he seemed unresponsive and disinterested in getting well, inquiries were made about his history. One sergeant on another ward said yes, he knew Taylor. The captain had lost two brothers at Spotsylvania. Further research produced Rafe's address and one volunteer sent a letter off to his parents advising them of their son's condition and suggesting that they come to Washington if at all possible. The letter ended up on the floor of the New York Post Office, trampled to shreds by busy men who were sorting other such missives. In Lanston Rafe's parents, still believing that he was with the army, wondered why he had not written.

A week went by and Taylor showed no improvement. He ate his food indifferently, responded but little to the bright greetings of the medical staff, and conversed not at all with the others on the ward. He did read incessantly, asking the staff for books on engineering, physics, chemistry, botany, and mathematics. They were able to produce few such texts, but Rafe read and reread whatever was available. It was discovered that he had been raised a Congregationalist and a nurse finally located a busy minister and brought him to see Rafe.

"Captain Taylor, may I present Reverend Billings?"

Rafe looked up, glared, said nothing.

The nurse was too weary to try to cajole the captain into greeting the preacher with proper respect. She sighed, walked away, and left the two men staring at each other.

Finally Rafe said, "Would you mind leaving, sir? I'm not interested in hearing about God's mysterious ways."

"Then we won't talk about God," the man said quietly.

Rafe blinked. At least the man wasn't a crazy Reverend Mitchell. "To be blunt, sir, I don't feel like talking about anything else either."

"Not even yourself?"

"That's right."

"Do you want to get well, Captain?" The spare young man drew up a chair next to the bed and sat down. "I asked you a question, Captain."

"I'm very tired, sir. I was about to take a nap when you . . ."

"Do you care about living?" the minister interrupted.

"No," Rafe answered shortly.

The minister's face remained composed. "Well then, do you care about your family? Living for their sake if not your own?"

"Now see here, Mr.—"

"Billings."

"Mr. Billings. I've spent three years acting for other people's 'sakes.' The town, the country, my family, the whole goddamned world. All I ask—and surely my request is not unreasonable—is to be left alone."

"To die?"

"I don't know."

The minister picked up a physics text. "I see you've still got one interest left."

Rafe said nothing.

"Are you planning to be buried with these books?"

"If they'll get me past St. Peter," Rafe mocked.

"No need to be sarcastic. It's evident that you're not a religious man."

"How perceptive you are." Rafe fully expected the minister to stalk off, but the man did not move.

He said to Rafe, "Then I take it your wish is to be left to die. You're not at all concerned about the future you'll be missing."

"Right you are, Reverend."

"You have no plans for marriage or children?"

"Right again."

"Did you ever have any dreams, Captain?"

Rafe shrugged. "Guess so."

"What happened to them?"

"Saw them shot to pieces."

"You saw your brothers shot to pieces. Isn't that what you mean?"

Rafe said nothing.

"Were the brothers the whole of your life, Captain?"

"I have a family," Rafe muttered.

"But they don't count at all?"

"Of course they count! Look, I don't need you with your stiff moral collar and your religious pieties to tell *me* what I ought to be feeling. You weren't in that war. You haven't the slightest conception of what it's like out there. If you don't leave here right now, Billings, I'm going to yell like a rebel until someone comes along and throws you out!"

The minister smiled broadly. "By Jove, you're coming to life at last! Your eyes are actually blazing. I'm going to get the staff and tell them to come see this phenomenon." The minister rose and took a step away.

"Get back here, Billings." Rafe smiled in spite of himself. The preacher reminded him of Pat.

Reverend Billings sat down again and said quietly, "No, I've never fought in a war. But I do have some idea of what it does to men. There's a whole ward upstairs of men who have lost their minds. I don't suppose you'd care to visit it."

"No," Rafe whispered.

"The reason I'm here, Captain, is to see that it doesn't happen to you."

There were a few more visits by Rev. Billings. At the end of two weeks Rafe had grudgingly decided that life was at least worth a try. He was discharged in the care of a Sanitary Commission volunteer, an elderly man who was traveling to Boston. They would go as far as New Haven together and then Rafe could take a train home. Rafe decided not to send a telegram to his parents since his arrival date could not be predicted. He walked out of the hospital on the second of June, promising the minister that he would stay in touch and thanking him for his patience.

"I'll go to church every Sunday," Rafe joked.

"Please don't. It would prove too much of a shock for God. He might cause an earthquake."

"Just what we need," Rafe said. "A lively catastrophe."

But Rafe's revived sense of humor did not last long. By the time he reached New Haven, two dismal nights later, he was again morose. He thanked his traveling companion and then stumbled around trying to make connections to Hartford. Hours later he was in the Hartford station, sitting on a bench and staring stupidly at the few people drifting through at this late hour. A sympathetic station attendant asked the weary-looking officer where he was going.

"Lanston, Mass.," Rafe replied.

"Have to wait till mid-morning."

"All right," Rafe said indifferently.

"Unless we can get you on a freighter. Shall I try?"

Rafe hesitated. He was anxious to get home, though he dreaded the prospect at the same time. His family in mourning, his brothers' empty room. But he was so tired, and he craved his own bed.

"Shall I try to get you on a freight train?" the man asked.

"Yes. Thank you, sir."

CHAPTER 14

E mily heard the story from the clerk Danny Winstead, who had heard it from a workman in the freight yards. She had passed the Taylor house to get from her house to the store but had not known that anything was amiss. Then Danny came in while she was setting out the wooden buckets of cheese.

"You hear about the Taylor boy?"

"Which Taylor boy?" Her heart thudded. Two of them were dead in Virginia and two were prosperous civilians who lived out of town. That left Rafe as the most likely newsmaker, and she did not want to hear what the news was.

"They found Rafe by the station four o'clock this morning. Lifted him off along with the freight."

"What?"

"He got a chest wound last month at Spotsylvania. It's a long story. The lists said 'flesh' but it was really his chest. Anyway the ride in the caboose was rough and Taylor wa'nt feeling none too good when he got here. Couldn't move to get off the train. The engineer—you know Flannery?—he said the boy was half dead."

"Oh my God!"

"But they say he's all right now," Danny said. "That new doc checked him over right there at the station, then they moved him home."

"He's all right?" she repeated, holding her breath.

"That's what they say. Surprised you ain't heard about this. Awful lot of commotion over on Maple this morning."

"I don't get up until six," she said absently. But she had wondered where Mary was when she came downstairs.

Emily removed her apron. "I'm going over there."

"Give them my—darned if I know what to say to 'em, Miss Stevens."

"I know." No one knew what to say to anyone anymore.

The last month had been like one long wake. Many local boys had been wounded and five had died—two in the Wilderness, three at Spotsylvania. Every church had had its memorial services, but there had been no burials because they could not bring the bodies home—no one knew where they lay. Jack Lawrence had lost an arm. Abby had gone to a Washington hospital to get him. They had arrived a week ago, worn and depressed, and the Stevenses had put them up. The next day Emily had driven them out to the farm of Abby's parents where the children were staying. Jack was pale and in pain, Abby tight-lipped, trying to look brave. Emily dropped them off, then drove over to the Lawrence farm to help Abby's brother Jeremiah ready the place. The youth milked cows and did other outside chores while Emily cleaned, baked pies and breads, changed bed linen, made soup, and dusted. She left before the couple came home, for she had not wanted to see the tears. She had seen enough tears this month to flood the Connecticut River.

There had been that night in June when the Taylors heard about their youngest boys. Their parlor, dining room, and sitting room had been filled with neighbors, all of them crying and tripping over each other. Only Matt had been totally in command that night. He had gone from neighbor to neighbor, whispering that he thought the Taylors wanted to be alone. Then he had led the lot of them two doors down to his new house, dispatching Emily to the kitchen to make coffee for everyone and sending Mary back to the Taylors' to do something for Marie and the girls. After that, Matt left the house and walked down to the telegraph office to wire the oldest sons. Finally, he returned to the Taylors' and took Charles for a walk out the Whitney Road where, as Matt put it later, "The man didn't have to act like no brave patriotic statesman. I set him down on a rock, gave him a lantern and some handkerchiefs, and come back here."

With these sensitive and expedient gestures Matt, without intending to, had acquired more stature on Maple Street than a hundred books of etiquette would have given him. Had the times been different, he would have been included at every dinner party from that day on. But no one in Lanston had dinner parties these days.

Tears, black crepe, and tolling bells. These were the symbols of Lanston in June, 1864. But here and there one might hear a young boy shouting, "And next month I'll be old enough to go! I don't care what Ma says. I'm going to get me a rebel scalp!"

Emily stopped in front of the Taylor house. Her hands were shaking and her stomach felt queasy. Please let him not be badly hurt, she thought. Please let him be like he was last summer, smiling, playfully asking her for a "field expedient" waltz.

Seeing Mary emerging from the Taylors' side door, Emily rushed over and said, "Mary, tell me what hap—"

"You're not going in there, are you?"

"I thought they might need some help."

"No, they got doctors up there. They don't need help, 'less it's doses of laudanum and that the doctors can give them."

"What do you mean? Aren't they excited? Rafe's going to live, isn't he? Well, *isn't he?*"

"Yes." Mary took Emily's arm and led her back toward the house. As they walked into the kitchen, she went over to the stove and lit the fire for coffee.

"Are you going to tell me what happened?" Emily demanded.

"There ain't—isn't—much to tell." Even in her preoccupation Mary was trying to use the grammar she felt was appropriate for Maple Street. "He doesn't talk much. He looks like death warmed over. And his eyes . . ." she trailed off.

"What about his eyes?"

"They look like the ones you see in daguerreotypes. Vacant, sort of. Like he was staring at a camera and not blinking. But it could be the dark circles make him look so bad. Hard to tell."

"Can he have visitors?"

"He isn't the way you remember him, Em. The Taylors don't want visitors."

"But why? Is he maimed? Has he lost any limbs? Danny didn't say he . . ."

"No, it's nothing like that. He just don't—doesn't—want to see folks." She paused. "He's just sort of—shaken, I guess. But I'm not going to carry any tales. The Taylors, they're saying he'll be in his room for a while 'cause he's been wounded. Me, I won't say different."

"My God," Emily said dully. And she wondered if Mrs. Harrington had been right when she said, "If a bullet doesn't get him his experiences will. . . . Some soldiers are driven plumb out of their minds."

For three weeks the town saw nothing of Rafe Taylor. The doctor invented reasons for prohibiting visitors. First Rafe was in too much pain. Then he was too tired. Then he acquired some mysterious disease with a long Latin name no one had ever heard of. It wasn't terribly contagious, the doctor said, but he didn't want healthy people exposed. During this time, what was left of the Taylor family resumed their affairs. Marie, dressed in unrelieved black, returned to the war committee's sewing circle, which met during the month of July in Mary's sitting room. She was quiet but polite, smiling wanly when some matron tried to interest her in the latest gossip. But she would say nothing of Rafe's condition beyond "Yes, it is contagious." And she said nothing about his spirits, though when pressed she had once mumbled, "He regrets that he is unable to leave the sickbed."

During the last week of July the men who had marched down Center Street three years earlier completed their terms of service and began coming home. Almost instantly the grim cloud that had hung over the town was lifted. Only a few men had reenlisted to help Grant take Richmond and Petersburg. The rest were hugging wives and children or planning weddings with their girls. Couples could not bear to wait any longer, and so the weddings were quickly planned. Between nuptials and parties, orders for food from the store tripled in a week, and the clerks were performing a regular catering service. With the men out making deliveries, Emily had to take over behind the counter, had to wire wholesalers in Boston for extra supplies and to hound railroad people to make sure the goods came in. She spent hours at the railroad station and telegraph office, and many more working into the night with accounts and inventory.

Christine Osbourne had been married the year before to her original love, Don Benton. He had sustained no wounds during the war, and he arrived just in time for his son's birth. For the Bentons, this July was especially sweet, but for Emily it meant she now had a christening to add to her lists of projects.

Though exhausted, she did try to see Abby as often as possible. The Lawrences were getting on well, Abby assured her. Jack couldn't do some of the chores anymore, but he did manage with his left hand and soon the children would be old enough to help. Abby was more buoyant than she had been in years, and since Jack seemed to be getting on, Emily decided that they would be fine. Her visits to the farm became fewer as Abby's spirits returned.

There was still a great deal to do, however. Emily had decided to start a library in three back rooms of their large house. She had been thinking about it ever since Mrs. Harrington had sold them the house, and now she had assembled a small collection. Each of the well-heeled families had contributed books, and Judge Williams' donation totaled twenty-five volumes. She wrote enthusiastic notes to Mrs. Harrington about the library. One of the chambers would be named "The Harrington Room," and so, like it or not, the widow was destined for immortality. The widow wrote back to say that she was deeply moved. There was not one acerbic comment in the long letter which described her absorbing work in Washington. She had certainly made the right decision in moving. At the age of sixty-six, the lady was finally mellowing.

With weddings at every other farm and company house, and reunited couples joyously flooding into church, Emily began to feel rather lonely. It was not because she didn't have beaux of her own. Barry and Jonas were still calling. But she was beginning to long for permanence. The next step, Emily decided, would be to try to see one of these men in a more romantic light. She was tired of working, tired of being tired. She wanted someone to take care of her.

Rosie concluded that Emily had come to her senses at last and began totting up the merits of the two men. It was Jonas, the music tutor, whom Emily should marry, Rosie declared. He was a bit of a fop but he and Emily had so much in common, after all. Music and—music and—

"And what?" Emily asked.

"Wait a minute. I'll think of something." Rosie thought and thought and finally said, "Anyway, he's handsome."

" 'Anyway, I'll make my own decisions."

In the fourth week after his arrival home, Rafe emerged from the house. He walked only as far as Prospect Street, but Rosie happened to be passing at the right moment. She reported to Emily at the store.

"What did he say?" Emily asked.

"He said 'hello, pleasant weather, and you look well.' "

"That's all?"

"He's become very quiet," Rosie said.

"How does he look?"

"Thin. Like last summer. But not sick. When was he cured of that disease? I didn't even know he was getting better. Everyone said it must be typhoid because it lasted so long."

Emily wondered if Rafe was up and about for good or if the doctor was going to have to invent a new affliction. She passed his house that evening, wondering whether to go in on the pretext of business with Marie. But she went home instead, almost afraid to see him, not knowing what she would say.

She found out the next day. He was standing on the common near the meeting house, looking off in the direction of the old ball field. Her heart pounded as she walked up behind him and said, "Hello, Rafe."

She startled him and he jumped. Then he looked at her for a long time as though trying to focus his eyes. Finally he said, "How are you, Emily?"

"I'm well. And I'm glad to see that you're better."

"Thank you." He smiled uncertainly.

What could she say now? She didn't want to offer sympathy about his brothers. This wasn't the right time. And she could not ask "What have you been doing for the past ten months?" nor "What were you thinking of when you looked at that ball field?" What could she say?

As she stood there thinking about it, a dove swooped in low over their heads, bound for a tree branch behind them. Emily never noticed the bird, nor the fact that the air in its feathers made a whistling sound. So she did not understand why Rafe suddenly shouted "down!" and flung himself prone on the ground, his hands over his head. She crouched beside him and asked urgently, "Rafe, are you ill?"

Slowly he picked himself up. He was sweating and breathing hard.

"What happened?" she asked.

He looked at her, frowned, and muttered, "Nothing." Then he saw other witnesses to this embarrassing spectacle bearing down upon him. And brushing past Emily, cursing under his breath, he walked rapidly toward Maple.

One of the men who rushed over was Constable Barrington. He asked Emily what had happened.

"I don't know. He was standing here talking and then he suddenly yelled 'down.' Yes, I think he said 'down.' It might have been 'round.' I'm really not sure."

"Was there any sudden noise?" Barrington asked.

"I didn't hear anything."

"Must've been a bird. You see a bird?"

"I don't remember."

"Bet he thought he was under attack by shell fire."

"Oh," Emily said. "Yes that might have been . . ."

"Take a long time for *that* boy to get back to normal," the constable said. "A long time."

For the first two weeks, Rafe had actually been in pain, but in the next week and a half he had simply not wanted to get up and face the world. He had not wanted pity or idiotic gossip, but most of all he had not wanted questions about the war. From the beginning he had told the family that he would not talk about it. They could discuss anything else they wished and he would, if interested in the subject, be happy to oblige them. But any mention of war and he would ask them to leave the sickroom. It was as simple as that, Rafe announced. In the third week he began coming downstairs late at night when everyone was asleep and sitting in the backyard. His thoughts at first were of nothing immediate. It just felt good to sit there under cover of darkness gazing at Orion and wondering how long it would take to travel to the nearest star. But by the beginning of the fourth week he had decided that he ought to be doing something about affairs here on earth—and particularly his own. And so he told Charles that he would spend the rest of the summer doing law clerk duties in his father's office. He would also—as was his father's wish—apply to Harvard Law School. Rafe did not want to be a lawyer. Science was the discipline he loved. But he did not know how one earned money at pure intellectual inquiry. He ought to work in one of the applied science fields. Physics interested him most, then chemistry. But he would go to law school for now, just to have a lucrative profession to fall back on.

Before he could help his father, he would have to get out of the house. It was an ordeal at first. There was Rosie, with her concerned looks. The memory of Emily and the episode with the bird upset him. He had cringed when he saw the pity in her eyes. All over town there were old men and little boys anxious to hear about the Wilderness and Spotsylvania. Rafe tried to be civil, but it was difficult to explain that he just could not talk about it. He found himself brushing past people and snapping, "I'm in a hurry." The Taylor family was subjected to a rash of complaints. Rafe was cold, Rafe was brusque, Rafe was rude to old men and little boys. Charles sometimes felt compelled to explain that Rafe was not himself. Because of the tensions he had been under he had forgotten his manners. People said that they understood, and a few of them did. But despite their compassion they could not help being indignant or hurt—as Emily was. And virtually everyone, by the middle of July, had learned to avoid the Taylor boy.

Rafe buried himself in his father's office during most of the daylight hours. Sometimes after work, he would saddle one of their horses and ride up to Dawn Hills. There he spent evenings with an obliging prostitute who did everything he asked her to do and never bored him with chatter. Most of his accrued army pay was spent on her services. What was left went for bottles of whiskey, smuggled into Dawn Hills from New York. He drank alone in his room at night. Once, feeling ill, he tiptoed down to the summer kitchen searching for some tea—a special brew concocted by Annie that had always settled his stomach. It was Annie herself who found him at five-thirty in the morning, slumped over the table, fast asleep. The teacup was still full.

Gently the elderly cook tapped his shoulder. "Rafe."

"Mmmmm."

"Rafe, it's after five in the morning."

"Hmmm?" He opened his eyes, looked around, and shook his head. "Must've dozed off."

"I'm thinking something else done the dozing for you. Mr. Taylor know you're drinking all the time?"

"Don't think so." Charles liked his fine wines and after-dinner brandies but he did not countenance hard drinking and had never in his life been drunk.

Annie said, "Well, it's a miracle if the family don't know 'cause I can smell the whiskey clear to the stairs."

"Leave me alone, Annie."

"No, I will not." She drew herself up and said, "Everyone else in this family's been pussyfooting around you thinking they're doing you good. Well, they ain't and it's time somebody was telling you so. You know what's wrong with you, Rafe?"

"No, but I've no doubt you're about to enlighten me." Rafe sighed and rubbed his aching head.

"You're too closed up. You'll not be talking about this and you'll not be talking about that and you'll not be talking about your brothers, God rest their souls. So there ain't nothing left to be saying, is there? But if you won't talk, at least you should be doing something besides working and drinking. Go on picnics. Go fishing. Meet some girls or visit your friend Jack Lawrence. Have you seen that boy since you got home? Or are you just sitting here, and him without an arm, needing someone to talk to!"

Rafe stood up. "I'm going to bed."

"Go right ahead. You go wrap yourself in the bed sheets

not talking and not thinking and not facing what's gotta be faced and then . . ."

"I have faced it," Rafe shouted. "I was there! What do you want me to do? Go back to the battlefield and dig up their bodies?"

Annie shook her head. He was poisoned inside, like a boil that wouldn't come to a head. And the whiskey only stopped the pain. It wasn't draining the poison. He had changed so much since childhood days! That boy had never kept himself locked up. He'd laughed, argued, boasted, cried, worried out loud—never caring what people thought, for he'd told her that admitting to his feelings made him enjoy life more. And she'd thought it made him stronger, too. He had used that strength to guide the boys. But now the boys were gone—and Rafe wasn't Rafe anymore.

Annie said gently, "Gotta be getting out and talking to people, Rafe. *Got* to."

"I don't want people. Not living ones, not dead ones, and especially not the living who urge other living to go out and kill. I'm sick to death of people, do you hear?"

"Then take walks by yourself. At least you should be working up an appetite. Maybe some of the hate in you will start seeping out in sweat."

So because Annie would give him no peace, Rafe began taking walks. The exercise did make him feel better, though his appetite did not improve. Once he got as far as Jack's house, but he could not go in. He did not want to see, to be reminded. Instead, he walked in a great semicircle around the west edge of town and, without realizing where he was, came out near the pond where he and his brothers once fished. He stood for a moment, remembering how Johnny and Bill had teased each other.

"No catches yet?" Johnny had said. "Why don't you give up, old man? Go be a fisher of men, like Peter."

Bill had retorted, "splendid idea, but I'll fish for women, thank you. And that's a sport you can't match me at."

"Wanna bet? You pick the girl and we'll see who wins *that* little game."

Rafe, tired of their foolishness, had snapped, "If you both don't shut up, you'll scare the goddamn fish." But looking back now he regretted having been impatient with them that day or at any other time.

He looked at the worn path for a moment, picturing the boys walking up the hill to the pond, fishing poles against their shoulders. As Rafe stood there the bright day seemed to grow dark and a numbing cold descended. He stared at the path, standing rigidly erect, unable to move. How long he remained there he did not know, but at last he began to walk away, slowly, not sure of where he was going, brushing past bushes and thickets and moving deep into the woods. He still felt numb, but as he tripped over a branch and fell against a pine tree the sharp pain in his head brought him to life. He cursed and began pounding mindlessly at the trunk. Then he started to cry, not in the furtive embarrassed manner of men at funerals but in outraged sobs. He picked up fallen branches and whacked them against the tree. He cursed himself aloud for not trying hard enough to save his brothers. Then he cursed his brothers for not listening to him. He swore and muttered and cried and tore at bushes until he was so exhausted that he had to sit down. His knuckles were bleeding and his eyes stung but he felt better than he had in months. When his heart slowed to its normal rate, he began to feel drowsy. Stretching out under the trees, he slept until night came and waves of mosquitoes woke him. Then he went home, and with an appetite he had forgotten he had, Rafe cleaned out the pantry.

Things improved after that. Rafe smiled more often, concentrated on some of his family's anecdotes, actually greeted friends like Emily when they passed in the street. He continued to take his walks. There came the day when he went to see Jack. The meeting was not an ordeal. He found that Jack was just as anxious as Rafe to forget the war. At first the men talked of cows, orchards, maple syrup, harvests, and hay. They ate Abby's blackberry pie and then cautiously began to talk of men they knew—of Pat, Kent, Joe Shepherd, and others. They laughed over old jokes and, when Abby was out of the room, reminisced about Pat's lectures on anatomy. Not once did they mention a battle. As Rafe was leaving the house, feeling full and good from the talk and the pie, he thought, I must tell Annie that I've rejoined the human race.

Rafe was improving, but he was still not himself. Emily saw him often now and he occasionally stopped at the house to chat with Mary. But there were few smiles for Emily, few personal words. And sometimes his behavior was outrageous.

One evening Emily and Jonas, her dignified black-haired music tutor, had been walking down the street bound for a charity function at Williams Hall. She was dressed in last year's yellow creation and Jonas too was impeccably attired. They were chatting softly together as Rafe stepped on to Maple Street from the common. He stopped dead in his tracks and stared at the elegant pair.

"This is Raphael Taylor," Emily said to Jonas. "Rafe, my escort, Jonas Whiting."

Rafe had been returning from a walk and was in shirt sleeves. His hair needed cutting, his trousers were rumpled, and he needed a shave. After looking Jonas over one more time he finally muttered, "Pleasure, Mr. Whiting." He did not extend his hand.

Jonas was from Dawn Hills and came to town rarely. He knew few people in Lanston, though he was acquainted with most of those on Maple Street. But he did not connect this unkempt young man with the prestigious Taylor family. And since they were standing in front of Judge Williams' house, he asked, "Are you the groundskeeper for the gentleman who lives here?"

"Why, yessuh!" Rafe bowed his head. "How'd you guess that, suh? Just got the job too. Sure would like to stand here talking to you fancy-looking folks but I gotta go spread some dung in the master's garden. Oh, *excuse* me, there's a lady present. Some *fertilizer's* what I mean."

"Oh Rafe!" Emily forced a light laugh, and turned to Jonas. "He's only joking. This is Charles Taylor's son."

"Oh, I beg your pardon," Jonas said.

"Ain't nothing," said Rafe. "Ain't nothing a-tall. Well, good night, folks." And with a bow toward Emily, Rafe walked on home, ambling like a colt.

Among Jonas' many faults was his short temper. "I did not find that spectacle in the least amusing," he snapped.

"No, I don't blame you." Emily sighed.

"Such an ill-mannered man. How unfortunate for the Taylors."

"He's not always like that. He's just home from the war and he's . . ."

"A pity our army has such specimens in its ranks."

"Now just a minute. Rafe is not a 'specimen.' He's a former army captain and he's seen action in practically every battle that's been . . ."

"That in itself is not ennobling, my dear. The worst hoodlums in shantytown have seen action."

"Have they indeed!" Emily set her hands on her hips. "And 'gentlemen' like you have not, I suppose."

Jonas' face turned red. "You are the last person I would have expected to suggest that I shirked my patriotic duty. You know that I tried to enlist." Jonas had a slight limp, the result of a childhood fall, and had been rejected by the army. "That you of all people would resort to such pettiness!"

"I said nothing about shirking duties. I'm just astonished that you would make judgments about my neighbor without knowing a thing about him. He's been wounded three times. He just lost two brothers. He nearly died himself."

"My regrets," Jonas said tonelessly, "but the man is positively churlish and I must say I find it distressing to be wasting this pleasant summer evening arguing about him. I see you so rarely, my dear. Now let us proceed to the hall and forget this unfortunate altercation."

"No!" she snapped.

"And pray why not?"

"I have a bad headache."

He arched an eyebrow. "Of recent origin?"

"How did you guess? Yes, it just came over me now."

He sighed. "Of course."

She was angry at Jonas and almost as furious with Rafe for putting her in a position where she was forced to see what a prig her music teacher was. Until now she had resolved to ignore many of Jonas's deficiencies. But that was no longer possible. Now she was down to one suitor: Barry, the shy thirty-five-year-old academy master. Occasionally Rafe saw her walking with him. He was never rude to Barry but he was decidedly remote and perhaps a bit jealous, she liked to tell herself. But if he was jealous, why didn't he court her himself? His "just neighbors" attitude was annoying—particularly after last summer's flirtation.

But Rafe would be out of her life soon enough, when he went back to Harvard. Now she must start thinking seriously about her future. Perhaps she should accept Barry's proposal. If she really tried hard, they might have a pleasant marriage. She would have babies and help him correct Latin papers. She would become a matron like any sensible twenty-four-year-old. As the first hot days of August dragged by, the idea became more and more appealing—to abandon her exhausting schedule and just to be a wife.

CHAPTER 15

Emily was returning from a visit to a sick friend of Mary's one Sunday afternoon in mid-August when she thought she saw a body lying under some distant trees. She was up at the northern end of town, where the street curled into the woods, and she had walked some paces past before the vision registered in her brain. With some trepidation she set out into the forest to ascertain if that glimpse of white had actually been a man's shirt and that army blue a pair of trousers. She wondered if the person was already dead. If so, was the killer nearby?

After working her way through a dense thicket, she saw that the man was Rafe. He appeared to be sleeping tranquilly, breathing regularly. His arm was outstretched and his hand covered a fern. His color seemed good, but she could not be sure that he wasn't sick or hurt. Perhaps he was suffering pain from the chest wound. Grasping her skirts, she stepped over a large log and knelt beside him. "Rafe?" she whispered.

He opened his eyes and smiled. His quick recognition led her to believe that he had been awake. If he had heard her approach, he must have thought it was an animal. "Emily! What brings you to the forest primeval on this glorious Sabbath day?"

"I thought you were dead," she said bluntly.

He looked confused and then grinned. "Oh. Sorry to have disappointed you."

She snapped, "Your sense of humor has gone from bad to reprehensible! I saw a body. It wasn't moving. So I came to see who was . . ."

"Sorry." He pulled himself up to a sitting position. "Thank you for your concern, but I'm fine. Just lying here enjoying nature's bounty. As for my crude sense of humor, I've been meaning to apologize for that incident with what's-his-name but somehow I always forget."

"His name is Jonas. Jonas Whiting."

"Yes. The elegant Mr. Whiting. I haven't seen him recently."

"He lives in Dawn Hills."

"Pity," Rafe said.

"I know how deprived you must feel. Well, having established that you're healthy, hearty, and your old acerbic self, I shall now attend to my business and leave you to your nature studies." She gathered her skirts and turned to leave.

"Don't go," he said.

"I'm busy, Rafe."

"Yes, of course. Busy Emily. I'll bet that if I asked you to sit on that log for ten minutes you wouldn't be able to do it."

"Goodbye, Rafe." She was not going to accept nonsensical wagers. But she walked away very slowly.

"Emily, please sit down and talk to me."

Affecting a resigned sigh, she sat on the log. "Very well. What shall we talk about?"

"I didn't have anything specific in mind." He clasped his knees with his hands. "It's just such a rare occasion being alone with you—without customers or committeewomen hovering about—and I'd like to make it last awhile."

"You could have arranged such 'occasions' long before this," she heard herself say.

He studied her face and without smiling said, "No, Emily. I didn't want to burden you with my problems. But

I'm in rare good humor today and I don't think there's too much danger of driving you away."

She smiled. "I can talk awhile." In a lower voice, she added, "It will get easier, Rafe."

"Yes, I think so. Being here in the woods helps. And I wasn't joking about 'nature's bounty.' Do you know how it feels to see so much life around me after all those years of . . ." He shook his head and said, "I love these woods. In the past month I've covered every inch of them. It was Annie's idea. She told me to take long walks."

"You do look better," Emily said.

"Would you like to see my favorite place? It's about a mile from here, up near the pond. There are eight trees, mostly pines, that grow in a rectangle. When you stand among them it's like being in a small room. I tried to destroy one of those pines once. Pounded at it until my hand was . . . But the next day I went back and it . . ." He broke off.

"You went back . . ." she prompted.

"Would you like to see the place, Emily?"

"Yes, I would." She wondered what it was he had done to the tree and why. But he seemed not to want to talk about it and she wasn't going to insist. From town gossip she had learned that one had to be careful when talking to Rafe. Above all she must remember not to mention the subject on everyone's lips these days: would Sherman capture Atlanta? A little boy had made the mistake of putting this question to Rafe last week. Rafe had told the child in army English what Sherman could do to himself and to Atlanta. Rafe had apologized at once but the child could not resist telling folks that Mr. Taylor cussed worse than anyone he'd ever heard and how come nobody made *him* wash his mouth with soap?

They said little to each other on the long walk out to the pine-studded area Rafe wanted her to see. There wasn't much to say, she supposed. There was no news of town that he would not have heard. Rafe had been home two months, he lived two houses down, and they saw each other almost every day. How strange then that they should be acting as though they had not been together in years. For that was the mood of this long walk. Shyness, uncertainty, quick glances and uneasy smiles. One or the other would feign absorption with a skittering squirrel or a posturing woodchuck, but neither was really thinking of animals. Emily would remark that the weather was dry and Rafe would say that rain was predicted, but neither was concerned about the elements. Mostly, during the mile-long walk, there were long silences.

This awkwardness evaporated abruptly as soon as they reached the tree room. Rafe took her hand and led her to the spot, then looked at her eagerly. "Isn't this beautiful?"

"Yes, it is."

The tops of the trees formed a roof and the floor was of dried pine needles and leaves. Outside the room, ferns grew in abundance along with weeds and a few berry bushes. But this place was, as he had said, a room in the middle of a forest. She was still standing in the center of it, looking around, when she saw him walk outside the room and examine what looked like a blueberry bush. He returned in a moment and said, "I tried to tear that bush apart but I didn't kill it, Emily."

Now curiosity got the best of her. "What happened here, Rafe? Please tell me."

"I was—upset one day and I stumbled in here like a maniac and tried to tear the woods up. But of course I didn't succeed. Look at all those leaves out there! Oh, they'll fall from the branches in autumn but they'll be back again next year. The pines and the cedars will still be green. They'll welcome the weeds, the buds on the bushes and on the maples over there. They'll urge the leaves along. Death in the woods is only temporary."

"And that's why you love them?"

"Yes. I know forests can be leveled for firewood and furniture. And in Virginia I've seen forests burn. But they grow back. They always grow back." He walked over to one of the pines and began stroking the bark. "I pounded at this one until my knuckles bled. A formidable opponent. Look, you can't see a trace of our fight."

He turned to look at her, then pulled her to him and buried his face in her shoulder. She held him, stroking his hair. After a moment he lifted his face and kissed her. His lips caressed her forehead, nose, and cheek, then moved to her mouth. He grasped her with one hand and with the other grazed her back, waist, and arms. The movements were swift, the touch light, and she felt as though she were being stroked by a warm breeze. He parted his lips and with his tongue parted hers. Then he led her to a grassy spot and pulling her down with him, began to kiss with urgency, breathing hard, stroking her basque.

He undid the top two buttons and then stopped abruptly. "My God, I'm sorry." He carefully buttoned the basque and then sat with his hands clasped around his knees. She too sat up, brushing at her hair.

Rafe now held his hands palms up and studied them as though to ask them why they had done this thing. He said, "This was not just—physical need, though of course that was a part of it."

She colored slightly and looked down. "What do you mean?"

"I mean I love you," he said.

She looked up quickly, her heart racing.

"I know this must sound like a way of justifying—what I just tried to do. But it's the truth. I love you." He paused, still studying his hands. "You know the sort of person I am, Emily. Unwilling to make long-term plans unless there's a reasonable chance of implementing them. I may have loved you for years. I don't know, never stopped to consider. What I do know is that I can see again."

"Can see—?"

"I can focus my eyes. I can look at you closely. For years I didn't want to look too closely at lovely things because I thought I might die and I didn't want to suffer any more than necessary. The less there was to give up, the better I could have faced . . ."

"Oh, Rafe." She shook her head.

"But everything's changed. I'm only now coming to realize it. I'm free. I can make my own future." He paused. "You're not promised to him, are you?"

"To whom?"

"Barry Wingate."

"Oh, Barry." She had almost forgotten the man's existence. "No, we're not engaged."

"I didn't think so. If I'd believed that you were planning to marry him, I would have done something about it before now." He paused. "What I said before—do you understand?"

"Why you didn't want to make plans?"

He nodded.

"I must have felt the same way," she said.

He thought she might be telling him obliquely that she loved him too—or that at least she felt a strong attraction. But he did not insist on clarification, for fear that he might be wrong. Instead he reached for her hand and caressed it gently and completely as though it were the whole of her body, turning it over, running his fingers along the wrist and thumb and into the cushion of the palm. He touched and stroked her slender fingers, then laid his hand flat in her palm, bending her fingers to cover his. She could see that he was trembling with the need for more. She too was highly aroused, wanting so badly to be kissed again that she could scarcely acknowledge the fact that she was in love with him. Thinking and considering would come later. Now she wanted to immerse herself in flesh and sensation. Still clasping his hand, she lay back in the grass.

Rafe stretched out beside her, kissed her, ran his fingers through her hair, then stroked the calico of her basque. He held her tighter and tighter still until she was moaning aloud and arching toward him. Then, gasping, he loosened his grip and said hoarsely, "Our—uh—clothes. Would you like to remove—" and he broke off abruptly. He didn't want to force her, but oh, God!

Emily guided his hand to the basque buttons. He undid them quickly, removed the bodice, then looked helplessly at the stays. Without a word, she showed him where to start unlacing. After some floundering, he accomplished the task and tossed the corset aside. Then he ran his hand under the chemise to feel her flesh. He was breathing hard, and as his fingers touched her, she gasped. The chemise was quickly discarded and he bent to kiss her breasts. When she felt his lips, Emily cried out.

Somehow they removed her clothing and his without once losing contact with each other, kissing and caressing the whole time. Then Rafe came to her.

She was not aware of how quickly he climaxed, never realized that he had stopped and rested. She had felt him inside her, had felt the increasing speed, had heard him gasp and felt him shudder, and now he had stopped for a moment to stroke her breasts. She had not experienced a climax but was not thinking about this. She was thinking only of him, of how good it felt to have him so close, of how she wanted him even closer, a spirit to drink and drink until she drowned in him.

Shifting his body slightly, Rafe began to stroke her in the place that was aching to be touched. The caress was gentle at first, then harder, and she felt herself being lifted to the limits of consciousness as she felt Rafe's rapid movements. For an instant she was aware of nothing, and then nothing became everything as she began to spend. She heard her voice and Rafe's hoarse moans. And she gasped and held his body, feeling him shudder in violent spasms which were so like her own. Finally they were still. She looked at his face, at his closed eyes, at his parted lips and tousled hair. And touching his cheek she murmured, "My love."

The forest was silent except for the songs of the birds. They lay side by side, eyes closed, absorbing one another through touch alone. She loved him so much that she longed to *be* him, or at least to be so close to him that their natures could not be distinguished. But at the same time she wanted to treasure his uniqueness. He had done things she had never done, felt emotions she had never felt, and it excited her to think that there was so much yet to discover.

After awhile they became aware of the late afternoon mosquitoes and agreed to put on some clothes. They decided to dress each other. When he told her that she had the easier end of the bargain, she retorted that if he thought *lacing* stays was a problem he ought to try wearing them. His answer was that it was women who insisted on wearing the damn things, and that they shouldn't blame men if the corsets cut off their breathing. Then she ordered him to stop talking and start lacing.

They returned again to the pine room and leaned against a tree, their arms around each other.

"Let's not tell the folks right away," he said.

"Tell them what?"

"About our marriage."

"You haven't asked me to marry you," she said.

"Oh. Will you marry me, Emily?"

"Yes."

"Now I've asked. The reason I'd rather not tell the folks is that . . ."

"You don't seem surprised that I accepted your proposal," she interrupted.

"Why should I be surprised? We love each other."

"Yes, that's true," she said smiling, disarmed. "All right, why don't you want to tell . . ."

"I'd like us to go to a justice in Dawn Hills and then come back here."

"Here to the woods?"

"Every afternoon for a while. No one would know. We'd go home every night, come here every afternoon. I could have you to myself first, and then we could tell them we're married. If we planned a regular wedding they'd be after us with questions, interfering, trailing us all over the map. I'm not ready for that. Are you?"

"No." But she did not want to elope either, did not want to be deprived of the white dress and toasts and "Oh what a lovely bride!"

She said, "Why don't we compromise? We'll be alone together now and get married later."

"Aren't you afraid?" he asked.

"Of what?"

"Of getting with child before the nuptials."

Emily was surprised at herself. She had never once given the matter a thought. Yet with Roger, visions of babies had been dancing in her head less than five minutes after spending.

Rafe said, "There's a device that's supposed to prevent such accidents from occurring, but I've heard it doesn't always work and I'd rather be safe and elope. The wedding would have to be a small affair anyway."

She knew why, of course. There had just been two deaths in the family. She said, "Still, I think your parents would be unhappy if we eloped."

He frowned, thinking of how much a wedding would cheer Charles and Marie. "You may be right."

"Let's just tryst here for a while," she said, grinning.

"Sounds glorious."

"You mean wicked and sinful," she said.

"Which means blissful. And later we can start the formal proceedings."

"Proceedings," she repeated. "That reminds me of court which reminds me of law. What about Harvard Law School, Rafe?"

"I won't go. I'll have a wife to support."

"What sort of work will you do?"

"I'll think of something." He sounded confident.

She had never before felt so devilish. There was something terribly exciting about playing the proper young lady at a bandage rolling meeting and then, two hours later, abandoning herself to wanton lust. Never did any of her associates miss her. If she was absent from the store, Danny assumed she was at a meeting. If she was absent at supper time, Mary assumed she had been delayed at the store. If she was absent at eight P.M., Danny or Mary or people at the Victory Association assumed she was rehearsing for the next concert. If she was not at the rehearsal, other musicians assumed she was in any of the several other places. Since these people did not meet together to compare notes, Emily did not have to account for her time. She would say to anyone who asked, "I was delayed with the usual business." No one ever suspected that the business was Rafe, and sometimes she would laugh in sheer delight over the double life she was leading. She would explain to puzzled onlookers that she was remembering some innocent amusing incident.

As for Rafe, his father was pleased when his son left the office at two or three in the afternoon. Annie had told Charles about the walks, and Charles himself could see how much these excursions had benefited his son. Why, the boy was improving with astonishing speed! He looked better, his posture had improved, his appetite had returned, and he was greeting the townspeople in gentlemanly fashion. Though Rafe did not discuss his own part in the war, he had begun explaining to the men on the common or at Stevens' Store how Sherman's flanking action had brought him to the gates of Atlanta or why Grant could not, at the moment, seize Petersburg. Rafe had changed overnight, and Charles, attributing the transformation to Annie's wisdom, joyfully increased the cook's wages.

Out in the pine room the couple made love and made plans. In the last week of August, Rafe told Emily that he could probably get a managerial position in one of the many factories along the Fort River. They could live in Lanston or Dawn Hills or in a town farther north depending upon his salary, the hours, the kind of house she wanted, and so on. She asked him to try to make it Lanston, provided that the hours were reasonable. Any small house would do, and she wasn't concerned about the salary. She thought it would be best to live near the folks, especially after the children came.

"I wonder if one's already on the way," Rafe mused. "I do want children."

"You've been using—that thing."

"Yes. But I've warned you, it's not foolproof."

She thought, but it's a lot nicer than seed spilling. She wondered if Rafe had guessed about Roger. If he had, he never asked about it. If he was disturbed, he never let it show.

But few moments were passed in thoughts of careers, children, or former lovers. Most of the time they were detached from the world, off in a land of trees and flowers, twittering birds, rustling bushes, and the sweet urgent sounds of lovemaking.

Rafe sometimes thought that he was dreaming. Real life just wasn't this perfect. No woman so lovely and responsive could come to him except in a dream. Nor was nature itself usually so obliging. Even when it rained, the roof of the tree room filtered out most of the drops. They made love one day during a downpour using Emily's petticoats and skirt to cover the pine needles. The moisture made their bodies slick and Rafe so thoroughly spent himself that he fell asleep at once. His brief dream was not of what he had but of what he feared:

His men were firing in volleys. The woods were burning and the forms of trees and troopers were outlined in the flames. Rafe kept yelling, "Cease fire! Cease fire!" and the flames moved toward him and the men kept shooting. He heard Emily's voice and he screamed "Get back!" but she stayed there and held on to him and then suddenly everything was quiet. It was a damp summer day, the men had disappeared, and he was with Emily. Rafe was certain that he had passed out on the battlefield and was dreaming of her.

She held him for a long time, pinching his arm several times to try to show him what was real and what had been the dream. Yet even when they were dressing and preparing to leave, Rafe was not certain.

"I keep thinking you're going to vanish and I'm going to wake up."

"I'll always be here, Rafe. Always."

She thought, I'm bound up in him. Without him I'm not complete. Whatever he is, I am. Whatever he does, wherever he goes, whatever he decides, I'll be with him.

In her mind she acknowledged the truth at last—Rosie had been right about love.

PART 4

CHAPTER 16

In the first week of September, every evening after returning from the woods with Emily, Rafe rushed home, dressed formally, and walked down the street to "call on" Emily Stevens. Matt and Mary, exchanging knowing glances, would sit in the parlor while Emily, feigning maidenly embarrassment, played the pianoforte and Rafe, acting the nervous suitor, nodded thoughtfully through her sonatas, twining his hands in agitation for the benefit of the beaming onlookers. Rafe had no doubt that Matt would give his blessing, but the couple had to make this look like a newborn courtship and both of them played the role to the hilt.

After making four such calls, Rafe decided to talk over his plans with his parents. He was supposed to be registering at Harvard at the end of the week, and he had to explain why Harvard would never be. In the library he announced to both parents his intention of marrying Emily Stevens "provided Mr. Stevens approved." Rafe said that while his decision might seem to the family to be rather precipitous, the fact was that he had been interested in Emily for many years but had refused to acknowledge his feeling until the war and its dangers were behind him.

Marie, who had been concerned about Rafe's lack of motivation, was happy over the announcement. Normally she would have cautioned him to wait, but the poor boy was utterly at sea and needed some stabilizing influence. Who better than the sensible and intelligent Emily Stevens?

Charles too was pleased. Emily was a cultured young woman, who, despite her undistinguished origins, would be a credit to his son. She was a fine example of what free education combined with hard work could produce. He was concerned, however, about Rafe's professional future. Just how did the boy intend to support a wife? There was the inheritance, of course, but this wouldn't last a year. Charles stroked his beard. He might ask his son to read law with him. It wasn't Harvard exactly but Charles could try to train Rafe for the bar while paying him a small salary for his assistance at the office. Already Charles could see the nameplate over the door of the small building on Center Street: "Taylor and Taylor, Attorneys at Law."

Rafe was saying, "I was speaking to Mr. Waite last week."

"Oh?" Charles wondered what this had to do with Rafe's wedding plans. Was he thinking of inviting the man? Waite was the owner of a machine works factory erected during the first year of the war. He was now one of the wealthiest men in Lanston and he never let anyone forget it. "Shoddy new money" was the way Maple Street dismissed Waite and his family.

"He's looking for someone to manage his factory," Rafe said.

"Ummm . . ." Charles was no longer listening. There were more important matters on his mind than Waite's employment problems.

"I want the job, Father."

"Excuse me? What job?"

"Manager. Of Mr. Waite's factory."

"What?" Charles' mouth dropped open. He gripped the arms of his chair.

Rafe sighed. It was time to tell his father his true feelings about the four sacred professions. "I'm sorry, sir. I don't want to study law. It doesn't interest me. And the ministry, as you know, is out of the question. As for medicine, I saw enough of that during the war to know that I'm not suited for it. That leaves teaching. I wouldn't have the patience."

"But a manager!" Charles croaked.

"I could do it, Father. I'm interested in the company, in machines and how they work. And my experience as an officer will help. I know how to get jobs done. I haven't discussed the salary yet, but I'm sure it will be adequate. Waite's Machine Works is expanding and . . ."

"Oh Lord!" Charles was still in shock. His son managing a factory for that plebeian Waite? Why, for generations the Taylors had sent distinguished professionals into the world—clergymen, state representatives, judges, professors, lawyers. And now Rafe was proposing to take a position as a manager of a *factory*? Not an owner, not even a stockholder, but—a glorified foreman!

Charles did not consider himself a snob. He was ready to applaud anyone who moved upward. Indeed, he was willing to welcome his future daughter-in-law with arms outstretched. But he did not applaud those who stepped down.

This attitude about man's obligation to better himself was in part based on Puritan precepts—beliefs so strongly rooted in New England tradition that even the most enlightened Yankee still at some level subscribed to them. According to Calvinist doctrine, God chose certain individuals to be saved. The rest were doomed to hell. It didn't matter how good or bad these people were. The decision had been made in advance and no amount of praying and self-denial would make a difference. No man knew for certain until the moment of his death whether or not he had been numbered among the elect but there were certain indications that gave him clues. If a man was wealthy or intelligent or in other ways successful this was a sign that God liked him. If a man was poor or shiftless or beset by waves of misfortune or if, having started from a high position, he found himself descending to a lower one, the Almighty was hinting broadly that his future would no doubt be with Lucifer.

To be sure, Charles would have vehemently denied that he subscribed to any of this Calvinist nonsense. Hadn't he been the one responsible for getting Mitchell to resign? He, along with enlightened New Englanders everywhere, now believed that a man—any man, no matter how undistinguished—could get to heaven simply by leading a moral life. But a Puritan streak ran through Charles. Logical as he was, and fully aware that Rafe as an agnostic was beyond redemption anyhow, he still could not bear the thought of his son's stepping down. Rafe must maintain the position for which he had been prepared these many years. Moreover, he must do something to benefit mankind so that his fellows too might rise.

Charles knit his brow. But wasn't being a good manager a way of benefiting mankind? Yes, but not to the same degree. Still, many distinguished men had gotten their start through similar ventures. Yes, but their descendents had attained to loftier positions. But what made a lawyer loftier than a manager? Because law required rigorous study, that was why. But what made "thinking" more noble than "doing"? Charles frowned.

As Charles agonized over this question, Marie exclaimed to Rafe. "It's a wonderful idea, Raphael. You'll stay in town, then? For a moment I was worried that you might leave."

Rafe said, "I don't know that I'll work there forever, Mother. A year or two, perhaps, until I know what I want to do."

Charles emerged from his ponderings in time to hear this last exchange. He had decided that tradesmen and senators, laborers and judges were equal in the eyes of God. There was no "higher" or "lower," no rank, no hints from the Almighty. He must keep telling himself this until he believed it in his heart. It might take forever, he thought dismally, but he must keep trying.

"So you want to work for Waite." Charles forced a conciliatory smile.

The wedding was set for November but Rafe and Emily were effectively married long before then. They made love every evening in the bedroom of the house they had bought on Laurel Street. It had not occurred to either family that the couple needed chaperoning while they fixed up their home. The place was so badly in need of repair that they could not conceive of the two having time for anything else. Once, when Mary dropped by unannounced bearing sandwiches for the hard-working pair, she was puzzled to see that little work had gotten done. She called out her presence and after a long while Rafe appeared in the upstairs hall looking disarrayed and flushed. So that was why the boxes in the parlor had not been unpacked. He'd been removing that dismal blue wallpaper in the bedroom. Then Emily came down for the unscheduled supper looking just as red and just as disheveled as Rafe. A dark suspicion crossed Mary's mind. She frowned, hoping she was wrong but thanking God that the wedding was but a few weeks off. After that, she advised Matt, Charles, and Marie to leave "the children" alone in the evenings so that they could "talk over their plans." In the daytime, of course, when Emily was alone in the house, parental help would be a good idea, she said.

It was an exquisite time for the young sinners. When Rafe returned from work, Emily would set out sandwiches, cheeses, and fruit while Rafe poured wine he had managed to buy through one of his workmen. They would eat quickly, then sip wine as they helped each other undress. They continued to drink when they were under the sheets, holding glasses with one hand and stroking flesh with the other, until the wine was set aside for the few minutes it usually took to achieve the first of the two climaxes they usually shared.

After two frenzied sessions (though Rafe would sometimes insist on three) they would lie in bed holding hands and talking. Rafe would tell her that he wanted to take care of her, that he meant to give her the most comfortable home and all the money she needed, that she must not worry about anything because he would be there to protect her. One of these speeches moved her to tears, and she struggled to control them. But he told her to go ahead and cry, that crying was good for the spirit and helped a person relax. She agreed with the theory but refused to cry and said that she did not need more relaxation. She was indolent enough, she said. There were rooms to fix up and a wedding to plan for and it didn't seem right to be so slothful. But the word "relax" seemed to be a favorite in Rafe's vocabulary. She guessed that this was because he had spent so many years under tension. She was not thinking about the lazy prewar days when he had fished at Barrett's Pond—days that would have bored her to stupefaction had she ever shared them with him. Rafe worked hard and enjoyed his job but his after-work pace was slower than hers, his time sense less acute, his goals less fixed.

Rafe thought of himself as a man of the present and of his fiancée as a what's-next woman. What would come next, he said to her, were babies, diapers and mayhem. She might as well be lazy while she had the chance.

They laughed a good deal during the pre-wedding days on Laurel Street. Since she still spent some time at the store and on her committees there were always amusing anecdotes to relate. Rafe had his own stories to tell about the workers he managed. Sometimes they would joke about living in sin. Emily wondered aloud why she had never guessed that Reverend Mitchell's tirades on carnal knowledge meant that such knowledge must be great fun. One night they recalled some of the preacher's wilder sermons, both of them rolling on the bed and laughing until their hilarity culminated in joyous lovemaking.

So happy were they on Laurel Street that Rafe actually forgot the war for long stretches of time and was able to immerse himself in pure sensuality. Elsewhere in the nation Grant sniped at Petersburg and Sherman occupied Atlanta. Elsewhere men writhed in agony in sweltering tents. But here on Laurel Street there was no hint of the rest of the world, only the dreamlike state for which warriors struggled. Here on the gleaming brass bed was the cause men ultimately fought for.

In October, Rosie dropped in at the house on Laurel, her two children in tow, and announced that she was moving. "To Connecticut. Ed just can't earn enough in this town to make ends meet. And with another baby on the way"—without embarrassment, Rosie patted her stomach—"we'll have to go where the gadget-making industries are."

"Connecticut!" Didn't anyone in this town ever stay put?

"Bridgeport or New Haven."

"It's so *far*, Rosie."

"I know. I know. But we don't have any choice."

What would she do without Rosie, Emily wondered. Foolish and misdirected as the woman could be, Emily had always welcomed her flattery, her effusions, her ability to cheer or to counteract the dourness that sometimes permeated the town.

"Don't worry," Rosie said, blinking back the characteristic tears. "I'm not leaving yet. Not until the wedding's over and I'm sure you're in the promised land."

On her wedding day Emily stood before the mirror in her white satin gown. It had a high neckline and full-length sleeves, but its cut was simple and its lace and pearl trim were confined to neckline and cuffs. Rosie had urged something fancier. Overskirts and undersleeves, ruffles and ribbons, embroidery by the yard. But the affair, Emily pointed out, would have to be small and dignified. And the dress should reflect this.

Emily felt a momentary twinge of guilt while admiring herself in the mirror. White was the symbol of virginity. But what else could she have worn, she asked herself. A black dress? A white dress with black dots, one dot for each wicked lapse? The thought made her laugh and she caught her reflection in the glass. The radiant, laughing bride. Symbolic, she thought. Their relationship had started with laughter in a small classroom.

There would be a light buffet luncheon following the affair but no music, aside from the march itself, and no untoward merriment. The Taylors were still in mourning. Out of deference to his parents, Rafe had agreed to a religious ceremony. The minister well knew that young Taylor was a heathen, but his bride-to-be attended meeting regularly, and so did all four parents. Thus the minister consented to preside.

The organist from the meeting house played a few chords on Emily's old pianoforte and then she was gliding into the parlor on her father's arm. There were involuntary gasps from the assembled guests. Those who had heretofore been skeptical of young Taylor's choice were persuaded of its wisdom on the spot. This was not the Emily of school days with the homely clothing, nor was this the mannish businesswoman of later years helping her father haul boxes into the store. This was a lady. Those older people who could remember Charles' marriage thought that Emily bore herself like the young Marie. And Rafe, the image of his father, was a youthful Charles Taylor. The boy would get over his foolish notions about working in trade and join his father as a professional. With one glance at his attractive young couple the older guests could predict their destiny.

When she entered the parlor, Emily saw none of the guests. She concentrated on the deep blue gown of Abby, her matron of honor, until she had walked up the aisle and was at Rafe's side. He looked unlike Rafe in the formal wedding clothes. He stood ramrod straight, towering over his oldest brother, who was best man. But as Emily cast sidelong glances at him, he seemed to loosen up for a moment. He smiled and whispered, "You look exquisite," then turned a grave face toward the minister.

It was a long ceremony. The minister, who loved to give sermons, was in his glory today. He began the proceedings with his own observations on the sacrament of marriage, then went on to quote at great length from both testaments. Emily heard little of this and Rafe even less. She was thinking of the slow, measured tones of a Mozart piece she loved, wishing she and Rafe were able to hear it now. Music expressed love as no other art could, she thought. And losing herself in remembered music, she was able to get through the sermon. Rafe was thinking of that first afternoon in the woods when, in his opinion, they had actually been married. He could see no connection between that divine experience and the "It is written" injunctions the minister was handing out. For Rafe the ritual was a test of endurance. Only when the vows were exchanged and the ring placed on Emily's finger did either of them concentrate on the actual ceremony.

The reception was small—Maple Street Families and a few old friends including Rosie and her husband. The luncheon was pleasant, the well wishers sincere, and the Taylors seemed cheered by the event. Mary and Matt were congratulated many times on the tastefulness of the parlor, the quality of the food, the utter dignity and rightness of the affair itself. No unruly guests, no spiking of the punch bowl, no inappropriate laughter, no flood of tears. Even Rosie, dressed in dull green silk, comported herself like a lady. Emily was happy to see how proud her parents were, but she could not help wishing that the times had been different and the atmosphere jollier. Oh, how she would have loved a crowded house and music and champagne and everyone in town here, including Christine, who would envy her stately figure, her elegant gown, the splendid house, and the banks of flowers. She wished too that Mrs. Harrington had been able to come in from Washington. But the widow had been recovering from a bout with grippe and had wired regrets.

So the wedding ended and the couple departed, Rafe walking in the erect posture he normally reserved for military reviews, Emily smiling uncertainly as befitted a nervous bride. They stepped into Charles' carriage, waved discreetly, and were driven the short distance home by Charles' gardener, dressed formally today and acting like a Beacon Hill coachman. As they walked into the house, Emily felt let down. The most prized day of a woman's life was over. It had all seemed so quick and so formal. Then they saw on the table in the front hall two bottles of champagne set in bowls of melting ice. Near them was a note.

Figured the bride would want a proper toast and the groom needed a proper welcome to the family. Wish I could have served this at the wedding.

It was signed, "Pa."

Emily grinned with delight as Rafe popped the cork. "Your father," he said, "is a great man."

They spent their two-week honeymoon in New York, at the St. Nicholas Hotel. They shopped, attended the theater, a concert, an opera, and they visited the standard tourist sights: the Croton Reservoir and Barnum's Museum. Rafe wished that Pat and Kent were here in the city. He had missed them over the months and wanted them to meet his new bride. But both men being noncombatants, they had reenlisted without hesitation and were still in Virginia.

Emily was stunned by the size of the city. It seemed even bigger than Boston. One could never, for a moment, be bored in a city like this. But even the delights of New York took secondary place to the chief pleasure of the trip—being with Rafe continually. There were no more conventions to shut them away from each other. They were free to be together twenty-four hours a day, to sleep together at any time, to conceive a baby whenever they wished. Emily wanted to be pregnant. Rafe was eager for children too, and the pair spent happy hours working on their project. What freedom they had! No more waiting while Rafe put on the device. No more doubts whether the condom had been effective. No more listening to determine if one of the family had barged into the house. Nothing but lolling about, exploring each others' bodies, dressing when they wanted to go out to dinner, waking up at whatever late hour they chose. No deadlines to meet today. Or tomorrow. Or at any time for two whole weeks.

It was nothing less than Roman decadence, and Emily knew it would not last long. When they returned home, life would be considerably more structured. But Rafe would be hers. And that was all that mattered.

She was amazed at the changes that were coming over her. Once so reserved, she could now utter sentiments without embarrassment, responding to Rafe himself, who could say "I love you" or "My world is in you" without hiding his face or protesting, as Roger would have done, that such words were foolish. From Rafe she learned an openness of expression that made being with him sheer delight. If only life could go on like this forever. No emotions held back, no misunderstandings, not even the *hint* of a disagreement. But she would not worry about the days when life might not be so blissful. Now she wanted to laugh and kiss and say "I love you" as often as she pleased.

CHAPTER 17

They returned to Lanston in early December. Rafe went back to work at the factory and Emily prepared to resume her usual jobs—organizing the library in her parents' house, attending meetings of the Victory Association, and of course supervising the store.

The store had always been known as "Emily's" even though her father owned it. As supervisor, she had been given carte blanche; her decisions were final. Therefore she was astonished to walk in the day after her return from New York and find the clerk Danny Winstead happily rearranging things.

"Why are you putting those barrels in the front room?" she asked. "And why have you moved the desk?"

"Well, I'm not the owner yet, I guess, but I didn't think anybody'd mind."

"You're not the owner *yet*?"

"Not till next week. Your pa said he wanted cash and I have to wait till the bank . . ."

"*My father is selling this store?*" She was shouting.

"Well—sure. Didn't you know?"

Fifteen minutes later she had reached Matt's factory and

was standing in front of the lathe, her hands on her hips. "You could at least have *told* me, Pa."

"Meant to, Em. Slipped my mind, I guess. I needed the money for new equipment here and I never thought you'd care one way or t'other since you're married now."

"Yes, I'm married, but that was *my store*." She caught herself. "I don't mean I owned it, but I built up the business, Pa." How could her father have been so thoughtless?"

"Guess you did at that. Sorry I didn't tell you about it, but honest, Em, it never dawned on me that you'd care so much about the old place. Husband to do for you and all."

In other words, Emily thought, her achievements were to be sold away as soon as a husband came to rescue her.

She walked home in a fury, propelled by her anger. Very well. Pa needed the money. But still, that was *her* store. He was right, though. She did have a "husband to do for her" and oughtn't to care so much about "the old place." No ordinary husband did she have, either. She had Rafe, her love, her very life, and she ought to be thinking not of stores but of the world she wanted to build for him. Of the house, the children . . .

But Pa had sold her store.

Oh, there were so many plans to make, so much to do. The rooms must be decorated to their taste. She must try those recipes the Taylor cook had given her. The fig pudding especially, with that cream sauce Rafe loved.

Pa had sold her store.

Emily made a cup of tea, then went into the parlor and looked around, admiring the bottle green drapes and the new russet chairs. She tried to remember if the patterned carpet she had bought in New York and was now waiting for was primarily russet or bottle green. The color of the sofa they were planning on buying would depend on this. Why couldn't she remember what color predominated in the carpet?

Now she stood up and walked from room to room, imagining the sound of children's laughter, imagining Rafe as a father. Her throat tightened in happy anticipation. And as she returned to the parlor she remembered the dominant color in the carpet. Russet. That was it. Therefore the sofa would be bottle green. She felt a surge of satisfaction at having her memory return and began wondering about other colors. Gold seemed the best choice. Small amounts of brick red might blend. There was a farm woman out the Bridge Road selling beautiful embroidered pillows. She would drive out today and get—but she had no money. She remembered that married women were given allowances. Lord, but these changes were hard to adjust to!

Not since she was seventeen had Emily had to ask anyone for money. At the store, Matt had told her that her wages would be ten percent of the profits. With this she could buy her bonnets, material, and gewgaws (Emily usually bought books) and not have to bother him. The other ninety percent would, of course, go for general household expenses. So Emily had drawn her pay weekly on the basis of percentage, and this had encouraged her to learn more about business. She had accumulated a tidy sum in the Lanston Bank. Much of this had recently been spent on her trousseau, but seventy-five dollars remained. As she realized that she must now operate on an income set by Rafe, and that not a dime of the money would belong to her, that seventy-five dollars assumed great importance. If she wanted to buy Rafe a small Christmas or birthday gift she could draw off the interest and be able to say that the money for the gift had come from her own pocket and not from his. That money, therefore, must remain in the bank for the rest of her life. She must remember never to dip into the capital.

Again she thought of the store, of the commissions that had once been hers, of the scheming and conniving to undersell Zeke, of the Irishmen telling her Stevens' Store was special. And again she tried to distract herself. Rafe's two ancestral portraits should be moved to the north wall. The oval daguerreotypes of his brothers would look better in the hall. . . .

By mid-December Emily knew she was pregnant. From the moment the doctor confirmed the news she was pampered like a princess. Marie Taylor was there every day, overjoyed, to Emily's surprise, at the thought of grandchildren. Was this the Marie who had lectured her daughters on postponing marriage? The Marie who in early war sewing sessions had emphasized the trials of motherhood? But Emily was too happy to dwell on her mother-in-law's abrupt change of philosophy. She was busy making plans for her little girl. (Emily was sure it would be a girl though Rafe and Marie spoke of "him.")

From the instant she was born, Emily would tell the child how much she was wanted and loved. She would tell her how pretty she was and how charming. There would be parties for all the little friends and she would make sure that her daughter's dresses were as fashionable as everyone else's. And she wouldn't neglect education. The child would learn great literature and great music at her mother's knee. Her daughter would become a woman so complete, so desirable, that men like Rafe would be there in abundance begging for her hand.

In March Emily dropped all outside activities and went into confinement, knitting and crocheting or reading, being waited on by a middle-aged servant of Marie's named Doreen who had been dispatched to take up residence in the Laurel Street house despite Emily's protests that she would prefer to do her own cooking and cleaning. She mustn't risk a miscarriage, Marie warned. Thoroughly bored, Emily finally found an outlet at her piano. She began working on a sonata, a composition that absorbed her totally. All through March she struggled over the andante movement and in the first week of April played it for her husband, who thought it exquisite. She knew, of course, that he was trying to flatter her and also knew that there was no future for women in music, but perhaps after the baby was born she could one day give a local concert and win some modest praise.

Before a week had passed, however, she was playing for an audience and Rafe was calling her incomplete work "A Hymn to Peace." For on April 9th, 1865, the two generals met at Appomattox and came to terms.

People were too happy that week to be concerned over the fact that an enceinte woman was appearing in public. As long as Emily tied her hoops to disguise her condition, Marie said, she would merely look plumper. At her family's urging, Emily played her hymn on the meeting house organ while men and women wept and Matt turned scarlet with pride. Later, standing on the common with Rafe, listening to the band play "The Battle Hymn of the Republic" and watching the boys prepare to set off firecrackers, she wondered if Rafe minded the accolades she was collecting while he, a war hero, was totally ignored. Looking at him she could discern nothing. He was actually smiling. Still, she thought, she ought not to overdo it. Their happiness was too important to jeopardize.

Her labor pains began on a hot July morning. It was the first experience in almost a year to cause her pain of any kind—if she didn't count the sale of the store or the death of Lincoln one week after the war ended. Since she knew that the pain would not last long, Emily resolved to grin and bear it. It was small enough payment for the joy of having Rafe and a little daughter too.

By four P.M. she could no longer grin and was scarcely able to bear it. Dr. Nelson kept assuring her that it would be over before she knew it. Her stepmother and mother-in-law soothed her brow with cool cloths while Doreen, the maid, offered a hand for her to grasp. Marie also encouraged her to cry out though she told her son later to go downstairs so that he wouldn't hear too much. But Rafe insisted on staying in the nursery across the hall.

Marie said, "You can't sit here and listen to that. Emily would be *furious* if she knew."

"Why?" He winced as he heard his wife's low moan.

"Because—well—giving birth is undignified."

"Undignified? Do you think I expect people to be *dignified* when they're suffering? In case you forget, Mother, I've been in a war. I don't know what childbirth feels like, but if it's anywhere near as painful as what I felt at Gettysburg and Spotsylvania I'm surprised she's so quiet."

"But to sit here and listen, Rafe. Your illusions . . ."

"I didn't marry an illusion. I married a woman. And my illusions are no more shattered than hers would have been if she had seen me then, clawing at the ground and whimpering like an animal."

Marie shook her head slowly, tears coming to her eyes at the thought of what her son must have suffered. Never before had he mentioned these things. Then she quickly collected herself. "Nevertheless, Raphael, I don't think Emily would want to know you were listening. She's a very proud woman."

"Perhaps she is. But she's also my wife. Since Nelson won't let me in the room, I'll stay right here."

"But why? What purpose does it serve?"

"It's just something I want to do."

Emily was beyond caring about her dignity. A pain had started—a pain more excruciating than anything she had ever known. It became worse and worse until the moan in her throat tore out in a scream. Then suddenly there was no more pain. There was Dr. Nelson shouting, "Fine!," then a slap, then a mewing noise, then Mary saying breathlessly, "It's a boy, Emily."

Her first reaction was relief that the baby was alive. How could any creature manage to live after going through a trial like that? Then she thought, a boy. She hadn't expected a boy but she was not disappointed. At first she was too weak to talk, but in the absence of pain her strength returned quickly. She said, "May I see him?"

"We're still busy here," said Dr. Nelson, who even at a time like this deemed it improper to utter the words "cord" or "placenta." Outside there was a furious banging on the locked door and Rafe was shouting, "Emily! Are you all right?" He had heard first a scream and then an ominous silence.

"Emily's fine," Marie shouted back. "You're the father of—of a son!" She burst into tears and rushed into the hallway, remembering to close the door so that Rafe would not see any blood.

A moment later Mary was standing beside the bed holding the naked child in her arms. She too was crying but she managed to say, "Take a quick look, Emmy. I have to bathe and dress him for his father."

Emily turned. The child looked like every other newborn she had ever seen. But what had she expected? Halos? Angels singing hosannas? She grinned at the baby, who was crying furiously at having been wrenched from his warm home, and she thought, but I never expected a saint. I wanted a child with spirit. And I have him. And I think I love him already.

Rafe could not be held at bay much longer, so Dr. Nelson, Doreen, and the nurse made quick work of cleaning up while Mary made the infant presentable in head-to-foot blue swaddling. When Rafe walked in, however, he did not look for the baby. He went directly to Emily's bedside and bent over her, clasping her cold hand. "How do you feel?"

"I'm fine. Really I am."

"You're so cold. Your teeth are chattering."

Dr. Nelson said, "That's perfectly normal. Don't worry about Emily. Worry about the problems of fathering." He beamed and nodded toward Marie who was now holding the baby. As Rafe turned to look at his son, his mother said, "The image of you, Rafe. A Taylor through and through."

It had been decided long before that the baby, if a boy, would be named for Rafe's brothers. Now, as Rafe looked down at his son, Marie cooed, "William Jonathan Taylor. What a big boy you are! Yes! You're proud of that, aren't you? Now don't make faces at me. No, I want you to meet your father. . . ."

Would she be able to do that, Emily wondered? To talk to a baby who didn't understand a word she was saying? And what about the other arts of motherhood? Now that she could actually see the baby, Emily was beginning to worry. He was so tiny, looked so utterly helpless. Upon her shoulders would rest the responsibility for making him strong, courageous, and independent.

Marie handed little William to Rafe, who held the baby awkwardly and swallowed with pride. Then Mary reclaimed the child and began to croon to him.

Suddenly Marie clutched the bedpost and began to sob. And in that instant Emily knew what accounted for Marie's grandmotherly zeal. She had lost two sons and now they had returned. Rafe fumbled in his pocket for a handkerchief and handed it to his mother. Emily thought, he too sees his brothers in the eight-pound baby. She tried to share their happiness, but she was hurt. The baby, after all, was half Stevens too and nobody had thought of that. But she kept her mouth shut. This was not the time to remind them.

In the months following Bill's birth, Emily was rarely alone with him, except in the small hours of the morning when she sleepily nursed the child. By day, when she was full of maternal enthusiasm, the two grandmothers were often joined by other Maple Street matrons. To get anywhere near the bassinet Emily had to fight her way past the admiring crowds. No sooner had the last of the visitors departed than Rafe was bounding in the door anxious to see "my son!" If Marie was expert at monologues, Rafe exceeded her by far. He would drone on to the baby about his day at work— foreman problems, machinery that broke down, what he'd eaten for lunch. Working with so many Irishmen, Rafe had absorbed a slight brogue and would affect such phrases as "I'm after thinking your mother'll be wantin' to change your diaper." With which utterance he would drop the wet child into his loving mother's arms and walk off whistling, "Kathleen Mavourneen." Emily asked him once where he had acquired the ability to chatter at an uncomprehending child. She herself preferred lullabies, she told him, and could not sustain monologues for more than ten seconds. Rafe had been holding the baby and grinning when she put this question to him, but suddenly he frowned and looked away.

"What did I say?" she asked.

"Nothing. I learned in the army."

"Oh?" she said. He was looking off into space, brooding, no longer watching the baby. She saw that he was troubled by some memory and did not want to tell her about it. "Rafe," she said, "the baby wants you to talk to him. He's waving his fist, waiting." She forced a laugh and kept on laughing until Rafe turned back to the baby with a strained smile.

In time the crowds tapered off, leaving Emily alone with the baby. Doreen returned to her employment at Marie's and Emily threw herself into motherhood with passion, bathing and powdering, changing the little outfits three times a day, trying to distinguish between false smiles and genuine smiles, looking on in wonder at every sign of progress. On the day he first turned over she shouted and clapped, and when he was able to pull himself up to a standing position she summoned all the grandparents to witness this triumph.

Marie's visits were becoming fewer and fewer as the novelty of William Jonathan wore off, but she was the first to arrive for Bill's stand-up performance. She laughed, then cried, then gave Emily this advice:

"You must learn from my mistakes, dear. Treasure your children while you have them. I—I was never really there for my Bill and my Johnny. And then"—sobs consumed her—"and then one day they were gone and—I never had a chance to make it up to them."

Emily handed her a handkerchief and vowed fiercely never to neglect her children.

Marie patted her hand. "I feel good knowing our little Bill is in loving hands." So saying, she dried her tears. She donned her kid gloves, smoothed back her hair, and departed for a club meeting, leaving Emily in a drool-spattered apron pondering the meaning of her words.

Rafe and Emily had been married for more than a year and so far they had not had an argument worthy of the name. She might sulk because he failed to appreciate a new arrangement of bedroom furniture. He might sulk because she wasn't up to sex seven nights a week. But somehow they managed to use normal speaking voices in making their grievances known. Yes, he did like the furniture arrangement but couldn't she bring his old leather chair back in? Yes, it was ugly but he was comfortable in it. . . . Yes, she *did* want his lovemaking but couldn't he lower the number of encounters to four a week? Women up all night with babies tended to get tired.

They had solved their problems neatly and she still loved him as much as ever. Not in the same heart-stopping way, of course. She was comfortable now, so comfortable indeed that she found herself thinking less about Rafe and more about other things. She had taken up pastimes that did not interfere with motherhood. Among these was a mania for news. She ordered Hartford, Boston, and New York papers in addition to Lanston's own *Weekly* and read them eagerly as the baby napped. All winter long, confined to the house with the baby, she dwelt on problems local and national. Could the United States survive with Johnson as president? He was, after all, a Southerner by birth, and Northern radicals would make trouble for him. And what could be done about educating the Southern Negro? Surely Congress ought to develop some decent programs. War veterans had become opium addicts while in service. Wasn't anyone going to cure them? And the mill owner in town was exploiting women. Shouldn't something be done?

When Rafe walked in the door at night she assaulted him with her questions. All during dinner and even as they were dressing for bed she would lament the state of the union and tell him that men ought to be doing something about it since they were the only ones who could vote. He endured it all patiently though he could give Emily no solutions. But one night he grumbled that he was too tired to consider such matters and couldn't they just go to sleep?

"Am I boring you?" she asked icily.

"I just don't feel like discussing the news every night. Couldn't you give me one day off?"

"Day *off*?" Her voice rose slightly.

"Yes." His voice was a shade louder.

"I see. Well, fine. Take a day off. Take a year off. I'll never disturb you again."

He grit his teeth, tried to explain. "I'm tired, Emily. Hearing the news every night is like reliving the day at work. It's exhausting."

"Then I'm to be quiet all the time?"

"Not *all* the time."

She stood up and stalked out of the bedroom, shouting over her shoulder, "There! Enjoy your solitude."

He was in no mood to placate her. What the hell did she expect from him anyhow? Was he supposed to become like his father, rampaging through the state effecting reforms? Wasn't it enough that he supported her, helped her with the baby, loved her with all his heart? He tossed in bed for another half hour, certain that she had by this time come to see his position. And finally he went downstairs to find her sitting on the russet couch biting her lip.

"Please don't misunderstand," he said. "I love you very much, Emily. But I don't love the whole world. That is, I can't deal with it at this time. You see, I was out there—in the world, I mean—for three years. When I came home and found you it was like walking into a warm house after being in a storm. I guess I need to stay in the warmth a little longer." He sat down beside her.

"Yes, I understand." Her voice broke. "Oh Rafe, I'm sorry."

He kissed her. "It's all right. Now come back to bed." And she walked up the stairs with him, vowing to be careful of what she said in the future, wanting to weep with relief because love didn't die with one argument.

She stopped hurling national problems at him and remained cheerful during dinner. But after two weeks of serenity, she began another study—educating the young child. Every night he was treated to discourses on ways to stimulate learning skills in babies. He tried to listen but found his eyes growing glassy. To be sure, such discussions weren't as depressing as the news recitals, but Bill, after all, was only nine months old and hardly ready for the alphabet. Couldn't she just let the baby play and gurgle in peace? Couldn't she relax a little bit and enjoy the meal she had made and later make love with the old passion? Well, perhaps she was feeling a little restless. It had been a long, cold winter.

On the first springlike day in 1866, Emily packed Bill into the pram and tore off down the street like a prisoner fleeing jail. She stopped first at her father's factory down near the river. Matt was very busy and he advised Emily to take the baby out of there, away from the sawdust. He promised to drop in the next night to see his grandson. Emily walked up the hill to Center Street and down to her old store. She was now a weekly shopper at Danny's, but she would never get used to the dust, the smell of cats, the tobacco juice on the dirty stove. Deciding to wait until Saturday to shop, she rolled the pram toward Maple Street to see her stepmother. Mary was busy sorting books. She was now the town librarian, looking after the collection Emily had started and receiving a modest fee from the town for her services and the use of her house. As one matron walked in to ask for a volume of Scott, Mary ushered Emily and the baby out, warning of book dust as Matt had warned of sawdust. Next Emily called on Marie, who was on her way out the door. Marie, now the assistant editor of the *Lanston Weekly*, was always in a hurry these days. She kissed her grandson, said she'd be over later that week, and glided down the street toward the printing office. There was no one else at home, for Rafe's sisters, heedless of their mother's advice, had both married men from Dawn Hills the autumn before. Sighing, feeling very much alone, Emily turned the pram toward the green.

Here on a bench, watching their children romp, were Christine Osbourne Benton and another young mother named Priscilla Peters.

"Hello, Emily," Christine said with an authentic smile. "Sit down and join us. Please."

Please? Had Christine actually said please to the former farm girl and store manager? Emily's first impulse was to arch an eyebrow and plead another appointment, but she felt obliged to say hello. The greeting led to a chat about baby Bill—a discussion which Priscilla joined—and soon Emily was seated on an adjacent bench rocking the pram and smiling stiffly.

In the year and a half since her marriage, Emily had deliberately avoided these women. In the past they had hurt her many times with their subtle condescension, and now that she was married to the son of one of Lanston's most prominent families Emily was determined to let them stew in their own pettiness. She and Rafe had had two dinner parties in the past year and Emily had seen to it that the guest list got into the newspaper so that the Christines and Priscillas could see the blanks where their names should have been. But now, as she talked with the women, it dawned on her that these snobs were at least available for conversation. She had more in common with them than with her relatives or the older Maple Street ladies like Dr. Nelson's wife. Christine and Priscilla spoke of teething and thumb sucking and feeding schedules and how to dress little boys. The three had an intense discussion about disciplining young children and Emily, whose son was the youngest child present, was able to learn a few things. After a while she noticed that she was actually enjoying herself—that she had long craved the company of mothers her own age. With Rosie gone and Abby busy on the farm, Emily had been lonely. Her old enemies had mellowed in their attitude toward her, and even as she puzzled over the reasons, Chris was giving her the answer.

"You've settled down, haven't you, Em?"

"I guess so."

Priscilla was more direct. "You're one of us now. At school you used to be so—distant."

"*I* distant? I don't recall . . ."

Chris interrupted. "Your nose was always in a book. You were such an 'intellectual.' But you've changed, Emily."

"Have I?" She didn't know whether to be flattered or insulted, pleased or indignant. She knew nothing except that she was able at last to talk to housewives about housewifely matters. And for this privilege she was ready to bury her doubts and some of her old anger.

She said, "I guess I *have* changed." And from here she moved carefully, her tone becoming warmer and warmer (this required some acting) until she had invited them to stop by for tea.

In the following weeks Emily was gradually admitted to Lanston's society of young matrons. They sat in one another's yards, watching their children and talking about their pregnancies and births. They strolled down to Center Street, talking about morning sickness and labor pains. Emily began to wonder why this subject consumed them all. She no less than the others was absorbed by it. Then she realized that giving birth to a child—any child but especially a man-child—was a woman's ultimate contribution to society. Every labor pain must be made important. And that final mindless scream must be savored in all its agony.

Having acquired a group of friends, Emily no longer needed to rely on Rafe for conversations. Dinners were quiet. She had talked herself out during the day. Moreover, being in the company of women made her appreciate the novelty of a man. There were moments when she and Rafe were as close as they had been during the first weeks of their marriage. The couple was happy.

Their second son, Michael, was born in January, 1867. Because the family was accustomed to the birth drama by this time, little fanfare attended the new arrival. They all kissed the baby, urged Emily's swift recovery, and went about their business. The new baby resembled Emily more than Bill had, and since the Taylors had not proclaimed him the reincarnation of anyone, Emily began to think of Michael as a Stevens. Though she believed she loved the two children equally, Michael was special. In his hesitant first movements she could see herself as a baby. She encouraged him so that he would not know what it meant to fail or to feel parental disapproval. Every cry was perceived by her as a plea for comfort, and she pampered him twenty-four hours a day. Once when Rafe suggested that she might be spoiling the child, she indignantly explained that new research proved that it was impossible to spoil an infant. This was not true, but Rafe came to believe it when he saw that Michael was a happy baby. The days beat on with the same gentle rhythm and no variation in pitch. Was it March already? April? Good grief! As a single girl she had always been acutely aware of time's passage. Now, dating a letter to Mrs. Harrington, she had trouble remembering the month. It must be contentment, Emily thought. With her marriage she had lost that compulsive awareness of time.

Rafe too was content. It was pleasant to sit in the parlor after dinner watching his wife nurse the baby while he told her hilarious anecdotes about zany old Mahoney down at the factory. With the older boy asleep, peace reigned in the house. The fire crackled, little Michael suckled, and as he reached the punch line of the latest Mahoney story, Emily's light laughter would ripple through the room. Once in a while she would tell him of her day too. Rafe didn't find news of household matters stimulating but he was interested in what the children had done, so Emily limited her contribution to evening talks to Bill and Michael. Any mention of Christine's new curtains or Priscilla's sewing circle would bring yawns from her husband.

At first Rafe had been disturbed by Emily's alliance with his former love. But Christine didn't seem especially concerned. Indeed, Emily had told him of a conversation in which Chris had admitted cheerfully that Emily was far more suitable for Rafe than she would have been. He knew she'd been exaggerating, of course. The woman might have conceded Emily's superiority, but she could scarcely have been "cheerful" in doing so. But Rafe nodded understandingly. If it made Emily happy to believe that Christine had actually forgotten those intense embraces and breathless words—well, her happiness was more important than the truth.

As Emily sat by the fire enduring the Mahoney stories, she developed a technique for keeping Rafe happy while thinking of something else. If he smiled a certain way, she knew he had reached the punch line and she forced out a chuckle. If his smile was less final-looking she knew that he was still building up to the climax and she parted her lips to suggest eager anticipation. Every so often she would worry that perhaps the romance was going out of their marriage. But she could not accept such a dreadful truth. They were simply revealing their true selves to one another. This was the mark of mature love, settled love. He might not be so stimulating as he once was, but she must not dwell on that. Love altered not when alteration found. And her love for him was true.

Satisfied with her conclusions, she would again drift away into reverie while the fire crackled, the baby suckled, and Rafe droned on.

In May, 1867, Rafe met a man named Paul Griffin, who was the owner of a locomotive manufacturing company that purchased tools from the factory. In Mr. Waite's absence, Rafe was giving him a guided tour of the place. Impressed by Rafe's managerial abilities, amazed by Rafe's comprehension of mechanics and physics, and anxious to have a Harvard man lend dignity to his firm, Mr. Griffin asked Rafe if he would be interested in locomotive designing. His company was located in New Jersey, he said. Would Rafe consider the move? Rafe hesitated. Would it be fair to Emily? Could he himself stand being so far away from all that was familiar? New Jersey? What did he know of New Jersey? In the moment's pause, Mr. Griffin embellished the offer. Would Mr. Taylor feel better about the move if he could invest in the company? Well, yes, Rafe said. That would be an inducement. Mr. Griffin pressed on. And would Mr. Taylor feel more comfortable if the company paid for a New York hotel suite for the family while they looked around for a house?

"New York? I thought the firm was in New Jersey."

"It is. A ferry ride across the Hudson from Manhattan."

"Oh!" Rafe brightened. Emily wouldn't mind that at all. As for him, he wasn't mad about cities, but all things considered it might be worth a try. Pat and Kent were there, after all, and he wouldn't feel like a total stranger. "I'll have to speak with my wife," he told the man, "but I think she'll agree."

She agreed before he had finished the sentence. New York! Concerts, theaters, museums, and libraries. Shops and parks and horsecars and commotion. Even the cobblestones throbbed with life. She had not forgotten a detail of that brief honeymoon.

They called the family together and broke the news. There were tears from Marie and sighs from Matt but everyone agreed that the move would be good for Rafe's future. Rafe sent off a letter to Pat Shepherd asking him about housing in the city. Then the couple began the tedious process of packing. They hoped to be in New York by the middle of June, which gave them a full month.

Pat's answer came back quickly. There was a brownstone for sale on East Tenth, just across the street from his office. A good neighborhood in the Washington Square/Fifth Avenue area. In the rest of the letter he filled Rafe in briefly on all that had happened since the last time he'd written, which had been two years earlier toward the end of the war. Kent had married Pat's sister Beth and they now had a child. His brother Joe had married a beautiful young widow with a four-year-old girl. He, Pat, had also married and now had a son. He and Kent shared an office in Kent's brownstone, Kent specializing in surgery and Pat in general medicine. It would be bully if Rafe could buy the house across the street from Kent's. For a small deposit the owner would hold it until Rafe arrived.

There was no description of Pat's wife or of his son. Rafe thought this was strange, but he congratulated himself on having predicted Kent's marriage to the lovely dark-haired girl he had met at Gettysburg. He sent off a check to Pat and resumed packing, looking forward to seeing his old friends.

When the initial exuberance had worn off, Emily left the babies with her stepmother and strolled around town for a last look. She walked down Center Street, once the focus of her life, and thought of how small and inconsequential it was, compared to the Broadway they would be living near. Pathetic, really. And none of the shopkeepers realized it. Glancing toward the common she saw two friends from her circle of matrons. The thought flashed through her mind that they were dullards and that she too had been a dullard with her monotonous prattle about pregnancies. Women in New York spoke of art and literature. She could not imagine them sharing news of their morning sickness.

On she walked, past Winter's Dry Goods and Lanston High School which was now a modern brick building (the old Lanston Academy was a cobbler's shop). She glanced over at Maple Street, still the center of town aristocracy, and she smiled. Fifth Avenue was where real aristocracy lived. The Astors would laugh at the likes of Maple Street. She hurried past her old store, which she could no longer bear to look at, and walked down toward the mill. As she neared the railroad tracks she began to see the ramshackle houses and the ill-dressed children. She thought, here we have something that is the same in small towns and cities alike—the poor. As she walked north toward the machine factory, she saw her husband sitting under a tree eating a sandwich and chatting with some workmen. Rafe noticed her, waved, and hurried to join her.

"What are you doing here, Emily?"

"Just taking a walk."

"You look upset."

"Just having guilty thoughts because I'm so glad to be leaving."

He smiled. "A town isn't a person, Em."

"No, but laughing at a town is like laughing at you and me and everybody we care about. It's like seeing our idols shot down. Or like finding out that a treasure is worthless."

"I've never known you to be so melodramatic, Em. This is just a place. A mixture of good people and bad, a blend of the tasteful and the tawdry. New York is no different."

"But it is, Rafe."

"It's bigger, but not different." He paused. "During the war I took a walk through the town, but my journey must have been different. I didn't find the town as a unit dull, only parts of it. Maple Street, for example, was complacent and predictable. Your store, on the other hand, was vital and exotic."

"Exotic?" She wasn't sure she had heard him correctly.

"Yes. The smell of spices and cheeses. The wares imported from the cities."

"You found my store *exotic*?" she repeated in amazement.

"Yes. And don't forget, Em, I'd been to many places when I came to that conclusion. To Philadelphia, Washington, Boston, Baltimore. In the army I'd met immigrants from many countries. Pat's regiment was full of them. And I still found your store fascinating."

On impulse she grasped his hand and said, laughing, "You and your blarney, Rafe Taylor." She was blushing like a young girl because Rafe had called her store exotic.

A red-faced man walked over and Rafe introduced him as Ed Mahoney. Was this *the* Mahoney, the comical foreman whose jokes and capers so delighted Rafe? Emily held out her hand, happy to meet him. "My husband has told me so much about you." She realized that she was no longer jealous of this man. Since Rafe had used the word "exotic" she'd been heady with benevolent feelings toward all mankind. But as Mahoney took her hand she stared at him. Had she been *jealous*? Was that the right word? No, she'd been *bored* by Rafe's stories. Why would she be jealous of Rafe's friendship with this man?

"I've got to be getting back to the office now," Rafe said. "A lot of details to attend to before I leave." He nodded toward Mahoney. "Ed here's taking over the job of manager."

"Congratulations," Emily said.

The two walked off, followed by other workmen who were chattering and laughing. Emily looked after them, puzzled by her feelings but certain that "jealous" wasn't the right word.

She had meant to take a direct route home but she found herself backtracking to the old store. She stood in front of it for a while, smiling foolishly, and then strolled home thinking that the town was a fine place indeed. It would be pleasant to come back and visit every summer.

CHAPTER 18

Two weeks before they moved, Rafe and Emily made a trip to the city to look at the brownstone Pat had mentioned. Free of responsibility, leaving the children in the care of grandparents, Emily felt young and adventurous. It was like a second wedding trip.

Rafe had wired ahead that he was coming to New York, and to his delight, there were three people waiting to greet them at the Fourth Avenue Station. The first to stride up was a tall, disjointed young man with light brown hair and a broad smile. He hugged Rafe like a brother, and Emily knew even before she was introduced that this must be Pat Shepherd. Next to Pat stood a lean rugged blonde man with a face as controlled as Pat's was mobile. Kent Wilson's greeting was reserved. A handshake for Rafe, a nod for Emily, and the words "Good to see you again," forced out through a stiff smile. Had Emily not been raised with the likes of Matt Stevens, she might have been offended by Kent's brusqueness. But hearing the New England accent she thought, "aha!" and adjusted her appraisal accordingly. She saw warmth in the man's eyes and concluded, he's utterly delighted to see Rafe again.

Kent quickly took a step backward, as though relieved to be concluded with the sentimental part of this reunion, and the dark-haired woman beside him stepped forward. She was Kent's wife, Beth Wilson. Her manner was warm and enthusiastic. She smiled, shook their hands, asked if the trip had been tiring, asked about the children. Beth was a handsome woman who appeared to be Emily's age—twenty-seven. Her full figure just missed being plump but she was tall enough to carry the weight well. Her blue muslin dress was simply cut and unadorned. A very attractive woman, Emily thought, but not the type to gloat about it.

Beth said, "We've planned a dinner for you. Can you stand us for another three hours?" Before Emily could answer, she added, "Perhaps you should wait before looking at that house. With us for neighbors you may decide against it."

But Emily was fairly sure that she would enjoy having a woman like Beth across the street.

The Taylors knew little about the relative merits of brownstones and had to be content with their friends' assurances that as townhouses went this one was a fine buy indeed. During their stay in New York Beth introduced Emily to neighbors on Tenth Street so that Emily could see for herself what her own future house might be like. Emily was not impressed. Why, every house looked alike! There wasn't one she visited that had a central hall. Some had halls on the right and rooms on the left. Others had halls on the left and rooms on the right. All were four stories high, and everyone except Beth used the same rooms for the same functions. Servants gathered on the ground floor, just below street level, in a room next to the kitchen. The first floor featured a parlor (some called it a drawing room) facing the street. This was generally reserved for visitors. Behind the parlor was a library or sitting room where the family actually gathered of an evening, and behind this, overlooking the mews, was a dining room. The last was directly above the kitchen so that food could be sent up by a dumbwaiter. The third floor was given over to the master and mistress of the manse and possibly an older child as well. Into the fourth floor were crammed the bedrooms of the servants and those small children they tended.

The interiors of these houses seemed greatly overdone. The classic look in rooms, which Lanston residents clung to, was definitely out. Too dull and old-fashioned, decorators asserted. The bounty of America ought to be exhibited, not hidden. And so every fixture was a lion or a cherub and every pattern in a room shouted down every other.

If Beth's house was simpler, it was partly because she had little time for decorating. Moreover, her rooms were not in their assigned places. The street floor of her brownstone contained the doctors' offices, the waiting room, and a small recovery room. Beth's dining room was below stairs next to the kitchen and her book-lined parlor was tucked into the third floor along with a master bedroom and a small laboratory. Upstairs lived Beth's baby, Kathy, and two servants. Until recently Beth's aunt, who had owned the place, had lived here too. (Good God, where had she fit an *aunt*?) But two weeks earlier the aunt had decided to move to rural Pennsylvania where her son and grandchildren lived. "Near Gettysburg," Beth explained, and Emily remembered Rafe telling her that Beth had been at Gettysburg just after the battle. Emily was about to ask her about that episode, but Beth was explaining the unfinished look of her house. After her marriage, she said, she had bought patterned carpets for each of these rooms. The sofas and chairs resting on them had been of solid colors, as had most of the draperies and curtains.

"I was afraid of clashing patterns," Beth said. "But I suppose that's old-fashioned."

Bureaus and chests had been added, but few little tables and even fewer knickknacks. She hadn't had the time, Beth explained apologetically. She helped both her husband and her brother in their offices and did microbe research as well. But one of these days she must fix up the house. Emily wanted to shout, "Don't touch it! Don't add a thing!" But she held her tongue out of deference to Beth. Perhaps one had to acquire a taste for the new style in rooms.

They spent three days in New York, staying at the St. Nicholas, the hotel of their honeymoon days. Emily was squired about by Beth and Beth's beautiful sister-in-law Diane while Rafe made arrangements for the purchase of the house and visited the locomotive works in New Jersey. Beth and Kent had two dinners for them. Pat had none, but as soon as Emily met his wife, she could understand why. Eileen was painfully shy and rarely spoke except when addressed. She was a thin, red-haired woman, attractive in every respect. Yet her way of averting her eyes or staring down at her plate detracted from her looks in a way Emily could not define.

The men did not dwell on war memories. Indeed, they went out of their way to avoid the subject, the war being too recent for the horrors to have been sifted from the triumphs. Their dinner conversations were of current and future enterprises. Kent and Pat spoke of advances in science and technology while Joe, the brother of Pat and Beth, who was in the insurance field, apprised Rafe of Wall Street matters with tips on investing. Emily thought that Joe Shepherd was one of the most attractive men she had ever seen. Tall, dark and weathered, he had large brown eyes that conveyed an impression of sensitivity. With his dark hair beginning to gray at the temples, he looked older than his twenty-six years. His wife matched him in perfection; Diane Shepherd was petite, blonde, and blue-eyed with exquisite features. Emily felt a trifle clumsy in her presence and so, she suspected, did Beth. But Diane was pleasant and bubbling with plans for helping Emily after the move. Emily liked her in spite of the fact that she had always distrusted beautiful women.

On the way home in the train, Emily discussed her new acquaintances. She wondered how Kent had come to choose Beth and she him. He was so taciturn, she so friendly. The same was true of Pat and Eileen, though their differences were so much more extreme.

Rafe knit his brow and said, "Yes, I noticed. Eileen's awfully reserved, isn't she? Makes Kent look like a politician on the night before an election."

"Perhaps she's just shy. Or perhaps she's become dependent upon medicines and couldn't wait to get home and take them," Emily said. Such problems were common in these days when opium-doused medications, available without prescription, were making addicts out of as many women as men. The women used "female complaint" as an excuse and the men spoke vaguely of old war wounds or stomach ailments.

"I don't know what Eileen's problem is," Rafe said, "but I think if it were opium she would have brought the stuff along to dinner. One thing I do know, though—Pat's become an inebriate."

"Really? I never would have guessed that."

"How could you be expected to? We all drank a good deal this week. But I knew Pat during the war, and the difference in his attitude toward liquor is startling. He held that glass as though it were the only friend he had. I don't remember seeing him put it down except to eat."

"He's a doctor, Rafe. Doctors can't work when they're drunk."

Rafe's smile was ironic. "He's no longer a surgeon. And you'd be amazed how well men can function under enormous quantities of alcohol."

No, she wouldn't be amazed. She remembered her father on the farm. But she had thought doctors might be different.

Rafe continued, his voice sad, "I've never seen him like this."

"Like what?" Emily remembered only a cheerful gregarious man.

"I can't explain it," Rafe said. "You would have to have known him before. He was the one everyone went to for advice." Rafe paused, thinking. "Now I have the impression that he's looking for help himself."

"What sort of help?"

"I don't know."

He leaned back in his seat, preoccupied, and Emily was struck by the fact that in three days away from home they had become so absorbed by the problems of another family. But problems were a sign that one was part of a group, and she was so glad to have a group to belong to (she had feared being lonely at times) that she left Rafe to worry about Pat Shepherd while she pondered changes she must make in her decor. A little more gingerbread, she decided. Not too much. It would drive her crazy. But enough to indicate that she was fashionable. The packing was almost complete but she vowed to rescue from the junk heap all wedding-gift bric-a-brac featuring cherubs and lions. How was she to know, when she buried the atrocities in the attic, that they represented the vanguard of fashion? Thank heaven she hadn't given them away!

In a few weeks they had set up housekeeping in New York. Beth found them a maid of all work named Kitty, who was installed in the servants' quarters, where she spent long hours fixing up the below-stairs room to her satisfaction. They as yet had no other servants. Forty-five years old, with such fierce pride in her work that Rafe called her the Irish Puritan, Kitty was so professional a servant that she would explain to Emily how she herself was supposed to be treated. When Emily attempted to help Kitty with an arduous or un-dignified task, the portly woman would gently point out that "ladies" did not scrub floors, that "ladies" gave their servants credit for knowing how and when to perform such tasks, that "ladies" as well as servants knew their place. Emily was at first intimidated by the woman's attitude. She reacted defensively, explaining that she had had a maid in Lanston and knew perfectly well how to treat servants. If Kitty did not prefer a more democratic arrangement, that was just fine with Emily. In New England, mistresses weren't so rigid nor servants so exploited, she pointed out indignantly. This, of course, was not true. The fact of the matter was that Emily did not know how to act with maids and was uncomfortable having them around. But she would no more admit this than admit that she had once done work more menial than Kitty could ever imagine. So she sighed loudly and muttered about New York's peculiar ways and said she would forego New England's superior servant-handling techniques if Kitty insisted on this stratified arrangement. Then, under the maid's tutelage, she set out to become a lady.

With basic furnishings in place, drapes up, and the nursery finished, Emily began unpacking the boxes of gewgaws.

"Oh lord," she grumbled to Rafe one night, kneeling on the floor in the hall and holding up a pair of dragon candlesticks. "I can't stand them."

"Then don't use them. There's gaslight in New York."

"It would be wasteful not to use them."

"Do you want to be wasteful or tasteful?" He chuckled at his rhyme, then bent down to open another box.

"You're a big help."

"Mmmmm," he said absently, extracting a pair of book ends from his own box of effects. Rafe was settled at work now. His new associates had none of Mahoney's charm, but Rafe had a challenging job to describe in detail. While he was too engrossed to take an interest in her decorating problems, she was expected to hang on his every word, and this one-sided arrangement was beginning to annoy her. She did not find the wasteful/tasteful joke in the least amusing and was about to tell him so when she saw him staring fixedly at a dog-eared pamphlet that must have been in his box of books. It was titled "The Soldier's Friend" and bore the stamp of the Sanitary Commission. Suddenly he dropped it on the floor, shaking his head as though to rid himself of his thoughts.

"Rafe, what is it?"

"Nothing." He rose, carrying some books and said, "Going to put these on their shelves." And he walked down the hall to the library.

Emily did not go after him. She had tried to do so in the past, telling him that talking about his memories or nightmares might help. Each time he had said irritably that any descriptions he might give would only nauseate her. And there was no sense in the two of them being distressed. In time she had ceased asking.

He had told her a few war stories, however, most of them accounts of camp life, of Pat's and Kent's antics, of the monotony that had driven them all to the brink of lunacy. There had been moments, he said, when he had felt like a baby confined in a crib.

She was curious about the pamphlet. What on earth was in it to provoke such a reaction? A letter from one of his brothers perhaps? But she would not invade his privacy by looking through it. She placed the pamphlet back in the box.

During the summer months of 1867 Emily continued to rearrange the furnishings and what Rafe called "gimcracks." She fretted over every room, determined that her house be fashionable yet easy on the eyes. By September she had accomplished a good deal. The conservative russets and bottle greens in the parlor were livened by flashes of red and yellow pillows. Two of Rafe's ancestral portraits, which Marie had given them, were featured on one wall (for greater effect) and she had not enough in the way of framed items to completely plaster the other three. She made do with what she had, however, and was pleased with the result. New Yorkers would doubtless call her Spartan until she'd accumulated a ton of knickknacks, but Emily would think of some way to suggest that she'd *planned* this room to be classic.

Beth Wilson, Diane Shepherd, and four members of Diane's sewing circle (or "tea group" as she referred to it) were invited by one afternoon in September. Sitting on Matt's finely crafted chairs, holding their china teacups so that not one drop fell on their silk visiting dresses, talking in well-modulated voices about the shops on fashionable Fourteenth Street, they were the very model of New York upper-middle-class gentlewomen. All of them had compliments for Emily's home. And one woman named Caroline said, "How quaint," as she sat in a prized Queen Anne wing chair given to Emily by her mother-in-law.

"Thank you," Emily said warily, wondering if "quaint" was supposed to mean hopelessly old-fashioned.

Beth asked, "Has it been in the family very long?" She was helping Emily with her debut by asking the right questions, though Emily had not asked her to do this.

"Why, yes," Emily said. "Since before the war." That meant the Revolutionary War, of course. She hoped they all understood this.

"Well, I do think our ancestors had more taste than we do," Beth declared. "The chair is utterly charming."

Emily gave her a grateful look, but she was beginning to suspect Beth's motives. Never had she known the plain-speaking Elizabeth to use the words "utterly charming."

Diane now turned to the group. "Emily's husband is from a distinguished New England family. Very close to the Lowells and the Adamses."

Emily blushed. This remark was rooted in a conversation at dinner the other night in which Rafe and Kent, who had both attended Harvard at different times, had said that they'd been ill at ease with the sons of old Boston families. Emily realized that Diane too was trying to embellish her background for the benefit of the group. But she involuntarily clenched her fists, hoping that neither of them would overdo it.

"Mercy!" said Caroline, smiling. "I had no idea we were in such rarefied company."

Emily forced a laugh. They *had* overdone it. "Oh good heavens," she chuckled, "it's nothing like that."

Beth said, "I don't understand your concern, Caroline. Diane, after all, was married to an Allister before she was widowed and I've never known you to comment on that. Emily and Diane are no different from the rest of us." Beth's voice resonated slightly with the tone a wealthy aristocrat might use in reassuring the masses that America was the land of opportunity. She was teasing and Caroline knew it, but the latter did wonder if Mr. Taylor's people were as well born as Diane had intimated.

Emily waited for questions to be asked about her family lineage, but the conversation soon took another turn. In the next two hours, however, she provided them with a version of her background that would sit well in groups like these. She said that her father had "done a little farming" and now "amused himself at furniture making." "Very Massachusetts," she added, giving the impression that Matt was one of those irascible old landed gentlemen who hated everything modern and loved to tinker with his tools. She told them also that her stepmother was a librarian and Beth said that her father was too. Then Emily broke the news that she had once been fascinated by general stores and their operations. Over her father's objections, she had managed one and had a "delightful little stint as a businesswoman." The bored heiress dabbling in the marketplace. She told them too of wealthy friends, among them Mrs. Harrington who had gone to Washington to battle for women's rights. This would appeal to Beth, who was a voluble apostle of Susan Anthony.

As Emily watched Beth and Diane exult over her furnishings for the benefit of the four young matrons, she realized that these two had either guessed that her history was less distinguished than she had indicated and were helping her to overcome the liability, or didn't care what her history was and simply enjoyed playing these games for socially ambitious people like Caroline. Emily could not tell.

The tea party was a great success. Diane reported that Caroline had removed a parasol from the wall of her parlor and added a bust of Nathan Hale to one of her cluttered tables. "She's trying to acquire a New England look," Diane exclaimed with glee.

"Do you think so?"

"Oh, I never thought I'd see the day when Caroline bowed to anyone. She's looking for a Queen Anne chair this very minute—and she used to think that all New Englanders except Bostonians were crazy backwoods Congregationalists. I *told* her you'd make New Yorkers look shoddy, but she wouldn't . . ."

Emily did not hear the rest of the sentence. Diane meant well, of course, and was on her side. But she resented the words "backwoods Congregationalists." Were Episcopalians like Diane and Caroline supposed to be superior? Who did they think had spurred the revolution? Who had been the first to lay down their lives for liberty? Episcopalians? Hah! None other than those backwoods Congregationalists. For the first time in her life she felt a warm surge of feeling for the dear old meeting house, and determined that future conversations at the tea group would be studded with references to Lexington, Concord, and the superiority of altarless churches in evoking feelings of true democracy.

While Emily concerned herself with her social position, Beth cheerfully went about her unconventional life. She had been born in a tolerant middle-class home. Her father, an Englishman educated at Oxford, took pantheism as his religion. Her mother had been an orphaned Irish girl from a poor immigrant family. Beth and her brothers were Catholics. Her family numbered Negroes among their friends and found it difficult to tolerate people of Caroline's ilk. Yet Beth, for some reason, liked to get back at them when the opportunity presented itself.

Beth rarely had time for tea parties and had made a special exception in Emily's case. Generally Emily saw Beth only in the evenings when one or another in their group was having a dinner party. Beth might also run across the street on an occasional weekday if there were few enough patients and her laboratory work was finished. But such occasions were rare. Beth was usually too tired for social calls. In addition to her medical work at home, she often accompanied Kent or Pat on middle-of-the-night calls, administering ether while the doctor set a leg or delivered a baby. Twice she had delivered the baby herself while her exhausted brother slept in another room.

Beth also helped her husband solve other problems. Kent's patients were often disturbed by his brusqueness or tactlessness, and Beth was forever having to smooth things over. But Beth's major triumph in the advice-to-her-husband area was the Lady Macbeth Incident. Two weeks after the tea party Beth stopped in to tell Emily the story. Kent had come storming home from the hospital a few days before.

"He found out that the chief surgeon was calling him Lady Macbeth because of the way he scrubs his hands and all the medical students were laughing behind his back. Can you imagine such stupidity? They don't believe in germs, Emily. The fools must think that Pasteur is a place where cows graze. Anyway, Kent was fuming over the Lady Macbeth epithet and I told him how to capitalize on the joke. At first he refused to do it, but then he relented. Yesterday he strode into the amphitheater holding his hands up and shouting at the medical students in this gravelly falsetto, " 'All the perfumes of Arabia will not sweeten these little hands.' "

"You're joking!" Emily began to laugh.

"No, it's true. The students fell out of their chairs laughing, the chief surgeon turned red as a beet, and when everyone calmed down Kent began to roar that if they cared a whit about saving lives they would *all* do well to become Lady Macbeths. Then he went on with the operation. And no one has laughed at him since. True, they won't wash their hands, but at least they've stopped laughing."

"And this was all your idea?"

"Yes. And he'd better remember to acknowledge me when he tells the story."

Lady Macbeth was a very popular character. The tea group also mentioned her when describing women who were too ambitious for their husbands—or, even worse, for themselves. Diane was particularly concerned about one friend named Eleanor who had bought a jewelry business on Fourteenth Street. "I've got to *do* something before everyone starts excluding her," Diane said gravely one morning over coffee.

"Do something about what?" Emily asked.

"Eleanor. She doesn't realize what she's doing. It's not as though she were a widow and *had* to open a business. She's married. And to a rich man."

"But what has this to do with her selling jewelry?"

"She doesn't need the money."

"I still don't . . ."

"It's just not done. Don't you understand, Emily? She's *ambitious*. She's putting some poor man out of work, when she ought to be giving charity to his family."

"What 'poor man'?"

"A *man* could have bought that place. A breadwinner with *children*. And she bought it instead. I just can't understand it. She's such a nice person, really, and I must talk to her before she's ostracized."

Emily was confused. What was Diane saying? That a comfortably situated woman who worked was responsible for the starvation of children? It was all very puzzling. Money was worshiped more than God, but only if a man earned it. If a woman had a hand in garnering a fortune, the gold was tainted.

"Do you think her husband's greedy?" Emily asked.

"Her husband? Why, no. What are you . . ."

"Then why is Eleanor greedy?"

"Because she's already got a husband to support her."

"And this means she can't work?"

"Of *course* that's what it means. Why are you acting so naïve about all this? You know the way things are done, Emily. Men make money and women run charities."

"There's no law that says . . ."

"Of course there's no *law*," Diane snapped impatiently, "but it's an age-old tradition. It's just the way things are."

Emily wanted to retort, but arguments eluded her. It was true that this was an age-old tradition and that it had seemed to work in advancing civilization. Each person doing his or her special jobs, always knowing one's place, one's role. But something in Diane's logic disturbed her, though she could not determine what it was.

Emily was at pains not to mention again her "delightful little stint as a businesswoman." Good heavens, they must have thought her a predator! She couldn't very well tell them at this late date that her work had actually been necessary for survival. She'd already implied that she had been well-born. How had she gotten into such a mess to begin with? Why hadn't she simply told the truth? She did not know. Emily could no longer understand why she did many of the things she did.

CHAPTER 19

The children were growing up now. Young Bill, two years old, had a capacity for mischief that astonished even Rafe, whose own record for getting into precarious situations had been a favorite family complaint. Michael, at ten months, was learning how to walk and promised to follow in his brother's footsteps. The pair of them kept Emily busy, but she enjoyed motherhood. She read them stories, composed little songs, invented games for Bill and less advanced challenges for the baby. Her main problem in childrearing was establishing discipline. Yet the morality poems written for children made Emily shudder.

Let children that would fear the Lord
Hear what their teachers say:
With reverence hear their parent's word,
And with delight obey.

Have you not heard what dreadful plagues
Are threaten'd by the Lord
To him that breaks his father's laws,
Or mocks his mother's word?

What heavy guilt upon him lies!
How cursed is his name!
The ravens shall pick out his eyes,
And eagles eat the same.

But those that worship God, and give
Their parents honor due,
Here on this earth they long shall live,
And live hereafter too.

Emily eschewed such poems and continued to use less violent threats, such as, "If you don't pick up those toys you won't get any dessert."

The servant, Kitty, found it hard to hold her tongue if she happened to be around during one of Emily's discipline sessions. One day she suggested to her mistress that the boy would end up spoiled if Emily didn't find a workable method.

Emily was indignant. "I suppose *you* have all the answers?"

"Begging your pardon, Mrs. Taylor, but I'm thinking five minutes in the corner would work like magic."

"But he'll get restless."

Kitty grinned. "Ain't you *supposed* to be punishing him? Sitting him in a corner's better'n shouting at him. After two times he won't be hearing the shouting."

"He certainly hears my husband," Emily said. Rafe could command obedience by striking his officer's pose and bellowing, "There'll be no more glasses of water. Now get back to bed. Is that clear? Forward . . . march!"

Kitty said, "Your husband ain't around all day. And when he comes he's bigger and his voice is deeper. Try sitting Bill in a corner, Mrs. Taylor. Sure, you'll see the difference."

Emily tried Kitty's method and found that it only made Bill wilder when he was finally released from the chair. She then tried Rafe's army commands and discovered that not only Bill but Kitty too could not restrain their laughter. Finally she came up with a new idea. She could see to it that opportunities for mischief were kept at a minimum by remodeling the nursery so that Bill could mess it up to his heart's content. Step one would be to remove the baby from the room until he was old enough to become a fellow destroyer. Her approach was considered unique, and several other mothers were persuaded to try it. Soon Diane had a "disaster room" fixed up for her four-year-old daughter and Beth was making plans to do the same when her baby Kathy was old enough.

The subject of parenthood dominated the women's conversations, but pregnancy, Emily noted with astonishment, ran a close second. Even Beth gloried in remembered agonies, and there was one conversation that Emily was sure she would never forget. One noon when Beth managed to get away from the office, she dashed across the street in time to join Emily and Diane for lunch. Over roast beef sandwiches, of all things, the three began talking about their deliveries. Diane said that her daughter had been born in wartime while her first husband was in the service. How lucky Beth had been to have her husband not only there but delivering the baby too.

"Lucky!" Beth exclaimed. "Kent was more nervous than I was and Pat couldn't even hold the ether cone steady."

"At least you had ether," Emily said. "My doctor didn't want me to have any. I thought I'd die."

"How long was your labor, Emily?" Beth asked.

"About ten hours."

"Mine was twenty-one." Beth sat up straighter, as though proclaiming herself the victor in the agony contest.

Emily persisted. "But I didn't have ether. You can't imagine what it feels like to give birth without ether."

"I can." Diane shook her head in sympathy. "I didn't have any. My doctor thought it would kill the baby."

"Oh," Emily said, defeated. Not only had Diane been without a husband; she'd been without ether too. And Beth was still winning in the duration-of-labor contest. Now Emily thought of something else. "My second baby," she began, stressing the word "second," "was even more difficult that the first. There are after-pains with the second that I can't even begin to describe." Neither Beth nor Diane had had a second child.

But Beth wasn't listening. She had been panting to get a word in and now she said, "I was sure Kent was going to resort to a Caesarean, but he managed with forceps. It's a wonder the baby and I survived." She sighed.

"Yes," Diane said, taking a bite out of her roast beef sandwich. "Well, you're lucky to have a doctor for a husband."

"Lucky! Kent was so nervous . . ."

Diane interrupted. "You've already told us he was nervous."

Beth countered. "And you've told me twice how lucky I am."

Emily was still searching for something to trump the forceps story, but on hearing this icy exchange she began to laugh.

Beth turned her glare from Diane to Emily. "What's so funny?"

Emily was surprised. Couldn't Beth, who was more inclined than any of them to laugh at herself, see the humor in this conversation? But rather than point out how foolishly she thought they were all behaving, Emily lied. "I was laughing at—at the memory of the grandparents in front of the cradle. They would never let me near the baby."

With that the three began complaining about how grandparents spoiled children and the subject was dropped. But not for good. Never for good. On subsequent occasions Emily would find herself groaning, "Oh no, here comes Beth's forceps story again," or "How many times must I listen to Diane relate the tragedy of the husband in the service?" Yet all the while she foraged in her mind for some new horror with which to embellish her own tales. And finally, in desperation, she had to resort to the weather. "It was so cold on the night Michael was born. Have you ever seen a New England winter? Why the icicles are so long that they drive themselves into the ground. . . ."

Emily's days were a blaze of activity but her evenings and Sundays were becoming very quiet. Rafe couldn't abide her chatter of the women, nor could she tolerate his talk of pistons and brakes. Conversation had deteriorated to the point where the children was the only subject left. To be sure, it was a lively one, and they could share a hearty laugh about Bill's latest word or Michael's skill with his toy drums. They were both loving parents. Rafe liked to roughhouse with Bill, carrying him around on his shoulders, or tease the baby, waving his watch fob and watching him grab for it. Both of them were excited when Michael took his first steps; they congratulated each other on having brought such precocious and intelligent creatures into the world. Surely no one else's children could equal their sons.

But eventually the boys were put to bed and there were long evenings when the Taylors sat in the parlor reading and did not talk at all. She would look up from time to time, wondering how Rafe was able to tolerate this vacuum, but if he happened to catch her eye he would usually smile a contented smile as though to say, "Isn't the silence pleasant?" Apparently Rafe was not disturbed at all.

In bed he still made fervent love to her, but her response was not what it had been in the old days. This sometimes troubled her, for she missed those wonderful transports. But she took comfort from knowing that her diminished drive was part of the normal evolution from girl into mature woman. The mature woman considered carnal relations a necessary duty and was proud of her inability to take pleasure in the act. But if she tried to explain this to Rafe, he would give her no peace. Rafe subscribed to the uncommon opinion that women had the same capacity for pleasure as men did. Hadn't Emily proved this in the era of the pine woods and the dalliance on Laurel Street? Therefore, if she was losing that capacity, the fault must be his. Unless she was tired. Was she tired? Yes, said Emily over and over again. Better to tell him this than to watch him struggle to bring her to climaxes that took forever to achieve and were never as intense as they once had been.

But the Taylor marriage, though getting duller than she wanted to admit, was utopian by comparison to Pat Shepherd's situation. His quiet wife, they had learned from family sources, was that way by nature. No, she wasn't on opium and no, she did not dislike Pat's family and friends. She was simply shy and had been that way even when Pat was courting her. As to *why* Pat had courted her, everyone reasoned that Pat had come home from the war looking for someone to cure his emotional wounds. He had been a sensitive doctor, appalled by what he had seen, appalled by the number of bodies he had been forced to maim during his surgery. He had sought a gentle woman, whereas before the war he had preferred high-spirited and defiant types. And he had married Eileen. She must have lulled him like a mother and rocked him all the way to the altar. She had remained a luller and a rocker, but since Pat hadn't remained a child, problems had ensued. He had probably awakened one morning to realize that he had married a withdrawn young creature eager to love him but unable to communicate with him. A religious woman who attended Mass seven days a week, leaving Pat feeling guilty because he wasn't religious at all. In short, a vague shadowy figure, all goodness and devotion but not quite human. The antithesis, in fact, of the kind of woman he was ordinarily drawn to.

All this had been communicated to the Taylors by Beth and Diane, Beth's mother, a younger brother named Sean, and by others who were close to the situation. Pat himself had said nothing and Kent angrily refused to discuss the subject, but Joe had been known to corroborate the theory with a nod and a shrug.

One night in January Pat came over to prescribe some medication for young Bill, who was down with a cold. Later he sat in their parlor drinking whiskey after whiskey. Though his daily alcohol consumption was enormous, Pat functioned well and rarely got drunk. But tonight, perhaps because he felt comfortable in Rafe's presence, he was no longer watching his intake and was blurting out things he normally did not discuss. When Emily walked into the parlor with coffee to sober him up, he was rocking back and forth in his chair saying, "I know it, but I can't stop. And usually I don't drink this much anyhow."

"You've got to try, Pat," said Rafe.

"I have."

"Then for God's sake try to find the reason for it. You weren't this way in the army."

"There isn't any reason, Rafe. I just like whiskey."

"You're sure that's all?"

"It's not her fault!" Pat snapped, unaware that he himself had been the first to mention his wife. "She's a good woman. A saint."

"I know she's a good woman. But maybe you feel guilty because you're not happy with saintliness. That's why you . . ."

"No! You don't know what you're talking about. You don't know anything. Just leave me alone, for Christ's sake. Leave me *alone*!" Pat smashed his fist against the armrest of the chair.

At this point Rafe turned slightly and saw Emily standing in the doorway with the coffee. He frantically waved her out and she tiptoed from the room wondering what was going to happen. An hour later Rafe walked into their bedroom and said, "I had to ask you to leave, Em. He wouldn't have talked if you'd been there."

"I understand," said Emily. "Were you able to help?"

"Not much."

"It looks to me like he's trying to drink himself to death."

Rafe nodded.

"Why can't he get a divorce?"

"He doesn't want to hurt her," Rafe muttered.

"Then his bottle's become his lover?"

"His bottle and assorted street women he finds when he's on a binge."

Good God, she thought. The man's beyond hope.

Yet within a few days Emily would look to the troubled young doctor for help of her own. As it turned out, Bill did not have a cold. At first Pat told them it was "a form of tonsillitis." Tonsillitis, both parents knew, was not a serious disease, so they managed to stay calm through four days of rising fever and sore throat. Rafe went to work. Emily administered wet rubs and plasters. Both were sure that the trouble would end soon. But on the fifth night Bill was worse. His temperature was rising and his breathing was difficult. Pat came in at seven, examined him hastily, then used a syringe to clear out the throat. Bill gagged and then yelled, "Go 'way! Go 'way!" Emily stood there watching, holding fast to the child's hand. Rafe was quite pale. When Pat had completed the syringing he motioned both parents into the hall.

"I'll leave him alone for a minute," Pat said, trying to smile. "He's mad at me."

Rafe asked, "What kind of tonsillitis *is* this, Pat?"

"Well," Pat said, "at first I thought it was follicular but it's not, actually. It's—does the baby have any of these symptoms, by the way? Last night he seemed perfectly normal."

"I think he's getting a cold," Emily said.

"Let me check on him now before I . . ."

Rafe said, "Just a minute. We were talking about Bill."

Pat said, "It doesn't make sense. There's been no epidemic in this area."

"Epidemic of *what*?" Rafe demanded.

"Well, I didn't want to discuss this until I was sure beyond a doubt . . ."

Rafe was almost shouting. "Will you *tell* us, for God's sake?"

Pat turned to Emily. "Have you kept the baby isolated? You remember that I told you . . ."

"Yes, I have. Please, Pat, tell us!"

Pat looked at the floor and then mumbled, "Bill has diphtheria."

Emily gasped and Rafe exclaimed, "Diphtheria!"

"Please try to be calm. Many children survive diphtheria," Pat said in reassuring doctor tones. "And in Bill's case we're lucky. The membrane hasn't spread too far."

"What does *that* mean?" Rafe asked.

"It means Kent can probably do surgery."

"Surgery!" Rafe shouted.

"It may be necessary. We'll wait a while, of course, but the membrane is blocking the trachea—the windpipe—and surgery may be indicated. Now let me check the baby." And Pat strode quickly down the hall.

Emily rushed into the room where Bill was tossing. She was breathing hard from the shock and fighting tears.

Bill muttered, "Mama, my throat. Hurts bad. My throat." He was gasping for air.

She pressed cloths against his feverish forehead and said, "I know, dear. I know."

Rafe entered the room behind her and stood at the foot of the small bed, his fists clenched into tight balls. When Pat came in a few minutes later, he hissed, "Do something! Please, Pat!"

"I've sent your maid for Kent," Pat whispered. "Try to stay calm, Rafe."

"What will Kent do?"

"Puncture the windpipe. That's all."

"Then he'll be able to breathe?" Rafe whispered.

"Yes."

"Thank God." Rafe exhaled loudly. "Is the baby all right?"

"Catarrh and swollen lymph glands."

"Not diphtheria!" Rafe hissed.

"It could be, Rafe. The symptoms differ from child to child. It could also be a cold, so let's tell Emily it's a cold until we're sure."

"All right."

Emily heard the two whispering but did not want to call Bill's attention to the fact. She walked to the foot of the bed and stood with them.

"Kent's on the way," Pat said. "And the baby's got a cold. Everything's under control. Don't worry. I wanted to send for Beth too but frankly, Emily, we can't have her exposed. She might bring it home to the baby."

Emily nodded absently, not really hearing him, and Pat walked over to Bill. He said in a soothing voice, "Here, I have something to make you feel better."

"No! No me-cine!" The little boy was choking but his mental powers had not abandoned him and he refused to swallow Pat's foul-tasting nostrums.

Pat bent over the boy, holding the bottle of medicine and a spoon. He said, "Did I ever tell you about the time your papa got sick in the army and wouldn't take his medicine?"

"No," said Bill.

"Well, he wouldn't. Dr. Kent and I had to hold him down."

"Papa wouldn't take me-cine?" The child smiled with delight. He was just like his papa.

Pat turned. "Isn't that right, Rafe?"

Rafe could barely talk but he managed to say, "That's right." He was puzzled. What was Pat trying to do? Make the child sicker by pointing out that his father too disdained remedies?

"I bet you'd still be afraid to take it," Pat continued. "I'll bet Bill can do better than you can."

Nor Rafe understood. "Better than me? He's only two and a half. I'm a grown man."

"You may be a grown man but you act like a baby when you have to take medicine."

"I do not."

"You do so. I'll prove it." Pat held out a teaspoon of the murky concoction. "I'll bet you can't even swallow it."

Rafe made a face, rolled his eyes, opened his mouth, took the bitter brew, then grimaced, groaned, rolled his head, and finally exclaimed, "I did it!"

"That was only a teaspoon," Pat said. "And you made a face. I'll bet Bill here can take two teaspoons and not make a face."

"I'll bet he can't," said Rafe.

But Bill murmured, "Yes, I can," and with that Pat shoved the medicine into his mouth, clapping and shouting, "Ha! You did better than your papa!"

Pat was so cheerful and Rafe such a good actor that Emily was lulled into optimism. Surely they didn't expect Bill to die if they could carry on like this. And Pat said that children could survive diphtheria. Certainly he believed that Bill would be one of them.

But even as she stood there, Bill was getting worse. His face was almost blue now, and the effort of breathing was so exhausting him that he no longer had the strength to speak. He simply lay there making agonized wheezing sounds and she thought he was going to die.

It was then that Kent rushed in, windblown, snow all over his hair and coat. He carried a medical bag in one hand and three nested basins in the other. Still holding the paraphernalia, he walked over to Bill, looked down, and frowned. Then he placed the basins on a bureau, filled each one with a solution of carbolic acid, dropped instruments into the first one, and tossed off his coat. Only then did he greet Rafe and Emily. "We'll do what we can," he said, putting on a surgical smock. "But if you insist on staying in here, then face the wall. I don't want any fainting." He turned to Pat who was searching through his own medical bag. "Got the chloroform?"

"Yes."

"All right. Let's see what's going on." Kent walked over to the child, gently removed the nightshirt, examined his throat, listened to the heartbeat, held his fingers over the nostrils, nodded, and then held the child down by the shoulders. He said, "The bare minimum, Pat," and Pat dripped chloroform through a cone. Bill struggled briefly, then was still. Kent again ordered Rafe and Emily to face the wall. This time they obeyed. Out of the corner of her eye, Emily could see the doctors at the bureau, plunging their hands into the basins. She saw Pat holding a wad of lint. Then they disappeared behind her. Rafe clasped her hand. For a while they heard only Bill's labored breathing. Then they heard Kent's muttered words: "There . . . all right . . . watch that retractor, Pat . . . good . . . he's coughing, coughing . . . watch it, *watch* it, Pat. Did you get any on you?"

"No," Pat said.

"Damn stuff is deadly. All right. Let's see . . . looks good . . . wait a minute . . . all right."

The parents heard Bill cough and they sighed in relief just to know he was still alive. There were more coughs, then silence. They heard Pat murmur, "Color's normal already." In a louder voice he said, "You may turn around, folks."

The parents rushed over to the bedside. They expected to see blood all over their son, all over the sheets. What they saw was a neat throat incision. Bill was sleeping soundly, breathing regularly, and his color was good. They turned to the doctors. Emily had tears in her eyes. She said, "Will he live, Kent?"

Kent mopped at his brow. "I think so." There were many possible complications with diphtheria but Kent felt no impulse to recite them. That was Pat's department.

Emily asked Kent, "And if the baby gets it, will you be able to do the same . . ."

"I don't know," Kent said. "Let's not worry about that now."

"Oh, how can I thank you!" she cried. "Both of you! I never thought you'd save him."

"Do you mean to tell me," Pat said smiling, "that you had no faith in the medical profession?"

"I didn't mean . . ."

"Why, we were the best doctors in the whole Union Army," Pat declared.

"And well known for our humility too," Kent said.

For once Rafe could not be lighthearted. He said, "This is a miracle."

As far as Pat was concerned, it *was* a miracle. For children with Bill's symptoms the mortality rate was 80 to 90 percent. But his thoughts were now on the baby, and while Kent cleaned up, Pat sneaked down the hall to examine Michael. He returned in a few minutes betraying no signs of alarm. Instead he suggested that Emily get some sleep before she wore herself down to the point where she was too sick to care for Bill. To speed her slumber along he gave her a dose of laudanum and told Rafe to march her downstairs to bed. It was now past eight o'clock.

When they had gone, Pat said to Kent, "The baby's getting worse. Vomiting, High temp. A very abrupt onset. That's typical in the younger ones. Last night he wasn't even *sick*."

"Any membrane?"

"Very little. In this disease every goddamn case has a different set of symptoms. He could die tonight or linger a week. He could suddenly get well and then die in three weeks of myocarditis. Or he could develop the membrane and have it punctured by you and either live for two minutes or eighty years. You never know."

The doctors made quick work of cleaning up. Kitty came in to sit in the armchair next to Bill's bed. She would stay here all night. She said, "You'll be seeing to the baby now?"

"Yes," Pat said.

"He's very sick. Will you be staying, doctor?"

"All night, if need be."

"God bless you, doctor." And turning to Kent she said, "Both of you."

The men walked down the hall to the nursery. Michael's temperature was very high and he was shuddering from chills. His glands were so swollen that he looked as though he had the mumps. While Pat foraged in his bag for medications, Kent suddenly lifted the baby from the crib and pressed his ear against the chest. He waited, holding his breath.

Pat looked up. "How bad?" he asked.

"No heartbeat."

"*No* heartbeat?"

"Shhh." Kent listened again. Listened. Set the baby down.

Pat stood at the crib and looked at the child, his mouth agape.

Kent said, "Must've been a coronary embolism. Can't think of what else could have . . ."

Pat said, "Embolisms are common. *Anything* can happen with this goddamned disease! I'd rather fight the plague than a case of diphtheria." He shook his head. "Christ, it was so *fast*."

Kent sighed. "Where's Rafe?"

"Putting Emily to bed."

"She's already asleep," said Rafe, entering the room. "How's Michael?"

Kent and Pat exchanged glances.

"How's Michael?" Rafe repeated, walking over to the crib. He looked down, touched the baby's arm, then looked at him sharply. Rafe's heart began to hammer. Why wasn't he breathing? Without turning to the doctors for confirmation, Rafe felt for the child's pulse. Then he stood up straight but did not turn around. He studied the baby for a long time. And when he turned Kent could see in Rafe's face the same dead expression he had seen in the tent at Spotsylvania.

"I'm sorry," Pat said, leading Rafe to a chair and sitting him down.

"It was very sudden . . ." Kent began, then broke off.

Rafe looked past them, his eyes blank, his lips slightly parted. Neither doctor moved and no one spoke. Pat reached into his bag for a flask of whiskey and offered it to Rafe. Rafe shook his head in refusal. Then he said, "I won't tell her until morning. She needs the sleep."

Pat nodded.

"She needs some sleep," Rafe repeated.

"Yes," said Pat.

But Emily did not sleep long. At ten that night, while Kent and Pat were down in the library trying to get Rafe drunk, she put on a robe and padded up the stairs to Bill's room. Kitty slept in the armchair beside him. Emily leaned over the bed, touched the child's cheek, and smiled. He looked good. She was sure he was going to live. Next she walked back toward the nursery and saw Pat coming up the steps.

"You're awake," Pat said.

"Yes."

"You're supposed to be asleep."

"But I'm not," she smiled. "I want to look in on the baby."

Pat positioned himself in front of the nursery door and called down the stairs for Rafe.

"Is something wrong, Pat?" Her first thought was that the poor man looked exhausted and had drunk too much. She too must help Pat in his struggle with alcohol. "Are you ill, Pat?"

He did not have to answer the question, for Rafe was now at the foot of the stairs. He bounded up, taking the steps two at a time. He too looked drunk and his eyes were even redder than Pat's. He said, "Why aren't you asleep?"

"I couldn't sleep. I can never sleep when the children are ill. But Bill looks better, so as soon as I check on the baby's cold, I'll try again."

Pat had disappeared into Bill's room to check his condition. Rafe and Emily stood alone in front of the nursery.

"The baby had diphtheria," Rafe said dully.

Emily did not notice the tense Rafe had used. She only nodded. She had half-expected that he might develop the disease, but had been sure Kent could perform a similar operation.

"He was very ill," Rafe continued. "The attack began abruptly and caused a heart—caused a heart failure."

She stared at him in disbelief, moving her head from side to side as though shaking it. He reached out to grab her, for he thought she was about to faint. But she turned swiftly, opened the door to the nursery, and strode over to the crib. No one had drawn a blanket over Michael's face, so at first he appeared to be sleeping. But he wasn't moving, wasn't breathing, and when she bent down to lift him, he was rigid and cold. She picked him up anyway, hugged him to her, then began to cry. Rafe gently removed the baby from her arms and led her back to their room. He sat on the bed holding her. She was sobbing and he hoped she would continue to weep until she was so exhausted that she sank into sleep. As he held her and stroked her hair, he kept thinking there was a force in the world that seemed bent on taking away everything he loved. But it wouldn't get Emily. He would see to that somehow. He rocked her in his arms, and held her more firmly.

She was thinking of the day Michael had been born. He had been the second, and people hadn't paid so much attention. So she had treated him as special. How many nights had she suffered with him through the colic? How many more through the teething? And where had she been when he needed her most? Asleep. Would he have lived if she had been there to hold the chubby arm and coax the crooked grin that was so much like Rafe's? Would he have fought off the disease and lived? Reason told her that it wouldn't have made any difference, but she wanted to think of him as he had been earlier today, kicking at his blue blankets and yelling for her to take him out of bed so that he could practice his new art—walking. Then she realized that he would never walk again, would never pull himself up in the crib or wave his arms for food, or smile, or cry. She wanted to hear him cry, longed for his outraged demands for food, for the angry pounding on the headboard that always brought her at a run with the sharp words, "You're as patient as your father!"

No more comparisons with Rafe. No more wondering what Michael's future would be. No more fears of spoiling him or bringing him up wrong. And no more dreams that he would be a president or a Beethoven or just a gentle human being. No more.

It was one o'clock of a bitter January afternoon. In the parlor the grandparents sat with the parents. They had arrived the night before. In the kitchen Beth was giving instructions to Kitty and to her own maid who had come to help. In Bill's room Pat had just dispensed the hated medication and was now foraging in his bag for the flask containing his own "medication." Coming in the door to pay their respects following the funeral were Kent, Diane, Joe, and other friends and neighbors. It was the ritual of death, the unbearable made bearable by distractions, the never-to-be-forgotten soon to be forgotten in the commotion. Emily had been afraid that she might not be able to stand it. But the stoicism on which she prided herself had lasted through the funeral and did not fail her in this hour.

Several women were whispering to each other, wondering why Emily felt it necessary to hold her emotions in check. And Beth, walking into the parlor, heard their thoughts. What was the fun of a funeral if there were no shrieks and sobs from the distraught mother?

Caroline, of Queen Anne chair fame, was more interested in who the mourners were than in the ways they manifested their grief. Her eyes fell on Charles and Marie Taylor, and she nodded as if to say, "Yes, they do look as though they'd be at ease with the Lowells." But her reaction to Matt Stevens was astonishment. She turned to Beth and drawled, "I gather that Emily's pedigree is not so distinguished as her husband's."

Beth was not certain she had heard correctly. "What did you say, Caroline?"

"Nothing."

"Did you ask me about Emily's *pedigree*?"

Caroline blushed and turned away.

"At a time like this?" Beth edged over and stepped on the hem of Caroline's skirt. "Come," she said for the benefit of onlookers who had been busy talking and hadn't heard the exchange. "Come help me with the servants, Caroline."

None of the others was aware of what was happening and Caroline was not about to risk ruining her gorgeous black silk by attempting resistance. She nodded, "I'm coming," and Beth removed her foot from the trailing skirt. Caroline exited into the hall with Beth breathing down her neck. She retrieved her wrap and started down the stairs to the street. Beth was hard behind, seized by the impulse to kick her into the gutter.

Outside on the sidewalk, Caroline turned on her. "How dare you! How dare you threaten me in front of all those people."

"Get out of here!" Beth shouted, then lowered her voice because they were attracting the attention of a passing pedestrian. "Don't you ever set foot in our houses again."

" 'Our houses!' How exclusive we are all of a sudden. The great Elizabeth Wilson, daughter of an Irish immigrant. And the magnificent Emily Taylor, graduate of a barnyard."

"You bitch," Beth growled.

"Elizabeth Wilson. Eloquent to a fault. No need for gutter language, Beth. You don't frighten me. No, and you don't intimidate me either with all your self-righteous posturing. Remember this, my friend. It was you and Emily who started it. The poseur and her gallant defender running on about Boston society."

"If we did it was only because you drove us to it. You're pathetic, Caroline. You have no other values to fall back on. Whereas Emily . . ."

"Whereas Emily is pretentious and evasive and transparent as glass."

Behind them a deep voice cut through the cold. "Beth, for Christ's sake get inside before you catch pneumonia."

It was Kent. Beth was furious with him for daring to interrupt her just as she was warming to a devastating retort. Caroline seized the opportunity to escape, and Beth stomped over to her husband. "How long have you been standing here?"

"Long enough," he muttered, taking her arm and steering her up the stairs into Emily's house. "I came out to smoke my pipe in peace."

"Oh, poor Kent," she mocked. "To be deprived of your precious peace and quiet."

"Don't turn your cat fights on me!" He slammed the door behind him.

"Cat fights!" she hissed, lowering her voice so that the mourners in the parlor could not hear her.

"Yes." He too lowered his voice. "What other name would you give to the likes of that? 'Irish immigrant . . . graduate of a barnyard'—Why are women so obsessed with people's backgrounds? What does it matter what Emily's history is or how other women judge it? I cannot for the life of me understand why you *or* Emily feel it necessary to justify this. You waste your lives defending things that don't *matter*."

Kent stopped talking. Beth had begun to cry. It was grief for Emily combined with outrage at Caroline's cruelty. Kent's remarks had simply been the last straw. She had burst into tears before hearing the words "You waste your lives defending things that don't matter." But Kent, thinking she *had* heard them and that this was why she was weeping, hastened to make amends. "Please don't cry, Beth. I didn't mean *you* waste your life the way most of them do. I don't mean you," he said again, thrusting a handkerchief at her.

Beth heard none of this. She was thinking of the things she should have said to Caroline and sobbing with rage. Kent was upset. He had hurt her deeply, he thought, clenching his fists. Why couldn't he learn to think before speaking? It was cruel to point out that women had only a limited contribution to make to the world of progress and ideas. This was why they spent so much time inventing foolish games about status. It was to keep them busy, to satisfy their need for competition. A natural instinct, competition, no matter what form it took. Too bad women did not—or could not because of society's strictures—put their brains to some useful purpose. But Beth had used her fine mind helping him. She had competed against the forces of nature to fight disease. He said, "You, after all, fight in *real* contests. What I said about wasting lives certainly doesn't apply to you."

"What?" She was still crying.

"Haven't you been listening?"

"No," she snapped. "I haven't heard a word since 'cat fights.' Furthermore I won't listen to *another* word!"

"How about, 'I'm sorry'?"

"*That* I will listen to."

And they walked back into the parlor, Kent sighing in relief

Mary stayed in New York with Emily for a while, assuming the responsibility for keeping Bill in bed until his convalescence was complete. Pat, who worried about complications, was most insistent that Bill not move from the bed for two weeks following the surgery, until every symptom had disappeared. The child did not know that his brother was dead (nor should he know, Pat warned, until he was up and about). Bill kept asking to see Michael. Mary would tell him that Michael was sleeping or that he had a cold, or that he was eating supper. Then she would distract him with a game or a story.

Emily was grateful for Mary's presence. She alone could not have handled the pleas for Mike. Nor could Kitty. Emily cried a good deal when not in the public eye, though she tried to be strong for Rafe.

They finally told Bill that Michael had died and that dying meant going to a far-off land to live among the birds and flowers. Bill sobbed when he heard that his brother had deserted him. Rafe was not equipped to give his son a satisfactory reason for the sudden departure, so Emily explained that all people eventually returned to nature but that Michael had elected to leave early. Bill didn't think Michael was bright enough to make such decisions, but after thinking about it he said, "I guess I teached him to be smart too."

And Emily said, "You did, and he was very grateful."

The arrival of Matt and Mary Stevens had caused comment among several women in the tea group, and in the weeks following the funeral, after Mary had gone home, they discussed the matter among themselves. It was obvious that Emily had been guilty of the sin of omission in describing her background. She hadn't exactly lied, they agreed. She *had* said that Matt had done farming and tinkered with his tools. But they'd been left with the impression of an eclectic, well-read Jeffersonian character, not the plain, tipsy, little-educated man they had met. They were angry over having been misled. Beth explained to Diane, who explained to the tea group, that Emily was guilty of nothing more heinous than editing her history in order to belong. She'd been afraid that New York might reject her, Beth declared, and there wasn't a woman or man alive who hadn't at one time or another resorted to similar ruses in order to be accepted.

Emily knew nothing of these discussions. At the funeral she had been too distressed to consider that sharp eyes might be drawing all sorts of conclusions about her. At the time Matt had simply been her father. She did not see a man who had drunk half a bottle of Pat's whiskey and who, in his grief, was murmuring drunken, incoherent sentences. She saw only the father she loved. And Mary was her gentle stepmother who was not aware of the overly correct observations of "manner" that betrayed a woman who had not been born to the same. But the onlookers had been very aware indeed. Middle-class to a fault, they set more store by these matters than did the more secure wealthy. And they were nonplussed when Emily emerged from the ordeal behaving much as she had before. How could she not realize that she had been *found out*, they wondered as they paid their customary calls.

But their hearts were forgiving. Emily had, after all, flattered them immensely by having gone to such lengths to p ase them. Caroline might see her as a counterfeit and a liar. The others saw her as Cinderella who, despite her high-born prince, still remained Cinderella. They could like her more now that they were securely superior.

Emily did not notice these changed attitudes. In the months following the funeral her mind was on one thing only: bringing more children into the world.

It was a need that both Diane and Beth could understand—especially in a mother who had just lost a child. Diane was obsessed with the need for more children. She had suffered one miscarriage since marrying Joe. Beth, though not obsessed, did want at least one more to be a companion for Kathy. They listened with full understanding to Emily's discourses on the joys of motherhood, which joys were increasing as little Bill moved from infancy to the age of comprehension.

"Do you know what I've discovered?" Emily said to them one day. "The whole of a woman's life is charted in her baby's first cry. Think of it. It means the mother is never again a separate person. Part of her is given over to the child the moment he is born. She's no longer alone. Nor will she ever be. If the child lives, she lives through him. If the child dies"—here her voice caught—"a part of her dies too. She has no sense of being an individual the way a man does. Rafe, for example, is a wonderful father but one thinks of him not as a father but as Rafe. I, on the other hand, am Bill's mother. Only incidentally does one think of me as Emily. Parts of me are gone, you see. Through my motherhood." She paused. "It's an awesome thought."

"A frightening one," Beth said. "I like to think that I'm intact."

"But you're not," Emily said. "Don't let the thought upset you, though. Think instead of the power women have. Yes, a mother does lose part of herself. But consider what she gains. Consider what she does for mankind. She nurtures and rears children who will carry on not only her dreams but the dreams of the father, the grandparents, all the antecedents to the beginning of time. Giving birth is insurance that a branch of the human tree will never die."

Emily elaborated on this theme until Diane grew misty-eyed from the implications. What, after all, was more important than the quality of generations to come? And who had control of this vital function? "Women!" she exclaimed to her husband later, as though this was a revolutionary new idea. And Joseph, who found the act of making children more immediately satisfying than the distant idea of generations, solemnly agreed.

The person most moved by Emily's hand-that-rocks-the-cradle-rules-the-world view of motherhood was of course her husband. He craved the sounds of little people. To him they evoked youth, innocence, laughter, and the peace that had suffused him before the war came along to shatter everything. His two little boys had given him a second chance to enjoy those happy times. And the death of his second son had shattered him.

In May, 1868, Pat Shepherd informed Emily that she was in the family way. It was a moment more poignant than the moment predicting young Bill's arrival. Then she had had dreams for the baby but they had been abstract fancies of a little girl in velvet dresses growing up to marry another Rafe. Now she was experienced—a professional mother, a woman aware of the phases of childrearing and the expertise required to cope with them. There was no greater challenge in life, Emily thought. And she was equal to it, anxious to undertake it. She would fill the sad house on Tenth Street with love and laughter.

PART 5

CHAPTER 20

By January, 1873, Emily and Rafe had five children: Bill (seven), Nicky (six), Peggy (four), David (two), and Adam (six months). Nicky had been adopted the year after Peggy was born. Emily remembered the date one winter afternoon as she went through her files looking for a misplaced meat bill and unearthed the boy's adoption papers. In those days, with only two children and a full complement of servants, she had become heavily involved in charity work—mostly with destitute adults and occasionally at a downtown orphanage. Rafe had found out that she was spending many afternoons in an area called The Five Points, the most notorious slum in all America. He had raged like a madman. Didn't she realize she could get *killed* down there? Well *of course* he approved of charities, but he was more concerned with keeping his wife alive. Couldn't she stay home and mend clothes for the poor or make Christmas toy collections on Fifth Avenue? Sighing, she had acceded to his wishes and had limited her movements to safe places. But she could not forget a brown-haired child who had been left one morning at the entrance to the orphanage and went by the name of

Nicky. She had asked Rafe if they could adopt him. At first she thought he had said yes only to placate her. But after taking one look at the urchins in the squalid place, he had muttered, "I wish we could adopt them all."

Emily put the adoption papers back into their envelope and continued to search for the meat bill. When Rafe had imposed limits on her charity work, she had plunged into childbearing and house maintenance with zeal. Two inefficient servants had been let go; the staff was down to Kitty and one housemaid named Moira. Emily did not want or need any others and retained nurses only for lyings-in. What was the point of servants if they usurped responsibility for everything and left the lady of the house feeling useless?

Before Emily could locate the meat bill, Moira came into the library and announced Mrs. Shepherd and Mrs. Mason. This meant Diane and their mutual friend Joan Mason, the wife of an attorney. Since the desk in the library was a mess, Emily would receive these two friends in the parlor. She told Moira to bring some tea and the remains of Kitty's magnificent fruitcake, left from Christmas.

Adam, David, and Peggy were napping; Bill and Nicky were at school. Emily had an hour in which to entertain before she would have to nurse Adam.

The talk was the usual talk. Diane complained about Joe's work schedule; Joan complained about the cost of keeping little girls in clothes. (Diane had two girls and Joan three.) Diane grumbled that her laundress had been two days overdue this week. There was a discussion about the new fashions and how women had to have perfectly flat stomachs to wear dresses with all that gathering in the back. How could women who had borne children have stomachs like that? wondered Diane (blonde and plump) and Joan (dark and plump). There were corsets, of course, but if a woman was too fat, whalebone stays were just as painful as steel ones. And both of them were too fat. And both envied Emily because she wasn't. Why wasn't she?

"I don't know," Emily explained almost apologetically. "I've always been thin. Even where I wish I were fat." She did not mention her breasts, but both women knew which part of the anatomy she was referring to.

The conversation now moved to the subject of getting money out of stingy husbands.

"Don't tell this to Beth," Diane cautioned Emily, "but I tried a new trick to get a dress from her brother."

Emily had never been able to determine whether Joe was cheap or Diane a spendthrift, for the only side of the story she ever heard was Diane's.

Diane said, "You know that blue taffeta I'm always wearing to charity balls?"

"Which blue taffeta?"

"How could you not remember? You've seen it so often I'm surprised you don't call me Taffeta Shepherd! The dress with that stupid bow on the train."

"Oh, *that* one." It was ugly, Emily thought. She wondered why Diane had bought it in the first place.

"Well, mercy, I'm just so *tired* of it! I told Joe I wanted a new velvet gown. There's the most marvelous new dressmaker on Thirteenth. Madame DuMonte. Terribly expensive, but straight from Paris and I just had to impress upon Joe the importance of having a DuMonte dress."

"And?" Emily asked.

"I tried being sweet. He wasn't in the least moved. I tried being logical. That was even worse. Finally Joan and I were invited to that Danworth affair"—she beamed at Joan—"and I asked my friend here if she'd comment loudly—in Joe's presence—on what a frump poor Diane had become. She did. And of course Joe and I 'overheard' her. And today"— Diane laughed—"I have an appointment with Madame DuMonte."

Joan said, "Now your husband's mad at *me* and can't understand why you still like me! That's the last time we'll do *that*, Diane." Joan sighed.

Emily cut in, annoyed. "You wouldn't have these problems if you'd just learn to balance your budget. Your husband would be so pleased that any extra money for a dress would be given cheerfully."

Diane pouted. "Oh, I'm so tired of listening to your complicated mathematical formulas on budgets, Emily. They don't ever work for me."

Joan said, "And you spend so much time at those books

that it hardly seems worth the effort."

"I don't spend that much time," Emily said. "And it isn't an effort. Rafe handles all special bills like medical accounts, birthday and Christmas gifts. All I handle are routine household expenses. It's a challenge seeing how much I can save by the end of a month."

"A challenge!" Joan's look was incredulous.

"Yes," Emily said. "It's rather like running a business. Instead of earning profits, one earns savings. I've been putting money into a special emergency fund for more than two years now."

"We know," Diane said. "And we can't understand why you don't salt it away and spend it on yourself the way every sensible woman does."

"Because then it would be gone," Emily said.

"What do you mean 'gone'?" Joan asked. "Think of all the bonnets you could buy."

"Money in the bank is more valuable than bonnets," Emily said.

"Why?" asked Diane, perplexed.

"It just *is*. Any businessman can tell you that a bank account . . ."

"Well, if it's business you want," Joan said, "why not set up an awning over the steps and sell the children's castoffs?"

Both women laughed. Emily did not laugh. For months she had derived great satisfaction from putting a dollar or more a week into her fund. Toward this end she had spent hours hunting down bargains or sending the servants to distant greengrocers, all so that she might save odd amounts like eleven cents. When Adam was born, she had approached Rafe gravely and asked for a suitable increment. He had said that since she never squandered money he would give her what she wanted when she wanted it. But she had refused. She would run the house like a business, and good businessmen did not accept charity. Rafe had been more puzzled than pleased by her thrifty independence, but he had given her the increment she asked for. She had continued to save. The total in the bank, after two years, was only $103. It could hardly cover any real emergency, but the money was tangible evidence of her efficiency as a housewife and she was as proud of this as of the $75 left over from her single days. But neither of her friends would understand this, so she dropped the subject.

The women droned on about other matters. They spent five minutes trying to remember the year Beth's son Douglas had been born. Was it '68 or '69? It had been winter, but which half of the winter? And finally they remembered that it had been '69.

Emily recalled Mrs. Harrington's visit a week earlier. The elderly widow had breezed in one afternoon between trains (from Washington bound for Boston) and had also reminisced about years past. But her focus had been different. According to Mrs. Harrington, the major event of '68 had been Andrew Johnson's acquittal; of '69, the completion of the transcontinental railroad; of '70, the passage of the Fifteenth Amendment; of '71, the arrest of Tweed; of '72, the General Amnesty Act for all but the leading Confederates. As Diane and Joan chatted on, Emily began to yearn for a refreshing breath of Harrington.

Diane and Joan were now discussing a mutual acquaintance who had shocked everyone by wearing a walking dress to an evening affair. Concealing a yawn, Emily announced that it was time to nurse the baby. As soon as the women had left she went back to look for the missing meat bill. Finding it at last under a heap of bakery accounts, she filed it in its proper place and did some swift calculations. She'd saved $1.17 this week. The total in the emergency fund was now more than $104. Emily was pleased.

The older children came barging in from school at four o'clock. This was always a pleasant part of Emily's day, for unlike her mother-in-law Emily liked the questioning phase of a child's development, the endless "whys" that enabled her to teach them thoughtfully about life. She and the boys went down to the kitchen where Peggy, four, was already "helping" Kitty with dinner. The boys had cookies and milk. Emily had tea. She asked Bill, the oldest, what he had learned in school today.

"We're learning about mammals," Bill said, talking with his mouth full.

"Oh, really? Did you know that whales were mammals even though they live in water?"

"Uh huh. Teacher told us."

"Mammals are warm-blooded animals," Emily continued. "Their hearts have four cavities. This distinguishes them from reptiles. Now birds, of course, also have warm blood but the internal structure of their bodies differs from that of mammals. Dr. Pat has a book that explains . . ."

"I know, Mama," Bill sighed. "The teacher told us about birds and all that." He took another cookie. "Can Nicky and I go out and play? It's not too cold."

"Well, *that's* something you don't know," Emily snapped. "Your *grammar*. It's *may* Nicky and I go out and play."

Kitty turned from the stove and smiled. "Sure there are a few things you can still be teachin' 'em."

Emily did not smile back. She waved the boys out and said yes, Peggy could go too. Then she turned to the cook and sighed. "The schools have taken over my job."

"And ain't that what they're for?" Kitty said agreeably, giving the soup another stir.

"My work will end when the baby is six," Emily said glumly.

"I wouldn't be saying that. It'll *start* to end maybe."

"Shall I keep having babies until I'm past childbearing age?"

"And why would you be wanting so many children?"

"So I'll always have someone to raise," Emily said. "It's hard to imagine, with a baby still not weaned, that the day will come when they're all grown up."

"Ah, but life will be so peaceful, Mrs. Taylor."

"Peaceful," Emily repeated. "Yes, I suppose it will." But what was she going to do with all that peace? Talk to Diane and Joan all day long? Work in safe charities doing safe work? Perhaps she should have another baby.

Rafe came home at seven, tired and preoccupied, muttering about some workman who had misplaced the diagrams for a new locomotive model. They had finally found the damned things after a three-hour search but work had been halted, time lost. Emily listened, glassy-eyed, hoping he'd tell her something exciting. News of the Westinghouse air brake, a miraculous safety measure, had absorbed her interest some years before. But there was little else in the technical area that she could appreciate. Changes in gauge sizes meant nothing to her since she could not go to the plant and see the results of these minor alterations. And Rafe, knowing how disinterested she was, went upstairs to change for dinner.

They were both thirty-two years old, and since both had darkish blonde hair, the occasional gray strands went unnoticed. In appearance they seemed no older than twenty-four and indeed looked much as they had on their wedding day. She remarked this fact as she saw him climb the stairs. Rarely did she study Rafe this closely. But tonight, possibly because of her chat with Kitty, she was in a pensive mood. As Moira settled the oldest children around the dining-room table and carried two trays up to the nursery, Emily stood at the window looking out onto the mews, remembering those days in the pine room; sneaking out of the store, skimming over the fields and into the woods to meet Rafe. How exciting those weeks had been!

At dinner Rafe reminded them that tomorrow he would be leaving on his trip to Philadelphia. Two of the firm's engines weren't functioning properly, and the railroad men were demanding that an engineer come down and do something. So Rafe had packed charts, instruction books for mechanics, and enough changes of clothing for a two-week stay. He always tried to keep these trips short, but problems were forever cropping up and two weeks seemed to be about average. He made two or three such trips a year and spent his time worrying about the things that might happen while he was away. The children might get sick and die, Emily might decide to visit some charity in the bloody Sixth Ward and get stabbed. The house might burn down, the laborers might rise and reenact the Draft Riots of '63. He was always relieved to walk in the door and find things just as he had left them.

Tonight the family endured his pre-trip litany:

"Bill and Nicky, you're not to cross the street unless an adult accompanies you."

"Yes, Papa," the boys chorused.

"A little boy on Twelfth Street was trampled by a horse last week."

"Yes, Papa."

"Peggy, you are not to sass your mother or the servants."

"Yes, Papa."

"All three of you are to keep an eye on David and Adam."

"Yes, Papa."

"And listen to your mother."

"Yes, Papa."

"Emily, would you pass the potatoes?"

"Yes, Papa," said Emily absently.

Bill and Nicky were consumed with guffaws. Peggy's soup sprayed across the table. Rafe threw Emily a devastating look which said, "How dare you make me look the fool in front of the children!"

Emily glared at the children who were still roaring. "That was *not* a joke," she said sternly. "I said 'Papa' by mistake." She took her napkin and sopped up Peggy's soup.

The rest of the meal was consumed in silence. But over dessert Rafe said gently, "I know you couldn't help laughing at your mother's mistake. But you must realize that this is a serious matter."

"Yes, Papa." Peggy dared to smile. She was four, the only girl, and Rafe's darling. She was also Emily's delight because she was high-spirited and had a keen sense of humor. Rafe complained that Emily spoiled her, letting her get away with antics that the boys would have been punished for. But Rafe was even more lenient.

Rafe now rang for the servants and said, "We will review the instructions for what to do in the event of a fire."

Emily groaned inwardly. Though Rafe struggled constantly to forget the war, he never attempted to undo his military training. She sat through the children's and the servants' recital of actions to take when the house burst into flames and hoped he would not go on to prepare them for floods, pestilences, and attacks of invaders from New Jersey.

The children passed the oral quiz on fires and Rafe dismissed them along with the servants. He said to Emily, "Sorry I lost my temper earlier."

"It's all right."

"You know I loathe these trips."

"I know."

"You've got the name of the hotel?"

"Yes?"

"And you'll wire me if anything goes wrong?"

"Yes."

"Kent is right across the street if you need any help."

"Rafe, he's been there since we moved to New York."

"I just wanted to remind you. Don't hesitate to wake him in the middle of the night. He's used to emergencies. And Pat's also standing by."

"Honestly, Rafe, you make it sound as though Attila the Hun is going to break in here raping and pillaging the moment he sees you get into the hansom. Stop worrying, for heaven's sake! We'll be fine."

"You won't go off on some mission with Beth to help the derelicts on Chatham Square?"

"I won't budge from the chair. I'll have Kitty tie me to it." She knit her brow. "But how will I get out when the tidal wave comes?"

"This is no laughing matter, Emily. Do you know what the crime rate is in this city? Do you know how many murders and . . ."

"I know! I know!" She waved her coffee cup in exasperation. What had happened to the carefree Rafe of her youth?

He sighed. "All right. Lecture's over." He looked down and murmured, "I'll miss you."

"I'll miss you, too."

"Shall we say goodbye properly?"

"At this hour? The children are still awake."

"Moira will see to them. Tonight their parents will go to bed early."

Emily had been planning to reread *Innocents Abroad*, but Rafe's needs were more important than a second helping of Clemens. She nodded demurely and said, "Shall we retire?"

As Rafe unlaced her, Emily's thoughts returned to the summer days in the Lanston woods. She closed her eyes and tried to remember how it had been then with the rustling trees and the birds, the sun glancing off the leaves. She turned to face him, trying to see him as the young man home from the wars. It wasn't difficult. In appearance, he had not changed. She tried to relive the emotions of those days, hoping he would not shatter the mood by saying, "and don't forget to keep the front door locked . . . and be sure to warn the servants not to open the door to strangers." But he did not intrude on her memories. He kissed her urgently with quick, probing flicks of the tongue. Then he led her to the bed and, without turning out the light, caressed her gently, as though discovering her for the first time, as though he too were remembering. It had been so long since she had been this excited and it felt good. When he entered her, she found her movements matching his, heard her voice as from a distance, and when he reached down to touch her she began to spend in intense, consuming spasms. Dimly she felt and heard his own violent pleasure. Then he moved from her and she lay still, exhausted but calmer than she had been in a long time. How had this happened? And why didn't it happen more often?

He turned to her and smiled, running his finger along her breast. "You were with me."

"Yes."

"It seemed very intense."

"It was good, Rafe."

"I'm so glad," he said. And he closed his eyes.

She thought, if only it could be this way all the time. And then she thought, but it's nice to know that it still can happen. Then she kissed his cheek and drifted into sleep thinking of the pine room at dusk.

CHAPTER 21

As it turned out, Rafe's concern proved to be justified. He had not been gone three days when Bill began running a fever. Since Bill shared a room with Nicky, the latter came down with a fever too and vomited twice. Peggy had developed a cough.

Ever since Michael had died, childhood epidemics had filled Emily with terror. One of the reasons she and other mothers wanted large families was that the mortality rate of babies was so high. Last year there had been bouts with mumps and measles. The year before it had been whooping cough. Every time the children coughed or vomited or showed the most benign catarrhal symptoms Emily would panic. Would it stop at this or would it lead to meningitis?

Pat came by three nights in a row to examine the three oldest. He assured Emily that the children had only mild colds, but she did not believe him until the fevers abated and the boys resumed their evening pillow fights. The baby and David, meanwhile, remained symptom-free and in strict isolation, though the problems of keeping them confined were driving Moira to the brink of lunacy. And there was no question of getting them out for a pram ride, since the weather this January was bitter cold.

On the fourth night of Pat's visits he said, "The boys will be fine. Bill's suffering malingerer's disease at the moment. I understand there's a test at school this Friday."

Emily smiled. "Malingerer's disease I can cure myself. How's Nicky?"

"Fever's down. Keep him home another day."

"And Peggy?"

"I think she's been faking this cough so that she can be one of the crowd." As the only girl, Peggy often mimicked her brothers, even in illness.

"Are you sure it's an act?" Emily asked.

"Is Peggy's name Margaret?" Pat grinned. He was as close to the Taylor children as to his own son.

Pat was carrying a basin that he had taken from the boys' room. Now, with a hasty "excuse me," he sank to his knees and was violently sick. Emily, frowning, held his head. Whatever the boys had contracted, Pat must have come down with it too. Yet Pat had been looking ill for months now, his face sunken and sallow, his eyes watery and yellowish. Always a thin man, Pat had lately become gaunt.

Pat stood up, weaving. "Excuse me."

"What's wrong, Pat?"

He shrugged. "Mind if I go downstairs and sit in the library?"

"Are you sure you wouldn't rather lie down? The guest room is . . ."

"I'll be fine," Pat said, moving toward the stairs.

As she bent to pick up the basin, Emily saw blood. "Good God!" she exclaimed aloud. She ran down to the library where Pat was already seated in a leather chair, his head back against the cushion, his eyes closed. As she rushed in, he opened his eyes and said, "I'm all right. Upset stomach."

"What's wrong? Not consumption!"

"Consumption? Where did you get that idea?"

"You vomited blood. I saw it."

Pat sighed. "No, it's not consumption. I'm calling it metastatic carcinoma of indeterminate origin."

"You have *cancer*?"

"No. I said I'm *calling* it cancer."

Emily understood. Pat had invented a disease to hide the fact that he was suffering from something else. It didn't take her a minute to guess what it was. She said, "Cirrhosis can be controlled, Pat. Proper diet and rest . . ."

"Not at this stage." His voice was cold.

She shook her head. "Oh, Pat. Why?"

"Why did I keep drinking, you mean? Please, Emily. Not you too. I've had enough lectures from Kent, my family, and your husband to last a lifetime—which, as it turns out, will be mercifully short. Anyway, I'm not drinking at the moment. Alcohol makes me sick." He began to laugh and he said again, "Alcohol makes me sick. How's that for irony? If only I'd gotten sick when I took my first belt."

There was a long silence. She looked into the yellowish, somewhat frenzied eyes of the dying man, swallowed, and turned away. Then she murmured, "What can I do to help?"

Pat shrugged. "You can do your best to give credence to the cancer story. I don't want my patients knowing that their lovable family doctor was a drunkard. The family will guess the truth, of course, though Kent's got a cancer history down in the records." He paused. "No one knows I'm ill but him and I'd like to keep it that way until my condition becomes obvious. A week or two, I think, should do it. No sense in upsetting the whole clan now. Nor Rafe either. Don't mention that blood to him, please."

"If those are your wishes. But are you sure it's hopeless? Isn't there any chance at all?"

"Kent will tell you there is, but Kent could never face death. He'll try every heroic measure in the book, though I've already told him I won't consent to surgery. But no, there's no hope. There have been several hemorrhages." He sat up, then leaned toward her. "Don't look so concerned. Please don't. Dying has advantages, Emily. Think of all the things I'll never have to worry about again. Bills and taxes and middle-of-the-night calls. The Grant scandals, Tammany corruption, crime, another war between the states. You poor folks will be chewing your nails to the quick while I sleep blissfully on."

"I don't understand you!" she exclaimed. "I've never understood this! Rafe used to tell me what you were like in army days. The source of strength for everyone. That you of all people would drink yourself to death . . ."

"When Rafe met me, I was twenty-three. A young bachelor, still riding the crest of my time."

"Your *time*?"

The dying man leaned forward and said to Emily, "Most people know a time that's right for them. For some it comes in adolescence. Others don't find it until they're old. For many, like Beth and Kent, the best time is now, the middle years. I think it's a mistake for people to force themselves out of their own golden age. The change must evolve naturally. If this doesn't happen, then a person should relax and suspend himself in his personal era. To hell with conforming more than you have to." He paused, then asked, "Is your time still to come, Emily? Or has it passed? And if it's passed, will you ever try to find it again?"

"I don't know," she said. "I'm not even sure what you mean."

"My time came in my early twenties, just after I graduated from medical school. I was excited and always in love—with women, of course, and with medicine too. Then the war came. In the last year and a half I suffered mentally. We all did, I think. The condition would have healed itself eventually, and if I had only waited for that to happen, I might have returned to my time. I would have chased women forever, first as a young lover, then as an older one. I wouldn't have hurt the women. Beth can tell you; I always chose women like myself who lived for the adventure of love and little else. Exciting chases, frenzied love affairs, disastrous endings. Immature perhaps, but this was my idea of living . . ." He broke off.

"Go on," she said.

He shrugged. "As I told you, the war interfered. I came home wanting nothing more than to crawl back into the womb." Pat cleared his throat. "Indelicate imagery. 'Scuse me."

"It's all right."

"Kent tried to tell me I was making a mistake, but of course I didn't listen. I married, and I've gone downhill ever since. I tried—for the boy, mostly. But it didn't help. It wasn't Eileen's fault. Promise me you'll never even *think* that. The fault was mine. Baby Pat lost his golden age and ceased to function." He shook his head. "I never meant to hurt her."

"I don't think you did hurt her," Emily said.

"What makes you say that?"

"She had God taking care of her." Emily knew at once that the remark was too flippant for the occasion, but there was no way of retracting it.

To her surprise, Pat chuckled. "She had God. Yes. You always were a wit, Emily, even when you weren't trying to be."

"I didn't mean . . ."

"I've always wondered what you were like."

"What I'm *like*?"

"I've only known you as a married woman. In a marriage parts of the individual are hidden. Funny, but I've always had the hunch that you were no more the marrying kind than I was. You seem—I don't know. Are you happy, Emily?" He held up his hand. "No, don't answer that. I want to believe that you're happy because I care for Rafe too and I think he's happy. His golden era is now, I think. Rafe was born to be a father. If only the two of you could always— God but don't I sound like the patriarch on his deathbed trying to reassure himself that the flock will carry on."

"You sound tired and sad. Oh Pat, I do wish you'd try to help yourself."

"It's too late, Emily. It really is too late for speeches of hope springing eternal. I do want to live—for my son's sake, mostly. But I won't." He paused. "Do me one favor, though. None of the others will be capable of it. They'll deny and deny the truth and keep telling me I'm going to get well."

"What is it you want me to do?"

"To say goodbye. I want someone to say goodbye to me."

"Pat, please."

"Say it."

She took a deep breath. "Goodbye, Pat. You—I'll never forget—you are a good man, Pat." The fragmented, totally inadequate sentence left her physically drained.

He rose and took her hand. "Thank you," he said. Then he turned and walked out.

Emily never again saw Pat alive. He kept working for two more days and then stayed home in bed. Awareness stole over the family slowly and Diane reported to Emily the facts and the reactions. Pat was ill. . . . Pat was vomiting all the time. . . . Pat wasn't getting better. . . . Beth thought it was consumption, Joe was alarmed, Kent was being maddeningly evasive. Everyone went to the house on Thirteenth Street to visit him but Emily kept inventing excuses not to go. Goodbye had meant goodbye. There had been something in Pat's manner that told her he did not want her to see him again. It was important that at least one of his friends remember him as he had been—in possession of himself and of his dignity.

When Rafe came home from Philadelphia—a week overdue—she told him only that Pat was ill. She did not know any more than this, she said, for the children had just recovered from colds and she had wanted to stay with them. Rafe went to see Pat and he came home upset. After visiting Pat for the second time, he muttered, "I'm sure it's his liver. Why can't he go quickly? *Quickly*, for God's sake!"

Rafe did not describe conditions in the sickroom but Emily had the details form Diane. Pat's slow disintegration had been an agony for him. And all who had been there to witness it suffered as well.

Pat lingered for more than a week, becoming more and more irrational. Then he sank into hepatic coma and died. When Emily and Rafe arrived at his house that night, they expected weeping and hysterical commotion. Instead, they witnessed profound relief. Eileen was asleep in her room. Beth was asleep in an armchair. Kent, with a calm Rafe had never before seen, quietly gave instructions to the undertaker. Pat Junior slept in Joe's lap. Pat's mother wandered about the kitchen. The others too were either sleepy or unusually calm.

There were tears at the burial, but these were drowned by a sleety storm that tore through the Brooklyn cemetery as though nature itself were outraged to see what had happened to Pat—and by his own hand. Afterward, in Pat's dining room, quiet prevailed as each person drew into himself and confronted alone the fact that Pat was no longer there. Looking from face to face, Emily wondered why a man who had been so loved, who had given so much love in return, would want to destroy himself. She would never, as long as she lived, understand it.

The death of Pat Shepherd had an unusual effect on Emily, and she could not define the reason. She had been fond of him, grateful to him, but had never actually loved him, could not even claim a sisterly relationship as Rafe claimed a brotherly one. Through the winter she often found herself remembering that last conversation, the agony of saying goodbye. And she never forgot the question he had asked: "Are you happy, Emily?" followed quickly by the words, "No, don't answer that."

Emily seldom stopped to wonder if she was happy or not. Such preoccupations were considered indecent, particularly in women who were admonished by all society, including their own sex, to live not for themselves but for their children. So as quickly as possible, Emily put the question from her mind. To help her forget Pat and the unnatural morbidness his death had generated, Emily began to read a great deal. She set herself a regimen of study. Shakespeare first. Then Milton. Then Immanuel Kant and Descartes. Then Darwin. Hour after hour she would stand at the parlor window looking into a slushy morning, concentrating hard on what one or another of these sages had to say. She tended to her household duties absently, talked to the children in Shakespearean English, communicated to Rafe or the tea group not about practical matters but about metaphysical speculations. If family and friends reacted strangely, she did not notice. They all seemed to be far away, dancing around the perimeter of her world, indifferent to the profound truths that were shaking her. It was not until March that she realized she was neglecting them shamefully. Slowly her eyes came into focus and she began to see everyone again. Only then did she wonder what had caused her to be absent so long. And she concluded that winter's confinement had made her a bit dotty.

In April she received a wire from Mrs. Harrington. The widow would be passing through New York again on her way upstate and planned to stay overnight at the Fifth Avenue Hotel. Emily wired back that she must stay in the Taylor guest room or not bother to stay at all. Then she invited Beth and Kent to a dinner for the elderly suffragist.

No other woman but Beth would fit in at such a gathering. Diane, Joan, and others cared nothing for woman's suffrage and might possibly offend the widow by intimating that she was associating herself with crazy ladies who wanted to wear men's trousers or put aprons on their husbands and send them to the scullery. The rumors circulating about women in this movement had been enough to cause wives to slam their doors in the faces of petition seekers with pious pronouncements that they had *husbands* to protect them and didn't need to go into vulgar voting booths where men spat tobacco and cursed and offended every sense of decency. Beth had once tried to collect petitions. She had reported that women believed getting the vote would bring the end of family life. Wives and husbands would murder each other because each favored a different candidate. When Beth laughed at these fears, wives pointed indignantly to the political arguments in New York which had led to stabbings and shootings. If women were to vote, families would be broken and society itself would be torn asunder by the angry hand of God, who had warned women what their place was and of what would happen if they dared step out of it. Gotham would become Gomorrah.

So the Harrington dinner was limited to the two couples and the guest of honor. Mrs. Harrington, now seventy-four, had lost a great deal of weight since leaving Lanston and looked younger than she had at sixty-five. She brought gifts: toys for all the children, a small brooch for Emily, and a set of pipes for Rafe, who never smoked pipes. She had visited the Taylors at least once a year since they had been in New York, as she was always traveling through the city on her way to Boston, Rochester or New Haven. Occasionally women's conferences were held in New York itself. The oldest children adored her. The babies were frightened of her booming voice. But she mothered them all with a mixture of hugs and insults, and she didn't treat their parents any differently. ("Emily, you're too thin. . . . Raphael, you have dark circles under your eyes. . . . Both of you are as set in your ways as a couple of Lanston coots.") No one minded the insults, for minutes after uttering them she might say, "Play that adagio movement from Bach, Emily. The one that made me cry that night in Williams Hall." Or, "Raphael, you are a perfectly marvelous father. Not a brat in the brood. However did you manage that?"

Of the group at dinner, only Kent seemed uncomfortable with Mrs. Harrington. He kept staring at her as though trying to fit her into his categories of patients. She stared back at him once but with full understanding in her eyes. Emily read her thoughts on Kent—typical suspicious New Englander. Then the widow went on talking as though he were not there.

Oh how she talked! Beth's face was flushed with interest, and Emily, though accustomed to the Harrington style, was also fascinated. Rafe's attention was divided between the lady's opinions and Kent's incredulous facial expressions. Once Emily saw Rafe wink at Kent as though to say, "She's the town eccentric. Just bear with it."

The widow spoke first of the valor of Susan Anthony. Miss Anthony and a number of female residents of Rochester had attempted to vote the previous November under the provisions of the Fourteenth Amendment. This amendment, passed after the war for the purpose of granting suffrage to Negroes, had consisted of five sections. Mrs. Harrington was concerned with the first two. Section one stated that all persons born or naturalized in the United States were "citizens" and as such could not be deprived of life, liberty, or property without due process. In the second section, dealing with the illegality of denying the vote, the word "male" was specified. Most lawyers reasoned that section two, by its use of the term "male," made it clear that theirs was the only sex under consideration. A few, however, thought that seciton one, by its use of the term "persons," gave *everyone* the right to vote. Section two, these liberal interpreters maintained, merely stressed that the privilege could not be denied to males.

Accordingly, some women were now attempting to test the amendment. Miss Anthony's case had garnered the most publicity. For trying to vote in Rochester's November election, she and other women had been arrested and released on bail. They were now awaiting trial.

"This will not end," said Mrs. Harrington, shaking her fist, "until women learn to revolt as men do. We must use men's tactics. We must raise a great howl from ocean to ocean, clamor and shout and riot in the streets if necessary!"

"Now really . . ." Rafe began.

"Don't 'really' me, Raphael! It's the only way any group in this nation ever gets attention or justice. Appeals to sweet reason, as the abolitionist movement showed us, did not work. What worked was war. I fervently hope we won't have to make war, but I assure you we will make very loud noises. They can toss us into jail and we'll howl and shout from there. For we will have our rights, Raphael. We *will* have them!"

Kent choked on his coffee. Beth's eyes blazed with revolutionary zeal. Emily's face was outwardly calm, but inside she was seething. She had always thought it a monstrous injustice that women, who were fully as intelligent as men, were denied the right to elect their own officers. But unless she had a Harrington around stirring her up, Emily tended to forget this indignity along with the other inequalities against women. Sometimes she went so far as to tell herself that the imbalance was in the natural order of things. Man was the protector, woman the nurturer. Over the course of history this system had worked. Diane had been right about that. Who was Emily to question it?

But as Mrs. Harrington continued to rage, Emily found herself glaring at Rafe. Why, *she* knew more about issues and candidates than he did! All Rafe seemed to do was growl that all politicians were corrupt. He'd actually missed voting in '70 and '71. And the only reason he'd gone to the polls in '72 was that it had been a presidential election. As for Kent, Beth had said he flatly refused to vote at all. He hadn't liked Greeley and he hadn't liked Grant and all Beth's arguments that he simply *had* to choose had fallen on deaf ears.

Neither man, however, was against giving women the vote. Both had gamely signed Beth's petitions, Rafe remarking that women at home had more time to study the candidates' platforms, Kent saying that if women wanted to take responsibility for the idiots in government they were welcome to it.

Mrs. Harrington continued. "They said women could not be freed until the Negro was freed. They said it was impossible for the two groups to be liberated together. *Why*, I ask you, was this *impossible*?" She did not wait for anyone to venture a reason but went on. "And now they're linking our movement with that of the reactionaries and the bigots. Why? Because some of us are indignant over the fact that immigrant males from Europe, who can neither read nor write, who know not a word of the Constitution nor the difference between a president and a king, are being herded into the voting booth by corrupt ward leaders in exchange for cash or whiskey. This while educated women get thrown in jail!"

Beth said, "Then suffragists are considered to be anti-Negro *and* anti-immigrant?"

"Yes!" Mrs. Harrington shouted. "And we're speaking of the same women who risked ridicule to get up on platforms and plead for abolition. The same who risked their lives on underground railroads. The same who organized charities and schools for Irish and German immigrants. Not only are we supposed to be reactionary bigots, my dear, but paradoxically we are also proponents of free love."

"Susan Anthony advocates free love?" Rafe exclaimed in amazement.

"No! No, Raphael!" The widow waved her hand impatiently. "Don't you pay the slightest attention to news of women's affairs? Her associate, Mrs. Stanton, has written articles on fairer divorce laws, means of controlling large families, and other very practical subjects. They call this free love. And of course she's attracted the attention of a few—a very few—who advocate a lower standard of moral conduct. But our enemies claim that *all* suffragists are libertines." Mrs. Harrington paused. "Back in the forties they connected the Brook Farm community with free love. Brook Farm, that innocent, glorious Arcady! My husband and I visited often. It was simply an experiment in community living. Its only objective was the unity of intellectual and manual labor *within* the individual. No union outside of marriage was *ever* sanctioned! But does the modern generation know or care about the real Brook Farm—the schools, the artists, the Margaret Fullers and Nathaniel Hawthornes? No, when one thinks of Brook Farm . . ." She broke off in exasperation and abruptly returned to the subject of suffrage.

"Now we have that turncoat Victoria. She's hurt the British movement and she's hurting ours." The widow speared a piece of beef with her fork as though stabbing the interfering monarch. "Her Majesty has said, and I quote, 'The Queen is most anxious to enlist everyone who can speak or write to join in checking this mad wicked folly of Women's Rights with all its attendant horrors, on which her poor feeble sex is bent, forgetting every sense of womanly feeling and propriety.'" Mrs. Harrington held her fork aloft. "This is Queen Victoria speaking. Did *she* refuse the crown because she was a member of that 'poor feeble sex'? Did *she* shrink from the 'attendant horrors' of presiding over the realm? The hypocrite!"

Mrs. Harrington was now quite red in the face, and Kent was studying her clinically, wondering how long it would take before she succumbed to a coronary or a stroke. He looked around the dining room trying to remember if he'd brought along his medical bag. He usually took it everywhere he went and had twice been summoned from his seat in the Academy of Music to attend someone in the audience. No, he couldn't see it. But they lived just across the street, and there was digitalis near at hand.

Mrs. Harrington finally fell silent and began to pick at her food, which was rapidly growing cold. The others followed her cue, Rafe looking vastly relieved because he was starved. Kent noticed with satisfaction that Mrs. Harrington's color was returning to normal. Perhaps there would be no emergency tonight. He had hoped to relax over brandy and enjoy the evening.

But the widow was by no means finished. Over the nesselrode pudding she had additional observations to share. "Have any of you noticed that most of the suffragists and prominent female reformers in America—the Grimkés being a notable exception—were born in the Northeast?"

"I've never thought about it," Emily said, "but now that you mention it, yes, it's true. I suppose women in the South were too isolated from one another to band together and organize reform movements."

Beth said, "And there's a tradition of chivalry there that has probably affected women's attitude."

"That's true, of course," Mrs. Harrington said, "but I was thinking in terms of the Puritan influence. Lucy Stone, Lucretia Mott, Harriet Stowe, Margaret Fuller, Dorothea Dix,

Elizabeth Stanton, Julia Howe, Susan Anthony, and so many others were born in New York or New England. Now, granted some of these women were Quakers and as such were given rights that no other religion will permit. But all of them—Quakers or not—were raised in an area steeped in Puritan dogma: work hard, get ahead, achieve the highest goals possible—and still keep working." She swallowed a spoonful of pudding and continued. "Well, men can follow those rules easily enough. They can strive to their heart's content. But women, who are raised with the same rules, grow frustrated when they see that there are limits. At some point they have to say, 'This is it. I can't surpass my man.' Puritan-heritage women have two conflicting rules. Succeed yet don't succeed. It's a wonder more of us haven't gone mad."

Beth added, "Particularly those women of the Calvinist-based religions."

Mrs. Harrington and Emily exchanged glances. Here were two such women. But the widow did not want to digress to the subject of Reverend Mitchell. She wished to pursue her original argument. "In other areas of the country, where the paradox is not so sharp, there are fewer disgruntled women. And in that sense the rigid old Mathers accomplished what they never intended. They made life so impossible that they drove women to free themselves."

Kent said, "Interesting point. But there are factors that you're overlooking." It was the first time this evening that Kent had spoken more than two words.

"Please explain," Mrs. Harrington said.

"The North is industrialized where the South is not. Industry separates couples. Men and women no longer work together, and the women left behind feel the world is passing them by."

"Interesting thought, doctor. One tends to think of industry in terms of the exploitation of the poor. But yes, there's this aspect too. Couples no longer work together. Some spouses scarcely know each other."

Rafe said, "But wasn't it Wyoming that first gave women the vote? Few Puritans and no industry in Wyoming."

"Ah!" said the widow. "I was speaking of the older leaders. You're referring to the new. Yes, the Western situation is unique in the world. There you have women pioneers who helped their husbands plant wheat, build soddies, fight Indians. They will not *stand* for husbands turning around and calling them scatterbrained fragile flowers. Western women will have the vote before we do. You'll see."

It occurred to Emily that if she had married Roger she might soon be casting her first ballot. If she could get from the farm to the polls.

The rest of the evening proved to be interesting. The subjects moved from the woman question to law and government to the state of the sciences to the philosophy of John Stuart Mill. Rafe, with each successive brandy, contributed increasingly profound views on beauty and truth. He and Beth debated Aristotelian philosophy while Emily and Kent discussed the implications of Darwin's findings. Mrs. Harrington swiveled her head, listening to both discussions, dropping into each an opinion, an epigram, or an apt quotation. When the evening was over Emily's head was reeling. So much had been said, so much news and so many ideas exchanged! She wished she had had time to record and examine every statement.

But the evening ended, and Mrs. Harrington retired. The next day the widow was gone and Emily was back in the parlor with Diane and Joan wishing those bits of talk from last night were candies in a box. Then she could nibble them throughout Diane's descriptions of the trim she was making for her daughter's green poplin.

Beth had been just as enthusiastic about the Harrington visit. A week later she met Emily on the sidewalk outside the house and thanked her again for the dinner. "Oh, you can't know how exciting it was. I haven't had so much fun in years. So much more interesting than charity benefits, don't you think?"

"Yes," Emily said. She too was tired of charity balls. They had nothing much to do with charity. They featured Strauss and gossip and brittle conversation in which the words "blind," "Thackeray," "Gainsborough," "insane," "Newport," "regatta," "orphan," "Chopin," and "Regency chairs" followed so hard on one another that they formed a cacophony too harsh for Emily's ears.

Beth said, "I wish I could remember half the things we talked about that night."

"Come in for a while and let's try."

"Oh, I can't, Emily. Didn't I tell you? Some society women have asked me to help set up a nursing school at Bellevue."

"Really?"

"I'm so excited about it!" Beth was a doctor in almost every sense but the name. She had read all Kent's textbooks, assisted him with the in-home surgery that most patients preferred to hospitals. She passed implements, handled retractors, administered anesthesia, and operated a gadget called a carbolic spray which spewed a mist of disinfectant into the air to kill all lurking germs. Little wonder they had asked her to help organize a nursing program.

"It'll be the first institution in the United States to be modeled on Florence Nightingale's principles," Beth continued. "You know that until now Bellevue's been staffed by drunken matrons who were given the posts as alternatives to prison sentences."

Emily knew. This was why Rafe had refused to let her do volunteer work at the city hospital.

"You see, nurses have to be more than caretakers," Beth said. "They need to study materia medica and obstetrics as well as patient care. They need theory in addition to practice. It's time doctors stopped treating them as maids and gave them professional status."

On and on Beth talked, enthusiasm radiating from every pore, and soon Emily grew annoyed. If she had time to jabber about the Bellevue school, why didn't she have time to rehash the evening with Mrs. Harrington?

"Did I say something to upset you?" Beth asked.

"No," Emily snapped.

"You look angry."

"Why would I be angry?"

"I guess it's that you're squinting. The sun's in your eyes. I do have to go, Emily. We must have you to dinner soon, though I can't promise you a guest like Mrs. Harrington." And off trotted Dorothea Dix, leaving Emily feeling alone and very disgruntled.

Her annoyance, Emily soon discovered, was not limited to Beth. By mid-May she was becoming irritated with everyone she came in contact with, most notably her husband. It had gotten so that she could not stand Rafe's jokes or his anecdotes about work or his infernal whistling or his careless habits—socks on the floor, treasured books lying open and face down. If he raised his voice while disciplining the children, she muttered "tyrant" under her breath. If he didn't raise his voice or bent one of the rules she hissed, "coward." Yet Rafe's habits weren't recently acquired. He'd been this way from the beginning. Way back when she'd been desperately in love there had been socks on the floor. And his jokes—why, his sense of humor had been the first quality she had noticed. There was only one conclusion; she herself must have changed. She wasn't certain why or how, but she was determined to try to see the family in a more pleasant light. She tried especially to be good to the children. They needed her guidance, though the older boys were beginning to turn to Rafe for manly camaraderie. On inclement Saturdays, Rafe, Nicky, and Bill would sit down in the kitchen eating cookies as fast as Kitty could bake them. Rafe told her that these gatherings evoked childhood memories, and Emily tried to sympathize. But she could not help being envious, watching the males sitting there laughing. Bill and Nicky rarely laughed for her. Generally they whined or argued for more privileges or dallied when they were supposed to be cleaning their rooms or suggested that their mother was too pedantic.

For a while Emily threw all her talents into preparing Peggy for life, teaching, preaching, lecturing, showing her how to care for the babies. And always she was hurt when Peggy edged out of the room to roughhouse with the older boys. That left David, two, and baby Adam. And these two Emily could handle without even trying to use her brain. Her message to David amounted to "You're supposed to *play* with toys, dear, not take them apart." Her message to Adam was "Just one more spoonful of oatmeal." At least the little boys needed her, but she couldn't help thinking that they too would end up in the kitchen with Rafe, laughing with their mouths full, planning lives of their own. And when it was over she would end up a widow in one of the boys' houses.

Old interfering granny, the family nuisance.

To shake herself out of these gloomy moods, Emily retreated into books as she had after Pat died. But she found
that she could not concentrate. She tried the piano and discovered that she was making mistakes But she still found a
measure of satisfaction in keeping the household books. She
concentrated on bargain hunting and penny counting, hoping that in time fascination with her family would return with
a surge. In the first week of June she saved a dollar and
thirty-three cents. In the second week of June, two dollars
and five cents. In the third week of June she sank to a yearly
low of eighty-five cents. After this she spent days tracking
down new bakers and butchers (in safe areas, of course) and
nights planning menus that were nutritious but inexpensive.
Rafe found her in the library one evening charting
month-by-month graphs of the price of fruits and vegetables
from the high in winter, when so much produce had to be
shipped in, to the low in summer, when almost everything
was in season. As Rafe looked over her shoulder, she was
superimposing the graphs for fish on the produce curves.
This was to be followed by meat. She looked up with annoyance at having been interrupted at her work before she
could get to the meat.

"What's this?" he asked.

"A new way of handling household accounts. It's more
scientific. I can glance at the chart and plan budgets around
the season. I'll be able to save more money."

"Why go to all that trouble? You manage very well on
the budget you have now."

"I want to do better."

"But why?"

"I just *want* to. That's all."

"Why don't you let me give you more money? Then you
won't have to . . ."

"I don't *need* more money."

Rafe shook his head. "But this is ridiculous! If you're so
determined to save a dollar or two a week for emergencies I
can just give you the . . ."

"I don't want you to give me a dime. I can run the house
by myself."

So Rafe left her alone with her graphs, and in the last

week of June she saved two dollars and fifty cents. It was an all-time record and she felt the need to celebrate. But there was no one to share her enthusiasm. Not a soul—least of all Rafe, who earned a good salary—would understand what this accomplishment meant to her. Two dollars and fifty cents!

During the month of July the family usually journeyed to Lanston. Rafe stayed for a week, then went back to the city until the weekend they had to leave. Kitty always went with them, leaving Moira alone in the city to tend to Rafe's limited needs. Emily and Rafe had agreed long ago not to spend whole summers on Maple Street. The grandparents, they thought, weren't used to five lively children and might prefer to spend some of the green months in peace.

Lanston was no longer a small town. Industries were springing up everywhere and there were now two business districts rather than one. Center Street still served the townsfolk and most of the farmers, but across the tracks in the industrial area, stores, blacksmiths, and other shops were going up rapidly. The babies and Peggy usually stayed at Marie's under Kitty's supervision. Emily and the boys stayed at Matt's, which was now half house and half library. Budget keeping had to be suspended, for the grandparents refused to accept money for food. To make up for this, Rafe and Emily usually brought them expensive gifts.

Though the grandparents welcomed the yearly visit, not one of the four was free to entertain the brood during weekdays. The men had their jobs and so did the women. Marie was assistant editor on the paper, Mary was busy in the library, and Emily, left with other mothers, sometimes felt that the only difference between Lanston and New York was that women here took their tea outdoors more often than in parlors. Otherwise the conversations were identical. Christine and Priscilla spoke of clothes, husbands' miserliness, pregnancies, and the problems of growing fat. Emily nodded and nodded and nodded.

On Sundays, however, things perked up. Emily, her father, and the five children piled into Matt's wagon and went out to see Abby. The men, the boys, and Peggy rode around the farm in haywagons while Emily and Abby talked.

Abby had more pressing problems than did the town

women, and Emily, once a farmer herself, was able either to empathize or to give advice. They talked of crop rotation, curing the diseases cows contracted (the Lawrences had a dairy farm), gardening, preserving foods, and the political ideas of New England farmers (too conservative, both agreed). But Abby was anxious to hear about life in New York.

"Tell me about your friends," she asked one Sunday.

Emily told her what she could of Diane and Joan, noting that Abby grew glassy-eyed during the narrative.

"And how about that doctor's wife?" Abby asked.

"Beth?"

"Yes. What's she been up to?"

"Just about everything," Emily said.

"She's practically a doctor, isn't she?"

"Practically." Emily's voice was flat.

"Imagine it! A woman in medicine! And not a midwife.'

"Yes."

"You don't sound very excited," Abby said.

"Why should *I* be excited? It's Beth's life."

"I know, but I mean the *idea* of it. I've read that more and more medical schools are thinking of admitting women. And the new nurses' training courses . . ."

"I've heard," Emily said shortly, getting impatient with the conversation. It was like talking to Beth herself.

"I guess you have heard." Abby shrugged, looking at Emily oddly. "Well, tell me what you've been doing. The plays, the balls, and so on."

Emily generally attended at least one function a week—a concert, the opera, a benefit or dinner or ballet. She said, "It's all very pleasant."

"Pleasant?" Abby repeated. "Just *pleasant*?"

"There've been some very good concerts."

"Well, *tell* me about them."

"There's not much to tell. I enjoy listening to music but what can I *say* about it except that it sounded good?"

Abby shook her head. "*Something* more, I should think."

"Really, there's nothing," Emily said. "Let's get back to what we were talking about earlier. It seems to me that if farmers would only learn to organize the way laborers do . . ."

Abby interrupted impatiently. "Why don't *you* organize them, then. You stay and organize and I'll move to New York where I'm sure I'd find things more than 'pleasant.'"

"Capital idea," Emily smiled. And Abby, studying her, thought, why she almost means it! Never would she have guessed that Emily could get so passionate about the plight of the farmer. For the moment, Abby was puzzled.

But Emily's passion was still her emergency fund. As soon as she got back to New York, Emily returned to her bookkeeping. All through August she devoted herself to the challenge of reaching the three dollar mark. In the last week of August she saved two dollars and ninety-three cents. It was close enough. She came out of the library that evening in a buoyant mood. And she was disappointed to see that the faces around the dining room table were glowering. Now that she thought about it, the children had been greeting her with scowls since the holiday had ended. And she could not remember the last time Rafe had smiled either. They talked occasionally about the children or the servants. And sometimes he made love to her in a perfunctory way and in silence. Otherwise he just drifted around the edges of her life as they had seemed to drift after Pat had died. How was it possible to spend all that time with a husband and family and not really be with them?

Emily made a firm resolution to concentrate on Rafe and the children. Over soup she asked everyone how they had enjoyed the summer. Peggy glanced at Nicky who glanced at Bill. Then the three of them looked at Rafe whose face was stony. Then Nicky said, "Summer was nice, Mama."

Next she asked Peggy if she liked her new muslin frock. Peggy said, "It's nice, Mama."

Finally she asked Bill if he was anxious for school to start. He said, "Yes, Mama, but why are you asking us all these questions?"

"Because I care about you."

"You didn't ask about us yesterday or the day before that or the day before that. All you did was tell us to do things."

"Enough!" Rafe barked.

Emily choked on the soup but managed to get it down. She said in a barely audible voice, "Because mothers are sometimes—preoccupied—doesn't mean they don't care about their families."

The children said nothing. Rafe studied his napkin. And when the tribe had left the table, Emily asked him, "Do they really think I don't care about them?"

"I should think the answer would be obvious."

"You're so reassuring," she muttered.

"What do you want me to do? Lie to you? You walk through this house like a ghost. No, let me qualify that. To the children you're a ghost who feeds and clothes and nods and never listens. To me . . ." he broke off.

"And what am I to you?"

"What am *I* to you?" he asked, his face angry.

"Are we going to volley this question back and forth for the rest of the evening?" she snapped.

Rafe stood up and went to close the dining room door. Then he sat in the chair normally occupied by Nicky. His fists were clenched. "It's become increasingly apparent that you don't give a damn about me."

"What do you mean?"

"You can't stand lovemaking. You can't even stand conversation."

He was right. There had been moments when she had been guilty of these crimes. But she did still care for him. And occasionally he was interesting. And there were times when she *liked* to sleep with him.

"Well?" he demanded.

"Well what?"

"So you won't even deny it!"

"*Yes* I deny it. Sometimes I *do* like to be with you."

He laughed shortly. "Oh, that's bully! Sometimes you like it. How often, Emily? Once a month? Once a year?"

"You're being impossible, Rafe."

He looked angry enough to kill. He said, "What in hell has *happened* to you?"

"Stop shouting at me."

"Shouting is the only tactic that seems to get your attention," he boomed.

"And you can stop baring your teeth."

"Jesus Christ!" He slammed the table so hard that she

gasped. "Can't you answer one question, Emily? I asked what's *happened* to you?"

"You're completely irrational," she finally said, not because she really thought he was but because she did not wish to answer this question or any that were likely to follow. She did not know how. "I won't sit here and be bullied by you!" she declared, standing up to leave. Rafe also stood and grabbed her arm hard. She shouted, "Let go of me!" He held on for a moment longer and then, sighing, let the arm drop. "I'll be sleeping in the guest room," she announced.

"I'll hardly know you're gone," he muttered.

"And what do you mean by that?"

"You're a bright woman. Figure it out."

She stared at him, her face contorted with rage. And she had thought she was being such a good wife in submitting to him when she did not feel like it. This was the thanks she got! "Go to hell" were her parting words.

CHAPTER 22

The ferry glided into the Canal Street dock. It was a warm day in early September. Rafe had removed his frock coat. The ocean air was cooling, and he took several deep breaths before disembarking. Glancing at his watch, he saw that it was just past seven. Late for supper, but it was just as well. For the past two weeks he and Emily had communicated only through the servants. He began to walk east. The Greenwich Street El rumbled overhead, spewing cinders over the hapless pedestrians. Rafe, darting under the tracks, began cursing aloud.

A minister was walking toward him. There was something familiar about his face. Then Rafe remembered, and he tore down the street toward the man. "Reverend Billings!"

The man blinked. "Yes, I'm Billings."

Rafe's face fell. "You don't remember me, do you?"

The minister knit his brow. "I'm afraid not."

"Rafe Taylor. Formerly Captain Taylor. A patient during the war." Rafe named the Washington hospital.

The man still looked blank but he tried to smile. "Oh . . . yes. How are you, Taylor?"

"You *have* forgotten. And we corresponded for months."

Billings shook his head. "Forgive me. There were so many soldiers."

"Spotsylvania. Chest wound. You asked me if I planned to take my textbooks to the world beyond."

A smile stole over the man's face. "Ah, of course! The heathen. You kept trying to get rid of me."

Rafe grinned.

"And later you promised to reform." He winked. "Have you?"

"Uh—give me time. Do you think we might have a drink, Reverend?"

"I'm sorry. I have to get to New Jersey."

"I work in New Jersey too. I'm an engineer."

"Then you found a use for the physics books here on earth?"

Rafe smiled. "Do you live in New Jersey? Perhaps we could . . ."

"I still live in Washington. I have a sister in Hoboken, though." He paused. "Well, how have you done, Taylor? Did you marry?"

"Yes. I have five children."

"And you were ready to turn over and die," the minister said, smiling. "You're happy, then?"

"Um," Rafe grunted, and the man took the monosyllable to mean "yes."

"I'm so glad. We used to pray so hard, hoping that you boys would survive the wounds of the mind as well as those of the flesh."

"I know that, sir, and I'm grateful."

"How many years has it been, Taylor?"

"Let's see. Sixty-four to seventy-three. Nine years, I guess."

"That long? It seems like yesterday."

"I know," Rafe said.

"I wish we did have time to talk."

"So do I, Reverend."

"Do you think you might write to me?"

Rafe nodded, though he knew he never would.

The minister scribbled his address on the corner of an old envelope, shook Rafe's hand, and sprinted off in the direction of the ferry. Rafe looked after him. Billings had helped him so much back in that hospital. Rafe had half-hoped the miracle might be effected again. Shrugging, he turned and began to walk east.

Rafe was lonely. He had never in his life known such isolation. Most of his friends were gone now. The men who had laughed over the campfires. His brothers. All of them gone. He had friends at work but none so close. And there was Kent, but Kent was sometimes remote.

He was on Tenth Street preparing to enter the house when he decided, "To hell with it. I'll see old stone face himself." He crossed the street to the Wilsons', thinking that anything was preferable to going home to silence.

A new partner had finally taken over Pat's practice, but he wasn't there now. The waiting room and Kent's examining room were also empty. But behind the door of the consultation room he heard a drawer slam. Rafe walked over and knocked.

Kent opened the door. Every time Rafe saw him, he marveled at the fact that Kent never changed. He still looked as he had in the service—blonde-grey hair in disarray, shirt sleeves rolled up, the rushed look on his face.

"Rafe." Kent motioned him to a leather chair and sat down at his desk. "What's wrong?"

"Nothing. That is, nobody's sick."

"Well, that's good." Kent plowed through some papers on his desk. "Excuse me a minute. I'm looking for a patient's record."

"Is the name Connell?"

"How did you know?"

"Because it's under my feet." Rafe retrieved the record and handed it to Kent.

"Beth's so busy these days," Kent muttered, scribbling something on the record. "The Bellevue school project. She usually handles these things." He paused. "What time is it?"

"Twenty to eight."

"Christ, no wonder I'm hungry. Wish she'd get home." He leaned across the desk. "If nobody's sick, what's the reason for this visit?"

"Just wanted to talk."

Kent looked puzzled. "To *talk*?"

"Talk. An art practiced by ancient tribes. It involves moving the lips up and down while simultaneously emitting sounds. Perhaps you've never heard of the custom." Rafe was irritated. If Pat were here now he'd be saying, "Glad you dropped in! Shall I get you a drink?"

"Go on," Kent said. "Anthropology is one of my favorite subjects."

"For God's sake, Kent, you might at least make me feel welcome."

"What do you expect? Ruffles and flourishes? I don't own a trumpet."

Rafe stood up. "Goodbye, Kent. It's been a delightful evening. We must get together again."

Kent was pulling a bottle of whiskey out of a desk drawer. "You're in a capital mood, I see." He opened more drawers, slammed them shut, and on his third try produced two glasses. "Sit down, for Christ's sake."

Rafe glowered but took his seat again as Kent poured him a drink.

"What did you want to talk about?" Kent handed him the whiskey.

"Nothing in particular."

"Oh?" Kent sipped his drink. "How's Emily?"

"Fine."

"The children?"

"Fine. Your children?"

"Fine," Kent said. "I trust the servants have fed them."

"Did I ask you how Beth was?"

"No, but she's fine. Shall we move on to the relatives?" Rafe smiled.

"Let's try Joe," Kent said. "He was over here the other night. Worried about the market and predicting a panic. You have stocks, don't you, Rafe?"

"Yes, and he's warned me too. I've been meaning to sell. Haven't gotten to it."

"You probably should. We don't own stocks. A little savings is about all. Joe told me to wait for the collapse and then rush down there to buy up oil and steel."

Rafe smiled. "Who does he think you are? Jay Gould?"

"I don't know. Can you picture me down at the exchange in my top hat making deals with the Commodore?"

They both laughed at this unlikely image and they drank for a while. Then Rafe, leaning back in his chair, said, "Kent, do you remember Jim Reynolds from F Company? My regiment?"

"Reynolds?"

"The one who was always worrying about his wife."

Kent shook his head. "Can't recall him."

"I passed a man on the street today who looked just like him." There had never been a Reynolds in F Company. Rafe had just now invented him because he needed some advice. He said, "Don't you remember the night we were all in my tent drinking? Reynolds was telling us how his wife had changed so. They'd been happily married for years. Five or six children. And all of a sudden she seemed to stop caring. I asked him if he'd been unfaithful or intemperate. He said "no." Then you asked him if perhaps she was in change of life."

"*I* asked this man about his wife's personal problems?"

"Don't you remember?"

"I must have been crazy."

"Well, the woman was only thirty or so, so it couldn't have been change of life," Rafe paused. "Could it?"

"Unlikely," Kent said.

Rafe continued with his story. "Poor Reynolds just sat there crying in his bourbon and none of us had a useful suggestion to give him."

"Nelson must have told him to give the woman his army pay and stop squandering it on bourbon."

"That was another thing," Rafe said. "She didn't want money either."

"Impossible," Kent said.

"Such women exist, Kent."

"Only in theory. Like the square root of minus one."

"Well, she didn't want money. That's all I can tell you."

"You've told me more than enough," Kent said. "Why are we discussing the story of a man I can't even remember?"

"No reason," Rafe said. "Just wondered if he and his wife ever found happiness."

Kent looked exasperated. "Let's pretend they did, shall we? He came home from the war with a dozen long-stemmed red roses and she was so overcome by this chivalrous gesture that she melted in his arms."

Kent paused to light his pipe, and Rafe, pouring another drink, studied him. How did Kent, who was not exactly congenial, keep his wife so content? Beth didn't even seem to resent the monumental work load Kent added to her household duties. What was Kent doing to make up for all this? Bringing her roses? Did Kent even know what a rose looked like? Showering her with expensive jewelry and new bonnets? Rafe had never noticed anything extraordinary in Beth's attire. What was Kent's secret? Could it be that he was a superb lover?

Rafe knit his brow and stared at the crusty doctor. Granted, he was handsome enough in a rugged way, and granted, he was lusty enough. During the war he had visited more brothels than either Rafe or Pat. But was he also a lover so skilled that all his liabilities paled when he and Beth were alone together? What was his secret? Was it a question of technique? Was it mere clinical skill? Or did he suddenly change from a short-tempered surgeon into a passionate Romeo, singing hymns to Beth's beauty in blank verse?

"What are you staring at?" Kent asked.

"Staring? Oh. Didn't mean to. Just thinking." He had no intention of asking Kent what techniques he used in bed. In wartime, when the partners had been prostitutes, such inquiries might have been possible. But not now.

Kent picked up his drink again. "How's the locomotive business?"

Rafe shrugged. "The usual problems. They assign me a budget that would scarcely build a buggy and tell me to make an engine. I say, Fine. Just one problem. We can't use iron. We'll have to make the thing out of burlap. They tell me that since I'm a stockholder I ought to know how stiff competition is. If we don't match or undersell Baldwin we'll be in trouble. I say, Yes, but I can't build engines at the price they want without the assistance of a fairy godmother. And so it goes. We're already in debt. Deeply in debt. Keep this confidential, Kent."

"Of course."

"If Joe's been talking to you, you must know the railroad industry's overextended. There's a possibility that we'll go under."

"Jesus." Kent shook his head. "Emily know?"

"No, I don't want to worry her."

"Yes, I know what you mean," Kent said. And they drank to the universality of the breadwinner's plight.

"Ever get tired of being an adult, Kent?"

Kent nodded.

"Wish I could take a day off," Rafe said. He pushed back his chair. "Well, before I get too drunk I had better take my leave."

"If I see Tim, you want me to ask him about Reynolds?"

"Who?"

"That army crony you were so worried about. You really *are* drunk."

"Oh, *Reynolds*. No, don't ask him. I might find out the man was killed at Cold Harbor."

Kent frowned. "You want some coffee?"

"No. I'll just walk for a while."

"Sure you're all right?"

"No," Rafe said. "I'm not sure. But thanks for the whiskey." And he lurched toward the door, wondering if he'd have enough energy to walk up to Broadway and buy Emily a dozen long-stemmed red roses.

"Rafe."

"Huh?"

"If the business does start to go and you need someone to talk to . . ."

"Yes?"

"I'm here," Kent said.

Rafe turned and looked at Kent. Then he nodded and quickly walked out.

Rafe visited three florists before he found one who had a dozen decent roses. At that, two of them were slightly wilted. Grumbling, he paid the man without bothering to bargain for a lower price. Then he walked home slowly, wishing he could have one more drink to get him through this. In view of the fact that they had not spoken in two weeks, he was dubious about Emily's reaction to the flowers. Would she see them as a bribe to get her out of the guest room and back into his bed? No matter what happened, he must remember not to follow the presentation of the flowers with a kiss or a suggestive glance. He would take the steps slowly. He would be more chivalrous, less sensual. He would pay tribute to her charms but not attack her like a starving man. More of the gallant cavalier and less of the hungry husband. Then, after a while, when she did come back to his bed, he must remember to love her as he had loved her in his youth. He must try to look upon her not as his wife but as a maiden to be wooed.

Emily was in the library mending, a basket of children's clothing beside her. When he stood in the doorway she looked up, frowned, then bent over her work again. She sewed rapidly but carelessly for she knew of no task more monotonous than this.

"Emily."

She looked up and said coldly, "What is it?"

Rafe marched in quickly and thrust the roses at her. "Here," said the man who had intended to make a courtly speech.

"Oh!" She shoved the needle into Nicky's shirt collar and put her sewing aside. "Oh, thank you. I—I'll get a vase." She laid the flowers on her chair, went down to the kitchen, and returned a few minutes later with a water-filled vase. Rafe was standing in the same place she had left him and in the same position. He reminded her of the statue of John Adams in front of Williams Hall. She busied herself cutting and arranging the roses, then placed them on an end table. "They're beautiful," she said.

"Thank you."

"Uh—why don't you sit down?"

He sat down stiffly and kept his eyes on the floor.

"I'm glad you did this," she said. "I wanted to—to do something too but the days went by and somehow . . ."

"I understand. And I apologize for that night. I didn't mean—whatever I said."

"I apologize too."

A long silence followed. Rafe looked at the floor, Emily at the flowers. Finally, when he could bear it no longer, Rafe said, "I haven't been paying enough attention to you. I'm sorry about it. I should tell you more often how proud of you I am—the way you keep the house, balance the budgets. And you've always done a marvelous job with the children.

Especially in educating them. You've deserved more tribute from me."

She swallowed and murmured, "Thank you."

"I'd like to give you more than flowers. I want to buy you new dresses and . . ."

"But I don't need . . ."

"Don't say you don't need these things. Every wife needs them. And you, of all women, deserve to feel special. You've kept yourself young and beautiful. I want to see you in velvets and jewels."

It would be pointless to tell him that she didn't think velvets and jewels were the answer. Perhaps she did require such accouterments and just didn't realize it. After all, they seemed to be the answer for almost everyone else. She smiled and said, "Thank you."

He had promised himself not to try to seduce her, so he rose and said gravely, "I think I'll go to bed early. Long day tomorrow. Good night, Emily."

"Good night. And thank you for the roses."

He walked up the stairs feeling relieved. They had made a start.

Breakfast was pleasant the next day, for the first time in weeks. When the children saw their parents at the table actually talking to each other, they glanced at one another with delighted smiles and were almost too excited to eat. Papa teased them and told jokes. Mama brought David and Adam down and fed the baby cereal from her plate. They were a real family again. Bill almost cried with relief.

Rafe was feeling buoyant when he strode into Griffin's Locomotive Works that morning. But his mind was such that he always kept domestic and business affairs in separate compartments. Pleased as he was by conditions at home, it wasn't long before he was neck-deep in the problems of the day.

It was a drizzly Thursday in mid-September. Rafe was discussing a diagram with a foreman when Mr. Griffin's secretary came running up to him. "The boss wants to see you, sir."

"Can't it wait?" Rafe glanced at his watch. Eleven-thirty.

"I'm explaining something to Frank."

"He asks you to hurry. A stockholders' meeting."

Rafe angrily shoved his hands into his pockets. He walked off with the young man. "Did he say what it was about?"

"A wire from Wall Street. Something about Jay Cooke."

"Cooke?" This was the most reputable banker in America. "What about him, Pete?"

"I'm not sure. I think he's closed."

"Closed the *bank*?" Rafe was stunned. Good God, did that mean there *would* be a panic? He hadn't sold any of his stocks yet. Not one goddamn share. Joe Shepherd and others had warned him to pull out. But he had delayed for one reason or another. No time to go down to Wall. No patience for digging through the papers. It had always been, "Tomorrow I'll get to it." And tomorrow had arrived.

The ghost-white faces in Mr. Griffin's office reminded him that his Wall Street interests weren't the only thing in danger. A major panic would plunge the firm into bankruptcy and he'd lose his investment in Griffin's Locomotive Works. He would be without a job, would not be able to pay the remaining mortgage on his house, and would end up shamefacedly asking his father for money. He, Rafe, who had determined to make his independent way in the world, who had once told his father he would never need financial assistance.

Not that Charles had much in the way of assistance to give. It was the best kept secret in Lanston that the Taylors of Maple Street had little money, though Rafe in discussing wills and inheritances with Emily had been forced to tell her the facts. The Taylors had taken little interest in landed holdings or business investments and had let valuable assets slip through their fingers. All that was left was some dense woodland five miles south of town. For generations the high-minded clan had cared only for education and for maintaining a standard of living that "suggested" money. But the fact was that there was not enough in the family till to support Rafe and his family for six months.

"We must not be alarmed," Mr. Griffin was saying.

Not alarmed? Then why the hell was he clutching his cigar as though it was his fortune that burned in his hand?

"I merely wanted to keep you gentlemen apprised of the situation. We must stand and wait."

Rafe thought, We're all doomed to pauperism and he's spouting Milton.

The minute the meeting was over, Rafe told Griffin he wasn't feeling well and was leaving early. He bolted for the door, raced into the street, hailed a hack and told the driver to speed to the ferry. On the way across the Hudson he tried to calm himself. It was still early. He might be able to unload the stocks. Rich investors would be happy to pick them up. There were bears prowling all over Wall Street, he assured himself.

Emily was not at home, and Rafe was glad. He emptied his desk, stuffed everything resembling a stock certificate into his bag, and then crammed other papers back in so that Emily, if she entered the library, would not see the mess and become suspicious. He darted from the house, leaped into a hansom, and told the driver he'd triple the fare if only the man would hurry.

The scene on Wall Street reminded him of the Battle of Spotsylvania. There was no room to move. Mobs were surging back and forth. Brokers were being trampled. Ambulances were rushing to and from the area carting victims off to the hospitals. Rafe thought of his ten thousand dollars (now doubtless plunging toward zero). Then he imagined himself being stampeded to death and thought of his poor widow. Finally he collected his wits about him. Perhaps the hysteria was unwarranted. Vanderbilt and other bulls might come charging into the arena and save them all. His own investments might miraculously be spared. Even if they slipped, the loss might be minimal. Be calm, he told himself, gritting his teeth.

He left the area on foot, gasping at the air as though additional oxygen might alter his fate. He stumbled into a bar and spent the afternoon sharing his fears with a fellow fool, a man who had invested thirty thousand dollars in Northern Pacific, the investment that had caused banker Cooke's downfall. Rafe was drunk when he reached Tenth Street, but not so seriously drunk as to prevent him from making a decision—which was to sober up and calm down before confronting his wife. It was imperative that Emily know nothing. And the place to collect himself would be at Kent's.

But Kent was out on an emergency and Beth didn't know when he'd be back.

"There were so many people hurt today," she said. "Plus heart attacks and a suicide. Thank heaven we don't own stocks." She paused. "You've sold yours, haven't you? Joe's been sounding the trumpet."

"And the faithful have heeded the call," Rafe muttered.

Beth nodded, assuming that Rafe had followed her brother's advice. She asked, "Anything particular you wanted to ask Kent?"

"No. Tell him—tell him I found out what happened to Reynolds."

"Who?"

"An officer we knew. Seems he died at Appomattox."

"I'm sorry," Beth said. "Just before the papers were signed?"

Rafe nodded. "Moments before."

"Oh, how tragic."

"Sad. Very sad." And with a solemn nod, Rafe plunged out of the office and into the street.

The children were outside playing when Rafe entered the house. The servants and Emily were nowhere in sight. He tried to sneak up to his room but Emily appeared on the third floor landing just as he was ducking into the sanctum.

"You're home early."

"I'm not feeling too well. I think I'll take a nap."

"The news has upset you?"

"News?"

"Oh, for heaven's sake, Rafe, they're already calling it Black Thursday. Don't tell me you haven't noticed."

"Oh, *that* news. Don't worry about it. No, I've just got a cold. The rain didn't help."

"Rafe?"

"Hmmm?" He pulled a handkerchief from his pocket and pretended to blow his nose.

"Did you sell them?"

"Can't we discuss this later? I think I have a fever, Em. If I can just take a short nap . . ."

"You didn't sell them," she said.

He strode into his room and sat on his chair waiting for the explosion. He looked up quickly and saw that her expression was unchanged. Shock, he thought. After a moment he asked, "Aren't you going to say anything?"

"What can I say?" Her voice was as placid as Barrett's Pond in mid-July. "How can I criticize you for something that's partly my fault?"

"*Your* fault?"

"If we hadn't had that fight, you would have unloaded those stocks two weeks ago."

"Don't be ridiculous. I had ample opportunity to make the transactions. If I could get to work, I was certainly able to manage a detour to my broker's."

"All right. Assume the responsibility if you prefer. But I insist on sharing my half of it."

He stared at her in amazement, wondering how she could be so calm. Perhaps she didn't realize that the amount involved was ten thousand dollars. He had acquired the stocks over the years, mentioning the amounts of each purchase. But he couldn't remember giving her cumulative totals. Perhaps she had never added up the figures. Buoyed by this thought, he was able to say heartily, "Don't blame yourself and don't worry. There's bound to be a rally."

She looked down and said nothing.

"Tomorrow everyone will start buying like sailors in port."

She nodded, still not looking at him. He tried to tell himself that he'd convinced her. Now he must turn her attention back to his imaginary illness before she went on to ask about the future of Griffin's Locomotive Works. He said, "I'd really like to take that nap now. Don't want the cold to get any worse."

She said softly, "We could go home, Rafe."

"What?"

"There's my father's house. We may have to live upstairs on top of the library but at least it will be a home. And there's room at your parents' too. If need be, we could split up the family until you found a job."

"What are you talking about?"

"Will you stop pretending, Rafe? We both know the facts. Why can't we just be honest?"

"*What* facts?"

"There's ten thousand dollars at stake and Griffin's is going to fail."

His heart thudded. So she *had* remembered the amount. But who the hell had told her about Griffin's? Clearing his throat to conceal his alarm, he asked, "What makes you think Griffin's is going to fail?"

"I read the papers every day. The railroads have expanded so rapidly that there was bound to be . . ."

"Griffin's is not 'the railroads,' Em."

"It's a small corporation that hasn't paid a dividend in years."

"But that doesn't mean we're doomed. We've had to invest in equipment and . . ."

"All right, but I also know . . ."

"No you *don't* know," he interrupted. "You're not a businessman. How can you be so sure that . . ."

"But I am—was—a business*woman*. I ran a store and I . . ."

"So you did," he said absently, "but I don't want you worrying about every sensational item you read in the papers. The papers are . . ."

"I said I ran a *store*," she shouted angrily. "I know a great deal about business, Rafe. We bought that place right after the Panic of '57 and I used to read every item on the economy that I could get my hands on. I wanted to know how businesses worked, why they failed, why they succeeded. I wanted to know everything I thought I had to know. I realize it was a small store, and I didn't need all that information, but I acquired it anyway. I understood that panic and I'm sure I understand this one. Now for *God's* sake will you drop this pretense so that we can decide what to do?"

Rafe exhaled loudly. "All right. There may be trouble. On the other hand, there may not be. If I do lose my job, I'll get another one in the soup-making industry. Plenty of people will be standing in line for soup."

"Be serious, Rafe. Do you want to go home?"

"I don't know. We can't leave New York without a thought to the consequences, Emily. There's the children's education to consider. And you love the city. You'd be unhappy."

She shrugged. "I'm no happier here than I was at

home." She knew immediately that this had been the wrong way to put it, so she rephrased the remark. "I mean I'd be just as happy in Lanston as I am here."

Rafe missed both the original sentence and the correction. He said, "I don't want to think about moving right now. I'm hoping that by tomorrow everyone will have come to their senses."

And there was a rally on Friday. Hetty Green, the richest woman in America, went down to the Street to pick up bargains. Vanderbilt managed to maintain the price of New York Central. But most people, like Rafe, were there to sell. The rally soon collapsed like a soufflé.

The New York Stock Exchange closed its doors on Saturday morning and kept them shut for ten days. By that time the plant in New Jersey was ready to declare bankruptcy and Rafe had sent letters to both Matt and Charles. They would be forced to return to Lanston, he said. Would either or both of them consider accommodating the family until Rafe could find work and buy a house of their own?

The fathers replied in a joint wire expressing indignation that Rafe could even use the word "consider." Rafe was to start packing and stop worrying. They followed the wire with a letter. The library would be moved from the Stevenses' to the Taylors'. They would divide Matt's large house into two living units. When Rafe was employed, he could buy his share of the house. Until then, he was not to concern himself.

A strange thing happened to Emily during the weeks of packing. She discovered that she felt calmer and more in control than she'd been during all the years when Rafe's future had been solid. They had lost all their money, and she knew she ought to be feeling wretched. Diane practically ordered her to cry, warning her that it was unnatural to be so stoical in this dark hour. But Emily did not cry. To the contrary, she found herself feeling unbelievably cheerful. She told herself that this must be an act—to hide her alarm from the children. Rafe, in his room, worrying, blaming himself, would say to her, "Thank God, you're there for the children. I can't bring myself to face them. I stand in awe of you, Em."

One night she told him half-jokingly that they could always fall back on her emergency fund. He looked at her with eyes so wracked with pain that she had to turn away. Then he buried his head in his hands and said, "All these years you saved while I threw money into worthless stocks. All those years of deprivation for your hundred and fifty dollars! How will I ever make it up to you?"

"It wasn't deprivation, Rafe. And you didn't throw money away. You invested it. For us."

"Oh God," he groaned. "Those graphs, those charts, the pennies you used to count in order to save a dollar a week."

"But I didn't do it only for the family . . ." she began.

"Running from butcher to butcher to get four cents off on a pound of meat."

"I did it for myself, mostly."

"Don't try to make it easier . . ."

"But I did! I saved that money for one reason only: to see if I could do it. It was a challenge that I welcomed. It . . ."

"Don't lie to me. I'd rather you accused me than lied."

Sighing, she left him alone. Never could she make him understand that the fund *had* been for herself. If the truth were known, it meant more to her than all his thousands. Why else would she be so blasé about his loss? But that was ridiculous. How could her silly fund be as important as Rafe's fortune?

Packing a four-story house was an awesome task, but she organized things well, kept the children's spirits up, even managed to place the servants with good families. She tried to cheer Rafe, but he would not be cheered. He didn't seem to want sex either. She had been certain he would need that consolation and had been ready to help him find release in this way. But Rafe never knocked on her door and seemed to prefer sleeping alone.

At last came the night of the farewell dinner. Beth gave it, inviting several couples who had been close to the Taylors. It was a dismal affair—for Emily as well as Rafe. She had, until now, been too busy to ponder the fact that she was leaving the city for good. But now, with friends seated around Beth's table, the realization hit her. She had come to New York believing that new worlds would open up to her. The miracle hadn't happened, but still, she was unhappy about leaving her friends. She looked from one face to the other until her eyes fell on Beth. No, she would not miss all her friends, she thought. Only Beth. But it wasn't right to feel this way. She should mourn the loss of all of them. Especially Diane.

At one point Beth cleared her throat and mumbled, "I wanted to say something, but I'm afraid I'll cry."

Kent said, "No need for dramatic farewells. Anything worth saying has already been said."

Rafe tried to smile. "Sentimental as always, I see."

Kent shrugged. "It's the truth, for God's sake."

And so they left it at that. Diane and Joe, Joan and her husband, and other friends tried to say goodbye as casually as though this were an ordinary evening. When they had gone, Kent poured more brandy. He told Rafe he was looking for a summer place and asked him to look for a cottage in the Lanston vicinity. Emily and Beth, meanwhile, were promising to write each other often. And then Emily and Rafe were leaving the Wilson house as though their absence would only be temporary.

"See you soon," the Wilsons said.

"Very soon," the Taylors replied.

And an era came to an end.

CHAPTER 23

They came home in mid-October. Had Emily been making the trip in any other season, the ride would have been tedious, with the whining of the children, the clatter of the wheels, the braying of the conductor—all contrasting harshly with Rafe's gloomy silence. But because she was near the window and able to watch the scenery, Emily was content. There was nothing to compare with New England in October. In other seasons trees were simply trees, summer green or winter black, and unexciting. In autumn, however, when nature dressed up for its farewell to warm days and harvests, New England blazed with color—yellow, orange, russet, wine, brown, and red. The warmth of the colors suggested warmth in the land itself.

They reached home in early evening. The four grandparents came to meet them. A light supper had been planned, for a heavy meal would certainly make the children ill. Rafe and Emily were astonished to see the changes the two families had made. The entire library had been moved to the Taylor house. The recently emptied downstairs room would, when the walls were rearranged, become a parlor for the young family who had the use of four bedrooms. Matt and Mary would have their own parlor. Kitchen and dining room would be shared.

The immediate problem was getting the weary children to bed in the summer cots the grandparents had set up to see them through until the furniture arrived. For Adam they still had the crib which had been used every July since Peggy had been born. For Emily and Rafe there was of course the double bed in the back bedroom. This was never removed after the summer holidays and it had been made up fresh this afternoon, Mary told them.

It was the first time Emily had thought about sharing a bed with Rafe. There was no room for a guest chamber here. They had not slept together in more than a month. First there had been the fight, then the financial collapse, then Rafe's depression. Abstinence was so unusual in Rafe that Emily had actually been concerned. But in the commotion she had pushed the problem to the back of her mind.

The children were put to sleep, and Marie and Charles, after helping to tuck the children in, finally went home. And by nine P.M. the house was quiet.

"You two must be tuckered out," Matt said as he rose from his favorite chair. "Maybe you want to sit here a spell. Mary and me, we're going to sleep."

Mary nodded and stood up. "You need anything, you know where to find it. Haven't changed the house much since summer." She paused, then said, "Sure nice to have you home for good." And with a smile, she followed Matt up the stairs.

Emily and Rafe were sitting on straight-backed chairs facing each other. She said, "Want some cider? I know where Pa keeps his cache."

"That would be nice."

She went down to the kitchen, opened an out-of-the-way cabinet, and found the cider. Pouring two glasses, she returned to the parlor. "Drink up," she said. And both of them drank. They did not, however, toast anything.

He said, "Think you'll be able to manage without servants?"

"Mary and I can share some of the chores."

"Mary works," he said.

"She'll be around evenings. Other housewives do it, Rafe. I can too."

"It won't be for long," he said. "I'll start looking for work tomorrow."

"I'd rather we unpacked first. And I want to get the rooms in order." She knew that it would take months for him to find a job. Factories along the river had laid off scores of men. It was better that he get settled in first so that the discouraging process of looking for a job would not be made worse by a household in pandemonium. She said, "Wait a week or two."

"All right. But no longer than that."

It was he who suggested that they retire. He carried the lamp and she followed him up the back stairs. After he set the lamp down on top of a highboy, they both stood and looked at the quilted spread.

"Looks like we'll have to share a bed," he said.

"Yes. It certainly looks that way."

"How do you feel about that?"

"How do *you* feel?" she countered.

"I'm rather pleased."

"And I'm not *dis*pleased," she said.

He sat down on the quilt and drew her into his lap. "I was afraid that if I rushed things you'd think I was a barbarian."

"Is that why you stayed away?"

"I had planned to be more chivalrous. And when I lost the money I couldn't implement the plan."

"Couldn't shower me with baubles or hire musicians to serenade me."

"That's right."

"Why don't we forget knights and maidens and just be husband and wife?"

But Rafe wasn't finished. "What I said to you that night about its making no difference if you were in my bed or out of it—I didn't mean that, Emily."

"I know you didn't."

"What I meant was that I thought you didn't want it— want me—anymore."

"Well, I do want you, so let's just forget the episode."

"Will you ever forget it?"

"Of course I will." And in that moment she meant it.

Rafe exhaled in relief. Then he kissed her hard. She was instantly aroused and anxious to be rid of the pounds of clothing she'd been wearing since they had left New York. He all but tore her dress from her in an effort to speed the disrobing, and he had to suppress curses when he found himself tangled in stays. But eventually she was stripped to her chemise. The rest of her clothes were piled in a heap on the floor. She did not stop to drape them over a chair. Instead she watched Rafe undress himself—a process completed in seconds—then pulled off her chemise. They fell into bed together.

The lovemaking was fast and over quickly. There was nothing of the courtly knight in Rafe's frenzied movements. But she didn't want a knight at this moment. She wanted a human animal, because she felt like one herself. And so, though they spent themselves quickly, both were thoroughly satisfied and totally exhausted. They slept well on their first night home.

Although the three-generation family was more the rule than the exception in towns and cities alike, Rafe had difficulty at first in adjusting to the new order. Mary and Matt were always tactful in giving advice, but Rafe read criticism into every syllable. Even when no words were uttered, Rafe would bristle. While Rafe was erecting two-by-fours one day to make a small study, Matt came up behind him to watch, "just watch." But Matt's physical presence, combined with Rafe's awareness that his father-in-law ran a furniture factory and knew everything about carpentry, reduced Rafe to bumbling incompetence. He hammered his thumb along with the nail and had to give up work for the day. It was Mary, finally, who saved the situation. Gently she suggested to Matt that Rafe be permitted to make his own mistakes. Later, talking to Rafe, she emphasized that they were so glad to have him home that in their exuberance they had probably interfered too much. He gallantly assured them that they were the most wonderful in-laws a man could have, but he was glad when the family left him alone to hammer his nails in peace.

Waite's Machine Works, where Rafe had worked before moving to New York, had escaped the impact of the Wall Street disaster. Prudent Waite owed no creditors and thus far had managed to maintain full employment, asking only that the employees prepare themselves for a pay cut should there be a falloff in sales. On hearing that Rafe was back, Waite stopped at the house one day to ask his opinion of a production problem. Since the parlor and study were not yet finished and the dining room table was heaped high with the children's school books, Rafe sat down with Waite at the kitchen table and began scribbling diagrams and equations on one of Nicky's old school tablets. Emily, setting coffee before them, noticed that Rafe looked more animated than he had in months. After Waite expressed gratitude for Rafe's quick appraisal and solution, he said, "I wish we could afford you, Taylor. We need a good engineer over there."

"Times are hard," Rafe said casually. "I lost a few dollars myself."

"Yes, I'd guessed," said Waite. And Emily, rolling the piecrust for supper, also rolled her eyes. How could he *not* have guessed? Why else would they be living in Matt's house?

"Most embarrassing," Rafe said. "Fortunately I did not suffer heavy losses, but there were others . . ." Rafe frowned.

Emily looked over at the kitchen table. Rafe didn't even blush as this outrageous lie rolled off his tongue.

Rafe continued. "And of course you know what happened to Griffin's Locomotive Works."

Waite nodded.

Rafe shook his head. "Ah well! It gave us the excuse we were looking for—to leave the city and find a suitable place here." He turned to Emily. "By the way, dear, did you get a chance to look at that Georgian house on Patterson Street? Sutter's place?"

Emily muttered in the direction of the piecrust, "Not yet, Rafe." She was afraid that if she turned, her red face would give her away.

"We'll look at it tomorrow," Rafe said. Turning to Waite, he smiled. "It's not as big a house as I'd like, but it has been well kept."

Waite returned to the original subject. "I take it you're

not looking for employment."

"I hadn't thought about it," answered King Midas. "First I'd like to find a house. Not an easy task since the children demand to stay here with their grandparents. After we've settled that issue I shall of course consider my employment. The leisure life can get monotonous."

"Listen to him!" Emily hissed to the piecrust.

"I hope you'll consider me first," Waite said.

"You have my assurances, sir." Rafe said heartily.

"I know you don't need the money," Waite said. He too assumed that Charles Taylor was extremely wealthy and that Rafe, if he chose, could indeed live a life of leisure. "But would you consider working for me now?"

"Money, sir, is always a factor. I'm a Yankee, after all." Light chuckle.

Waite grinned. "Aren't we all? But I could only afford a modest salary." Waite then quoted an amount.

"I see," said Rafe, shaking his head. "Not possible."

Waite upped the amount by ten dollars.

"Still unthinkable, sir." Rafe laughed drily and Emily held her breath, hoping he wouldn't laugh himself out of a job. Mr. Waite finally quoted his top offer. Rafe walked over to the window, turned, affected a resigned sigh, then nodded slowly. There were handshakes, Waite's delighted grin, and Rafe's controlled smile. But the minute Waite exited, Rafe exhaled loudly.

"I feel reborn," he said.

On a crisp Saturday afternoon in late November Rafe and Emily went to the Lawrence farm for a visit, leaving the children with the grandparents. Jack took Rafe out to the barn to show him a prized horse and Abby suggested that she and Emily go for a walk rather than sit over the teacups as they usually did. It was a chilly day, but they walked briskly as they had done in school days. Emily was pleased to find that she could retain such vigor after all those years of sitting on Tenth Street.

"How does Rafe like his job?" Abby asked.

"I think he's happy."

"And you? Have you gotten over the shock?" Abby and

Jack were the only ones, aside from parents, who knew the magnitude of Rafe's financial loss.

"What shock?" asked Emily absently.

"The panic." Abby looked at her friend oddly.

"Oh, the panic. Yes, I'm over it." Suddenly Emily lowered her head and looked away.

"Em, what is it? Are you in debt?"

"No, of course not." Emily covered her eyes with her left hand and strode along quickly.

"Something's wrong. What is it?"

"You reminded me of an incident I'd rather forget."

"I'm sorry," Abby said. "Can you tell me?"

"I— don't know. Don't know if I can explain. That night when Rafe told me he lost the money, he was so upset. So very upset. And I—do you know how I felt?" She shook her head.

"You were angry at him. You probably felt like murdering him. And I'm sure he understood your reasons."

"No, that's just it. I wasn't angry. Quite the reverse. I was almost exhilarated. So many thousands had been lost and I—all I could think about was showing everyone how strong and brave I was. I was more efficient than I'd been in years—calming him down, making all the arrangements to move. I smiled through the whole catastrophe."

"I don't understand. What are you ashamed of?"

"Don't you see? I thrived on Rafe's misery."

"No, I don't see." Abby stopped in front of a white birch and grabbed Emily's mittened hand to halt her. Emily was crying. Not since they were children had Abby seen Emily cry.

"He worked so hard for all that money," Emily sobbed, "and I never cared a hoot. I cared more for that stupid emergency fund than for all his thousands. Poor Rafe. If he ever knew . . ."

"What emergency fund?"

Emily told Abby about her savings project, then said, "I believed my pittance was as important as his thousands. At least I *think* I believed that. Oh, I don't know what I'm saying. And I don't know why I'm crying." Emily unbuttoned her coat and floundered in her skirt pocket for a handkerchief. She blew her nose and said, "Let's forget this conversation."

"No," Abby said, leaning against the birch, her hands on her hips. "You didn't 'thrive on his misery,' for heaven's sake. You assumed control and you liked the feeling. After all, you were once in control of a store and of half the committees in town. Of *course* you smiled through the ordeal. You probably thought this was your last chance."

"Good God, what a thought!"

"Will you stop wallowing in guilt, for heaven's sake? Come . . ." she tugged Emily's arm. "Let's walk some more."

They set out down the Blake Road toward Whitney, passing the hayfield where Roger and Emily had floundered in snow twelve years earlier. The trees along the road were bare and the leaves under their feet brown and limp. The dismal pre-winter aura was on the land, yet Emily felt soothed by it. She was reminded of the years when she and Abby, Roger and Jack had tramped the three miles in to school.

Abby said, "All right then. You enjoyed taking charge for a while. What of it? You were never ashamed of those feelings when you were young."

"No, I guess not. But . . ."

"And I think I know why. You were born a farmer and were used to working hard. Out here people can't say that the man is chief and the woman just flits around spending his money on lacy petticoats. I know men would like to *believe* that, but it's not true and they know it. On farms couples share the business, the profits, the trials—well, everything. As you and your Pa did, first on the old place and later in the store. If you'd married Roger . . ." Abby broke off.

"If I'd married Roger?"

"You would have had the partnership, Not that you *should* have married him, Emmy. After all, you always hated farms, and Rafe was much more suitable for you. There was only one problem. You were used to independence and prestige—and to feeling necessary. I think that's the key word. When you visited us summers I used to wonder if you did feel necessary. Rafe earned all the money; the servants took charge of the children. And you—well, if it had been Christine, she would have loved the arrangement. She was born to this sort of life. But you—a farmer, a store manager . . ." Abby sighed. "You used to do so many things. You never stopped. I sometimes wondered if some old Puritan ghost was breathing down your neck hissing 'work, work, work.' But you loved it." She paused. "Then you married and gave it all up. Just like that. At the very least, I thought you'd talk your father out of selling the store. But you didn't. You never batted an eye. You settled into Laurel Street like a dreary old matron and began to knit. I couldn't *believe* it!" Abby wrapped her scarf more firmly around her neck. "I used to think Rafe ordered you to act this way. But I knew Rafe. At least I thought I knew him. He didn't seem the type to yell, 'And don't you leave this house!' "

"No, he didn't. Not then. If I'd stayed much longer in Lanston I suppose I would have found some way to take up my old life. But we moved to New York, and Rafe was always in terror of my running around to city charities. The streets are dangerous."

"How dangerous, really?"

"According to Rafe there are thugs on every corner."

Abby nodded. "Jack told me Rafe was very protective of his brothers. I can imagine how well he guarded you. Well, moving to New York certainly didn't help matters. At least here you could have done some of the unconventional things you did as a girl and no one would have thought anything of it. Small towns tolerate their characters. But there you *had* to conform, didn't you? Last summer, when you sat here fanning yourself and telling us about Diane and—Joan was it?"

"Joan."

"I thought, 'Good grief, how can she stand it? Day after day of tea and boring people!' Not that I didn't envy you the clothes, the servants, the operas, and so forth. Of course I envied you. But I knew you didn't envy yourself because when I mentioned Beth and her work you got that tight-lipped look that I've recognized since we were children. It was envy, Emmy. Beth was actually doing things. You, on the other hand, had to *invent* challenges. Like the sacred emergency fund."

Emily shrugged in silent agreement.

"So it's settled," Abby said.

"What's settled?"

'The store. You'll just have to buy another one. The town's growing by the minute."

"I have children, Abby."

"Then wait till Adam's out of diapers and hire a nurse."

"But there's Rafe."

"What about him?"

"Suppose the store were successful," Emily said.

"Yes?"

"Suppose I made too much money?"

"More than him, you mean?"

"Or even less. Think of his pride."

"Oh, I see." Abby nodded. She too was careful about such delicate matters.

"Maybe in ten years," Emily said. "When Rafe owns a factory of his own."

"Ten years is a long time," said Abby. "But it's up to you."

Emily had no intention of telling Rafe that she wanted someday to buy a store. For one reason, the day would be far in the future. For another, he'd just returned to work himself. If she approached the subject now, his first assumption would be that she thought him inadequate as a provider. No matter how many ways she explained it, his pride would be shaken.

After they returned from Abby's at eight that evening, she put the children to bed, did some mending, and set about her Saturday night ritual of planning menus for the week. Rafe went into his unfinished study to work on some diagrams. At about ten o'clock she walked into the study and asked, "How do you feel about roast lamb tomorrow and cold lamb Monday and Tuesday?"

"Fine."

"You don't mind lamb three nights in a row?"

"No."

"Because on Wednesday your sister's coming. Jessie and Dan hate lamb. And Thursday's Thanksgiving. We'll be at your parents'. By Friday . . ."

"Fine."

"Are you listening, Rafe?"

"Can't this wait, Em? I'm working."

In the old days she would have shrugged and walked away. Tonight she heard herself say, "You're working. I see. And I'm *not*, I suppose?"

"Excuse me?" He looked up from his charts, plainly irritated.

"Planning menus plus cooking plus doing all the dishes. That's not *work* as far as you're concerned."

"Of *course* it's work, but it's hardly a subject to keep us up until midnight."

"But those diagrams there do constitute a subject worthy of midnight oil."

"My diagrams bring in *money*, Emily. And money is a worthwhile subject, yes."

"Whereas food is *not*?"

"Money *buys* food, for Christ's sake!"

"Really? Why, I never knew that!" She opened her mouth to indicate astonishment.

Rafe threw his pen down in exasperation. "What the hell's gotten into you tonight?"

"Tell me more about money," she said. "I can't get the subject through my poor little head."

"Did you have any cider out at the Lawrences'?"

"No, I did not."

"Then what the hell . . ."

"I don't like your patronizing attitude, that's what the hell. As you know, I too have earned money. Do you, by any chance, remember Stevens' Store?"

"Of *course* I . . ."

"I'm glad you do. Because there's going to be another one very soon. To hell with your pride. Do you ever worry about mine?"

"Pride? Store?" Rafe slapped his forehead as though to jolt himself to consciousness. What the deuce was she talking about?

"Don't worry. I won't ask you for a dime. I'll borrow the money from Pa."

As he sat there staring at her, she suddenly saw herself through his eyes. Why, he hadn't the slightest idea of what she meant. She had simply exploded like one of those cannon balls that goes off years after a battle is over.

"A store?" he croaked.

She wanted to say calmly, "Let me explain this logically and sequentially." Instead, she heard herself blasting, "Yes!"

"With five children at home?" His face was crimson with disbelief.

She had planned to add the qualifier about waiting until Adam was older. Instead she shouted, "Yes!"

"*With five children at home?*" he repeated, bellowing.

"I'll hire a servant!" she bellowed back.

"You can't be serious." He stood up, stalked to the parlor door to shut it so that Mary and Matt would not hear them, then sat down hard on a chair near the fireplace. "Where did you . . . how did you . . ." he broke off, shaking his head as though to clear it.

"I want to share the work," she said. "I don't want you carrying the weight of the world on your shoulders—or your superiority either." She sat down on the couch.

"So that's it! Did I do something to make you feel inferior?"

"Did you do *something*? You've done many things. Let's start with the roast lamb incident. A little girl asked her papa if he'd like lamb three nights in a row. Papa said he was busy doing important things and told the little girl to run along."

"Christ! I thought we left these status concerns back on Tenth Street with the tea group. Now I find you've transferred all the pettiness to your marriage."

"Call it pettiness. Call it whatever you like. The fact is that you do consider me your inferior and no, I don't like it one bit. Do you remember how you once described the army, Rafe? The chain of command, the colonel's ridiculous orders, the feeling of being like a child in a crib? Well, you enlisted for only three years. I've been in it for nine, and there's no end in sight."

"The army? You compare your lot with being in the *army*?"

"At least you were an officer. I'm a corporal with only five children under me."

"Of all the ridiculous parallels. Have you forgotten the purpose of the army?"

"Battles," she said. "Well, every childbirth is a battle and thousands of women die. But I'm talking about boredom and tedium. The very stuff of army life. And rank. You're keenly aware of rank, Mr. Taylor. *Captain* Taylor. It might be the army heritage or it might be your sex. Do you remember the day Waite offered you the job and you said, 'I feel reborn'? As though staying home with me were a living death?"

"Now wait a minute . . ."

"Or the night you said it didn't matter if I was in your bed or out of it?"

"You promised you'd forget that incident!"

"I'll never forget it. You might as well know that right now."

"What I meant was that you didn't respond to *me*."

"I *know* what you meant. But it still made me feel like nothing. And that's what we're talking about. My rank."

He blinked. "Have I always made you feel this way?"

"Not always and not necessarily deliberately. Before we were married—before I became your property—I was pretty much your equal."

"Damn it, you sound like Mrs. Harrington! Have I ever said you were my property?"

"No, but the law says so. You're too polite to point it out, but you're well aware of your possessions."

Rafe stood up and paced from one end of the parlor to the other. Then he stopped in front of her. "So all these years you've felt inferior, put upon, my property. Why, may I ask, did you marry me in the first place?"

"I loved you. Love was supposed to propel a woman through anything, even if 'anything' was contrary to her basic nature. I wanted to believe love could do that. After all, that's what Jane Austen, *Godey's Lady's Book*, Rosie, Charlotte Brontë, Shakespeare, every dime novelist and every fairy tale spinner in the universe maintained. I saw evidence to the contrary in almost every marriage. But did I assume the storytellers were wrong? I did not. I assumed the love hadn't been 'true' to begin with.

"What an idiot I am!" she exclaimed. "Year after year, worrying about love. And all the while denying that there are other things in life. Ambition, for example. Heavens, but that's a dirty word, isn't it? Women are forbidden to have it. But I'm possessed of the trait. And I no longer find it shameful."

She looked over at him, her eyes blazing. He was staring

back, open-mouted, and she could not tell if he was sympathetic or angry. Nor did she ask. She said, "Why do we *do* it, Rafe? Why do we listen to public opinion and never—or rarely—examine our own beliefs? I'll wager that if three sufficiently influential people came forth next week and claimed that eating in public was a revolting act, most of us would immediately start wondering if this were so. Finally some would come to accept the idea. Then more people. And if no one objected loudly enough, the whole world would begin eating in the privacy of a closet. . . . Rafe, are you listening?"

He was staring at the wall, his mouth set.

"What is it, Rafe?"

"I'm tired."

"But this is important."

"We'll discuss it tomorrow."

"Rafe . . ."

"I said tomorrow." His voice was flat, emotionless. He rose and left the room slowly, and she sat there, shaking her head, wondering what had gone wrong. Was it something she had just now said or was his anger left over from the beginning of the conversation? In any case, he could have told her. Normally he would have shouted. But Rafe wasn't even talking.

Through most of Sunday Rafe was distant and preoccupied. In the early afternoon he sat near the fireplace in the parlor studying the diagrams he'd been working on the night before. Emily busied herself dusting and did not try to continue last night's conversation. She would wait until he was in a more receptive mood.

The day was unseasonably warm, the window was open, and the happy babble of children drifted in. One of the new games they had been taught by friends was called "Yanks and Rebs." Emily had seen them play it, looking on in the absent way of mothers, wondering if Nicky was going to stumble over that stone as he charged or if Peggy was going to knock over young David as she countercharged. To Emily, who knew nothing of real war, this was another game like hide and seek or baseball.

Rafe, who was usually at work while his children frolicked, had never been exposed to this latest sport and he wasn't listening now as Bill and Nicky told Peggy and David that the latter had to play rebels because they were the youngest and because Peggy was a girl. Only older men could play noble Yankees. Feisty Peggy retorted that she wouldn't play a rebel unless she could win the first battle. A loud argument ensued in which the older boys finally agreed that Peggy and David could win. Emily nodded with approval at her daughter's spirit, but she was getting weary of the noise and decided to walk down to the kitchen to make herself some tea. As the shouting and rebel yells commenced, Emily walked into the hall. Suddenly she heard Rafe exclaim, "What are they doing out there?"

"Playing Yanks and Rebs," Emily called back. Her impulse was to keep walking, but Rafe's tone had sounded odd. She turned back to the parlor. Rafe was now standing at the window, his fists clenched.

At that moment, Peggy shouted, "Boom!" and Bill, clutching his stomach, howled, staggered, and fell to the ground. There was another "Boom!" from David, and then Nicky crumpled to the earth, screaming with blood-curdling gusto. Now Emily saw Rafe grasping the window sill. The blood was draining from his face. Before she could assimilate what was happening, Rafe turned and staggered into his study where he sat down on a chair and lowered his head to his knees, reaching weakly for the desk drawer with the bottle of brandy in it.

"Rafe, are you all right?" She had followed him into the study.

He nodded, gasping for air.

"Brandy? Is that what you want?"

"Um." He raised his head and reached for the brandy she was taking from the desk. While she steadied his hand, he drank from the bottle. Then he rose and slowly walked back to the window. Nicky and Bill, now resurrected, were charging Peggy and David. Rafe tried to shout, "That's enough!" but his voice was not yet strong enough.

"I'll tell them," she said, and as he sat down on the couch she shouted, "You children play hide and seek! . . . Yes, hide and seek . . . Never mind why. I'm giving you an order!" And she slammed the window shut.

Sitting down beside Rafe, she asked, "Were you thinking

of their being in a war some day?"

He shook his head. "I was thinking of my brothers."

"Tell me," she said softly.

Rafe said nothing.

"Were you there? Did you see them?"

"I saw one of them. After he died." Rafe paused. "Johnny."

She had never known that. No wonder he had nearly blacked out. As she imagined Rafe finding Johnny dead on a battlefield, she shuddered involuntarily. She touched her hand to his forearm as though in comfort, but he did not notice. He stared straight ahead and continued to drink. After a few minutes, he said, "I used to ask the rebel what he thought of the cause."

"What rebel, Rafe?"

Rafe told her about the unconscious man in the tent at Gettysburg. Now, after all these years, she learned what that Sanitary Commission pamphlet had reminded him of.

"Of course the poor bastard had no answers," Rafe said. "But I saw for myself where 'honor' had gotten him. And that was answer enough. When I came home on leave, I urged my brothers not to join. I literally begged them. And Bill just looked at me, the arrogance of youth all over his face. He said, 'We're not *asking* you, big brother. We're *telling* you.' Those were his words. Oh, they put me in my place all right! And I told them both to go to hell. But I didn't mean that. Damn it, I didn't mean *literally*."

"Of course you didn't," she said softly. "You loved them, wanted to protect them. Don't tell me you've been suffering guilt for the past nine years."

"No," he said. "Not guilt. I just wish I hadn't said certain things."

"We all feel that way after people die," she said. "But the important thing is that you did love them and they knew it."

"Love," he muttered sarcastically. "I've lost more people in the name of love. Maybe I'd have better luck with hate." He was still drinking.

"What are you talking about?"

"Never mind." He started to rise, but she held fast to his arm. "Let me go. I have work to do."

"Not until you explain what you just said."

"Later, all right?"

She said, "What do you mean you've lost people in the name of love? Not me. You don't mean *me*."

Rafe didn't answer.

"Are you talking about last night? All I meant was that there's more to life *than* love."

"Grocery stores, for example?"

"Achievement," she corrected.

"To be sure." He drank more brandy.

"You don't understand at all. You really think I've stopped loving you."

"That's exactly what I think. How can an abstraction like 'achievement' explain all the problems in New York?"

"I think that 'abstraction' can explain a great deal."

"You can't be serious."

"Oh, yes, I can."

Rafe stroked his mustache and thought of Kent. Had the man actually been a master seducer or did his "charm" lie in sharing his work with Beth? "I wish I could believe it were that simple, Emily."

"All I can tell you is that back in the days when I *was* achieving—in the store and before that in school—I felt—" Suddenly she turned to him and said, "There's something I don't think I've ever told you. About school."

Rafe looked over and saw that her head was averted. She seemed almost embarrassed to look at him. "What is it?" he asked.

"When I was a little girl—No, not little. Actually I was fourteen . . ."

"Yes?"

"We sat next to each other."

"I remember."

"I loved you very much," she whispered.

"Then? In school?"

"Yes. You were so carefree. So witty and irreverent. You were always making me laugh, and I adored you."

There was a long silence. Then he said softly, "I never knew you felt that way."

She looked up and forced a crisp voice. "Of course not. I was at great pains to keep it a secret. Especially since you were always gawking at Christine."

"Oh *that*."

"Yes, 'that.' I was devastated, of course, but I got over it, and after three months or so I transferred my passions to I can't remember who. I tried to hate you but I couldn't. Eventually I resigned myself to the fact that I'd have to like you. You were very likable and I wanted you as a friend." She paused. "So we were good friends for years, and then you came back in '64 and I fell in love all over again. And still we were friends."

She thought, that summer idyll was what Pat would have called her golden age. She had had it all then. Work, excitement, friendship, and love. A good balance.

"Then we were married," she said. "I stopped being Emily and tried to be what everyone told me a wife should be. In the meantime, you were still grieving for your brothers. When we lost Michael I thought you would never get over it. Then you became more protective than ever. I understood your reasons, but I chafed under the restrictions. I wanted to rebel but I didn't. What model wife would defy a good husband? So I kept my mouth shut—kept my mind shut, actually—and kept on having babies. It was the only activity left. Other things happened. Misunderstandings. And now here we are. Are we the same two people who married each other? Are we still friends?"

Rafe did not answer.

"But I think we could be," she said. "Not exactly the same, of course, but close enough. If I had more external challenges. If you stopped trying to shield me from all life's dangers . . ."

"From *all* life's . . ."

"From most of them, then. Were you there to hover over me when I walked three miles in to the academy? I sometimes plowed through snow, Rafe, never thinking much about it, thinking only that a special person would be sitting there in the back of the room near the coat racks. And that he would make me smile."

Rafe murmured, "If only I'd known how you felt."

"But you didn't know, did you? And I loved you anyway. Do you understand what I'm trying to say?"

He nodded, but she knew he wasn't thinking about the importance of independence. He was thinking of her long winter walks, her youthful adoration.

After a moment, he said quietly, "Where did you want to locate the store?"

Her mouth fell open. "I—I don't know yet."

"Take your time deciding," he said. "That will give me time as well—to assimilate all this."

She caught her breath. He was serious. He was really going to try. But thinking about it, she remembered that Rafe had always tried. Year after year he had done things that the world might not deem heroic, but he had done them. There was heroism, though, in taking a horsecar and ferry to work every day, in being a good father (even if he *was* too protective), in trying to cheer a wife who was unhappy for reasons even she did not understand. The lovely roses and the efforts at chivalry—they hadn't been what she needed exactly, but he had tried so hard. Other members of his sex were extolled for going West with the cavalry or for making fortunes in business. Rafe had foregone opportunities to be that kind of hero, and in doing so he became the more valorous.

Overcome with emotion, she turned to him and hugged him, parting her lips for a kiss.

He grinned. "All this affection—for a grocery store?"

"It's not the store, Rafe. It's you."

He looked at her for a while, then closed his eyes and kissed her. At that moment, they heard the back door slam and thought that one of the children had come into the house to ask for a drink. She started to rise, but Rafe restrained her.

"Stay with me, Emily."

She touched his face, her fingers grazing his cheek. "I'm here," she said.

ACKNOWLEDGMENTS

This book was written with the assistance of many people who gave opinions, advice on plot, and valuable research information. These include my husband, Clifford, our children, Jennifer and Christopher, my father, Frank Smith, and my parents-in-law, Leona and Ernest Thompson. Hope Dellon, my editor at St. Martin's Press, who is possessed of the unusual combination of perspicacity and tact, helped me immeasurably. James Seligmann, my literary agent, gave valued advice and bolstered my confidence. And seven generous people assisted in the research. They are Marguerite Schall, Sylvia Broderick, Gil Wester, Rosemary Moore, Joyce Terrio, Debra Delaney, and Sheila Ceder.

HISTORICAL & ROMANCE

0426145763	Margot Arnold THE OFFICERS' WOMAN	75p*
0352303875	Antoinette Beaudry TROPIC OF DESIRE	£1.50*
0352302216	Clare Darcy CECILY	85p*
0352302224	GEORGINA	85p*
0352397799	LYDIA	75p*
0352396822	VICTOIRE	70p*
035239708X	ALLEGRA	95p*
0352395192	LADY PAMELA	95p*
0426186060	Elisabeth Kyle FREE AS AIR	75p
0426189051	DOWN THE WATER	75p
0352302429	Petra Leigh GARNET	£1.50*
0352302615	CORAL	£1.25*
0352303549	ROSEWOOD	£1.50*
0426177932	Barbara Michaels SONS OF THE WOLF	60p
0352395044	Jean Plaidy MARY QUEEN OF SCOTS (NF)	95p
0352302119	THE RISE OF THE SPANISH INQUISITION (NF)	75p
035230216X	THE GROWTH OF THE SPANISH INQUISITION (NF)	75p
0352302488	THE END OF THE SPANISH INQUISITION (NF)	75p
0352303476	A TRIPTYCH OF POISONERS (NF)	80p
0352395656	Antonia Van-Loon FOR US THE LIVING	£1.25*

BARBARA CARTLAND'S ANCIENT WISDOM SERIES

0427004209	Barbara Cartland THE FORGOTTEN CITY	70p*
0427004217	L. Adams Beck THE HOUSE OF FULFILMENT	70p*
0427004225	Marie Corelli A ROMANCE OF TWO WORLDS	70p*
0427004233	Talbot Mundy BLACK LIGHT	70p*
0427004241	L. Adams Beck THE GARDEN OF VISION	70p*

† For sale in Britain and Ireland only.
*Not for sale in Canada
♦ Film & T.V. tie-ins.

GENERAL FICTION

		Cyril Abraham	
Δ	042607114X	THE ONEDIN LINE: THE SHIPMASTER	80p
Δ	0426132661	THE ONEDIN LINE: THE IRON SHIPS	80p
Δ	042616184X	THE ONEDIN LINE: THE HIGH SEAS	80p
Δ	0426172671	THE ONEDIN LINE: THE TRADE WINDS	80p
Δ	0352304006	THE ONEDIN LINE: THE WHITE SHIPS	90p
		Spiro T. Agnew	
	0352302550	THE CANFIELD DECISION	£1.25*
		Lynne Reid Banks	
	0352302690	MY DARLING VILLAIN	85p
		Michael J. Bird	
Δ	0352301481	WHO PAYS THE FERRYMAN?	85p
Δ	0352302747	THE APHRODITE INHERITANCE	85p
		Judy Blume	
	0352302712	FOREVER	75p*
		Barbara Brett	
	0352303441	BETWEEN TWO ETERNITIES	75p*
		Jeffrey Caine	
	0352302003	HEATHCLIFF	75p
		Ramsey Campbell	
	0352304987	THE DOLL WHO ATE HIS MOTHER	75p*
		R. Chetwynd-Hayes	
Δ	0426187539	DOMINIQUE	75p
		Jackie Collins	
Δ	0352395621	THE STUD	75p
	0352300701	LOVEHEAD	75p
	0352398663	THE WORLD IS FULL OF DIVORCED WOMEN	75p
Δ	0352398752	THE WORLD IS FULL OF MARRIED MEN	75p
		Catherine Cookson	
	0426163796	THE GARMENT	70p
	0426163524	HANNAH MASSEY	70p
	0426163605	SLINKY JANE	70p
		Tony Curtis	
	0352302194	KID ANDREW CODY AND JULIE SPARROW	95p*
		Robertson Davies	
	0352396113	FIFTH BUSINESS	95p*
	0352395281	THE MANTICORE	£1.25*
		Alexander Edwards	
Δ	0352396881	A STAR IS BORN	60p*

† For sale in Britain and Ireland only.
* Not for sale in Canada.
♦ Film & T.V. tie-ins.

GENERAL FICTION

Δ	0352303603	Henry Edwards **SGT. PEPPER'S LONELY** **HEARTS CLUB BAND**	75p*
	0426188330	Joy Fielding **THE TRANSFORMATION**	95p*
	0352396857	Terry Fisher **IF YOU'VE GOT THE MONEY**	70p
	0352395273	Ken Grimwood **BREAKTHROUGH**	75p*
Δ	0352304979	Robert Grossbach **CALIFORNIA SUITE**	75p*
	0352301880	D. G. Finlay **ONCE AROUND THE SUN**	95p*
Δ	0352305142	Peter J. Hammond **SAPPHIRE AND STEEL**	75p
	0426165209	Brian Hayles **SPRING AT BROOKFIELD**	70p
Δ	0352304030	William Johnston **KING**	£1.25*
Δ	0426183746	**HAPPY DAYS:** **No. 1 THE FONZ AND LAZONGA**	70p*
Δ	0426183827	**No. 2 THE BIKE TYCOON**	70p*
Δ	0426184386	**No. 3 DEAR FONZIE . . .**	70p*
Δ	0426186222	**No. 4 FONZIE GOES TO COLLEGE**	70p*
Δ	0426187296	**No. 5 READY TO GO STEADY**	70p*
Δ	042618825X	**No. 6 FONZIE DROPS IN**	70p*
Δ	0426188764	**No. 7 THE INVADERS**	70p*
Δ	042619019X	**No. 8 FONZIE, FONZIE SUPERSTAR**	70p*
	0352303956	Heinz Konsalik **THE WAR BRIDE**	85p
	0427003210	**THE DAMNED OF THE TAIGA**	75p
Δ	0352398981	Jeffrey Konvitz **THE SENTINEL**	70p*
	0352301643	Dean R. Koontz **NIGHT CHILLS**	75p*
	0352303328	Pat McGrath **DAYBREAK**	95p

† For sale in Britain and Ireland only.
* Not for sale in Canada.
♦ Film & T.V. tie-ins.

GENERAL FICTION

△	0352396903	Lee Mackenzie EMMERDALE FARM (No. 1) THE LEGACY	70p
△	0352396296	EMMERDALE FARM (No. 2) PRODIGAL'S PROGRESS	70p
△	0352395974	EMMERDALE FARM (No. 3) ALL THAT A MAN HAS . . .	70p
△	0352301414	EMMERDALE FARM (No. 4) LOVERS' MEETING	70p
△	0352301422	EMMERDALE FARM (No. 5) A SAD AND HAPPY SUMMER	70p
△	0352302437	EMMERDALE FARM (No. 6) A SENSE OF RESPONSIBILITY	70p
△	0352303034	EMMERDALE FARM (No. 7) NOTHING STAYS THE SAME	70p
△	0352303344	EMMERDALE FARM (No. 8) THE COUPLE AT DEMDYKE ROW	70p
△	0352302569	ANNIE SUGDEN'S COUNTRY DIARY (illus)	£1.25
△	0352396164	Graham Masterton THE MANITOU	70p*
	0352395265	THE DJINN	75p*
	0352302178	THE SPHINX	75p*
	0352395982	PLAGUE	75p*
	0352396911	A MILE BEFORE MORNING	75p*
	0352301562	N. Richard Nash EAST WIND, RAIN	95p*
	0352395060	CRY MACHO	95p*
	0352303778	THE LAST MAGIC (Export only) Excluding Aust.. N.Z.. S.A.	£1.50*
	0352302720	Anaïs Nin DELTA OF VENUS	95p*
	0352303271	Alan Parker PUDDLES IN THE LANE	70p
	0352300809	Molly Parkin LOVE ALL	70p
	0352397179	UP TIGHT	70p
	0352302151	GOOD GOLLY MS MOLLY (illus) NF	£1.25
	0352302631	SWITCHBACK	75p
△	0426190866	Larry Pryce THIRD TIME UNLUCKY	75p
△	0426189647	FINGERS	60p

† For sale in Britain and Ireland only.
* Not for sale in Canada.
◆ Film & T.V. tie-ins.

Wyndham Books are obtainable from many booksellers and newsagents. If you have any difficulty please send purchase price plus postage on the scale below to:

> **Wyndham Cash Sales,**
> **P.O. Box 11,**
> **Falmouth,**
> **Cornwall**

OR

> **Star Book Service,**
> **G.P.O. Box 29,**
> **Douglas,**
> **Isle of Man,**
> **British Isles**

While every effort is made to keep prices low, it is sometimes necessary to increase prices at short notice. Wyndham Books reserve the right to show new retail prices on covers which may differ from those advertised in the text or elsewhere.

Postage and Packing Rate
U.K.
One book 25p plus 10p per copy for each additional book ordered to a maximum charge of £1.05

B.F.P.O. and Eire
One book 25p plus 10p per copy for the next 8 books and thereafter 5p per book. Overseas 40p for the first book and 12p per copy for each additional book.